THE
AFTER
HOURS

THE AFTER HOURS

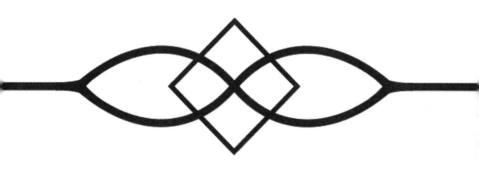

ASPEN ANDERSEN

CamCat Books
2810 Coliseum Centre Drive, Suite 300
Charlotte, NC 28217-4574

This is a work of fiction. Names, characters, places, and incidents are either products of the author's imagination or are used fictitiously.

© 2025 by Aspen Andersen

All rights reserved. Printed in the United States of America. No part of this book may be used or reproduced in any manner whatsoever without written permission except in the case of brief quotations embodied in critical articles and reviews. For information, address CamCat Books, 2810 Coliseum Centre Drive, Suite 300, Charlotte, NC 28217-4574.

Hardcover ISBN 9780744311525
Paperback ISBN 9780744311532
eBook ISBN 9780744311549
Audiobook ISBN 9780744311563

Library of Congress Control Number: 2024941166

Book and cover design by Maryann Appel
Interior artwork by Danler, Kesu01, Nevarpp, Vasaleks

5   3   1   2   4

FOR R & Z.

I'D SPEND ALL MY
AFTER HOURS ON YOU.

Dear reader,

I want you to be able to immerse yourself fully into this novel, and therefore it is my duty to inform you of the potential triggers in the content. This novel contains off-the-page sexual content, depictions of mental illness, physical illnesses, violence, blood, death, murder, attempted murder, attempted sexual assault, and mentions of suicide. Nothing contained herein is, or shall be construed as, an attempt to represent, bring unjust attention to, or otherwise categorize the experiences of victims of the crimes committed on the page. Your psychological safety comes first—please take care while reading.

—AA

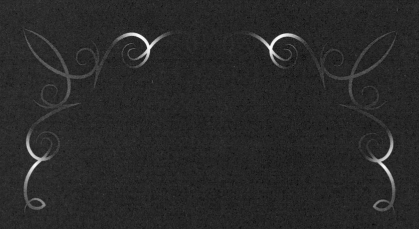

PART ONE

"People like us, who believe in physics,

know that the distinction between past, present and future

is only a stubbornly persistent illusion."

—Albert Einstein

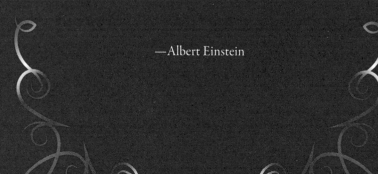

CHAPTER ONE

B IRTHDAYS ARE SUCH a weak way to benchmark time's effect on humans. The notion that you are somehow different than you were the day prior, just because the calendar we chose to tell time happened to make a lap that day. Yet there is never any significant change to the fabric of one's being between the two points in time. We humans even openly admitted that it was a flawed system, given the need for a leap year every four years.

I knew from experience that the moments that change us have absolutely nothing to do with the date and everything to do with how those moments play out.

My own birthday also happened to signify the end of the school year, the beginning of summer. Despite my own lack of enthusiasm for the occasion, my mother always went over-the-top celebrating me and, later, my stepbrother Justin as well. The year we turned nineteen, and our first summer home from college, was no exception.

Coming back home invited a cascade of complex emotions and memories that I knew I had to distance myself from. Any progress I had made toward shedding this place came undone as I found myself sinking back into the cocoon of my childhood and teenage years, without any of the security that it used to offer. Being back in this environment made me feel like I was somehow caught in a standstill. Unable to move forward yet without a place to stay back in.

"You ready for this, Sloane?" Justin asked with a smirk as he trailed me into the kitchen.

"Not one bit," I replied, grimacing as I grabbed a fruit platter off the counter.

Justin put an arm around my shoulders. "Come on, sis. My idiot friends may be idiots, but they've grown up. Besides, nobody remembers stuff that happened in high school." Justin chuckled, squeezing me and nearly causing me to drop the platter.

I wriggled out of his embrace. "Were you able to figure out if he's coming or not?"

Justin pursed his lips. "I heard her telling Dad to be nice. I don't know if she was talking about him or someone else."

I cursed under my breath. "That's him." There was only one person my mother needed to remind her husband, Neil, to be nice to.

Justin grabbed a platter of small sandwiches, and we returned to the backyard.

I relieved myself of the fruits and glanced around the party. While our backyard was nearly full, I cared to interact with only one guest—my best friend, Rebecca. I spotted her on the patio having a conversation with Neil.

"Gymnastics coach, impressive!" I heard Neil say as I made my way over to them.

Rebecca smiled sheepishly at my stepfather. "I guess."

"I wish the birthday girl would find a job this summer," Neil sassed, shooting me a teasing grin. He had been on my case since I arrived back home, but I knew he meant well.

"Oh, because the birthday boy is so gainfully employed?" I retorted sarcastically.

"Hey!" Justin protested. "I will have you know that I will be working my butt off at this training camp!" Justin's excuse for a lack of a summer job this year was that he had instead signed up for a football training camp for college players.

"Touché." Neil smiled and raised his glass in my direction before taking a sip.

"Besides, Dad, lay off Sloane. She's top of her class. She deserves a break." Justin shot me a knowing look that only I could see before bowing out of the conversation.

I gave him a grateful smile back. Justin was the only member of my family who was on my side of this debate.

Justin and I were ten years old when my mother and his father got married. We got off to a rocky start. Having both been only children, the transition to having a sibling was rough, which fueled the feud between us. By the end of high school, things had changed, and the dust had long settled.

After our little sister, Amanda, was born, we had developed a silent understanding that it was mutually beneficial for us to be friends. Justin now had his moments when he would act as my overprotective brother.

"All I'm saying," Neil continued as Justin walked back toward the house, "is a little nepotism never hurt anybody."

I cringed at Neil's persistence. If I wanted a summer job, I wanted to earn it on my own merits.

"Neil, can you go figure out what is going on with the speakers?" my mom interjected with a huff, scurrying up to where the three of us stood. She did not stop to wait for Neil's response, instead beelining for the house, indicating that her request was actually an order.

"Yes, darling."

Neil raised his glass once more in our direction, before heading over to the DJ booth that had been set up for the party.

"Ugh, I can't believe I have to go tomorrow," Rebecca whined. Her coaching job was in Las Vegas, four hours away, and she was going to be gone for most of the summer. Neither of us was looking forward to it.

"I know. I'm still mad at you," I joked. "Want me to come over later and help you pack?"

Rebecca scoffed, acting offended. "What makes you think I'm not already packed?"

I cocked my eyebrows, grinning as if to say "nice try."

Rebecca rolled her eyes, smiling. "Yes. Yes, *please*, I need help. Ugh!" We both burst out laughing.

Music started playing across the yard just as the string lights came on, offsetting the dusk settling upon us. I noticed my mother stalking toward me again, her eyes already telling me she needed me to do something for her.

"Sloane, where are the napkins? Come on," she trilled, still not bothering to stop as she shot off to her next task.

Rebecca and I shared a glance.

"Sorry, sorry. On it!" I called after my mother.

I sauntered into the kitchen but didn't see any napkins right away. I was digging through the various bags that had held supplies for the party, when I spotted the front door opening.

A dark-haired guy peeked his head through the door and looked around. He didn't notice me right away where I stood in the kitchen. The air left my lungs as his voice rang through the foyer and into the kitchen, and as my brain registered the sound, the recognition sent me spinning.

When he did notice me, he apologized, "Sorry, I knocked, but I don't think anyone heard—"

Thomas Salinger entered the foyer, closed the door behind him, and was now officially inside my house for the first time in over a year. I hadn't even recognized him without his signature thick-rimmed glasses. I found myself peering to get a closer look at him. I reluctantly made my way into the dining room but stopped in the doorway leading into the foyer. I didn't think I could stand being much closer to him than I already was. The theoretical distance that had formed between us was so vast that even being in the same space as him felt wrong.

"What the hell are you doing here?" The words came out of my mouth automatically.

Tom grabbed his upper arm with his opposite hand, shielding himself. I knew this was a compensatory trick he had conditioned himself to do instead of crossing his arms.

I hated that I knew that.

"I was invited," he answered.

"Who could have possibly invited you?" I said angrily, emphasizing that whoever it turned out to be would be in for a world of hurt.

Anything to match the hurt he had caused.

"Well, your mom, I guess," he said, awkwardly.

I couldn't understand why in the world my mother would send an invitation to Tom, knowing full well that we were not friends anymore. However, she didn't know the real reason I stopped being friends with Tom, so she probably didn't realize the weight of sending out that invitation.

"Well consider yourself uninvited." I didn't know where the hurtful words were coming from, and they felt foreign on my tongue despite the hatred I felt toward him.

"I wasn't going to come. I thought it was a mistake—" Tom started.

"Then why did you?" I spat.

"Well, I was hoping we could talk," he said, and I recognized all too well the hint of sadness in his voice.

"Talk? You and me? On my birthday of all days?" I said, indignantly, glaring at him.

"I'm sorry, this was clearly a mistake," he mumbled and spun around, reaching for the door.

"Yes, it was. As was our whole friendship, so we have nothing to talk about. Get the fuck out of my house." I didn't need to add that last part, as he was already on his way out. But I couldn't stop the hatred from infecting my words. I felt tears stream to my eyes at the finality of the words. I had never gotten to say them to him. I had never gotten closure.

"Hey, everything okay in here?" Justin entered the foyer through the family room, looking confused.

"I was just leaving," Tom said dryly, swinging the door open behind him. He avoided my eyes as he turned around and headed out the door.

I forgot all about the napkins, instead sprinting to my room and ignoring Justin's questions that followed me up the stairs. I was relieved that nobody except Justin had seen him. I tried to think of a reason why Tom would have thought today was a good day to try and talk to me. After a year of no contact. Not that talking could fix anything. What he did was unforgivable and had tainted every memory that I ever had with him, a huge chunk of my childhood memories.

What made me even angrier was that he had seemed so calm. Unbothered. As if our friendship breaking up in the way it did hadn't affected him at all. He was different; he had broadened a bit and put on some muscle, he was wearing different clothes and didn't have his glasses. His hair was longer, and he generally seemed more relaxed and confident. Like he had lived a lot more than twelve months in the year since we had spoken. The feeling of being at a standstill came rushing back, along with a fresh wave of a different anger that I hadn't allowed myself to feel for a very long time. A desperate wrath over everything that could have been if things had gone differently. I had lost a lot more than just my best friend the night Tom betrayed me.

A wave of nausea threatened to overpower me, and I could feel a throbbing headache coming on. I wasn't sure if it was because of seeing Tom or if I was legitimately getting sick. Once in my bathroom, I wet a washcloth, attempting to cool myself down without sacrificing my makeup. My mother had insisted on taking me to have it professionally done earlier that day and would throw a fit if I ruined it. I closed my eyes and leaned with my elbows on the counter. A few breaths, and I lifted my gaze to get a look at myself.

Directly behind me was the outline of a hooded figure dressed in all black. My heart thrust against my chest as I spun around, but in those milliseconds, the person was gone. It happened nearly every time I stood in front of a bathroom sink and mirror, followed by a single word.

Run.

The voice of the black-clad figure who had saved me from what could have been so much worse, before disappearing into thin air, echoed in my head once again. Taunting me, just like it had done for the last twelve months, since the night of my high school graduation. That single syllable saying so much more than one word. I knew that voice. I just didn't know whom it belonged to. But that person saved me, possibly even saved my life.

I turned around hesitantly, glancing in the mirror. I cursed under my breath as I saw a trickle of blood start to seep from one of my nostrils. I let out a defeated sigh.

I knew being back in this environment would send me spiraling. I had somehow shrunk back into the version of me that I had been around this time last year. A year ago, I was fresh out of high school, still heartbroken over a boy I'd had a fling with the summer before senior year. Still making myself small to avoid my bullies' attention. Still reeling from my best friend betraying me. But if this was my anxiety taking on a physical manifestation, I needed to seriously reconsider how I was going to spend this summer.

Just as I had the nosebleed under control, a soft knock came from my bedroom door.

"Sloane," Rebecca said as she opened the door.

"Hey, sorry—I just needed a quick break," I said, even though I knew I didn't need to provide Rebecca an excuse for my absence.

Rebecca took a deep breath before giving me an apologetic look. "Your dad's here. I was sent to get you."

My heart sank. I was already overwhelmed and had been hoping he wouldn't show up. But I knew that was naive of me. The few times my father had shown up for important events in my life, he had always been extremely late.

I reluctantly followed Rebecca out to the backyard and saw my father standing by Neil, making polite small talk. He spotted me, and a smile spread across his face. I made my way over to him, self-consciously wiping at my upper lip a few times to make sure my fingers didn't come back stained with red.

"There she is: the star of the show!" he boomed. He was being extra nice to me, and I knew why. He had an ulterior motive for coming to the party.

A few weeks ago, he had taken me to dinner and offered me an internship with his firm over the summer. He was a lawyer and a workaholic, the main reason my mother had left him, which had consequently led to him being an absentee dad. He'd been waiting for me to become old enough to be able to share the real love of his life with me: his work. I knew it was a gesture to try and excuse the years of little contact, the lack of father-daughter bond. He was trying to bond with me over the only thing he knew how to love. He had even sweetened the deal by promising that I really only needed to show up when I felt like it.

The problem was that I didn't even know if I wanted to be a lawyer anymore. My reasons for wanting to be one were completely different from his. In fact, I despised everything his firm stood for. He was mainly an attorney to the rich and (sometimes) famous, but also handled publicity scandals for them.

I thought it was the absolute worst way to put a law degree to use. It wasn't a fight for justice, it had no precedent-setting cases, no passion, no fighting for the wronged and oppressed. Just fights for the rich and famous to either keep them rich, keep them famous, or both.

I had been fully intent on declining his offer. But I felt like something in me had shifted when I saw Tom. He had been so distant, like he had completely moved on from everything we had been for almost half our lives. Like our friendship had never mattered.

Meanwhile, I was still reeling from its end. Coupling this realization with the fact that Rebecca was going to be gone all summer made me feel like I was being left behind, a feeling I was all too familiar with. I was sick of being that girl. I needed a change.

"I'll do it," I said, before I had fully finished crossing the lawn to where my father and Neil stood.

My father's smile broadened. "Really?" As I reached him, he pulled me into a one-armed side hug.

"Don't get too excited; this is me abusing my position as your daughter," I said, half kidding, half not.

"Well you are fully entitled to that," he laughed.

Neil winked at me, satisfied.

My mother came up behind Neil, beaming.

"Did you tell her yet?"

"Tell me what?" I asked.

"I have something for you. A birthday present," my father said as I stepped back from his embrace.

My mother let out a squeal. "Oh come on—I can't take it anymore!"

"Come with me," my father said, heading back toward the house. I followed him; so did Rebecca, my mother, and Neil. By the time we reached the front door, Justin had joined our group with a smirk on his face like he also knew something I didn't.

My father opened the front door. "After you," he said, gesturing for me to exit first.

I walked off the front porch onto the lawn, and in the driveway stood a shiny, deep-red four-door hatchback with a huge white bow on the hood. My jaw dropped.

"Don't tell me that's mine," I said, turning around to face my dad and the rest of the group that had spilled out onto the lawn behind me. Rebecca was jumping up and down and clapping her hands. She was probably more excited than I was.

"All yours." My father smiled. I could tell he was elated to be able to give me such a huge present; it was the only way he knew how to show me he loved me.

The fact that my mother seemed to have known meant that he had cleared it with her beforehand. Years ago, she had told him to stop showering me with absurdly huge presents and extravagant gestures in attempts to replace a real father-daughter relationship.

I walked over to my father and hugged him. I wasn't comfortable hugging him, but I was genuinely thankful and, to be frank, I would have hugged a stranger if they had given me a car. The new car sat next to my old one. At sixteen, I had scraped together pennies to be able to afford it—something I had always been proud of. Now it just looked like a heap of scrap metal.

"Consider it a tool for the internship!" he added, pleased with himself.

My heart sank for what seemed like the umpteenth time that day. I realized then and there that he would have probably shown me the car as a way to get a decision out of me regarding the internship. But I had told him yes before even greeting him. I mentally kicked myself, wondering where the rashness I had been feeling a few minutes earlier had come from. The car was a bribe, but I had spared him from even having to use it as one.

"Thank you, Dad. It's awesome," I said, trying very hard to match my excitement to everyone else's. Another wave of nausea swept over me as I went over to examine my new mode of transportation, and I found myself longing for the night to be over.

CHAPTER TWO

When I arrived at my father's office on Monday morning, my father spent about fifteen minutes with me before rushing off, claiming he had a meeting. I should have known that my father was too important for me to actually work with him directly.

I was therefore left with the office receptionist, who looked less than enthusiastic to have me dumped on her. Her tour of the office consisted of rushing around, half-heartedly showing me where the restrooms and the cafeteria were, but mostly chatting up lots of people, refraining from introductions and only mentioning me once.

"Oh yeah no. This is Shannon, Becker's daughter," she said to an older lady in the accounting department who asked if I was there to replace her. I thought about saying "my name is Sloane," but I couldn't muster the energy for the confrontation.

After the uninformative tour, the receptionist dropped me off at my desolate-looking cubicle that was stacked with banker's boxes. Thankfully, my first task was something I could easily sink into and keep myself busy with. I had about one hundred boxes of physical files that I needed to organize. Some of them were older than me, from when my father started the firm. I took a late and long lunch, hoping to have as little left of my day as possible when I got back. As I arrived back at the office, I turned the corner and spotted my cubicle—and immediately knew something was off.

All the files I had stacked, labeled, and categorized that morning were strewn about the desk, the floor of the cubicle, across the piles of to-be-tackled boxes I had stacked behind my chair, and out of the cubicle and onto the floor of the hallway. Nothing was where I had left it, nothing was in order, and I had no idea if any of them were missing.

Frustration flared up in the pit of my stomach as I chewed the insides of my cheeks.

But then I noticed that my computer monitor was on, a video playing silently on full screen.

The shock of realization nearly knocked me over as I rushed to the computer, pounded on the space bar to pause the video, and quickly turned the monitor off, desperate to make the visual disappear as fast as humanly possible.

I glanced around, praying to any deity that would listen that no one had noticed.

Oh gosh, what if my father has been here?

I wondered if this was some sort of hazing ritual, this being my first day, but found it hard to believe that something so tactless would be done in this otherwise sterile environment. The video was not only very inappropriate for work, but it also nudged something in me that I didn't want to think about.

Whoever had scattered the files I was working on had obviously pulled the video up as well. I looked around, my breaths short and shallow, to see if anyone had seen me. Mine was one of only six cubicles, and I had not seen anyone occupy the other five that entire day. I went over to the area across the hall to the person sitting in the nearest occupied cubicle.

"Hey, sorry to bother you, but did you happen to see anyone come by my desk?" I asked the youngish woman who was typing away on her keyboard. She barely looked up to acknowledge me.

"Nope, why?" She gave me a once-over, with an expression that looked as if I smelled bad, and then turned back to her screen, not bothering to wait for my response.

"Someone made a mess of the files I was working on while I was out at lunch. I was just wondering if you noticed anything, since you can kind of see my desk from here."

She craned her neck to see past her cubicle partition and looked over to my desk across the hall. "I would clean that up if I were you," she said, instead of answering my question. The words sent a shockwave of rage through me.

"Thanks. Hadn't thought of that," I said sarcastically.

As I turned to walk back to my cubicle, dreading the cleanup effort ahead, a man rounded the corner at the other end and started walking toward me. He locked eyes with me and, as he did, a jolt went through my body. We continued to close the gap between us, his features coming into focus, and the jolts just kept coming, twisting my insides until I had to bribe my breaths into my lungs.

He was handsome, with light-brown hair, short on the sides and longer up top, swept to the side. He had a sharp nose and oval face and his eyes were friendly with a mischievous glint, like he was hiding a funny secret. I could tell that if he were to divulge said secret, his smile would be the kind that would stop you in your tracks from across a room full of people. As he approached, my heart thumped louder and louder, a whooshing in my ears threatening to drown out my thoughts. I had never in my life had such a visceral reaction to seeing someone for the first time. A tiny thread at the back of my mind tugged at me incessantly.

This man is going to be important in my life.

"Uhm, Ms. Becker? Hi, Eric Baxter," he said as he nervously fixed his tie and walked up to me, hand stretched out awkwardly. I shook his hand,

and it was the weakest handshake I had ever known; he had barely touched my hand before he let go. It was as if my hand was something disgusting that he picked up off the floor, eager to shake off.

"Hi. Please, call me Sloane," I said, clasping my hands in front of me, not knowing where put them after the handshake.

"Sloane," he said, and my name rolled off his tongue as if he said it every day. Yet, he looked like he was either extremely embarrassed about something or just unbelievably uncomfortable in his own skin. His eyes were a bright green, and I found myself wishing he would stay still. Something about him made me want to examine him, commit him to memory.

I was certain I had never seen him before. I had defiantly shut down any opportunity to interact with this part of my father's life up until now. I frantically searched the far corners of my mind for any piece of recollection. Had I met him at school this past year? Perhaps at a bar? My stomach flipped as I thought back to the rare occasions I had allowed Rebecca to drag me out on the town during our first year at college. Her attempt to make me move on from my embarrassingly long heartbreak that I had brought with me from high school. Reluctantly, I had played along, Rebecca playing the role of my wingwoman expertly, but I had never allowed myself anything other than few drunken kisses. Nothing that should have triggered this outlandish feeling of recognition yet unfamiliarity. I kicked myself for purposely deciding to not remember any of their names. But I never thought I would find myself in this position.

You know this man. This man knows you.

"Well, it's very nice to meet you, Sloane. My office is right over there," he said, pointing down the hall behind him. "If there's anything you need, please don't hesitate to ask. They just upgraded me—I was made a law clerk a few weeks ago, but I've been interning here for a few summers now, so I know my way around." He smiled, and my breath caught. The knot in my stomach tightened so painfully it was borderline rude that my body could betray me this way. I couldn't understand where it was coming from; I had had plenty of crushes throughout my lifetime—but this wasn't that—

simply being smiled at had never invoked anything close to this. He wasn't even my type.

I shook it off. There was no way I knew him; I probably just had confirmation bias. That morning, before rushing off, my father had gushed about some guy named Eric, who was apparently his prized protégé, earning the nickname "Mr. Make-It-Go-Away." He was supposedly extra brilliant for his young age, so it surprised me how old Eric actually looked. I would have guessed at least late twenties if not early thirties.

"Nice to meet you as well. I appreciate the offer," I said. My eyes shot nervously to the mess at my desk, which was to Eric's left. My stomach did another somersault, but then relief washed over me as I confirmed that I had indeed turned off my computer monitor before leaving my cubicle.

"Whoa," he said as he spotted the wreck. "What the—?"

Thank goodness. He hasn't been over here yet. He didn't see the video.

"Yeah. It was like this when I came back from lunch. Did you by chance see anyone come through here?" I asked.

"No, sorry." Eric looked around at the papers with a concerned expression. It crossed my mind that maybe this Eric was to blame for the state of my cubicle, and that the only reason he was talking to me was to throw off suspicion. "This is so weird. So you didn't leave it like this?" he asked, sweeping a hand through his hair in a manner that indicated it was a habit.

"No, of course not." I chuckled to try to diffuse my indignation, my heart still pounding. Whether it was his presence or the embarrassment of having my workspace in such a disarray, I wasn't sure.

An awkward silence filled the space between and around us. The soft ambient noises of the office, fingers tapping on keyboards, printers whirring, distant conversations, made the silence even heavier.

"Well, I better get to it," I said with a slightly exaggerated sigh and a small smile as I stepped into the cubicle, careful not to tread on any of the files on the floor, letting him know that he could leave if he wanted to. I needed to fix this mess and clear my head of the effect his presence had on me.

"Can I help you get this straightened out? Off the floor at least?" Eric asked as he bent down to start picking up a few sheets that littered the hall.

Against what my body was telling me, I replied, "Sure, thank you," and got busy scooping up files and stacking them in neat piles on my desk.

A few moments into the task, I found myself face-to-face with him as we both stood up clutching handfuls of paper.

"Sorry," we both said at the same time, with nervous laughs as we did the stereotypical dance trying to dodge one another, somehow always aiming for the same direction as the other. The cubicle was maybe thirty square feet, and Eric's figure filled out the space between the partition wall and the stack of boxes that took up most of the open space within it. I had planted myself firmly in front of my computer, utterly aware that if someone even accidentally nudged the power button on my monitor, the video would show up. As he turned to go right, I turned to go left, and since we were facing each other this meant brushing up against each other.

"Excuse me," he muttered under his breath, and shot me an awkward smile as he quickly jerked away. It was only the back of his hand against my forearm, but I could have sworn it felt like a zap of current, followed by the distinct buzz of a tuning fork ringing in my ears.

As we finished getting all the papers off the floor, Eric quickly shuffled out of the cubicle. Maybe it was in my head, but it felt like he was breathing easier now that he wasn't so close to me. I sure was.

"Hey, I can take you to the security guard and see if he can't pull up the cameras for you. To see if someone was lurking here who shouldn't be," Eric suggested.

I didn't have to think twice. Glancing at my monitor once again to make sure it was off, I answered him, "That would be great."

༄༅༄༅༄༅

We stood behind the security guard's chair in his office. The building itself had its own security team and a robust system, but our firm had its own in-office guard that monitored the office cameras. The security guard, Herman, was a chubby, younger-looking guy with friendly eyes, possibly in his late twenties. His uniform was tight in many places and lose in others, his expression always cheery. He swayed a little bit when he walked, and he walked painfully slowly, like he possibly had a bad knee. Not really someone who could scare off intruders. But he had a bat in his belt and a booming voice.

"I don't see anyone I don't recognize," Herman said as he scrolled through the video from the front lobby camera in the timeframe I had advised, from approximately one thirty to three p.m. The timeframe had, of course, exposed my very long lunch, around an hour and a half, and I couldn't help but think how typical it was that the first time I decided to break the rules, I needed to confess to it not even thirty minutes later.

"Are there any cameras over the south wing of the floor?" Eric asked.

"So this one goes down the south hall, but it barely catches the cubicles," Herman said, pointing to the screen. He was right; it showed the hall that led down to the offices and conference rooms and sat between my cubicle and the unhelpful coworker's desk. But you could only see the outer partition of my cubicle and its entrance. I let out a silent sigh of relief knowing that my computer monitor was not captured by any of the cameras and therefore, the video wouldn't show up.

"Scroll back to one thirty on this view," I said.

Herman started scrolling. I saw Eric and me walking backward to the entrance of my cubicle, us picking up some of the mess inside the cubicle, moving back out into the hallway with Eric reaching down to pick up the few papers that had made their way onto the hall floor. Then, Eric and I stood in the hallway talking, shook hands, and Eric walked backward down the hall toward his office and the conference rooms. A part of me felt like I was having an out-of-body experience—and that it was somehow wrong to be watching my interaction with Eric back with him and the security guard. Like it was incongruously intimate for the commercial screens in front of us.

Next on the reversed footage, I could be seen in the corner of the screen talking to the unhelpful coworker, her disinterest in me and my affairs even more apparent in fast rewind, as she barely seemed to move her head in my direction once. I disappeared out of view into my cubicle, my desperation to shut down the monitor neatly hidden behind the gray partitions. Then I could be seen standing in the hall surveying the paper mess with a blank expression before walking backward down the hall and out of sight.

Herman kept scrolling, and the video showed little traffic along the hall. A few people who Eric and Herman claimed to recognize strolled past my cubicle lazily, coffee cups in hand.

"Wait, stop, go back for a second," I said.

Herman obliged and let the tape play.

"Look." I pointed to the hallway floor as the tape played.

The time stamp said 1:37:48 p.m., and the floor of the hallway was clear. Then, at 1:38:03 p.m., the papers appeared on the floor.

"Weird," said Herman. "Let me check."

He scrolled further backward, all the way to 1:28 p.m. when I was seen leaving for lunch. No one made their way down the hall in between.

"That's super weird, man," Herman said in a casual, unconcerned voice.

"But there's no other way into that cubicle area. It's closed off with a wall on the other end. Unless someone was highly aware of the camera placements and actually climbed over the partitions. But I would think someone would have noticed that, right?" My question was more directed toward Eric than Herman, but Eric stayed silent and didn't take his eyes off the screen. One of his arms was crossed in front of him, one hand at his mouth and chin. His eyes looked more worried than I wanted them to be.

"Yeah, I don't know what to tell you man," Herman replied. "Maybe someone turned up the AC and the wind blew your papers?"

I couldn't tell if Herman was genuinely trying to be helpful or if our request was just boring him, because anyone who laid eyes on the chaos knew that something as simple as an AC draft could not have caused it. I of course knew of another piece of evidence that proved that this was an intentional thing—the fact that someone had also messed with my computer—but I wasn't going to share it with them. Thankfully, Eric didn't need any convincing either.

"No, this was not an AC gust. Can you scroll back to where the papers fell down?" Eric asked, not removing his hand from his chin.

"Sure." Herman scrolled back to 1:37 p.m. and then wiggled the video back and forth so that the papers appeared and disappeared over and over.

"Okay, thanks man, you've been super helpful," Eric said, indicating Herman should stop.

I was disappointed; I wanted to know who had been at my desk. I *needed* to know who had been there.

We walked in stride back in the direction of our respective workspaces, and Eric made nervous small talk apologizing that our security camera quest wasn't more fruitful. He halted in front of an office that had a piece of printer paper taped to the door. It read Eric C. Baxter.

"No worries. Thank you for all the help. It was nice to meet you," I said, aiming for finality, but Eric was staring at me with a mix of concern and discomfort.

"Uhm," Eric started as if he didn't know what to say. "You uhm—" He tapped the area between his upper lip and nose. "You have a nosebleed."

Mortified, I felt around below my nose. My hand came back stained with bright-red blood.

"Oh my gosh, please excuse me," I said, and hurried off to the restroom.

As if this day wasn't awkward enough already.

CHAPTER THREE

ONCE BACK AT my desk, I forced my computer to shut down by holding in the power button, not daring to turn the monitor back on. I then safely rebooted it without any surprises popping up on the screen. After the fact, I wished I had at least checked whether it was playing from a website or a file on the computer.

This was no random act. That video was meant for me, and only me.

I didn't see my father at all the rest of the day, and I had a feeling that if the whole summer was going to be anything like that first day, it would end up being a colossal waste of my time. When it was finally time to go home, I tried to put it behind me and forget that I'd ever signed up for this mistake.

I walked out of the building and toward the parking structure where I had parked my new car; I had almost reached the corner of the block when an all-too-familiar voice called my name.

"Sloane?"

I turned around and froze. Standing about twenty feet away from me was a face I had tried so hard to forget, even though I knew very well that day would never come. My heart pounded as Dylan Archer walked toward me.

"Hey," he said as we approached each other, his voice buttery with a slight hint of raspiness. Only he could say a dull, single-syllable word like *hey* and make it sound like a siren's song.

A gust of warm wind slapped me in the face with his familiar scent, another thing I had worked very hard to forget. The furious flashbacks induced by his mere presence were magnified in the wake of his scent, and for a split second my knees felt like they were giving in. Nausea pricked at my throat.

"Hi." I sounded like I had been sprinting. "You're back in town?" I asked, trying to sound as if his answer didn't matter to me in the slightest.

"Uhm, yeah. I'm transferring." He reached his arm back and rubbed the back of his neck in the same irresistible way he always had. "It's really good to see you. What are you doing down here?" he asked, meaning the downtown area.

I didn't know why I felt the need to cover up the fact that I was working for my father. Maybe because he hated Dylan. "Oh, just shopping." My voice was too squeaky to hide my lies. "What are *you* doing here?" I was genuinely confused.

"Yeah, same here, shopping," he said. I could tell that he was lying too. "How have you been?"

Part of me wanted to crumble into his arms and tell him how awful this past year had been. Tell him everything I had been through after Tom's betrayal. Tell him how I still missed him, and that any feeble attempt at dating had paled in comparison to what we had had.

I felt pathetic, still being so affected by and pining for a guy who I could barely call a high school sweetheart, so I kept it cool. "I've been great."

I could have sworn I saw a glimpse of disappointment in his eyes, but it was probably wishful thinking. "Good, I'm glad."

"How about yourself?" I asked innocently, although I didn't need him to answer. I stalked his Instagram more than any other and knew he'd been doing just fine. Him and Private Profile Girl had tons of fun together.

"I know you said I'd learn to love it, but New York's not for me," he said, which came as a surprise to me. He continued, "I'm glad to be home."

I couldn't recall ever telling him he'd love New York; he was a born and bred Californian with an allergy to colder weather, but now was not the time to bring it up. "Well, welcome back," I said.

"Thanks." He smiled a small smile and glanced at his phone. "Shit, I have to go. Do you maybe want to grab coffee and catch up sometime? Soon?"

Grab coffee.

It sounded so mundane. It was something we had never done. We as an entity, Sloane and Dylan, were not capable of simply "grabbing coffee." We began and ended with explosions.

I still wanted to say yes, more than anything. But the thought of him and me keeping a civil conversation for the time that it took to drink a cup of coffee seemed impossible. I thought of my father, the fact that I was working for him, and how it would complicate everything if he found out I'd so much as spoken a word to Dylan. I thought of the fresh start I had wished for at my birthday party just days earlier. I thought about what it had felt like when Dylan left, and I knew my heart was in no place to feel like that again, anytime soon.

But the words came out of my mouth by their own volition. "Yeah, absolutely. Text me."

"Awesome." Dylan smiled, reached for his phone again, and said, "Listen, this is awkward, but I got a new phone and a new number when I moved, and I kind of lost your number." He chuckled awkwardly as he handed me the phone.

So that's why you never texted, asshole.

Why did you not know my number by heart?

And if you didn't, how come you didn't reach out through the half dozen social media platforms I have?

Losing someone's number in this day and age was not an excuse anymore.

"Oh, no worries," I said, again with the squeaky voice, and smiled as I punched my number into his phone, handing him mine to do the same with his new number.

"Thanks," he said, and smiled wide, gripping his phone as if it suddenly held more value than before. "It was really good seeing you."

"You too." I smiled back before he turned to leave.

As I went on my way, my anxiety took over. I couldn't believe that all it took for me to let him back into my life was a simple, accidental encounter on the street. Rebecca was going to be livid.

When I finally got home after wrangling the afternoon traffic, I changed out of my work clothes into yoga pants and a faded black hoodie. It was worn and ugly, but it was the softest article of clothing I owned, and since the string was still intact in the hood, I wasn't willing to consider it a lost cause yet. I flopped down on my bed, wishing my body was as exhausted as my mind was. This day had been one weird happening after another. The further removed I got from seeing the video on my work computer, the more I wished I had investigated what it was.

It can't be what I think it is.

I didn't have time to linger on it, as my phone started buzzing on my nightstand.

"Finally, the mighty lawyer-in-the-making Miss Becker graces me with her virtual presence!" Rebecca said as we got on a video call. I hadn't been responding to her texts all day, overwhelmed with the newness—and weirdness—of my first day at my job.

"Sorry, boo. How are you doing?" I answered.

"Ugh, I'm so tired. I just want to sleep in my own bed!" Rebecca wailed. She was lying down, one hand holding her phone, her opposite forearm lying across her temple. "My roommate is the most obnoxious person on the planet. She sleeps with a white noise machine and three diffusers. Three. Each with a different essential oil."

"You poor thing," I mocked.

"What I would give to be able to trade places with you. You're so lucky to get to be in an office! Wear heels all day, skirts, look cute—ugh!" Rebecca said. She was much more of a girly girl than I had ever been.

"I hate to break it to you, but I wore flats," I said.

Rebecca sat up and gasped, acting offended. "I disown you. Tell me all about it."

We spent a while talking about our new jobs, comparing and contrasting. Rebecca immediately looked up Eric when I told her about him and was obsessed. She couldn't believe how cute my new coworker was. I told her how I felt like I had seen him before, and the weird circumstances under which we met, but I of course left out the video. We spent some time dissecting it, but Rebecca didn't recognize him at all. She was, however, convinced he must have a crush on me, and didn't listen when I told her he had just been trying to be helpful.

"You're being ridiculous, Sloane. You think he can't have a crush on you from the moment he lays eyes on you?" Rebecca sassed, arching an eyebrow.

"No—What? Of course not," I retorted, wondering if that was maybe all this was. That I had just instantly developed a crush on this guy and that explained my brain short-circuiting at the sight of him.

Rebecca groaned and shifted how she lay on the bed. "Sloane. You're his boss's daughter—he probably had a thing for you before he even met you. How do you not get it?"

I rolled my eyes, making sure it was visible to Rebecca. "This is *not* like that."

Rebecca huffed and shot me a look as if to reiterate that I was being naive. "You seriously need to get back out there. College has made you a spinster!" she teased.

I bit my lip. I knew I needed to tell her. She was the one who helped me through the heartbreak, after all.

"What?" she pressed. "I cannot believe you don't think he's hot."

"I ran into Dylan," I blurted out, grimacing.

Rebecca gasped. "What! He's back? Oh my gosh, when?"

"Just as I was leaving work earlier." I sighed. "He asked me for coffee."

"No, Sloane. No. I will not allow it. You cannot go down that path again after everything! You spent longer getting over him than you were with him."

I winced at that fact, both because it was true and it was embarrassing. Dylan and I had only been a thing for a mere four months, the summer before my senior year of high school. The summer before he was supposed to start college at UCLA.

"He said he was transferring back here. That he's done with NYU."

"Oh, so *now* he's too good for NYU, but when you two were dating, he listened to daddy dearest and moved away?" Rebecca continued, her expression grim.

"It's not like that, Becks. He never wanted to go to NYU in the first place. He's probably just finally able to stand up to them now. And you know it wasn't his dad; his grandfather calls all the shots in that family." I tensed as I thought back to the awful moment I watched Dylan's grandfather lay down the law, the old man red-faced and sputtering. The moment that marked the end of us. What I hadn't known was that the rumor mill at school was going to spin it so that it looked like I was the one who drove him to move across the country.

"Whatever," Rebecca snapped, bringing me back to the present moment. "He should have had the balls two years ago. You are going to decline politely whenever he texts you." Rebecca held the phone closer to her face so I could only see one of her eyes, making it clear that she was glaring at me.

"Calm down. I'm not saying that I'm getting back together with him." I held up my hand to stop Rebecca from interjecting. "We never talked. We never got closure. That was probably why it was so hard. Remember how many times I whined about not getting closure? I feel like he and I both deserve a talk."

Rebecca frowned. "Okay, well. He hasn't texted you. Maybe he won't. Please don't get your hopes up."

"I'm not," I lied.

Rebecca narrowed her eyes at me in an exaggerated fashion. "I don't believe you. You are a hopeless addict for that guy. I don't think I have it in me to perform another detox."

She was right. I had been getting my hopes up, just a tad. I hated myself for it.

"Relax, I won't cross any boundaries," I said, and when Rebecca still didn't look convinced, I added, "That is, *if* he ever texts me. Maybe he won't. And that's fine."

I was still lying.

CHAPTER FOUR

THE REST OF my first week in the office was thankfully less eventful than the first day had been. The second week had me feeling more rooted as I got into the cadence of the workplace. The need to ask the haughty receptionist tedious questions, only to get unhelpful answers, decreased rapidly as the days went on.

By Thursday of that second week, I could definitely tell that Eric was finding reasons to swing by my cubicle. I would have been lying to myself if I didn't admit that Rebecca's words from the prior week were definitely polluting my thoughts.

I cannot believe you don't think he's hot.

And I would also have been lying if I didn't admit that I liked it when he went out of his way to talk to me.

There was a client meeting that afternoon, and my job was to get coffee and water, hand out the agenda, but otherwise observe silently. Just before lunch, Eric was showing me where to gather what I needed for the meeting.

"Here's where we keep the beverages for client meetings," Eric said, opening a fridge with a crystal-clear glass door in the employee lounge, full of bottles you would not find at your normal grocery store. The bottom two shelves held wine. As if he had spotted me eyeing them, Eric continued, chuckling, "Although we don't serve alcohol at daytime meetings."

"Got it," I replied.

"And for coffee, there's usually someone who fills up these urns here." He walked to the counter of the lounge kitchenette, where three coffee dispensers stood. "Just check which one has the most coffee in it and grab that one and some cups. Here." He opened a top cabinet revealing rows of nondescript white mugs with varyingly faded versions of the firm's logo on them.

"Simple enough," I said.

"I'm sorry," Eric said, and smiled at me, his eyes twinkling with something between pity and embarrassment.

"For what?" I piped, my voice coming out higher than I wanted it to.

"For asking you to be a glorified waitress." He eyed me as he closed the cabinet again, and as he let his gaze linger on me, I became hyperaware of every breath I took.

Forcing air into my lungs, I waved a hand at him both to pivot from whatever territory this conversation was headed into and to brush him off. "Don't worry about it."

"No, really. I know you're capable of much more." He leaned on the counter in front of the sink and crossed his arms, but his gaze stayed on me. "If it makes you feel better, I also had to do this for a while."

I paused, trying to read him. I didn't know why he was concerned over what tasks he was delegating to me. He wasn't being awkward, like he had been the prior week.

But he was definitely being weird. He had no idea whether my capabilities went past fetching coffee. And I couldn't shake the feeling that he was a little too comfortable staring at me. We stood about three feet apart, both leaning on the counter in the otherwise empty lounge. My nervousness got the better of me the longer I remained silent, and I grabbed the first joke that came to mind.

"I've done worse things for money."

Eric looked amused with my answer. "Have you now?"

I realized my joke had a terrifying amount of ways of interpreting it, so I quickly reeled it in. "Getting coffee beats scraping gum off the bottom of movie theater seats any day."

"True," said Eric. "I didn't know you worked in a movie theater."

I wondered why he felt like he should've known. It wasn't like I had submitted my résumé to get this job. Nor would he have read it.

"Yeah, summer before junior year. I still can't eat popcorn." I laughed despite being slightly on edge, like I always seemed to be around him.

"That sucks. Hopefully you won't get sick of coffee this summer." He winked at me.

"I could never get sick of coffee," I said, mock-offended. My heart leaped with pride that I was able to be quick on my feet despite his smile nearly knocking me over.

"Speaking of, I could use some," Eric said as he took a step toward me. I was standing underneath the cabinet that held the mugs. Without hesitation, Eric leaned in over me to reach for one.

His thigh brushed against my hip, ever so gently, but the touch sent a wave of sparks through me, like nothing I had felt before. He looked surprised as he realized just how close he was to me. I was frozen in place but managed to tilt my head back to meet his eyes.

"Sorry—" he began.

He was so close to me, his scent filled my senses. He was wearing a fresh cologne that didn't remind me of anything I had smelled before, which made it all the more irresistible. It was like a rainy ocean breeze that carried with it the faint scent of a wood bonfire and tropical flowers. I could see a shadow of a stubble on his jawline, and in that moment I discovered why it was such a coveted phenomenon. I held my breath as my stomach twisted and twirled.

Tension danced on the tightrope that tethered our gazes for just a moment. His eyes drifted down to my lips, scanning my face and coming back up to meet my eyes.

"No, you're fine!" I said when I couldn't take it anymore, ducking and stepping to the side.

Sweat dewed my hairline as I turned away from him and headed to the beverage fridge, quickly becoming busy with loading bottles onto a rolling cart.

"See you after lunch," Eric said from behind me.

I acknowledged him without looking in his direction, waiting to hear his footsteps drift away.

The excitement in the pit of my stomach made my nerves tingle. It quickly turned into nervous shaking, and to my despair, was replaced by an all-too-familiar wave of nausea.

***

My stomach grumbled as I set up the refreshments on the bureau along the conference room wall. I hadn't been able to eat much at lunch; I was too nauseous. I reminded myself that I had gotten through every nausea spell before this, so I could power through this one too.

The clients started filing in, four of them, music producers in some type of feud with a record label. I hadn't read the entire file. Eric wasn't there yet, and I offered them drinks, each of them choosing sparkling water in tiny glass bottles.

The nausea worsened the more I moved, and my head was spinning. As I reached to open the second set of bottles, my vision blurred. Clearing my throat harshly, I gritted my teeth and proceeded to wield the opener.

I barely registered the earsplitting crash as one of the bottles slid off the bureau and onto the floor, shattering.

The clients went silent, the one closest to me cocking an eyebrow and giving me a displeased once-over, letting their gaze linger on the mess at my feet. I could feel all eyes in the conference room on me as the blood rushed to my head and my vision tightened to a pinhole.

"I'm so sorry. So sorry," I muttered, bending down to pick up the pieces.

I was rushing and my vision still wasn't complying, hence the inevitable happened. I jabbed my palm directly into a razor-sharp corner of the bottleneck piece.

Wincing, but trying desperately to hide what a train wreck my execution of this simple task was becoming, I looked at my palm. Blood was seeping out of a wide cut along my life line. I didn't usually mind blood, but something was off. I realized drops of blood were also landing on my skin, not from the cut, but instead coming from my nose. There was so much blood. I looked around at the clients, all still staring at me, and a shiver ran through my body as every pore seemed to ooze cold sweat. The pain of the gash struck me suddenly, piercing and deep, as the adrenaline of my humiliation started leaving my system. I knew the glass hadn't gone through my hand, but it sure felt like it. I dry heaved and knew I couldn't hold it in any longer.

I didn't stop running till I reached the restroom, opening one of the stall doors so fast that it slammed against the stall partition loudly. I quickly locked it behind me, dizzy as I wrapped my injured hand with toilet paper. The blood seeped right through. I pulled my hair back as well as I could with my other hand, leaning with my elbows on the toilet seat, staring into the half full bowl, wishing my body would give me relief from the nausea.

A single drop of bright-red blood landed in the middle of the toilet water, quickly diluting and dispersing, becoming pink, then beige, then clear. I let go of my hair and touched my nose with my uncut palm, and it came back soaked with red.

As I stared at all the blood, I started seeing spots again and felt an intense need to close my eyes. I squeezed them shut, and as I did, a ringing started in my ears.

Breath coming in shaky gulps.

The buzz in my ears unbearable, eyes sealed shut.

A wicked case of pins and needles erupting on my back, spreading out from my spine and to my sides as it moved upward.

I clawed at my shirt, gasping for air as my face, neck, and chest suddenly burned with heat and cold sweat erupted across my body.

And then it was over.

Just like that.

My heart rate slowed, my breaths came easier.

Did I just have a panic attack?

I stood up and collected myself, adding a couple layers of toilet paper to my makeshift bandage. I peeked out of the stall and made sure no one was in the restroom before I made my way to one of the sinks. The faucet was touchless, with a motion sensor to stop and start the water flow. It didn't turn on when I placed my hand under it. I waved my hand and knocked on the sensor, but nothing happened. I tried the next sink, and the next. None of them worked.

I knew there were manual levers on the backs of the faucets intended to override the motion sensors in case this happened. I tried the lever on the sink I was at, but still nothing happened. Annoyed, because I desperately needed to wash my hands and splash some cold water on my face, I figured the water must have been shut off due to maintenance. I cleaned up as well as I could with dry paper towels and rewrapped my injured hand.

I stopped for a moment at the sink and hung my head, clasping its sides to brace myself. I tried one more time with the faucet, leaning my head down toward the sink to see if I could spot another valve that could get the water flowing.

Run.

An image of the black silhouette appeared once again, their voice ringing in my mind. I staggered away from the sink, nearly falling over, shaking from the flashback. Blinking my eyes furiously as I stared at myself in the mirror, my eyesight blacked out for a moment as I squinted to make my form come into focus. No one was behind me, but the sound of the word was etched in my brain.

I had no time to compose myself. I had to get out of there. Away from that sink that was playing mind games with me. I hurried to the door and peered out.

A person was standing at the other end of the brightly lit hall with their back toward me, walking away, just about to turn a corner. No one else was in sight so I decided it was safe for me to slip out and back toward the part of the floor where the conference room was without being seen.

But something caught my eye about the way the person was standing. I realized they hadn't moved in the few seconds I had been surveying the hall. One foot rested slightly off the ground, as if they were frozen midstep. I waited a few more seconds, and they still didn't move.

"Hey! Is everything okay over there?" I called.

I headed toward them, in the opposite direction of the conference room.

"Hey, are you all right?" I asked again when I was about halfway to them. They didn't respond.

I reached the person, a middle-aged man not that much taller than I. He was definitely not a mannequin, despite standing extremely still, with a nonchalant, ordinary look on his face. His eyes looked directly forward; he had one hand in his pocket and the other completely still by his side. His right foot was still hovering off the ground.

There was a still, eerie silence about him.

"Sir? Do you need any help?" I asked quietly.

I noticed then that he wasn't blinking, and his eyes had a lifeless sheen to them. His chest wasn't rising and falling either. Against my better judgment and all common sense, I placed a finger under his nose to check for his breath. Nothing.

I backed away from him, running every possible scenario through in my mind, wondering if I should be yelling for someone to call 911. Was this some spooky lifelike robot the firm had procured for some outlandish reason? Was he a magician? Why was he completely alone in the hallway then?

My breath came in rattling gasps as I slowly backed away from him. I walked quickly around the corner to look for someone—anyone—to come help me. To tell me that I wasn't crazy or in any danger. I reached the end of the next hall, made a right turn, and headed toward the cafeteria where there were bound to be people at any time of day.

I had sped up to a brisk pace which then made for an extremely ungraceful stop when I reached the cafeteria. There were indeed quite a few people there just as I had expected, but it was completely silent.

No one in the cafeteria was moving. They were frozen in all types of stances, some midaction, some inactive, some sitting, some walking. A cafeteria employee stood utterly still, holding a large square plastic tray full of dirty dishes and glasses.

It looked heavy, and he was holding it with his hands outstretched, not something that was easy to do while still for a long period of time. None of the normal cafeteria bustle was audible.

"What is going on?" I said into the void. No one so much as blinked.

I went up to a couple of ladies who were seated at the table closest to where I was standing. It was like walking inside a photograph. One of the ladies was smiling and her lips were pursed as if she were saying a *W* sound. The lady sitting across from her had her mouth clamped as if getting ready to say *B*, her eyebrows were furrowed, and she held her left index finger high, about to interrupt the other woman.

Neither woman was blinking. Neither woman was breathing.

My vision narrowed as I backed away from the table. I took one more glance across the room before spinning and bolting out of there. I shot back down the way I came, rounding the second corner with a skid. The man I had seen in the hallway was still right where I had left him, in the exact same position, as if petrified in place.

I sped up even more once I reached the other side of the office floor, closer to the conference room I had ungracefully left a few minutes earlier. The only sounds were my heavy breaths and my feet stomping on the travertine tile. When I reached the conference room, my heart sank. Inside,

Eric and the firm's clients weren't moving. Eric stood by the conference table, clasping a stack of manila folders lightly with both hands, holding them perpendicular to the table in front of him as if to tap the bottom against the table to straighten the papers. Except the stack was suspended about three inches off the table, and his thumb and the rest of his fingers were not tight enough around the files to be holding them at that level. The files were floating midair.

The panic attack I had in the restroom paled in comparison to what was happening in my body when I realized that everyone around me seemed to be affected by whatever was going on. I was the only person who wasn't. I went up to Eric and nudged him, knowing that if this were indeed a practical joke, I would look like an absolute fool. Eric staggered and swayed a bit to the point where I had to steady him to prevent his stiff body from falling over.

I ran to the large windows that lined one side of the conference room and looked down to the street below. Nothing was moving. Cars lined the streets, completely motionless, and not because of traffic. A line of flagpoles flanked the courtyard between the tower I worked in and its sister tower next door. The flags were stopped midwave, slightly wrinkled and curved, but still tugging away from their flagpoles and rising perpendicular to the ground beneath them.

I had to be losing my mind, there was no other explanation. The nausea, the nosebleeds, the headaches . . . I had to have a brain tumor or something to be having these hallucinations. That was the only logical reason. This was a hallucination.

Tears crept onto my lower lash line, and I buried my face in my hands, slumping into one of the chairs at the conference table. My mind raced through all the issues that had seemed so insurmountable in the past. I found myself wishing that something as boring as an ex-boyfriend, or an ex-best friend, or malicious high school rumors, were still my top problems. It broke my heart. Anything was better than having my mind taken from me like this.

Scrubbing my face, I looked up and placed my chin on my knuckles, elbows on the table, staring straight ahead. The clock on the opposite wall caught my eye, and I noticed that the hand indicating seconds passing wasn't moving.

I stared at it for a while, waiting for it to start moving, but couldn't dwell on it for too long as a strong jolt of nausea threatened at my throat and yanked me back into action. Even if I was hallucinating, or even just having a nightmare, which at this point I was hoping it was, I wasn't going to vomit all over the conference room. I had already bled all over it.

I stumbled to my feet and ran into the hallway and in the direction of the restroom. Halfway down the hall, it was as if someone had blindfolded me—except it was my own eyes doing it. They squeezed shut of their own volition and the ringing started back up in my ears. No longer able to see, I grasped out to my right, trying to find the wall to steady myself.

I tried my best to keep going, to inch my way forward by letting my fingers guide me over the crevices and door jambs of the wall, but when the pins and needles feeling started stemming out from my sacrum once again, I couldn't take another step. I couldn't call it a pain, but it was debilitating nonetheless. As if I were being carved through with a strong shockwave of electricity. And just before I thought I couldn't take it anymore, it stopped again.

I let out an audible gasp; I had been holding my breath without realizing. My eyes shot open, and I saw that I was barely steps away from where my eyes had closed. Sounds of life around me came rushing back to my eardrums so they quivered and ached under the pressure of it all. In fact, all my senses seemed to have jumped into hyperdrive.

A movement in my peripheral vision caught my attention and I spun to the left. The man who was walking down the hallway, the first frozen person I had encountered, was looking over his shoulder at me, an unamused and confused look on his face.

He didn't stop to stare and was quickly around the corner and out of sight, fully mobile, breathing and blinking.

I gathered my things and left the office without saying goodbye to Eric. I sent him an email apologizing for the mess in the conference room, explaining that I had cut my hand badly and was going to go see if I needed stitches. I probably should have done just that, but I wasn't going to. I wanted to go home, get under the covers, and never come out.

I felt like a fool, but it was better than the truth.

Or whatever I had just experienced.

CHAPTER FIVE

Once home, I ran to the downstairs bathroom and barely made it to the toilet in time. The relief of giving in to the nausea was almost instant, but not long-lived. A bright-red drop of blood hit the toilet seat and the floor as I stood up to flush.

"Fuck my life," I muttered under my breath.

I sat on the toilet, stuffing toilet paper up my nostrils. As I waited for the bleeding to stop, a string of texts came in from Rebecca.

Rebecca: I wanna quit. I wanna come home! These kids are monsters!

Rebecca: My roommate's mom brought her hamsters here and now the smell is even worse

Rebecca: Oh and she stayed in our room in my roommate's bed all week!

Rebecca: They were up at 6 a.m. doing yoga right next to my bed and blasting the heat!

Rebecca: It's 115 degrees outside! Go outside for your Bikram!

With a pang of guilt, I cleared my notifications, promising myself to answer her later. I typed "nosebleeds, nausea" into the search bar. The search returned a few hundred million results, the top one being "pregnancy."

I sighed uncomfortably, forced to breathe through my mouth, muttering to myself, "Well *that's* definitely not it."

I hesitantly typed out the word *hallucinations* to add to the search. I then proceeded to delete and retype it about eight times.

Only roughly one hundred thousand results. I clicked the top one; it read:

There are sixty-two conditions related to: nosebleeds, nausea, hallucinations.
Narcotic Abuse
Schizophrenia
Carbon Monoxide Poisoning
Pancreatic Cancer

I closed the website and locked my phone before reading any farther. If I wasn't already going crazy, I would definitely make myself crazy trying to diagnose myself.

༶༶༶

"What's up?" Justin entered the family room around dinnertime that evening. He flopped himself down on the couch opposite me, snagging the remote from where it lay between us. I didn't really care; whatever had been on the screen had merely been background noise to my doomscrolling. However, before he commenced hijacking the content playing on the TV, his gaze lingered on me for a moment longer than usual.

"You, uhh—you all right?" he asked, his eyes flicking between the TV and me. I didn't know when exactly Justin had become keenly attuned to my mental state and was surprised it had lasted through our first year away at college. I assumed the events of senior year had something to do with it, and I oscillated between loving and hating him for it.

"Yeah, just tired," I answered, trying to sound nonchalant, trying to sound as if I hadn't just had a psychotic break at work. I hid my cut hand in my pocket. I turned the conversation back to him. "You?"

"Same. I'm so glad it's the weekend," he said, letting out a deep sigh as if he had had a hard workweek.

"Hard week at the office?" I teased.

"Shut it, career girl. You wouldn't last through one of my workouts." Justin had gotten a football scholarship and moved up north for college and didn't want to "fall out of his groove" while he was home for the summer, hence him attending the training camp in lieu of a job.

He flicked through channels seemingly aimlessly, landing on a news station that was in the middle of its sports segment. Sometimes I envied his simplicity.

After a while, I mistakenly thought I was in the clear, having evaded Justin's suspicions that something was wrong. I bristled when Justin spoke without taking his eyes off the TV. "So the other day, at our birthday, what did Tom want?"

My chest tightened.

"Oh, you know. Just trying to reconnect probably. I didn't give him the time of day." I tried to hide the fact that my breath shook on its way into my lungs, my heart doing its best impression of a pickax on their surface, hoping Justin wouldn't sense my unease.

"I still don't get why you guys let that thing ruin your friendship," Justin said, glancing over at me and locking his eyes with mine. His face did that thing where he looked like he was judging me, but I knew it was out of concern.

I broke our eye contact, pretending to scroll on my phone. "Trust me, we would have grown apart anyway."

Justin shrugged and turned his gaze back to the TV when he realized he wasn't getting through to me.

THE AFTER HOURS

"I just thought you guys would get past it. Maybe laugh about it one day."

I scoffed to hide the guilt coursing through me, knowing that what Justin thought ended my friendship with Tom was a lie. As more and more time passed, I realized the lie I told was probably a way for me to stay in denial about the true reason my friendship with Tom ended. The lie also protected Tom.

Justin and I had been sitting in the exact same spots we were sitting in now, one year ago, the day after we graduated from high school, when I had told him that lie. I hadn't allowed my mind to go there for quite some time, but as I zoned out over Justin's sports segment on the TV, I found myself already there, unable to pause the flashback from playing through my mind.

"Don't shut me out," Justin pleaded.

"I'm fine," I spat.

"You're not fine." Justin trailed after me down the stairs.

I grabbed an ice cream pint from the freezer and sank into the family room couch. I switched the channel from whatever Justin had been watching and he didn't protest, so I knew he was dead set on talking.

"Is this about what happened at the party? I knew I should have—"

"No, I don't care about that," I interrupted. He sat on the opposite end of the couch, facing me. I stared straight forward, avoiding his gaze.

"The gash on your head looks gnarly. Did Tom take you to get checked out? Are you going to tell me what actually happened?" he asked.

At the sound of Tom's name, tears sprang up for the hundredth time that day, dancing awkwardly, warm on my swollen lower lash line.

"Just some guy being an asshole. I fell and hit my head trying to dodge him."

Justin peered his eyes at me, and I knew he didn't believe me. "That shouldn't upset you this much."

"Just stop, Justin." My voice was harsh. I felt bad, because he was just trying to help, but I couldn't have him pry out of me what really happened.

"Was it Dylan?" he asked, softly. Oddly enough, for the first time in months, my devastation was not because of Dylan. It was a welcome change, albeit this was in its own way a lot worse.

"No! Why would it be Dylan?"

"Then what the hell is up with you? When you texted me last night after you left you said you were totally fine. Don't make me regret not coming after you. And I spent all day covering for you; the least you owe me is an explanation."

There he went again with the brotherly guilt. Despite the rocky start to our relationship, Justin had become fiercely protective over me over the past few years.

It was the only way he knew how to show that he cared about me.

"You couldn't have done anything even if you had come after me. I make my own mistakes," I said, still not taking my eyes off the TV. I immediately regretted letting on that I myself had done something to cause my decrepit state.

"What, Sloane? What mistake could you possibly have made?" I could tell he wouldn't let up.

I knew I had to give him some hint as to what was going on. I pondered telling him what really happened at the party, but a nameless Woodoaks High douchebag just seemed so trivial compared to everything else that had happened after the party.

Justin would notice some changes eventually; I was never, ever going to speak to Tom again, and that would change a huge part of my life. I just couldn't tell him what actually caused it. Trying to form a sentence to describe what happened, even if just in my head, would end me.

I turned to face Justin, tried my best to force a believably assertive look, and willed my voice not to break. "I fucked up my friendship with Tom. We can't be friends, ever again."

"What?" he asked incredulously. "No, Slo, it can't be that bad. You and Tom barely even fight. I'm sure this is something you guys will get over." He maybe didn't understand my friendship with Tom, but he understood how strong it had been.

"No, this is final. It'll never be the same." Normally, saying those words out loud would have broken me, but I remained composed. I didn't have the energy to feel. I was outcried and exhausted and I just wanted to get this conversation over with.

"I'm actually fairly certain you guys have stayed the same since the fourth grade—"

"I slept with him," I blurted out, the words rancid on my tongue, looking Justin straight in the eye, my expression deadpan.

I hoped he couldn't tell how much of the truth I'd left out.

Justin's jaw dropped. This was probably the last thing he expected, for a multitude of reasons. Not only was it improbable due to the nature of my friendship with Tom, but it was also an awkward subject for us to talk about. I knew Justin saw me through slightly rose-colored glasses.

When he didn't say anything, I gave him a "What are you going to do about it?" look, shrugged, and turned my eyes back to the TV.

Justin let out a frustrated sigh and rubbed his temples with one hand, avoiding looking at me. "Did he—" he said before pausing, clearly uncomfortable. "Did he do something you didn't want?" I could tell he didn't fully believe me and was trying to find any reason to justify the situation in this mind. His rose-colored glasses immediately placed the blame on Tom.

"No." I held up my hand. "I told you—this was my mistake. Don't try and twist this." I felt bad for continuing to lie, but I had to see it through to protect the truth. "And don't you dare breathe a word to a soul, living or dead." I couldn't risk my lie getting back to Tom.

"I just—" He shook his head, still shocked. "Were there feelings between you guys? I just don't get it."

"No, nothing like that. Just stop. It was a drunken mistake; it happens. It is what it is, I'm over it, you should get over it."

Justin looked at me, worried. I hated that in order to keep the truth hidden, I had to lie and change Justin's perception of me drastically. But it had to be that way. Because what had really ended my friendship with Tom had come the morning after.

If a genie appeared and offered me three wishes, all three of them would be to change what happened that night.

Tears sprang to my eyes as the memory hijacked me. Before Justin could notice, I made my way upstairs to my room. Once there, I couldn't cry. I let out a frustrated growl, longing for the release. I crawled into bed, pressing one of my pillows into my face as I screamed. My hands dug into the material, clasping into such tight fists that I could feel the gash in my hand start to bleed again. I knew this stress had to have something to do with being back in this environment, with even Justin back home, back in the atmosphere so similar to the one last year, coupled with seeing Tom, seeing Dylan . . .

But I had started feeling off way before my birthday. Way before Tom showed up.

I started hyperventilating, thinking about the diagnoses I had read about. Something was happening to me. That much I knew.

I removed the pillow, but I still felt like I couldn't get enough oxygen in my lungs. My field of vision narrowed, and I knew that at the very least, I was having a massive panic attack. I tried to get a look at the gash on my palm, but my eyes wouldn't focus. Tinnitus struck both of my ears at once for a split second, but then they immediately felt on the verge of popping, my eardrums quivering under pressure from either in- or outside my body, I couldn't tell which.

I squeezed my eyes shut, which seemed to help a little. My heart skipped a couple of beats, harshly, like I was startled by something even though I sat alone in the silence in my room.

The sensation of blood furiously expelled, warming my chest.

A vastness behind my eyelids, incomprehensible.

Feeling as if every nerve in my body was clawing its way through my skin, exposed to the elements.

And then it all stopped. I felt fine apart from being still slightly short of breath, and my eyes were having a hard time adjusting after reopening them. It seemed darker than it had been before I closed them. The sun had just been setting as I left the family room. A wave of terror swept through me as I wondered if I had blacked out, since it seemed like the sun had set entirely in the time I had my eyes closed. I looked around to see my bedside lamp turned on, and I could've sworn it hadn't been when I had first entered the room. The silence in the room was now deafening with the acute absence of the overpowering tinnitus. Yet, I couldn't shake the feeling of another presence in my room. One that hadn't been there when I closed my eyes.

That's when I heard the toilet in my bathroom flush.

Someone was in my bathroom.

The terror in my body multiplied at this realization. I heard the water turn off and the door handle move. I had frozen for too long. I had nowhere to go but under my bed.

The person exited my bathroom, leaving the door slightly ajar. They made a sound that was most definitely a yawn and walked over to the bed, their bare feet inches away from my face.

I held my breath, clasping my hands over my mouth, squeezing my eyes shut. I couldn't breathe quietly with the amount of panic that was coursing through my body.

The person disappeared up into my bed, and as I opened my eyes I saw the mattress sink above my head. I still had my uncut hand over my mouth, forcing my breaths to slow down so they wouldn't make even the slightest sound.

A ringing phone vibrated above me, sounding like a fly buzzing through the mattress. The person lying on the bed spoke. "What's up?"

The voice struck a chord in me that I didn't know I had. I knew that voice, but I had no idea where from. It almost sounded like my mother's. It couldn't have been my mom; she was downstairs, and this person had come out of my bathroom.

I heard static as the phone was placed on speaker. "What time are you heading over here?" This voice was one I knew all too well. Cold sweat spread from my forehead down the back of my neck and shoulders.

It can't be.

"Soon, I just finished dinner." The person in the bed stretched and yawned and the person on speakerphone added, "Don't tell me you're tired."

"Don't worry, I won't fall asleep during the movie. I know you hate recapping for me. I'm just full."

I knew this conversation.

I knew who hated recapping movies I fell asleep over.

What I didn't know was what in the world I was experiencing.

"Actually, I was hoping we could scrap the movie idea. That's why I called."

I wanted so bad for this not to be what I thought it was.

"Scrap the movie and do what?" the person on the bed asked.

"Well, Pete's having an after party, and he kind of invited us." The person on the phone sounded like he was wincing, bracing for a blow.

"Excuse me, who are you and what have you done with Thomas Salinger?"

Me. It was me who said that. It was my voice.

"Oh come on, Slo! It's senior year, we're supposed to be going to parties. Catch some senioritis, would you? And since it's at Pete's house, there won't be any idiots there. Just a small gathering."

And the voice on the phone was the last one I wanted it to be. Tom's.

"Dude, I thought we were in this together. Mutual defiance of societal norms and forced socialization with unkindred spirits!"

"And we are! We defied the societal expectation of dressing up and feeling uncomfortable in a gym for hours drinking spiked punch and not dancing by not going to prom. But that doesn't mean we can't celebrate graduation."

I remembered this conversation all too well. I had lost track of how many times I had replayed it in my mind. If I could have just changed this one thing, Tom and I would probably still be friends.

"Tom, I love you, but I cannot stand being around kids from school more than I absolutely have to."

"I told you, none of the kids that have been giving you a hard time will be there. It's just a small group hangout. And if there happens to be an outlier then I'm right there with you. And we can leave whenever we want."

Dreaming. I must be dreaming. I must have thought about this conversation so exhaustively that it was now the headliner in my dream theater.

The person on the bed above me groaned. The slats above my nose creaked as she switched positions on the bed.

"I don't know why the hell you want to go so much because I'm not buying this senioritis crap, but if it means a lot to you, fine," my voice said.

"I love you!" the voice on the phone said.

"I hate you."

"Okay, do you think you can be ready in thirty minutes? I want to stop by the drive-through and grab a burger or something."

"You haven't eaten yet? It's almost nine."

"Mom and Dad left for Italy, remember?"

This was becoming too much to handle. I had never had a dream this detailed. I knew it was true: Tom's parents traveled a lot. They had barely made it home long enough to catch his graduation before they were off again. But this felt too verbatim. Too real. Too accurate, to be a dream.

The girl on the bed let out a long, slow breath. Everything in me wanted to scream at her to say no. I had wished over and over again that I had not gone along with Tom's suggestion.

Tom's voice echoed her with a sigh. "I don't want to make you do something you don't want to. You can say no. But honestly, you know how fast the rumor mill churns at school. I wouldn't worry about people bothering you about Dylan. People must have forgotten about it by now."

A combination of grief and shame stung in my chest and tears ran uncomfortably down from the outer corners of my eyes, past my temples and into my hairline. The only thing that could make a high school heartbreak worse was being dragged through the mud for it. Dylan Archer and I had broken up, or rather, been forced to break up, right before senior year started. During my senior year, school had become completely unbearable for me. Obscene gestures were made every time I walked down the halls. Guys asking how they could book the "Archer treatment," the main rumor being that I had caused him to want to move to the other side of the country for some explicit reason. As if that was somehow, at the same time, a good thing. I had come back from gym one day to find the contents of my gym bag doused in lubricant. Unwrapped condoms were flung at me during class when the teacher wasn't looking.

Breathing quietly became increasingly difficult as the atmosphere of the scene playing out in front of—or, above—me, took over every fiber of my being. I was swept up by a peculiar feeling that had been especially strong around the end of high school. Feeling like the person who had been with Dylan was light-years ahead of the person I was when I was around Tom. Like time was passing at different speeds with different people. I was growing up, but only bits and pieces at a time, while other parts were still the same and hadn't changed since elementary school. I liked being able to escape into a nostalgic cocoon with Tom, where time stood still. But that never happened again after graduation.

"No, you're right." The girl on the bed shifted and I saw her feet swing to the floor on my left.

"Yes!" Tom's voice sounded on the loudspeaker. "Pick you up in ten."

"You said thirty!" the girl yelled.

A triple beep sounded as the call ended, but the girl's feet didn't move. My eye was drawn to something on the second toe of her left foot. A toe ring. The same one I still donned. The toes even had my favorite nail polish color, bright but deep aquamarine.

Those are definitely my toes.

The person with my toes walked out of the room and closed the door behind her. My body ached. I wanted so much to stop her. What she was about to endure was the worst night of her—my—life. But I was too terrified to do anything.

This must be another hallucination. Like what happened at the office. There's no other explanation.

THE AFTER HOURS

I writhed my way out from under the bed and bolted to the closet, stepping in and closing the door behind me, leaving only a tiny crack. "Holy shit," a whisper escaped me as I enjoyed a few breaths of air gulped at normal volume. The relief didn't last long, as the person—me, my clone, whoever—came back moments later. And I remembered, that if this was indeed graduation night, then that person was about to rummage through the very closet I was standing in, hoping to find something to wear.

As she opened the closet, I held my breath and pressed my back against one of the closet's side walls, hiding behind my longer dresses. I could just catch a glimpse of her—and it was me all right.

An inexplicable pang of grief struck my chest as I surveyed her in the bits and pieces visible to me. I felt like I was seeing someone who had been dead for a long time. I wanted to burst out of the closet and hug her.

I guess I really am no longer the same person I was before that night.

Graduation Me didn't look for long in the closet and didn't notice me, thankfully. I peered through the crack by the hinges of the door and watched as she pulled on the outfit that I had thrown out after that night.

This is it. This is the breaking point. I have officially lost it.

Graduation Me got dressed and left the room. I let my knees buckle, my back sliding down the wall until I sat on the floor of the closet. I let out a single, long, rattling breath, willing my eyes to not fill with tears. What I was seeing felt *so* real.

You aren't even going crazy. You already are batshit crazy, Sloane.

When I finally felt ready, I climbed out of the closet and cracked my bedroom door open the tiniest possible amount to survey the hall. When the coast was clear, I tiptoed out onto the landing, glancing down into the foyer. I took care to not fully approach the railing, so that I could easily fall back if she was down there. I heard a familiar honk outside, followed by my own voice calling goodbye from the foyer, and the front door slamming shut.

I waited a few more moments, making sure no one was in the foyer before making my way down the stairs as quickly and quietly as possible, dashing across the entry hall and into the dining room. I peered through the curtains, but the darkened front yard was empty.

"Hey," an unfamiliar, childlike voice chimed from behind me, causing my heart to attempt to catapult out of my chest.

I let out a yelp and spun around to face the source of the voice.

Before me stood a girl, quite a bit younger and shorter than me, with thin, white-blond hair and huge brown eyes. Her face was perfectly rounded, eyebrows as white as her hair, and her jaw was set in some kind of imperious determination. I fumbled with my phone, trying to dial 911.

She held up her hands and smiled softly before speaking in an utterly innocent, childish tone. "I know you're scared. I'm here to help. I promise I'm not going to hurt you."

"Sloane? Did you forget something?" My mother's voice sounded from the other side of the house.

My eyes darted from side to side, calculating a route of escape, phone slipping in my hands. But the girl was too fast. She took three quick steps toward me and grabbed my hand.

A shake went through my body, and suddenly I felt as if my eyelids were being pushed down, like when you're uncontrollably sleepy and just can't keep them open. They snapped shut as I felt a little shiver climb up my spine and goosebumps grow outward from it. A buzz rang in my ears. A strange compilation of white noise and dull bass, a sensation I felt in my eardrums more than a sound that I heard. Eerily similar to the panic attack I'd had moments earlier in my room, the pressure on my eardrums went from a squeal to a throb, and then it was over.

The girl spoke again, and I felt her hand loosen its grasp on mine. "Open!"

I opened my eyes to find myself in the exact same spot, only it was sunset again, and red-golden light spilled through the dining room curtains, as if a fire burned right outside. The stark contrast of going from no natural light to the blaze of the sun hanging on by a thread sent my head spinning.

The girl smiled cautiously as she stepped back from me, as if I were a rabid animal. "I'm just going to leave this here, okay? You can call my dad whenever you're, like, ready to talk, and stuff." She placed what looked like a business card on the dining table and then beamed, squeezing her shoulders up toward her ears for a beat before adding excitedly, "Welcome back to the Present, Sloane."

And just like that, she vanished. She didn't dissipate or dissolve. There was no spark of light, poof of smoke, or gust of air. She was just there and then not there, within the same second.

CHAPTER SIX

T HE BUSINESS CARD felt just about as real as the girl who had appeared before my eyes in the dining room—not at all. Yet, I held it in my hands, willing my brain to register it as a sign that what I had experienced was, in fact, real.

>ADRIAN LEX CURATORIAL SERVICES
>*Curating moments.*

The peculiar slogan was followed by a phone number. The girl had said to call her dad—which made even less sense.

But what had made sense, was how she had welcomed me back to the present. Because she had—whatever she did had reset the out-of-body experience I had been having. Replaying the events of graduation night back in front of me as if I were a fly on the wall. Except of course, I had still been in my actual body. There had been two of me. When I had returned to my room, everything was restored to normal. I was the only Me there. I had still been too freaked out to sleep in my own bed and ended up spending the night on the family room couch. Which meant I hadn't slept well at all. Which is probably why my reflexes were off at work the next day.

"What's up?" Eric chimed from behind me as I sat on one of the chairs that had been set up in the firm's lobby. An all-hands meeting was scheduled, the only actual invite on my calendar that week.

I flinched and stuffed the business card in my pocket before looking up at him and smiling as inconspicuously as I could. "Hey."

He grinned as he sat down next to me. The meeting didn't start for another fifteen minutes, so no one else was there yet. I had just decided to escape my busywork and get there extra early to grab a seat toward the back.

Once seated, Eric leaned in and whispered, even though no one was close enough to hear him, "You know you're not actually required to show up to this meeting, right? It's really just the partners patting each other on the back, dropping a bunch of corporate speak, and making empty promises on their commitment to climate change and social justice."

I flashed my eyes in his direction after he finished. He somehow looked more handsome today than he had the prior week. I wondered if he had gotten some sun over the weekend. His skin had a healthy glow about it, his shoulders not as tight as they had been the day before. He wasn't wearing a tie and, whether deliberately or not, the top button of his shirt had come undone.

Biting my lip, I whispered back, "Yeah, but remember, my dad is one of those partners."

Eric smirked, raising an eyebrow, still whispering as he responded, "Oh, I know just how important you are, Ms. Becker."

My heartbeat seemed to be churning out flames, threatening to reveal themselves on my cheeks as a blush.

What am I doing? I am in no place to start dating someone right now.

"Want to help me finish setting up the AV equipment?" he asked, standing up. He motioned to the makeshift platform stage that had been set up along the lobby wall.

"They have you doing that?" I asked, confused, but also standing up immediately.

"Ehh," he said, shrugging. "One of those intern tasks that I haven't yet been able to shake."

The stage looked like something out of a convention hall, a carpeted portable stage complete with a thick, beige curtain backdrop that hung from steel poles mounted to the stage. It matched the aesthetics of the rest of the office.

In the middle of the stage was a large TV on a portable stand, a bundle of unconnected cords dangling from its back. Eric ushered me to follow him behind the backdrop. I did, trailing him in the two-foot-wide space created by the stage and the wall. He parted the heavy curtains behind the TV and got busy untangling the cords, handing me a couple of microphones.

"Hold these, please."

When he was sufficiently satisfied with the state of the cables, he reached through the curtain once more and turned on a receiver with a tiny antenna attached to it. I could hear people starting to file into the lobby.

"Flip them on for me for a sec," he said, his voice light and cheerful, peering in my direction, one hand still reaching through the curtain for the receiver.

I switched both microphones on, showing him the blinking red light on both of them.

"Hmm," he said, tapping each twice with his fingers. "We want that light to stop blinking." He turned back to the receiver.

I leaned on the wall, and my phone buzzed in my pocket. I shifted the microphones so that I held them both with my bandaged hand, leaving my good hand free to fish my phone out. The text was from Rebecca.

Rebecca: Chat at lunch?

The microphones slipped, and as I pressed them against my body to keep them from falling, they clanged together. This resulted in a loud crash over the speakers, followed by a high-pitched whine. Eric must have managed to get them working.

Displeased murmurs rose from beyond the curtain.

I shoved my phone back in my pocket, mortified, and fumbled with the microphones, trying to shut them off. But the combination of the slippery bandage and my slow reflexes instead caused me to nearly drop them both. They banged together again as I ungracefully caught them an inch from the ground, causing another ear-piercing crash to reverberate throughout the lobby.

"Sorry," I said, wincing. "Damn bandage."

Will I ever be able to have a day on this job where I don't make a fool of myself?

"Don't apologize." He smiled that same irresistible smile he'd worn my first day in the office, and I felt my knees buckle. He closed the short distance between us in one step. He grabbed one of the microphones and stretched the hand holding it as far out as he could behind him.

The whining ceased immediately, replaced by the chatter of the critical mass forming on the other side of the curtain. He used his thumb to flick the microphone off and brought his hand back in front of him. He was still smiling, half laughing under his breath.

I, however, couldn't function. My back was pressed up against the lobby wall. He stood facing me, less than a foot away. The tight space definitely compounded my perception of the closeness, but just like in the lounge the other day, I had to tilt my head up to meet his eyes.

This man is going to be my undoing.

His chuckles died out, and he too seemed to realize how close we were standing. Yet, neither of us did anything to increase the distance between us.

He placed the hand that wasn't holding the microphone next to my head on the wall behind me. He clamped his lips as intensity shone in his eyes. They drifted down to my lips, and I held my breath. Glancing back into my eyes, he paused as if he were asking permission before letting his gaze drop again, inching closer to me.

What the heck am I doing?

A loud creak sounded above us, and this time it wasn't the microphones. Eric pushed himself away from me as we both looked up. The horizontal pole holding the curtains up was coming loose at stage left—sliding out of its brackets with a metallic groan. I braced myself for the rapidly failing assembly to fall on us. It might not cause a lot of damage, but it would definitely expose us to the people in the lobby.

Next thing I knew, it stopped. The poles had aligned themselves back in the bracket, right in front of my eyes. I blinked a few times, checking my focus, confusion plastered on my face.

"Phew, that was close." Eric chuckled.

I let out a breath I didn't know I had been holding, forcing a laugh as I said, "Yeah. Phew."

※※※

"Hey there," Eric said as he peered around the corner of my cubicle partition midafternoon, startling me. I had been staring at the business card again.

"Hi. Did you need anything?" I answered. I saw a flicker in his eyes telling me that my response wasn't exactly what he had hoped it would be. Realizing I came off short, I quickly added, "I mean, what's up?" as I felt my cheeks warm.

"I was wondering if you wanted to grab some coffee that doesn't taste like mop water." He chuckled. He leaned lazily against my cubicle partition, a small smile engraved on his face.

I stared, trying to get a read on him. The coffee at the office really was awful—but was he asking what I thought he was asking?

He didn't even wait for my response. "Come on, it's Friday, everyone's checked out anyway." He paused and sent me a small sideways smile. "It's the least I can do." He gestured toward my bandaged hand, and I rubbed it with my opposite hand, embarrassed.

"It wasn't the coffee's fault though. I blame the bastard water bottles."

"All the more reason to let me buy you a cup." I looked up at him to see him smiling in a way that obliterated my usual feeling of wanting to sink into the ground when I was around him. His smile had a way of doing that, I was learning.

But my brain didn't let me bask in how his smile made my insides melt, instead commencing an overanalysis of what he meant by "buy you a cup." This was quickly followed by a feeling of self-loathing as I realized I was getting my hopes up.

"Sounds great," I replied, hoping it wasn't too forced.

I hadn't listened at all during the all-hands, instead sharing glances with Eric who had taken a seat in the row in front of me. It made it easy for him to turn his head and catch my eye with his gorgeous smile. I'd try to focus on what was being said—only to catch him staring at me, laughing under his breath when I noticed him. I'd then attempted to ignore him but couldn't stifle my own laughter when he started quietly making fun of what was being said on stage, acting like he was falling asleep, rolling his eyes. He didn't seem at all concerned that someone might spot what he was doing The stupidity of what I had nearly let happen that morning hit me like a forcefield. And now I had agreed to have coffee with him.

I had to stop this unintentional and completely out-of-the-blue crush in its tracks.

༶༺༶༺༶༺

Eric said he knew of an interesting coffee shop a couple blocks away, and I didn't want to reveal my unfamiliarity with downtown, so I let him lead the way. Even though it was close to the end of the workday, the sun still blazed in the sky, heating the pavement and the breeze between the skyscrapers. Even when we happened to be walking along the shady side of a building, the air was still scalding, dry but dreadfully heavy. I regretted not leaving my blazer in the office, but that would have meant parting with the business card in my pocket. My hand slipped into the pocket as often as it could while going unnoticed by Eric, just to make sure the card was still there. Every time I was assured it was safely tucked away, I became convinced that it had clung to my hand as I pulled it out of the pocket, fluttering away with the breeze, lost forever within a few seconds of me letting go. Which resulted in me sticking my hand back in the awkwardly positioned pocket and frantically grasping at the card once more.

When we finally reached the coffee shop, I was a little unimpressed; it was a tiny joint selling organic coffee and gluten-free pastries. The interior decorations screamed "try-hard." They were obviously trying to be super artsy and woke, but they were really just a jumble of vintage-looking knick-knacks with no overall coordination. We got a table on the second-floor mezzanine overlooking the main area of the coffee shop.

"You don't live with your father do you?" he asked, just as we were sitting down.

I had been about to take a sip of my coffee, but stopped, surprised at his brashness to get straight to the personal questions. I figured it was obvious that my father and I did not have the type of relationship a father and daughter who lived together had.

"No, my parents divorced when I was four."

"Yeah, I figured. He's married to his job, that man!" Eric said. My face must have given me away as he immediately apologized, "Oh, sorry, I didn't mean it like that."

"Oh no, you're exactly right. That's why they got divorced." I laughed.

"Oh." He let out a breath he had obviously been holding and chuckled. "Good to know. Do you have any siblings?"

I paused—I had been an only child for so long, and for so long I hadn't counted Justin as my brother out of spite, so I needed a second to formulate the answer.

"Yes, my mom remarried, and I have a seven-year-old half-sister. I share her with my stepbrother."

"Wow, lucky you."

Eric took a sip of his coffee, his expression cemented in a curious half smile, as if he somehow found these mundane facts about me fascinating. It still gave me a feeling that he was hiding a funny secret that he was about to divulge at any moment.

"Lucky?" I asked.

I'm really not this interesting.

"Yeah, I hate being an only child. I'd take a step and a half sibling any day over no siblings," he answered, his tone matter-of-fact, but his eyes looked shy, as if he was nervous what I would think of him. I hadn't ever thought about my siblings that way, but I figured my life would be even lonelier than it already was if I didn't have Amanda and Justin.

"That's a cute way to look at it." I cocked my head to the side, resting it in my palm, elbow on the table, studying him. His smile was contagious; my cheek muscles hadn't worked out this much in months.

His smile spread even wider. He chuckled as he leaned back in his chair, one arm on the backrest, the other arm outstretched and grasping at his coffee cup on the table. His eyebrows shot up for a second before he joked, "I love being called cute."

"Wow," I scoffed, letting the word drag on before bursting into laughter. "Way to make it awkward dude," I added, although that was perhaps the exact opposite of what was happening. We both continued laughing, eyes pinned on each other, probably annoying the people around us, but we didn't care.

As our fit died down, Eric sighed happily before resuming his questioning. "So how old is Justin?"

His words struck me and ripped me out of my post-laugh high. I frantically rewound my thoughts.

"How did you know his name?" I asked, nerves on edge.

Eric raised his eyebrows for a split second as if surprised by the question. He brushed it off. "Uhh—What do you mean?" He shot me a look as if I was being silly. "You just said it." He chuckled and took another big gulp of his coffee.

I decided not to press the matter. My memory probably wasn't serving me. "Well, he is exactly one day younger than me. Yes, we were in the same grade in high school."

Eric laughed as he picked at the sticker on the side of his coffee cup with his thumb, his eyes drifting to meet mine before he said, "That must've been really weird."

"Yeah, it really was, actually," I said, my voice breathier than I intended.

It had been really weird, and no one had ever thought to acknowledge that before. It was like he was reading my mind.

What is this feeling?

I held his gaze. Eric bit the inside of his lower lip as he sent me a sideways smile. Not the sweeping smile that could take my breath away, but its effects were just as profound. I felt heat bloom on my cheeks, and I became acutely aware that he didn't feel as uncomfortable as I did. Like he was more used to holding my gaze than I was his.

Seriously, what is this feeling?

As soon as my brain stumbled upon a question to ask him, I blurted it out, relieved to break the loaded silence. "So how did you earn your title, Mr. Make-It-Go-Away?" I smirked, happy with my quip. I hadn't mentioned that I knew his nickname.

He acknowledged the jab with a nod and a chuckle. "Well, that is a great question." He leaned in, both elbows on the table, and took a swig of his coffee before proceeding. "I guess because making things disappear into thin air is my expertise." He gestured with his hands after putting the coffee cup down, imitating an explosion.

Unsure whether he was dodging the question or just being funny, I continued, "It seems to me like that would take a lot of years in the field to master."

"Nah, I guess I just have a . . . talent for making people see things my way. I'm also a very good people reader; my intuition hasn't failed me yet," he said, nonchalantly, cocky even, as he tapped his temple with one finger and winked.

I could tell he was implying that he had read me already. If that's what he thought, then he was severely mistaken about his skill.

"Oh, how so?" I humored him.

"Well, if you figure out what motivates people then you can stop them in their tracks. Most of the time it's a simple, universal fix—money. But sometimes, when people are out to ruin a reputation, their intentions can be from a very personal place. I've always been able to find that place."

He was convincing as he elaborated, and I hoped I never had to reveal anything to him that could possibly put him in a position to start analyzing my motivations.

"Excuse me for just a moment," Eric said, before I had formulated a response. He stood up, heading toward the restrooms.

I welcomed the quick conversation break, so I was startled when I felt a hand on my shoulder just a few moments after Eric left. Whoever had touched me had given me a slight electric shock, but it was probably because I wasn't expecting to be touched. I was so startled that it sent a shiver through me. I closed my eyes and tensed a bit to help the shiver pass before turning around to look behind me.

A young woman stood behind me with an unsettling, hungry expression on her face. She had long, strawberry-blond hair that cascaded down to her midriff in large, bulky waves. She was wearing rather grungy clothes, light-colored jeans, and a black cargo jacket over a white tank top. She looked slightly unhealthy—gaunt, pale. Like someone who was abusing drugs but hadn't been doing it for long enough to begin to notice that it was affecting their appearance. I wondered if she were homeless and had wandered unnoticed into the coffee shop, yet she looked too freshly showered to be homeless. Her eyebrows were almost nonexistent, they were such a light color. They hung low over her icy-blue eyes that seemed to pierce into my skull. A slim, pointy nose sat wrinkled above a large, wide-set mouth that proceeded to twist into an evil sneer.

Before I even had a chance to ask her what she wanted, she reached over to my coffee cup on the table, yanked it up and splashed its contents all over my hair, face, and clothes. I gasped; thankfully the coffee was iced and not burning hot. The young woman laughed the most malicious laugh I had heard outside of children's cartoons. Had I not been so caught off guard, I probably would have found her laughter quite comical.

Wiping the sticky substance from my eyes as I yelled obscenities at her and stumbled to get up to face her, I noticed her laugh had turned into a coughing fit. She covered her mouth with one hand, and it came back drenched with blood. She took one look at her hand, wiped it on the side of her thigh, and went back to smiling, her teeth and lips stained with red.

She moved with lightning speed, shoving me back into my chair and wrapping her arm around my neck in a split second. My head was thrown back, and all I could see was the coffee shop's dilapidated ceiling tiles obscured by her red curls as she leaned down and placed her head on my shoulder. She smelled of rose petals and, oddly, a faint waft of vinegar. It made a nauseating combination. I could feel her breath on my ear as she whispered, "Watch where you're going, bitch."

As she let go, a jolt of pain pierced through me, knocking the wind out of me. Eyes closed, I staggered sideways out of my chair and fell to the ground, making a heavy sound as my head collided with the floor.

CHAPTER SEVEN

S HE WAS GONE when I opened my eyes. I winced as I shot up to a seated position. I turned my head every which way, and she was nowhere to be seen. I growled in frustration, wiping coffee out of my eyes. I wanted to cry; the combination of fear and humiliation stung like acid in my veins. It was as if everyone who was sitting on the mezzanine had just then noticed me. No one had so much as blinked or come to my rescue when the woman had me in a chokehold.

"Did none of you actually see that?" I was yelling, probably louder than I should have, and made a sweeping gesture toward my chair and where the young woman had been. "Thanks so much for the help," I said, my voice laced with indignant rage. None of the other coffee shop guests offered up even so much as a hand to help me up, most of them looking away, but not before giving me a "you're crazy" look.

I felt crazy.

"Hey—what happened?" Eric was back from the restroom.

He helped me stand up and I took off my blazer, reaching for the napkin stand on the table to continue drying off.

"Some—I don't know! Some homeless person or something came in here and poured my coffee all over me!" I could tell that if I kept talking, I would burst into tears, and that was the last thing I wanted. This was already humiliating enough. Was this going to be the new norm now? I couldn't go to work without making an absolute fool of myself in front of my coworker every single day?

"Wait, what?" Eric was handing me napkins, looking me up and down and back at my empty coffee on the table.

"Some chick—woman, person—came in here and just poured my coffee all over me and then put me in a chokehold!" I was still talking way too loudly, and the people around us were exchanging furtive glances and rolling their eyes at me. It didn't stop me from continuing, frantically looking around to see if I could spot her. "She—she had long curly red hair, she was coughing blood, super pale, she was wearing a black jacket—"

"Excuse me, sir, what seems to be the problem here? Miss, is this man bothering you?" An employee had noticed the commotion and come upstairs.

"No, he is not the problem here," I began.

"The problem seems to be that you guys allow mentally ill people to waltz in here and attack your customers." Eric's voice was icy. I had never heard him speak like that before. His tone and the look in his eyes made it seem like he was talking to a squished bug under his shoe.

It had the desired effect on the employee, who seemed to cower under his words, "I—I'm terribly sorry, sir. We can't always control who comes in here. We are in downtown. How about a free coffee the next time you guys come in?"

"I'm sorry, but from what I saw, your girlfriend spilled that coffee on herself as she fell off her chair. Just saying."

The voice came from behind me, and I snapped my head back to see who had the nerve to be butting in to the situation. It was a woman sitting two tables away from us. She sat with her computer and a stack of books, with earbuds in. She had taken one out and held it as she addressed us.

Her comment enraged me. If she had seen what happened, why didn't she at least offer to help me stand up or ask me if I was okay? I knew she could have just not been looking. But that was nearly impossible with the vantage point she had of our table—she was looking right at where I sat.

Eric was first to speak, and despite my agitation, I couldn't help but notice that he didn't correct her when she called me his girlfriend. "I did not ask you what happened. Sticking your nose in just to contradict is not helpful unless you have proof. You better learn that or you're going to make one hell of a crappy lawyer."

The look on the woman's face was priceless. She opened her mouth as if to say something, but instead she put her earbud back in and returned to her screen, giving Eric a seething look.

I glanced quickly at her stack of books, and I recognized some of the titles from my Intro to Law syllabus that I had enrolled in for the fall. I couldn't believe how perceptive Eric was. And how quick he was to formulate a comeback.

Eric turned to the employee. "Thanks, but I don't think we will be returning, with the type of crowd that comes in here." I saw him aim his gaze at the wannabe lawyer as he said those last words.

I couldn't resist and stole another look at the woman as I gathered my purse and my phone from the table. She had obviously still been listening despite the headphones because she couldn't contain herself.

"Oh real classy, douchebag!" she called after us as we walked down the mezzanine stairs.

As the adrenaline left my body, the traitorous rush was replaced with an unsettling recognition. Something about the way the redhead moved, how acutely her presence dissipated when I looked for her, felt familiar. And I didn't like it one bit.

"Are you okay?" Eric asked me once we were outside, his voice velvety as his eyes scanned me.

I looked around to see if I could spot the strawberry blonde. I knew it was a long shot; based on the speed she managed to escape the coffee shop with, she was probably miles away by now.

But was it speed, or what is something else?

"Yeah, totally fine. Just... sticky." I laughed.

Eric laughed at my comment as well. "I'm sorry our date got cut short! Let's get back to the office, and you can get cleaned up."

I froze in my tracks and looked at him, confused.

Did he say date*?*

He looked flustered, and as if he had read my mind, blurted out, "Coffee date, work date. You know, like 'it's a date!' type thing, not to imply that—"

A smile crept up onto my face. I couldn't help it. It was so refreshing to see him be the flustered one.

"Don't worry, I won't tell my dad," I teased.

Why are you being a tease? You know better this time around. Idiot.

Eric laughed nervously and let out a sigh. "You see right through me, Sloane Becker. Thank you."

Too busy desperately trying to hide the fact that my heart was attempting to collapse my lungs with its beating, I didn't ask him what he meant by that. I needed to play it cool. I couldn't let Eric sense even the slightest bit of interest from me. I had no doubt in my mind anymore: something *was* there, and I had to do everything in my power to shut it down, not encourage it.

After the havoc my father wreaked when he found out I was dating Dylan, I didn't want to know what he would do if he found out something was going on between one of his other employees and me.

"Uh, Sloane? You uh, it's happening again," Eric said awkwardly and touched the spot below his nose.

I immediately covered my own nose, mortified that this was happening in front of Eric *again*. As if I wasn't already a mess. My mouth filled with the metallic, bitter taste of blood.

I let out a frustrated growl. "Could you?" I asked, voice muffled behind my hand, indicating whether Eric could hop into the restaurant we were walking next to, to grab napkins. He gladly obliged. When he got back out, he handed me some way-too-fancy-for-a-nosebleed napkins, with an encouraging smile on his face.

"You'll be just fine," he said. "It happens."

Something about the warmth in his voice when he said it just made me want to believe it.

We proceeded, and for the first few steps, Eric placed his hand on the small of my back, ever so gently.

And despite knowing better, I let him.

༺༻༺༻༺༻

By the time I had completed a fairly unsuccessful attempt at getting cleaned up in the office restroom, it was already almost five o'clock. Thankfully, the nosebleed had stopped, but my hair was starting to get crunchy where the coffee had dried. My shirt had coffee stains all down the front and back and my slacks were spattered as well. The stains had dried on the walk back to the office, so I gave up any hope that they could be salvaged. Maybe my mom had a trick or two up her sleeve. I made a mental note to come up with a story other than the real one to tell her why my clothes had essentially been drenched in coffee. I was not looking forward to that conversation.

The conversation I was dreading more was the one that I knew needed to take place between Eric and me. I knew that if I wanted to be taken seriously at this internship, and by my father, I had to stop letting my ill-advised crush run amok with my head. Maybe Eric's kind words and protective gestures after the incident at the coffee shop were nothing more than that—kind and protective. But something about them was making my heart flutter in a way it hadn't for so long. And whether I was reading into things that weren't there, or if I was sensing the beginning of something, I needed to nip it in the bud. Partly, to make the correct move career-wise, but also, to prevent myself from setting any expectations that were bound to disappoint me.

I stopped by Eric's office on my way out and knocked gently on the door when he didn't notice me. His smile when he looked up and saw me was the same as the one he'd exhibited the first time I met him. The kind of smile that made me weak in the knees, but I wouldn't let my mind go there.

"Don't report me to HR, but you look terrible." He laughed.

"Very funny." I sat down.

"I thought you had left already," he said.

"Actually, I was hoping we could talk," I said, trying not to come off as ominous.

He let go of the computer mouse and leaned back in his chair. "Okay, what's up?"

"I wanted to clear something up, so that you don't get the wrong idea about me," I began.

Eric laughed. "I did not see that coming. I thought you were going to quit on me." He seemed relieved and I laughed with him.

"No. Not yet at least." I teased.

Stop it.

"I just—" I began, wishing I had rehearsed my speech better. "I really want to do a good job here this summer. And so far I'm not exactly excelling. I want my father to take me seriously, and I have to rebuild my reputation with him to some degree, and that means I need to tread carefully."

"It's not like those things were your fault."

I bit lip as my clasped hands gripped each other tighter.

"Do you know who Angus Archer is?" I asked, doing a one-eighty in my approach to make him see what I was saying.

"Yes, of course I do. He defended that movie producer who killed his partner by poisoning him. What was his name?" Eric swept a hand through his hair as he leaned forward on his desk, looking at me with intrigue in his eyes. My own hands ached to touch his hair. His words caught me before I sank too far into my daydreams. "Oh, I remember, Spencer something."

I shook off the rest of my out-of-context thoughts, determined to get my point across. "Then you know my father was the attorney for the victim's family, and that ever since then, he and Archer have held an inexplicably stubborn grudge against each other?"

"That explains a lot. I heard a rumor that your dad had someone disbarred because they left here to go work for Archer." I could tell Eric was trying to hide his amusement.

This was news to me, but I hid my surprise, determined to keep the conversation on track.

"Well, did you hear the rumor about his daughter dating Archer's grandson?"

Realization crept slowly onto Eric's face. It was almost comical, maybe even a tad forced.

"You didn't."

"Let's just put it this way: the only time my father and Archer have been able to stay civil in a room together was when they were in mutual agreement over the fact that Dylan Archer and I should be kept as far apart from each other as possible."

Eric laughed, leaning back in his seat. "I would have loved to be a fly on the wall for that conversation."

I didn't return his gleeful reaction. "So you understand why I want to do a good job?"

"Yes. Yes, of course I do," he said warmly while smiling as if he knew more than he was letting on. "We all have a past, Sloane. I don't think your dad agrees with me on this, but I choose to judge people by their present."

I let out a breath I didn't realize I had been holding. "I guess I didn't realize how much mine is following me around."

Eric smiled knowingly. "They tend to do that. And it's a good thing too, otherwise I'd be out of a job! But if you'd like to humor me, it's not often that I'm on the receiving end of gossip about my boss. Do you have any more details on what the gripe is between him and Archer?"

"You would have to ask my dad," I said, staring down into my lap.

"So it definitely goes beyond a romance between you and the grandson? Intriguing, Becker."

I rolled my eyes at him. I was, of course, cutting corners quite a bit in this recollection of events. It could have been a much more interesting story. I wondered if in time I would ever reach a place where I could tell the whole story. Maybe even laugh about it. I doubted it, but the power time has over one's emotions was unpredictable and interminable, so I hadn't given up hope yet.

For the time being. Even though it had been nearly two years, it was still too fresh, too humiliating.

"Well thank you for sharing that with me. And for what it's worth, I've only told him great things so far," Eric said.

"I appreciate that," I replied with a smile.

Eric's expression changed, and he suddenly looked exhausted. "So I was going to email you, but I guess I'll tell you now. I just got a phone call before you walked in here," Eric said, changing the subject.

"Oh?"

"Yeah, I just have some stuff I have to take care of next week, so I might have to take some time off." I could tell he wasn't particularly excited about whatever it was that he needed to do.

"Hope everything is okay," I said.

"Yeah, it will be," he said, and turned back to his screen. "Get home safe, Sloane."

"Thanks," I said, and stood up and made my way to the door, but something stopped me. I felt an immense need to make sure he was okay before I left him. The feeling was foreign in my body, and I wondered if I was allowing myself to care too much, too quickly. I turned around to look back at Eric. "Hey, are you sure you're all right?"

Eric pressed his lips together before answering, "Well, not really. But I'll be okay. I just have to deal with something from my past. See? I told you everyone has one." I could tell he was trying to keep a light note in his voice, but it wasn't very convincing.

"Okay," I began, not wanting to pressure him. It really was none of my business, but I couldn't help asking, "Is there anything I can do to help?"

"No. Thank you, though. I just have to go and redo this statement I made years ago in a case. Not work related but uh"—he took a deep breath before he said the next words—"ex-wife related."

The conclusion I had jumped to at his words was obviously written on my face, because Eric started laughing.

"Okay no. You owe me this story," I said, sitting back down.

Eric was still laughing. "Oh lord, what have I gotten myself into?"

"Spill it, divorcé," I laughed.

Eric's laughter died out, but he was still smiling. "Widower, actually." He fidgeted in his seat, fixing his blazer as he sat up straighter.

I froze for quite a while; that was the last thing I was expecting.

"Eric, I am so, so sorry. I shouldn't have asked—"

"It's okay, really. It seems like a lifetime ago. We were super young, and I knew we were never going to last. It's just a paper trail at this point." Eric smiled, and I felt guilty that he was having to save face for my sake just because I needed to stick my nose where it didn't belong.

"How long ago did she—?" I hoped Eric wouldn't make me finish the sentence.

"It's been over three years now. Way longer than we were married."

"I see." My next question was on the tip of my tongue, but Eric answered it.

"In case you're wondering, they don't think I killed her. It's just asset disputes. Her parents sued me for her assets, I sued them back, blah blah blah. Boring stuff, I promise," Eric said.

"Okay." I smiled. "I really am sorry though."

"Totally fine." His smile was still hiding something. I could not wrap my head around the fact that the man—guy—who sat in front of me, was only twenty-three years old. He seemed to have lived a lifetime longer than he should have, and it made me sad for him. In fact, he seemed older than he had been just a few hours earlier at the coffee shop.

What made me sadder was that my plan had completely backfired. Not only had I pried out of him something that had essentially brought us closer, but I had also failed at not setting expectations. I yearned to know him better. Get to the bottom of why he somehow felt familiar and foreign at the same time.

But until I figured out what was going on with me, that couldn't happen. And I knew what the first step needed to be.

After leaving the office and finally locating my car in the gargantuan parking garage, I got in, locked the doors, and started the engine to blast the air conditioning.

If I don't do this now, I never will.

I fished the business card out of my pocket and held it up to the steering wheel as I dialed the number. I held my breath as it started ringing. Just as I was about to hang up and abort the whole thing, a pleasant male voice answered.

"Adrian Lex Curatorial Services. Adrian Lex speaking." I could hear the man's smile through the phone.

I audibly gasped, my body finally remembering to inhale, which led to a stutter. "Uhm—yeah—uhm—hello. My name is Sloane Becker. I uhm—your card was uhm—left with me. I think by your daughter?" I exhaled as silently as I could as I listened to the blood rushing in my veins.

"Sloane, how wonderful to hear from you," Adrian said on the other end. "First off, is everything all right this very moment? Are you safe?"

His questions surprised me, and I wondered if he was used to people being more panicked when they called him. "Yes, I'm safe. I guess I just wanted to—"

"No need to explain. You probably have lots of questions. When would be a good time for us to meet?" His voice had an almost eerie calm to it, and part of me wanted to hang up, block the number, rip up the business card, and forget that I ever entertained this craziness.

"Yeah. As soon as possible, please," I replied, before I could talk myself out of it.

PART TWO

"The eternal present is the space within which your
whole life unfolds, the one factor that remains constant. Life is now.
There was never a time when your life was *not* now,
nor will there ever be.

Secondly, the Now is the only point that can take you
beyond the limited confines of the mind.
It is your only point of access into the timeless and
formless realm of Being."

—Eckhart Tolle

CHAPTER EIGHT

T HAT SATURDAY MORNING, I pulled up to the Highland Park house that the man on the phone, Adrian, had given me the address to. The street was lined with craftsman-style houses, with the exception of one Spanish mission style on the corner. Mature palms and jacaranda trees stood proud between the uneven sidewalk and the dilapidated curb. Along with a fresh blanket of bright purple flower petals, the trees cast a shadow over most of the asphalt, which was flanked with way more parked cars than the street should comfortably fit. I proceeded to squeeze my car into a tiny spot halfway down the block from my destination.

The house was a shade of dark green with maroon accents; it had a low-slung roof with gables perpendicular to the street and one shed roof dormer out front. The small garage stood off to the left at the end of a long driveway against the property line. The front yard was in need of some gardening, with succulents and high straw-like bushes covering every inch except the path that led up to the welcoming porch. The porch railing was made of stacked stones and housed comfortable-looking furniture. Nothing about the house's exterior, or the street it sat on, indicated that something abnormal was within its walls.

Yet, there I was, about to meet under just about the most abnormal circumstances I could fathom.

It dawned on me that what I was doing could potentially be extremely stupid. Yes, the person who offered to help was just a young girl, which had caused me to let my guard down. But if this Adrian person was out to hurt me, he might be using the girl to lure me in.

I shared my phone's location with my mom. Just in case.

There was no doorbell, so I knocked hesitantly on the dirty glass pane of the front door. I felt the old boards under my feet shake slightly as I heard someone come bolting toward the door on the other side. A girl's voice boomed from inside, "Coming coming coming!"

She flung the door open with a huge smile on her face. "Hi!" She was definitely the same girl who had been at my house.

"Come *in*!" she insisted before I could return the greeting, ushering me in while yelling, "Dad! Sloane's here!"

"So I figured, Maddie." A middle-aged man made his way toward us, crossing through a dining room situated to the right of the front entrance. He was drying a white plate with a blue checkered dish towel. He was thin, with caramel-brown hair that was peppered with gray streaks, one of them very prominent. He had a full beard, trimmed short, also gray in patches. The gray patches added dimension to his face, telling more stories than just the lines of his wrinkles. He smiled in my direction, his narrow-set eyes twinkling.

"Very nice to meet you, Sloane. Welcome, have a seat." He gestured to the dining room table that sat in the middle of the room to my right, decked out with coffee and pastries. The furniture matched the wide mahogany molding that framed all of the room's walls and windows.

I sat down against the wall facing the entryway; I hated having my back to doors.

"Please, help yourself. I'll be right with you," Adrian said before disappearing back into the kitchen. The girl was already digging into the pastries: donuts, fritters, and muffins. I poured myself a cup of coffee.

"Thank you so much for agreeing to see me on such short notice," I said to Adrian when he returned from the kitchen.

"It is absolutely our pleasure," he said, matter-of-factly. "I'm just so very glad you accepted our offer to help you." Adrian smiled warmly as he sat down, and I found myself thinking that this man had the perfect demeanor and presence to fool a victim of some sort, which is what the rational side of my brain was telling me was happening.

"I don't really have a choice," I muttered.

"You must have so many questions. And you've probably been experiencing some unusual happenings lately, correct?" Adrian held the tip of a ballpoint pen to a notepad, waiting for my response.

"Yeah—yes. To put it mildly," I stuttered.

He scribbled something on the notepad. "Have you been experiencing any unexplained symptoms lately, such as nausea, headaches, nosebleeds, pins and needles, chills, rapid heartbeat, or even panic attacks?"

"Yes. Yes, I have." I wondered if I had been signed up for some experimental drug without my knowledge since the symptoms he was describing were so spot-on.

"Good. Good." He scribbled away on the pad. "For how long have you been experiencing them? An estimate is absolutely sufficient."

"Uhh, I don't know, uhh—maybe a month?" I said.

"A month," Adrian repeated after me as he wrote. "Good! Your manifestation symptoms shouldn't last much longer, and should at least start to decrease in intensity very soon."

Cold sweat slithered across my forehead. "Manifestation symptoms?"

"Yeah! For your powers," Maddie, mouth half full of pastry, chimed in.

I shot an incredulous look at the girl's father. "Powers?"

"Well, Sloane, it seems you have been bequeathed the power to manipulate time, and Madeline and I are here to assist you with the transition."

His expression didn't waver from the slight smile.

I raised my eyebrows, mouth slightly open, looking back and forth between the two of them. Maddie still had the biggest smile plastered on her face, and I could tell she was holding back lots of things she wanted to say.

And then I just started laughing.

And laughing, and laughing.

Exasperated at first, and then a belly-holding, trying-to-catch-my-breath, falling-over-backward laugh. When I recovered, I said the only thing I could possibly say to the absurdity of the situation. "Okay! You got me! 'Smile, you're on *Candid Camera*' and all that! Who put you up to this? Was it Rebecca? Justin? Ooh, even better—was it my father? The firm really is hazing me, aren't they? Hah!" I kept laughing.

"Believe me, you're not the first person I've helped that mentions that show. But you must know they've been out of production for quite a few years now," Adrian responded with his own little laugh.

"Okay, you can drop the act. If it's not *Candid Camera* then some internet series... thing. Like a short video to try and go viral, right?" I kept laughing, but the more I rambled and they stayed deadpan, the more I started to worry. "No, seriously, who set you up to prank me?"

"You just said yourself that you've been having manifestation symptoms. We're not shitting you," Maddie said.

"Language, Madeline," Adrian said, without looking at her, and proceeded to scribble something.

"So what, you're telling me you guys are time travelers? Please, do share this evening's lottery numbers." I let the sarcasm drip from my words, eyeing the front door as I contemplated just walking out.

Adrian looked at me and spoke sternly. "Rule number one. We never Jump into the future."

"Yeah you *never* go there." Maddie mimicked Adrian's grave face. "And if you're in the Past and you know something about someone's Future, you never, ever, tell them what you know."

Adrian nodded in agreement.

"As Time Wardens, it is our most sacred and important duty to protect the Pattern, and that starts with preserving the Past, and fortifying the Future, at any cost."

I swallowed and sipped air I didn't realize I was missing. I wanted to continue laughing, but there was no amusement left in my body to over-rationalize with. They were dead serious.

When I didn't say anything, Adrian fidgeted in his seat, clasping his hands in front of him on the table, and shot me a small smile before continuing, "We are called the Lunai, that's L-U-N-A-I. It's an old name; it's nothing formal. In the past, our ancestors told time using the sun and moon. We are directly influenced by the lunar phases, hence the nod to the moon in our name. The closer the moon is to Earth, the more easily we can access our powers."

Fair enough. I'll humor this.

He continued, "There are not very many of us, less than ten thousand in the world. The powers are only meant to be passed on from person to person, as to not oversaturate or overpopulate. Surprisingly, people are often only thinking of one person when they die, so our population doesn't grow very rapidly. Which is good. We are tasked with an enormous honor and privilege, being the Wardens of the Pattern. Let's just say that there is such a thing as too many cooks in the kitchen when it comes to protecting the Pattern of Time, so to speak."

I gave him a confused look indicating I didn't understand, so he continued, "The powers aren't passed randomly. They pass from one human to another at the time of a Lunai's death. The person and, rarely, persons whom the dying Lunai is thinking about when they leave this existence is the one who inherits their powers."

My expression didn't change. I had no idea what he was talking about.

"So, one of *you*, thought about *me*, when they uhm–died?"

"It appears so," Adrian said. "Who in your life passed away recently?"

I shot a glance at Maddie before looking back at Adrian, wide-eyed. "No one."

"Interesting." Adrian took a sip of his coffee. "I guess it doesn't come as a surprise to me since you didn't contact us; we had to seek you out."

"You mean—" I began.

"Normally, when someone intends to pass on their powers to a person, they have a transfer contract. This allows them to reveal themselves before passing on, making the recipient aware of the powers beforehand. In case of unexpected deaths, we encourage everyone, contract or not, to leave a note or message, usually included as a sealed letter accompanying a traditional will, instructing their inheritor to contact their nearest Curator to explain what's going on," Adrian explained.

"The only reason we found you is because you Slipped about a year backward and I Sensed it, so we came and got you." Maddie spoke extremely fast. I could tell she was probably a pretty isolated child. She seemed to be bursting at the seams to talk to me.

"Madeline, what did I say about not bombarding Sloane with information? She doesn't know half of the things you are saying, honey." Adrian's voice was soft but stern.

"Sorry." She sank into her chair.

I stared at the father-daughter duo, wondering how I got myself into this mess, yet not able to shake the curiosity that was slowly growing.

"So, crash course, sorry," Adrian began, addressing me again. "I am what we call a Curator. There's one in most major cities. We also have Consuls in every country, and all states here in the US."

"So do you always just know when I use my"—I felt so silly saying the word—"powers?"

Adrian smiled slyly. "Sensing is actually a bonus perk that Madeline has. But let's stick to the basics, shall we?"

"Please," I said, hoping my utter confusion wasn't translating as frustration.

"Normally, I like to give people some time to adjust before jumping into training. But you're rather—uhm—incident prone. So I think we should really try and get some control right away."

"Incident prone?" I asked.

"Like when you Slipped the other day. We don't want that happening. Care to tell us what you were doing right before you Slipped?"

"I'm guessing *slipping* is slang for time traveling?" I asked, uncertain.

"Well, not exactly," Adrian said, "When you Slip, it's involuntary. You can Slip into a Stop, or as in your case the other day, you Slipped right into a Jump, which is why you found yourself in the Past, about a year ago."

What he was saying made sense, if you believed in all this stuff.

"I'm sorry. And you want to know what I was doing right before I did that slipping thing?" I asked, trying not to sound impatient.

"Yes, right before you Slipped, where were you, what were you up to, and what were you thinking?" Adrian asked.

"I was just in my room. I wasn't doing anything special."

"What was your state of mind? What were you thinking about?" he pried.

I tried to remember exactly what I had been thinking about, not that I was eager to divulge this to a total stranger. "I thought I was having a panic attack."

"Any particular reason why?"

I wondered if I should share the fact that, according to these rules he was telling me, I had in fact Slipped twice that day. Once at the office and once at home.

"I had an extremely stressful day at work. Weird stuff was happening, I cut my hand pretty badly. And I thought I had some bizarre illness."

"All right, I can see where that can cause some upset," Adrian continued, his reaction clinical. "Do you connect this in any way to the date that you found yourself Slipping to? Do you know the date you Slipped to?"

Realization dawned on me. I hadn't only been worried about my physical and mental health. I had been lost in an intrusive flashback about graduation.

"Yeah. Yes, actually. I was feeling sad about that particular night. Something triggered a memory of a horrible thing that happened," I said, my voice small.

"Well, there you have it," Adrian said, and I was glad he wasn't making a big fuss or prying further; my explanation seemed to have sufficed. I looked over at Maddie, who was enthralled by the whole story, her mouth slightly open. She reminded me of what I imagined Amanda would look like in a few years.

"So you're saying that now I'm going to time travel whenever I feel upset by something? Because if so, I don't want these powers," I stated.

"No, you don't have to worry about Slipping over every single thing," Adrian said in a reassuring tone. "That's why we're here. We're going to help you recognize the signs of your Slips and teach you tricks to prevent them from happening. It also gets easier once your powers mature a little bit. You will have a lot more control and will be able to call on them only when you need them." Adrian sipped his coffee while eyeing me over the brim of his cup with a patient look of amusement. The type of look you'd give a young child. His kind eyes made me want to trust him, but I was still skeptical.

"Yeah, like me for example, I haven't Slipped since I was, like, eight. And I'm eleven," Maddie said proudly.

"That's impressive." I smiled at her. I had no idea whether it was impressive or not, but for some reason, I really wanted to show this little girl some kindness. She beamed back at me.

"So I know this is a lot to take in at one time. But I just want to make sure that this was the only time you Slipped, right?" Adrian asked.

"No actually, I don't think so," I said. It was better to come clean.

Adrian asked me to elaborate on what had happened, where I had been, and what I had been doing and thinking leading up to the supposed Slip. It made perfect sense to him as I described the frozen, unbreathing people in the office, that I had accidentally Stopped time due to being in a state of panic, compounded with the intense physical pain of the cut in my hand.

"I'm going to ask you to try and stay away from situations and memories that are particularly potent, emotionally. Whether they are unpleasant or pleasant. Sometimes strong positive emotions can also cause Slips."

THE AFTER HOURS

My mind wandered to Eric for a split second and three sensations happened in my body nearly simultaneously. First, butterflies in my stomach. Second, incredulity at those butterflies that made my heart beat a bit faster. Third, nerves along my spine tingling in response to the shock and quickened heartbeat.

"You okay, Sloane?" Maddie asked.

"Yeah, yeah, I'm fine." I smiled and shook it off. "I think I just felt something."

"Did it start in your spine?" Adrian asked.

"Yes! Like pins and needles in my spine." I was so glad someone knew what I was talking about because it was such a strange sensation, and the internet had not been helpful at all.

"What were you thinking about?" Adrian smiled.

"My ex," I lied.

Adrian nodded and seemed amused with me. "You're going to need some practice getting them out of your head, I see."

I laughed. "Yeah, I guess."

Does this mean I need to get Eric out of my head?

"So when I . . . Slip, or . . . Stop." The words were awkward on my tongue. "Does it affect anyone else? Like could my family be aware when this happens to me?"

"Not unless you have skin-to-skin contact with them. Then they would be affected by whatever Stop or Jump you are making. But it's imperative that you do not reveal your powers to anyone. If you feel yourself starting to Slip, you must get away from any physical contact," Adrian responded.

I thought about the redhead in the coffee shop, how she had been seemingly invisible to the people around us. How she had so deliberately kept skin-to-skin contact with me. I shivered at the thought of her hands on me, invading my personal space.

"What about other, uhm, Lunai? Do they automatically have time Stop for them or—?" I wanted to describe what had happened in the coffee shop to get their take on it, whether the redhead could have potentially been a time traveler, but my segue didn't take, as Maddie suddenly and instantaneously disappeared and reappeared on the opposite side of the room from where she had been.

"Nope!" she chirped.

"Whoa!" I exclaimed.

Adrian rolled his eyes.

"I just Stopped and walked over here and Started again. Doesn't affect anyone unless you're touching!" She had a smug smile on her face, obviously proud of her trick.

I took a deep breath, still unsure I wasn't being pranked with some high-tech optical illusions. "Okay. Makes sense."

Absolutely none of this makes sense.

But still—doesn't it?

"We have covered a lot of ground. I don't like to inundate new Wardens with information the first time I get to speak with them," Adrian said, and shifted in his seat as if he were uncomfortable or tired.

I actually wish you would inundate me a bit more.

"No reading material?" I asked pointedly, trying my best to cleanse my voice of any sarcasm.

"Not quite yet, at least. Your homework for now is to come up with a routine, or ritual, something to reset you and center yourself when you feel like your emotions are becoming overwhelming. It can be anything you want. A mantra, something you say to yourself, or an act. I know some people like to have a glass of ice water. Some people meditate. Some people listen to a special playlist. Find what centers you, and you're already well on your way to being Slip-free."

Adrian said this as if this was something easy. Something that I could order online. As if I wouldn't be constantly doing this if I actually had a clue what to do. As if I hadn't already searched endlessly and unsuccessfully for this magic trick to control feelings.

CHAPTER NINE

A FTER I FINISHED work on Monday afternoon, I walked through the unusually thick air toward my car, mentally prepared for the hour-long commute ahead. It had been raining on and off all day, and petrichor hung in the air.

It felt out of place among the normally dusty skyscrapers of downtown Los Angeles, but I welcomed it, breathing deeply through my nose as I strolled.

As I got onto the freeway, I scrolled around on the car's screen that my phone was hooked up to, trying to find a different playlist to listen to. I made a mental note to mention how much I loved the car the next time I saw my father, whenever that would be.

I was about fifteen minutes away from home when I was startled by an emergency alert. A notification filled the car's screen as my phone wailed. I knew I shouldn't have, but the car screen didn't show any details of the alert, so I glanced at my phone.

Emergency Alert
Severe weather warning until Mon, 6/30 10:00 p.m. PDT.
Remember, Pull Aside, Stay Alive. —NWS

"Huh," I said to myself, glancing out the windshield and in the rearview mirror. I didn't see anything out of the ordinary. The showers we had been experiencing were certainly out of the ordinary for late June in Southern California, but nothing that could be categorized as severe. I wondered if it was a glitch in the system.

Just then, I rounded a bend in the freeway that took me around the hills that split one part of the city. Then I saw what the alert was talking about. Enormous, thick, dark-gray cumuli loomed to the north. Lightning flashes bounced furiously around within them, threatening to strike the ground. A wall of rain hung like a curtain from beneath the clouds like a glitch in the cityscape in front of me.

I switched away from my phone's music app and turned on the radio instead. A female voice was speaking hurriedly, a twinge of panic in her voice.

"... *the Secretary-General of the World Meteorological Organization in Geneva has released a statement saying he is stunned at the turn of events here in the southwestern region of the United States, and has called all hands on deck for an investigation into the formation of the superhurricane, and how it went undetected by their teams of experts* ..."

The radio cut off as a call came in from my mom, which I answered immediately.

"Hi, Mom."

"Sweetie, are you on the road?" My mom's voice was twice as panicked as the voice on the radio, but even so, I could tell she was toning it down for my sake.

"Yeah, I'm almost at the exit. There's no storm where I am." Just as I said the words, large, aggressive raindrops started splattering my windshield. I decided not to divulge this and further worry her.

Neil's voice, farther away than my mother's, sounded over the car's speakers next, dancing between nervousness and excitement. "Did you guys hear that? They're calling it a *super*hurricane. Nothing that has ever made landfall on the East Coast has ever been given that title."

"Neil. Sloane is driving. Don't scare her," my mother said.

"Sloane, get home. You're missing Dad having a field day." Justin's voice came over the speakers, followed by bellowing laughter.

Neil was one of those overly practical types of humans who found pleasure in, and didn't mind sacrificing their free time for, taking preventive measures for extremely unlikely scenarios. Justin had said once that Neil hadn't always been that way, that his doomsday-prepper mindset had intensified after Justin's mom died. Neil had outfitted our house with a state-of-the-art security system, a backup generator, and a stockpiling area in the garage that held at least a year's supply of canned food, water, and other household necessities. We had always made fun of him for it.

"You will thank me for my generator later when the power goes out," Neil retorted.

"Sloane, honey, please be safe okay? It's not raining too hard here either, so you might make it before it gets too bad." It wasn't clear whether my mother was convincing me or herself.

"Yep, I'll be careful. Promise, Mom."

"Love you, sweetie."

A second call announced itself on the screen. The rain was gaining intensity at a frightening pace, but that wasn't what caused my heart to leap.

I did a double take, but it was definitely Eric's name on the screen.

"Love you too Mom," I said hastily, and with a pang of guilt, switched calls. "Hi, Eric."

I heard him exhale. "Sloane. Hey. You okay?" He wasn't as panicked as my mom, but the concern was apparent, and my heart took another jump.

"Yeah, yes. I'm almost home."

The traffic started slowing down, and I had to increase the speed of my windshield wipers. But I couldn't help the smile creeping up on my face. I knew I should have been scared, but my brain would not register anything else.

Eric called me because he's worried about me.

Another breath. "Okay, great. Just thought I'd check on you—you know, I knew you were driving, and this weather is looking wild—" he rambled.

My smile just grew wider. "Yeah, I'm still driving." I hoped I came off carefree, not careless.

"Be safe, okay?" Eric said, his voice smaller than I had ever heard it, despite my volume being turned up high to combat the sound of the rain pelting my car.

"Always," I piped.

"I'll see you tomorrow? Unless—if the weather continues—then obviously, you probably won't come in. Anyway." He laughed at himself and sighed. "Ahh, I'm being an incoherent idiot, Ms. Becker. Look what you've done to me."

I bit my lip to stifle the squeal that wanted to come out. I was having the hardest time concentrating on driving. Flipping my windshield wipers up to the highest setting, I barely noticed the cars that were on the side of the road, stalled with their hazard lights flashing.

"I'll see you soon, how about that?" I said, once I'd composed myself. My cheeks hurt from smiling.

"I like that. I'll see you soon, Sloane." I heard his smile almost clearer than I did his words.

"Bye, Eric." I fought back a giggle.

What's wrong with me? I should be scared right now.

"Bye, Sloane." Once again, my name sounded like a serenade when he said it.

I let Eric be the one to hang up. A strong gust of wind slammed into my car from the left, jerking me back to reality. I slowed down a little to prevent the car from swerving, and realized I was one of very few cars left on the freeway.

A lightning bolt shattered the sky directly in front of me, so close it nearly blinded me. The rain poured even heavier, drenching my windshield completely to the point where I couldn't see out at all, despite the wipers being on their highest setting. I slowed down to a crawl and quickly set my GPS to navigate home. It showed that I was only a quarter mile from my exit.

I let out a breath through pursed lips and said to myself, "I can do this. Surface streets will be better."

A thought crossed my mind, taking me by surprise.

I wonder what would happen if I could Stop right now.

I pushed the thought away, needing to focus. I inched forward for the last stretch of freeway. As I exited, I realized my folly when I saw that the parkway that led to my neighborhood was close to being flooded. The water probably reached halfway up my tires, and I could feel them struggling to gain traction.

"Ugh, freaking—" I muttered as my tires spun turning onto the parkway. "Inept Californian," I spat, at myself.

I tried my best to keep calm as the water sloshed and splashed across the windshield, making it impossible to see more than twenty or so yards in front of me, the sheer force with which the water poured bordering on arrogance. The storm was somehow still gaining force, and terror tugged at me as I felt it threaten to steal my control over the car. A combined feeling of fear and relief hit me as I realized how dumb I was being out on the freeway. But I was off the freeway now, and only a few blocks from home. I could make it.

The world was a blur of the color of water. The gray of the asphalt, and the beige of the surrounding hillsides were simply backdrops to the cascades. Except for one spot in front of me in the street. A spot of light orangey-red visible in the gray torrent.

Despite going way slower than the speed limit, the figure closed in alarmingly fast. I swerved to my right, slamming on the brakes, my tires drifting in the deep water.

My heart leaped into my throat as I registered a stinging sensation in my spine, and before I could react, my eyes shut. My body began to shake uncontrollably, and it took everything in my power to keep my hands on the wheel.

My front tires thudded against the curb to the right and my car came to a halt with its front half on the sidewalk. When my eyes finally opened, my stomach twisted when I saw that I had missed a light pole by mere inches.

The rain had stopped. Or rather, been immobilized. It hung in chaotic arrays all around my car. The streams on my windshield and windows were seeping down to their resting spot, leaving the panes clearer.

I glanced to my left through the driver's side window. Standing in the middle of the street was the redhead from the coffee shop. Perfectly, eerily, lifeless and still.

I let out a breath I had been holding, thanking whatever powers, *my* powers, that I had been able to Stop. Not only did I not want to crash into her, but I also needed to get away from her. I had no idea how she found me; we were thirty miles away from the coffee shop in downtown. Did she know where I lived? Was she stalking me? Why was she on foot, especially in this weather?

My car was still running, so I shifted into reverse and prepared to back down off the sidewalk. Thankfully, there was enough space between her and the median so I could drive past her and away. I figured I might be able to drive home within the Stop—Slip—whichever it was, and I had a sudden longing to fast forward until I was at a point when I could actually use these powers deliberately. Then I could use them to my advantage in moments like these.

But as I was about to place my hand over the passenger side seat and turn to look behind me, I felt something brush against the back of my neck, tickling the edge of my hairline. Or rather, it was like a finger had been placed there, and was now being lifted.

I jerked my head to the right and behind me and let out a scream.

The redhead was sitting in my backseat.

My head snapped back to the left. The redhead was still standing frozen in the street.

There's two of them.

"I thought I told you to watch where you're going, bitch."

My glance at the redhead in the street lost me precious milliseconds. In the blink of an eye, the redhead in my backseat placed her left hand on my forehead, shoving my head back into the headrest. Her right hand pressed a small knife against my throat. She was otherworldly strong, and her arms didn't waver as I clawed at them, kicking my feet into the floor, trying to wrench away from her grip.

I caught a glimpse of us in my rearview mirror. I could have sworn she held a scalpel.

"Who are you? What do you want?" I shouted, my voice strained from the pressure she was putting on my windpipe.

"Isn't it obvious?" She smirked, her eyes on fire as they met mine in the mirror.

I growled and dug my nails into her forearm, while reaching with the other hand behind me, trying to grasp at her hair.

"Look. *Look,*" she said as she forced my head to the left, digging the scalpel farther into my neck. I could feel the hot sting of the blade and wetness spilling down to my collarbone. My line of sight was now directed out the driver's side window once more, staring at the blurred vignette of the other redhead standing in the street. "*Look at me!*" she roared as she slammed my head harder against the headrest. "Are you looking?" she snarled, sucking in breaths through her clenched teeth as she craned her neck to try and see my eyes in the rearview mirror.

I felt a jolt, and I realized that my car was still in reverse. The car had rolled backward, its front tires dropping off the curb and landing back on the street. It proceeded to roll backward down the slight incline in the parkway. I slammed my right foot on the gas, the tires squealing as my car hurtled back down the way I had come. Thankfully the street was empty; no one else was out driving in the dangerous weather but me. The rain still hung heavy around my car, except the droplets my car came into contact with. Through the windshield, I could see where my car had carved a tunnel through the raindrops.

The acceleration had the desired effect, and the redhead grunted as she hung on to me and my seat. When I felt the car couldn't go any faster in reverse, the engine protesting with a whine, I slammed with both feet on the brake.

The redhead lost balance and fell backward, her head slamming against the back of the seats.

As fast as she had appeared, she was gone. Both from the street and from my car. No flash, no zap or zoom. She just disappeared. The lack of her presence was abrupt, yet she left chaos in her wake.

The faint scent of vinegar and roses still filled my car as my eyes slammed shut and a searing pain shot through my core. When they opened, a thousand drops attacked the outside of my car as time Started again. I turned around in my seat, scanning the backseat of my car with hungry eyes, breathing heavily. I needed to convince my brain that the vision of an empty backseat was, in fact, the truth. My alarm bells were still firing, my brain refusing to register that I was safe.

For now.

I gagged as I felt something warm and wet pool on my upper lip, metallic-tasting droplets seeping into my mouth. I glanced at myself in the rearview mirror to see a steady stream of blood flowing from my nose, slithering down my jaw and chin to join the blood starting to crust on my neck.

CHAPTER TEN

EVERY FIBER IN my body knew it had been the same person as the one who attacked me in the coffee shop. And she probably had the same powers as I now did—it was the only explanation for how there were suddenly two of her and how they both disappeared into thin air. I knew of only one way I could get to the bottom of who she was and what she wanted, and it meant getting better at controlling these powers. Whatever the cost.

I was sitting at the Lexes' dining table that Tuesday evening, the day after the bizarre hurricane hit Southern California, coffee cup in hand and notebook open in front of me. As hesitant as I had been the last time I visited them, this time I was eager to learn as much as I could, as fast as I could. If only so that I could get rid of the horrendous symptoms that I now knew to be manifestation symptoms. I had felt nauseous all day at work, and my brain had been foggy ever since the incident in my car the day prior. Which was why I had told my mother a white lie and said I would be working late, to catch up before the long weekend. That Friday was the Fourth of July, so my lie had been totally believable. At least, that's what I had convinced myself to counteract the intense self-loathing I felt as I typed out the untrue texts to my mother.

"Just know that you always have a safe haven here. If you ever feel overwhelmed and feel like you need help, or even just a break from your powers, you are welcome here," Adrian said.

"You can give me a break from the powers?" I asked excitedly. I was about to say, "Why didn't you say so already?" but Maddie interrupted.

"*Dad*," she whined, "we didn't tell Sloane about the Sanctuary."

"The what now?" I asked.

"Sorry, Sloane. I'm getting ahead of myself. What I meant by safe haven here is the institute we have in our basement."

"Institute?" I pressed.

"Every Curator has a Sanctuary that serves their region. It's farther underground than normal basements like you're used to. Its placement within the earth fortifies the space and prevents the moon's pull on us, so our powers don't work down there. Or they are, at the very least, significantly dulled down."

I gave Adrian probably the millionth blank stare of the day, and he realized I had no idea what he meant.

He looked flustered. "So, you know how I mentioned that the moon affects our powers? Your powers are going to be stronger during a full moon and weaker on new moons, waxing and waning accordingly with the phases between."

"Moon's not gonna be full for over a week," Maddie said gleefully. "You'll be fine!"

I could tell she was being helpful, but this comment terrified me.

"Are you serious? Do I need to, like, lock myself up during a full moon or something?" I asked.

Adrian and Maddie both laughed, making me feel a bit left out, but Adrian recovered quickly and reassured me. "No, don't worry. It really isn't

THE AFTER HOURS

as big a deal as one would think. Some people need to align with the moon phases to really harness their power if they're trying to use them for specific purposes. A specific Jump. Other people don't need to rely on the moon as much. If you're employed by a Council and carrying out certain tasks, you might want to utilize moon phases to facilitate some precision in your Jumps."

I found that Adrian, as professorly as he was, had a sort of youthful glee about him when he got to explaining the nuts and bolts of this whole thing. It was adorable.

"Council?" I asked, but got cut off by Maddie.

"Come on!" She was already standing, a blueberry muffin in one hand, her other hand beckoning for us to follow her.

The entry hall split the house in half from front to back. It had mahogany board and batten along both walls that ran perpendicular to the front of the house. The staircase to the upper level ran against the wall to the right once you walked in, its handrail and treads made out of the same wood. Where the staircase began, the hallway narrowed as it led to the back of the house.

Maddie skirted along the staircase and took a few steps down the hall. She stopped and faced the left-hand wall, waiting for us to join her. The wall looked ordinary, except for the fact that it was pretty much bare, save the decorative woodwork. No pictures or artwork hung anywhere along the moss-green wallpaper above the wood which, once I noticed it, I thought was strange, since the rest of Adrian and Maddie's house was in general fairly well lived-in and seemed to contain a lot of memories, as if someone had lived there a long time. I then noticed that one of the wood panels across from where we were standing was slightly more worn on one side than the others.

Sure enough, once Adrian was firmly by our side, Maddie reached out and pushed the faded panel inward and around itself, spinning it along an axis in its middle so that its backside now faced us. This revealed a metal plate with a single illuminated elevator button, incongruously modern against the mahogany. When Maddie pressed it, the panels to the left of the hidden button made a loud clicking sound and pushed outward and then farther to the left. The door was immaculately hidden within the joints of the boards and the seams in the wallpaper. Behind it, a metal elevator door slid open with a soft chime, revealing an elevator cab.

"Whoa." I gawked.

"Pretty cool, huh?" Maddie said, smugly.

The elevator ride seemed endless, and I knew we were going much deeper than a regular basement. The doors finally opened to reveal a hallway with bare concrete walls. The lighting was dim. Traditional-looking interior doors dotted the walls at irregular intervals all the way to the other end of the hall. The doors all stood ajar and revealed sparsely decorated, yet homey, bedrooms.

I also definitely felt that we weren't above ground anymore. My chest was a little bit lighter, my nerves weren't threatening to short-circuit at any possible moment, and my head was clearer. The ground felt more solid under my feet.

As if he had read my mind, Adrian spoke as we were about halfway down the hallway. "You may feel some relief from your symptoms down here. Some say it feels like a fever breaking or a headache dissipating. It's different for everyone. But it's another benefit of staying here at the Sanctuary."

I started to wonder if I might actually take him up on that offer someday soon, if the symptoms didn't start letting up. We reached the end of the hallway, and Adrian and Maddie turned to the left toward a set of thick, wooden double doors that were accented with heavy black hardware. Adrian pulled out a set of old-looking keys and unlocked the doors.

As they swung open, I couldn't believe my eyes.

Behind them was a grand hall, multiple stories high, its structure, walls, floors, and ceiling made entirely of smooth, gray stone. It reminded me heavily of a church, with a bay-shaped space at the far end that housed a raised platform. Except the main space of the hall was not filled with pews but with round banquet tables set up in seemingly no order, as if for a wedding reception minus the white tablecloths and flowers. The hall was also wider than in traditional churches. To the sides, thick columns framed off the middle space and reached all the way up to the intricately vaulted ceiling above. Behind the columns were spaces with lower ceiling height and balconies above, going four stories up.

I noticed then that the balconies' back walls were completely covered with bookshelves that straddled the odd door, so the balconies actually served more as walkways to reach the bookshelves and doors that led off into mystery rooms on the levels above. The first floor of the hall also had doors on the side walls; some stood ajar revealing office-type spaces, surprisingly and contrastingly modern. One of them gave a glimpse into what looked like a kitchen. Up against one of the side walls, tucked under a second-level balcony, was a space that reminded me heavily of my home's family room. A couple of inviting couches, a coffee table, and a TV stand with a large TV all fit on top of a plush-looking area rug that defined the area.

What struck me as the most odd thing about the space was the lack of windows. I realized we were far underground, so windows were out of the question, but the space felt too grand to not have any windows leading to sprawling views, or at least some colorful stained glass.

"Welcome to the Los Angeles Sanctuary, Sloane," Adrian said, gesturing with both hands around the space.

"What is this place?" I said, awestruck.

"We mainly use this as a meeting space. Sometimes celebrations. Birthday parties. Christmas parties," Adrian said.

"You celebrate Christmas?" I asked, without thinking the question through.

"We're time travelers, not robots!" Maddie piped from one of the couches. She had plopped herself down on one of them and was flipping through a media menu with a remote, chomping down the blueberry muffin from upstairs, which I was surprised had survived the trip down here.

"This is amazing," I said, because it was. My mind shot to the redhead, and wondered if she attended parties here. I still hadn't found a good moment to mention her. I had no idea *how* to mention her. As much as I wanted to trust Adrian and learn from him, I wasn't sure I could explain what had happened without sounding like a raging lunatic, not to mention the issue of Maddie constantly being around. I wasn't exactly going to bring up attempted murder in front of an eleven-year-old.

"It's not much, but it's ours. It's a safe space for us Lunai to convene, study, and relax. The rooms upstairs used to house more bedrooms." Adrian pointed to the doors leading off the balconies. "Back in the day, a lot of Lunai lived here full time, or stayed for longer periods of time if they were transitioning between territories. New Wardens would come here for relief from their manifestation symptoms. They're mostly empty now; we've been meaning to update the furnishings."

When Maddie started streaming a TV show, I couldn't help but ask, "You have Wi-Fi down here?"

"Again, we're time travelers, not cavemen!" Maddie croaked, her mouth full. I kicked myself for the ignorant question.

"We try to keep the place updated with modern conveniences. No cell reception means we rely on internet connection. We can't expect people to sever themselves from the world, even if they would like a break from their powers."

Adrian made his way over to the platform at the head of the space and proceeded to turn the pages of a thick leather-bound book that sat on a table in the middle of the platform. The pages creaked as he turned them. They looked to be made out of parchment, or just extremely old paper. They were yellowing and frayed at the edges. Once Adrian reached the page he was looking for, he retrieved an inkwell pen out of his shirt pocket and scribbled something down on it. Something in me wanted to wince at the act. A book that looked that old and important should only be written in with a quill.

"Do you have a middle name, Sloane?" Adrian asked.

"Uhm," the question caught me off guard, "Renee. Sloane Renee Becker. Why?"

"Just making a note of you in the Horolog." Adrian turned his head toward me briefly and smiled. "Birthday?"

"June 3, 2006. Horolog?"

"Come have a look." Adrian gestured for me to join him on the platform.

The book gave off an even bigger air of importance the closer I got. Adrian had written my full name and date of birth across the top of a left-hand page, close to the middle of the book. I noticed the pages were less weathered toward the end of the book. Every page had a sigil at the top, lines that extended into a horizontal infinity symbol, with a diamond placed at its center. Two of the diamond's corners were encapsulated by the infinity symbol's loops, the other two sitting above and below the symbol's center.

"Is this a log of every, uhm, Lunai?" It felt weird saying the word.

"Yes and no," Adrian said. "The Horolog contains names of Lunai, the roles of each Time Warden, but only those in my territory. So you will see those who have called the Los Angeles Sanctuary home. A complete record is held with the Consuls. I'll notify the California Consul of you later today, via a much more mundane method. I just like filling this book out. Call me quirky."

I chuckled to myself. "And what method would that be? Carrier pigeon?"

"Email," he answered. "But the Horolog also contains our code of conduct and our Laws, to the extent that we know them. I wasn't really intending on unloading all of this right away though. I know it's a lot to take in."

"Can I look?" I asked, indicating the Horolog. Something about it drew me to it, something more than just my regular love of books.

"Of course," Adrian said, sliding it in my direction on the table.

I flipped through the pages gingerly, their parchment-like quality fragile under my fingertips, their crackling sound utterly enticing.

If only I knew the redhead's name.

Past the pages with names inscribed, I came to a stop at a page with a diagram on it. It was hand drawn and looked like something you would find in the works of historical mathematicians. Pythagoras, Hypatia, Euclid. It had a circle in the middle, and two lines leading horizontally to each side of the page. The circle was marked with the word *praesenti*. Under the line to the left of the circle, the word *praeteritum* and to the right, *futurum*. Above each line, as well as the circle, were formulas.

To the left of the circle, it read:

$$(TEMPUS^2 + TEMPUS) + AEVUM = NOVUS\ AEVUM$$
$$PALMUS\ VITAE = NOVUS\ PALMUS\ VITAE$$

To the right, it read:

$$(TEMPUS \times 2)^2 + AEVUM = NOVUS\ AEVUM$$
$$PALMUS\ VITAE - TEMPUS = NOVUS\ PALMUS\ VITAE$$

Over the circle:

$$(TEMPUS \times 2) + AEVUM = NOVUS\ AEVUM$$
$$PALMUS\ VITAE = NOVUS\ PALMUS\ VITAE$$

"What's this?" I asked.

"Oh," Adrian began, looking caught off guard. "I hadn't intended to introduce you to that part yet."

"Dad, don't patronize. Sloane's smart." Maddie stalked over to take a look at the page I had open. "Oh, this is easy. It's how you age outside your Present."

"Correct, Madeline," Adrian said, back to his usual soothing voice. "I guess I can explain."

He tugged a small notebook out of his shirt pocket, flipped to a blank spread, and began to scribble. "This diagram represents the Past, Present, and Future," he said, pointing to the word below the left line, then the circle, then the word below the right. "The formulas loosely translate to this, where *time* is the number of moments you spend in a Stop or Jump." He pushed the notebook in my direction.

Past Jump:
$(time^2 + time) + age = new\ age$
$lifespan = new\ lifespan\ (no\ change)$

Future Jump:
$(time \times 2)^2 + age = new\ age$
$lifespan - time = new\ lifespan$

Stopping:
$(time \times 2) + age = new\ age$
$lifespan = new\ lifespan\ (no\ change)$

"Jumping and Stopping affects our bodies in different ways. We haven't figured out the exact cause of it, but we know it has to do with the amount of After Hours your body experiences, and the toll they take."

"Sorry, the amount of after hours?" I asked, still staring at the formulas he had transcribed, nowhere close to understanding.

"When we as Lunai create new time by Jumping or Stopping, they become what we call the After Hours. They are moments created *after* the Pattern was created, the Pattern of Time, that is." He scribbled the words *After Hours* and *Pattern of Time* below the formulas on the page as he spoke, indicating they should be capitalized.

"Gotcha," I lied.

"So these formulas are an illustration of the extent we currently know about how it affects us humans. So when you Stop for instance, you continue to age while you're in the Stop." He pointed to the formula under the word *Stopping* before opening a new spread in the notebook. He sketched a straight line, halted his pen, drew the shape of a drop of water starting where the line ended, came back up to have the pen meet the line again, and continued with the straight line level to the beginning part.

"When you Stop, you're still within the moment in which you Stopped. But you're not yet in the next moment. You create a pocket in the Pattern. Therefore, you continue to age because your body exists in the Stop, but when you return and Start again, your body outside the Stop has also aged because of the pocket you create and inhabit. Hence why your new age after the Stop is your age before you Stopped, plus twice the amount of time you spent in the Stop."

It was starting to make sense. "Everything comes at a price, I guess," I remarked.

Adrian nodded. "But the price gets steeper when you Jump." He flipped back and pointed at the formula for *Past Jump*. "When you Jump to the Past, not only are you aging like you would in Stopped time, but you are also creating an After Hour in the Past. You're essentially docking points from your Past self, which leads to your body aging at an even more accelerated rate. Which is also why being in a Jump for too long can be dangerous. Not only could you possibly change something, and thereby alter your Present as you know it by the time you return, but you're also aging every instance of yourself between the Jump and your Present. Hence the compounded time here." He pointed to the exponent next to the first *time*.

He opened yet a new page in the notebook and sketched a straight line over the first page and continued into the right-hand page. His pen swooped down, but instead of a drop shape, the new curved line went back to the left page, cut up through the straight line, made a half-moon shape over it, and went back down, back along the curve to the right-hand page, and joined back where the straight line ended and curved line began.

"People who spend too much time in the Past come back, like, exhausted. Like, imagine being fifteen, but in, like, a twenty-five-year old's body," Maddie said. I couldn't help but laugh at her sassiness.

"So I'm guessing Future Jumps are even worse?" I asked. Adrian had flipped back to the formulas, and I pointed to the one that said *Future Jump*.

"Correct. It should be mentioned that we do not have an exact science to measure this since people's lives are at stake here, so we do not perform experiments. Rather, the Horolog is a collection of what we've consistently observed through the centuries and has yet to be disproven, rather than proven."

"Sounds like science to me," I said, and couldn't contain a chuckle.

"Touché." Adrian shot me a smile before he continued, pointing to the formula. "We are unsure of what causes it, but in addition to aging at the same rate as you would in a Stop and a Past Jump, a Future Jump essentially attacks our cells as if everything that has yet to happen between the Present you're Jumping from and the Future you're Jumping to starts to happen all at once. Which is why—"

"We never Jump to the Future," I finished his sentence.

"Exactly. It's also why Future Jumps are incredibly hard to maintain, should one attempt it."

"I remember you saying something about not being allowed to tell someone if you know about their Future. Why is that?" I asked.

"Good question," Adrian said as he picked up his pen. "While it mostly has to do with the ethical standards we want to uphold, it also has a lot to do with this." He picked up from where he had left off in his drawing, continuing the straight line to the right from the shape that represented a Jump, all the way to the edge of the page until the tip of the pen flicked off.

I shot him a puzzled look.

"The Future is unwritten. The Pattern is less forgiving. We can't divulge something that we don't know for certain will happen. If you Jump back to yesterday and tell that version of me that we'll be having this exact conversation the next day, that's simply what this version of you experienced. Yesterday's version of me might then go and do something like not text you back when you text me later that evening, hence canceling this training session and this conversation. So by communicating the Future, you're essentially altering the Past, and we all know why that's not okay. Does that make sense?"

"Yeah, absolutely," I answered. "But what does this mean then?" I pointed to the line in the formula that was identical between *Past Jump* and *Stopping*, but different for *Future Jump*. "What's this about a lifespan?"

Adrian took a deep breath. "What has been observed in those few souls who have pursued the fool's journey of Future Jumping is that not only have they aged considerably when they return, but their lifespan has been cut short by the time they spent in the Future."

I furrowed my eyebrows. "But how would they know that?"

"By seeing the Future, duh." Maddie was back on the couch, munching on something that was not the pastry she'd brought with her downstairs. I wouldn't have been surprised if she had a secret snack stash down here.

"They would confirm their existence at a certain point in time and then recheck after a certain amount of time spent in the Future, only to find themselves having met an untimely demise. It's inexplicable but astonishingly accurate," Adrian said.

"Will I have to take a test?" I asked, trying hard to retain everything I had just heard.

Adrian laughed. "No, not at all."

"Thank goodness. I suck at tests," I said.

"Ugh! I would *love* to take a test for once!" Maddie was making her way to join us again on the platform, her proclamation dramatic. "It sounds so brilliant. Cram sessions. Memorize facts. Spill it all on a piece of paper that then gets graded. And then you never have to think about it again. You can be all, like, 'Look at my *A*, losers.'" She made a peace sign with two fingers.

"That's *exactly* what's terrifying about them," I said, jokingly matching her theatrics with exasperation.

"Madeline is homeschooled. She thinks regular schooling is fascinating," Adrian said as he closed the Horolog and returned the black inkwell pen to its place in his pocket.

"Trust me, Maddie, I would kill to have been homeschooled." I gave her a knowing look.

"Ugh, all you Temp normies say that!" She rolled her eyes at me.

"Well she's not a Temp anymore, Maddie," Adrian said in a corrective tone.

"Temp?" I asked, my eyebrows raised, surprised at being called yet another term that I didn't know the meaning of.

"Sorry, it's what we call people who are not Lunai," Adrian excused Maddie, but she interrupted him.

"Well she was a Temp when she got to go to school, duh." She proceeded to roll her eyes at her father.

Adrian's hurried explanation still left me wanting, which he seemed to sense.

"It's short for Temporal. We Lunai are able to exist outside time, whereas Temporals are bound to time. Hence, Temps."

I laughed and wondered if they knew how it sounded. As if regular people were just temporary staff in life. But I decided not to mention it; they must have gotten the pun at some point. But Adrian set the record straight, again answering my thoughts.

"It's also sort of an inside joke at this point." He laughed like a dad telling a dad joke that only he thought was funny. The kind of laugh that obligates you to laugh with him. It was something I had never experienced with my dad, only my friends' fathers and Neil. Despite the jokes usually being cringeworthy, they were always heartwarming in a way that they filled you with joy regardless. I laughed with him, but also at the thought of a bunch of time travelers commiserating over the stupidity of a bunch of Temps.

"Can I keep these?" I pointed to Adrian's sketches in his notebook.

"Absolutely," he said, tearing out the pages and handing them to me.

It had started raining heavily again by the time we had said our goodbyes and I was headed home. Despite the precarious situation the storm had put me in the day before, I loved the rain, especially since it was so rare where I lived. The city changed instantly, its normal scorched, dusty surface glistened under the drops, and every facet felt fresher afterward. The buildings cleaner, the trees greener, the air a little bit lighter.

The rain, however, was not the reason a smile stayed plastered on my face the whole way home that evening. Something about Adrian and Maddie felt right. Like their presence was the antidote to something that I couldn't quite put my finger on, something that had been bothering me. Because just like the air I breathed, I felt a little lighter.

I promised myself that the next time I saw them, I'd ask Adrian about the redhead.

Seeing the Sanctuary, the massive library, the Horolog, the welcoming spaces that Adrian kept reminding me were available to me anytime I needed them—the combination of it all—made me feel less alone. But it also piqued my curiosity. I felt any last dregs of fear dissipate. Maybe this was something I could really hone. Control. Master.

CHAPTER ELEVEN

THE LIGHTNESS DIDN'T last long, as the farther I got from Adrian and Maddie's house, the heavier I felt. It was almost ten o'clock when I finally got home. I should have been tired, but I couldn't sleep. I was lying on my bed inspecting the notes I had gotten from Adrian when an intense wave of nausea—and somehow, shame—swept through me. I had been nauseous again all day at work, but not like this. This nausea was accompanied with a now familiar feeling of pins and needles in my spine. I shook violently, trying to remember Adrian's words of advice for what to do to counteract a Slip. I willed myself to stand up despite the shaking and went to my bathroom to grab a glass of water.

It didn't help.

I placed the glass I drank from back on the bathroom counter, my eyes avoiding the mirror. My phone buzzed in my pocket, and I reached for it with a trembling hand. The notification on the lockscreen indicated a text from Rebecca.

Rebecca: Help me come up with an elaborate, irrefutable excuse so that I can quit tomorrow without looking like a jackass that does not involve lying about my grandma dying or some other dark shit.

I started to type a response, but my shaking hands caused me to drop the phone. I tried to catch it but fumbled, my elbow hitting the glass. The phone landed in the sink. The glass fell off the edge of the vanity and hit my toe, so it didn't break, but it hurt me enough to send me over the edge and into the Slip I was fighting. Before I was able to bend down and grab it, my eyes sealed themselves and everything went dark.

A throbbing bass sounded, the pressure threatening to make my ears pop—and then the sensation was over.

I knew what had happened. This was just like when I had cut my hand in the office.

Still slightly shaky, I tried to persuade myself that I didn't need to panic. I at least had an idea of what to do to get back to the Present, even if I wasn't very good at it.

But first I had to figure out whether I was merely in a Stop or I had Jumped somewhere. Thankfully, I didn't need to wait long for my answer, as a familiar set of voices sounded from my room.

"You haven't eaten yet? It's almost nine."

"Mom and Dad left for Italy, remember?"

Not this again.

Annoyed at my evident obsession with this night, I wondered how in the world I found myself here yet again. I hadn't even been thinking about it this time.

When I had gone to the bathroom to get a drink of water, I hadn't bothered closing the door. Now the door was just slightly ajar. I reached for the knob and turned it as gently and slowly as I could, letting the door settle into the jamb before releasing it just as slowly. Once I was able to release my grasp, I hurriedly locked it. I was fairly certain nobody was coming my way, but I couldn't be too cautious.

THE AFTER HOURS

There were two of me out there.

Tom's voice still rang clearly from the phone. "I don't want to make you do something you don't want to. You can say no. But honestly, you know how fast the rumor mill churns at school. I wouldn't worry about people bothering you about Dylan. People must have forgotten about it by now."

"No, you're right." It was my voice.

"Yes!" Tom's triumphant voice rang from the device as the speakers crackled. "Pick you up in ten."

"You said thirty!" Graduation Me yelled.

A triple beep sounded as the call ended.

I pressed my ear against the bathroom door. I needed to hear enough to know when the coast was clear.

After some receding footsteps, I heard a shuffle and a low groan that could only have been me getting out from under the bed. I then heard my closet door slide shut, hoping and praying I had remembered everything correctly and neither version of me out there was about to try and attempt to go into the bathroom I was in.

Next, I heard Graduation Me come in, rummage through the closet before finding a satisfactory ensemble of jeans and a nondescript top, changing her clothes and leaving, closing the door to my room behind her.

Next, the closet door slid open yet again, and other Me made her way out of the room pretty much completely silently.

I knew what was happening downstairs. Maddie was about to show up and scare the living shit out of me.

I emerged from the bathroom and peered out my window, but didn't see anything. Familiar bustling came from downstairs, and I realized that my whole family, including myself who was waiting for Tom to pick me up, was there, and not frozen in a Stop. I had been very lucky that Maddie had found me before they did.

I had to get myself back to my Present as soon as I could. From what I had gleaned from Adrian and Maddie, it wasn't healthy to stay long outside your Present. And I certainly did not like the idea of aging at more than twice the rate. But I wasn't sure where to begin.

I made my way out of the bathroom and sat down on the edge of the bed, trying to conjure up a way to get myself out of this Slip. I heard a familiar double honk outside and knew Graduation Tom was here to get Graduation Me. A voice downstairs called something, and the front door slammed.

I remembered every detail of this evening so well. But thinking about the fact that there had been two additional versions of me in my room that night, and I had been completely oblivious to it, scrambled my brain. This changed everything.

After hearing the front door close, I snuck a peek out the window, making sure to keep my head low. Sure enough, Graduation Me was walking out to Tom's green crossover that sat idling by the curb. It took everything in my being to not go running out after her.

"Sloane? Did you forget something?" I heard my mother call downstairs. She heard me just before Maddie had brought me back to the Present.

If I remembered graduation night correctly, and I was sure I did, Tom and I had swung by a drive-through mom-and-pop diner five minutes away, before heading over to the party at Pete's house. The dinner run had not taken more than half an hour, forty-five minutes tops.

Against all of Adrian's warnings and my better judgment, and before I could stop myself, I snuck out of my bedroom into the hall.

I might as well take advantage of being here.

I contemplated the best way to get out of the house undetected. The master bedroom of our house did have a balcony with a spiral staircase leading down into our side yard. But it never came in handy when sneaking in or out, because it was directly adjacent to my mother and Neil's bed, and I wasn't sure whether one of them was in there. I also hated using the spiral stairs. They were one of the few things that were original to the house and were rickety and weak-feeling. Add to the fact that I'd always been intensely afraid of heights, and it just didn't make for a good combination. So I decided to take my chances with the front door.

I tiptoed down the stairs and dashed across the foyer to the front door, but I hadn't been stealthy enough.

"Honey? I thought you left already?" my mother's voice called from the kitchen.

I froze, hand on the front doorknob and a humming in my ears, different from the one caused by a Slip, wiping out any sensible thoughts of how to get myself out of the situation. This version of my mother was mother to an eighteen-year-old Sloane. She might notice that I wasn't that Sloane anymore.

I quickly slipped the hood over my head as my mother emerged from the kitchen drying off a wine glass with a towel. "Why did you change? I liked the peachy top you were wearing earlier."

I ran with my mother's assumption. "I realized it's a little chilly. Came back to grab a sweater."

"You have tons of cute sweaters sweetie; you need to throw that one out," my mom said without looking at me, holding the glass up to the light to inspect for smudges.

"Well that's not going to happen any time soon." Not for another year at least.

※※※

I power walked, putting as much distance between myself and the house as fast as I could without looking like I was fleeing a crime scene. In my black hoodie, that would have stirred all of the neighborhood watchdogs. I shrugged the hood off about a block away from my house.

As I slowed down, I noticed I had inadvertently started walking an all-too-familiar path. To walk between my house and Tom's, you could either take the sidewalks along the streets, or a much shorter way along a hiking trail that looped along the hillside around the neighborhood. Next to the path, at about a midway mark between our houses, was a bench. It was perched at a lookout point with a perfect view of the surrounding hillsides and neighborhoods.

This was "our" bench. Ever since we were kids, if one of us was coming over to the other's house, we used to meet there and walk together the remainder of the way. Our initials had been carved into the top plank of the bench's back for almost a decade.

I hadn't been to the bench—in the Present or Past—in the year since Tom and I stopped talking. As I stepped onto the sandy gravel trail, I stopped and looked down the path toward Tom's house. I did not want to go there, physically or mentally. I did not want to see our initials, I did not want to relive my last memory of being there. Especially not in a Slip. I had no idea if it could send me further into a tangle of Slips I wouldn't be able to come out of.

I veered in the other direction. I had a feeling where I was headed. I wasn't entirely sure, but something tugged at me to keep going.

Pete's house was farther away from my house than Tom's, located in the adjacent neighborhood across the parkway, close to where Rebecca lived. As I waited for the crosswalk light to make my way over the wide road, I noticed Tom's car coming up to the stop light. Just as the little white human figure illuminated, indicating it was safe to cross, I pulled up my hood again and scurried over, utterly aware that I was just feet away from Graduation Me.

I still couldn't resist the urge to glance through the windshield as I was right in front of the car. I knew it was stupid, not only because I was risking exposure, but also because it broke my heart all over again.

Graduation Me and Tom were laughing up a storm. I was drinking a milkshake, and he was chowing down a burger. A deep bass rhythm emanated from the vehicle, but I couldn't place the song, which was a kind of relief, since I didn't want any reminders, and I didn't want to further taint any music. I let my eyes linger on Graduation Me. She looked so happy. Yet she had already gone through an excruciating breakup, and an even more excruciating senior year. I knew the stinging, searing pain she was currently feeling behind her smile. But in hindsight, that paled in comparison to the way Graduation Tom was about to break her heart.

I half jogged the rest of the way across the street, knowing that they would soon pass me on my left, so I kept my face down, watching my shoes hit the sidewalk. I knew that Graduation Me hadn't noticed anyone strange on the way to Pete's house. I would definitely have remembered seeing someone who looked like me. But there was always the chance that I would change something. And that would not be good.

I turned onto a paved walking trail that snaked through Pete's neighborhood, a shortcut that would keep me away from the streets where I could be spotted. I reached an alley between two houses that led out to the sidewalk opposite Pete's house and stopped just out of sight, behind one of the cement block fences.

I peered around the corner and just barely caught a glimpse of Graduation Me and Tom walk up to the house. Graduation Me was trailing him hesitantly. I knew this already of course. The party at Pete's was far from the chill get-together that had been promised, so I had been reluctant about going in. The house was bursting at the seams, and before Tom reached the front door, it flew open and the muffled sound of bass exploded loud and clear into the night sky. A boy and a girl stumbled out, too preoccupied with each other to notice Tom and me as they maneuvered to a bench on the porch.

I wondered what harm it could possibly do if I went and did something to make them turn around. Set off Tom's car alarm or something. Call the cops on the party. Anything to just nudge Graduation Me away from the series of events that were about to transpire.

I wondered whether my phone even worked. I pulled it out of my pocket, and sure enough, it had the date of my graduation day, June 7, 2024, plastered across the lockscreen. I opened my messages, but they were up to my Present date. The latest one was the one from Rebecca that remained unanswered. I made a mental note to ask Adrian how this whole thing worked. If I didn't get control over these Slips anytime soon, at least it would be helpful to have an indicator as to where I was Slipping to.

I leaned into the tall stone wall next to me. I had a perfect vantage point of the house from the alley, but I was unlikely to be seen unless someone was really looking. I let my mind play back the events contained inside the house like a reel, slowing down and pausing at moments I wanted to examine, embellish. Skipping over parts that I was sick of.

A part of me didn't want to go back to my Present. A masochistic, self-absorbed part that wanted to relive these moments over and over outside my own head, in a feeble attempt to justify my actions that night. Convince myself that none of it was my fault. Keep it at the front of my mind where it was currently being held anyway, triggering the amygdala as if it was part of the Present, instead of the Past where it belonged.

Suddenly, the absurdity of the situation hit me, and I realized how incredibly dangerous this truly was. If I was spotted, it could cause a ripple effect into my Present and the Future that I would have no control over.

A popular song that was all the rage last spring started blasting to a roar of cheers from inside the house. The tune was insanely catchy, but I had never liked it that much. I remembered the moment it had come on. Every time I had heard it thereafter, I had remembered the scene in vivid detail, despite trying so hard to disconnect the two. Just like with all top-forty songs, its popularity dwindled over a matter of weeks. Now, hearing it for the first time in months, the memory of what was going on in the house in front of me hijacked me. Devouring me and capturing, like it had so many times before.

The situation inside was already a little out of control; I had never seen a house so full of people. It became clear to me that the guest list consisted of way more people than what could constitute a "chill get-together." There were even people who weren't from our school, and I recognized some as being from the neighboring high school, Woodoaks High, but I had no idea who most of them were.

Red plastic cups littered the sticky floor, loud music blared, and multicolored lights that seemed to have no specific source flickered and blurred the lines between people. Tom and I made our way through the crowd silently, him ahead of me. He kept looking over his shoulder at me, and I felt a weird relief to see that he didn't look as comfortable being there as he had been eager to go.

I was glad that there were people there who didn't know who I was, diluting the crowd and minimizing the amount of evil looks I got. When Tom looked at me for the fifth time, confused, I spotted his friend Pete just in front of him, and pointed him out.

"Tommy boy!" Pete yelled when he saw Tom, clearly drunk.

"Petes!" Tom replied. "You said it was a chill hang."

"What are you gonna do?" Pete answered, his voice slurred. He made a smug gesture before he continued, "I'm a great host. Who am I to deny people?"

"Hey, I'm going to walk around for a bit, see if I can find Rebecca," I yelled into Tom's ear. He didn't protest. Tom and Rebecca had a silent understanding that they both loved me and had to share me, and therefore tolerated each other. Not dissimilar from what Justin and I had with Amanda. I rarely mixed the two of them, as they didn't blend well. While they were never mean or rude to each other, they just didn't know how to act.

I made my way through the crowd out to the backyard and sure enough, Rebecca and her crew were there.

The cheerleaders and I also had an understanding. I don't know if Rebecca had something to do with it, but they left me alone, and vice versa. They let me tag along, and sometimes I could tell that they envied Rebecca of her relationship with me. Their whole gang dynamic was superficial, and I wondered if any of them had any real confidants, any actual close friends.

"Sloane!" Rebecca exclaimed as soon as she saw me.

"Surprise," I said, and couldn't help smiling at her reaction.

"What the hell?" she asked as she hugged me, clearly surprised to see me.

"Get this," I said.

"What? Hell froze over? Flying pigs?"

"The works. Tom actually dragged me here," I said, eager to share this outrage with someone who knew the absurdity of it.

"What? You're kidding!" Rebecca gasped.

"Nope, he's in there with Pete."

"Pete is so *drunk!*"

"I know," I said, laughing.

We stood talking on the back patio of the house, one of many groups littering the backyard. Some guys I had never seen before were standing close by us for quite a while, talking in relatively hushed tones, glancing over in our direction every so often.

I tried to shake it off, tell myself I was being paranoid, but when one of them clearly pointed at me and started laughing, I lost it. The rumors about me had obviously spread outside of my school's bubble.

"What the fuck are you looking at, dweeb?" I yelled. Rebecca and her friends didn't hear me over their own yapping.

My lash at the dude backfired and just made him laugh harder. Then he started to approach me. Terrified, I elbowed Rebecca to get her attention.

As the guy closed in on me, he looked me up and down, his eyes hungry. His expression alone felt like it was invading my privacy.

"So," he started, sleaze dripping off his tongue. He was tall, blond, heavyset, eyes small and sunken into his skull, his jawline broad and sharp. His neck was thick; the rolls I had spotted on the back of it were peeking around the sides.

"What do you want, Quasimodo?" Rebecca said, before he could get another word in.

He licked his lips and gave me another glance up and down. Totally ignoring Rebecca, he proceeded, "You that chick Archer had to move across the country to get away from?"

I didn't understand how he managed to say his words as if they were somehow a good thing.

"Nope, not her, piss off," Rebecca chimed. Her friends had now stopped talking between themselves and were watching, death stares shooting like *lasers at the guy. As much as I hated their cliquish ways, I was thankful for them in that moment because I wasn't on the receiving end.*

"Oh no, it's you all right." He laughed as he stepped closer, and when he was so close I could smell the stench on his breath, he continued, drawling, "I heard you were such a freak in the sheets, but you became so clingy, he had to put a continent between you guys. I heard you locked him in your room for days." Even though I knew he was humiliating me, the emphasis on his last word conveyed more—he was intrigued.

"Fuck off! Right now," Rebecca yelled and pushed him.

"Hey, hey now," he said, smirking while throwing his hands up in the air and taking half a step backward. "Feisty little sidekick you got there Becker. Does she join you from time to time?"

Rebecca was about to bulldoze into him, but I stopped her.

"We got a problem?" Tom's voice came from my right.

The guy halted. He got one glance at Tom and his face turned to disgust. Still in a calm manner, he said, "Nah, no problem. Just having a discussion about—" He paused, and licked his lips again, looking up and down my body yet again, and each time he did it felt more and more like his gaze was actually touching me. "Mutual interests."

I felt Tom's arm close around me. He placed his hand firmly on my hip and pulled me in tight.

"I assure you, she and you have no interests even close to mutual." Tom's voice was grimmer than I had ever heard it.

The guy took two deliberate steps toward us, and within the space of two seconds he loomed over us threateningly. "I wouldn't be so sure about that, lover boy." His face contorted into a snarl at his last words. Then he walked away into the house, his posse following him.

After he left, I felt like I could breathe again. I buried my face in my hands and tried to take deep breaths.

"Are you okay?" Tom asked, holding my shoulder, trying to see my face. Rebecca was stroking my back. I could see out of the corner of my eye that she and Tom were trying to communicate by mouthing words. They barely

communicated with fully functioning voices, and I could tell they were frustrated.

"I'm not only the school slut, I'm also the town slut now," I said, pressing my fingertips on my eyelids.

"No, no. Hey," Rebecca said, coming around to face me and grab me by the shoulders. "You are not. That guy probably does this to all girls. He's the scum of the earth."

"Let's just go home, Sloane," Tom said, pulling on my arm.

"No—no. Absolutely not," I said, looking up. "I have thrown all my fucks away. I'm staying," I said, and I didn't know who I was trying to convince, them or myself.

I went to the kitchen to get fresh beers for everyone. When I came back, Rebecca was already in a heated conversation about what an asshole the guy had been. Even her friends, who normally acted as if I didn't exist, were agreeing with her, and turned to me to chime in things like, "Such a loser, seriously, Sloane," and, "Don't listen to what his ugly ass has to say."

"Thanks for swooping in, lover boy," I said, quietly, so only Tom could hear, bumping my shoulder into his and laughing.

"Lover boy, at your service," he said with a bow, in his best impression of a superhero voice. We tapped the necks of our beers together and changed the subject.

Even though I had decided to put my game face on and move on from the whole ordeal, I became seriously self-conscious. Every glance in my direction set off the guy's words in my head.

"He had to put a continent between you guys."

A new song started playing, met with a roar of excitement. Girls exclaiming, "*This is* my *song!*" and various groups of guys singing along loudly. Everyone seemed to love this song more than their own mothers, except me.

No one really noticed as I excused myself to go to the bathroom and headed upstairs. I stayed for a tad longer than it normally would have taken me, at least until the song ended. And then a couple more songs. I wanted to be alone for a small while and recompose myself.

A girl's voice on the other side of the door, claiming she was about to pee her pants, prompted me to stop hogging the bathroom.

After a moment, I opened the door but immediately jumped back, gasping as horror racked my body.

"Hey, thanks man," a voice from my left startled me out of my stupor. I had sunk down to a sitting position on the ground with my back against the brick fence that was shielding me from view from Pete's house. I looked up to see a car pulled up to the sidewalk about fifty feet from where I was. A group of three guys who were most likely party guests stood and spoke to the driver through an open window. A brown paper bag concealing what could only be a bottle of alcohol emerged from the window, and the guy who spoke handed a bundle of cash into the vehicle.

The car took off at a ridiculous speed, tires screeching. The guy who held the bottle straightened out and crumpled the bag down to below the bottle's neck before unscrewing and taking a large swig of the amber liquid. His friends cheered for him as he passed the bottle along.

They started walking back to the house, and as the guy who had the first sip turned his face in my direction, recognition shook my body with the force of a freight train.

"That wasn't very nice of you earlier. How you responded. Don't act like I couldn't have you if I wanted to," he said into my ear as he barged into the bathroom, pushing me backward with his body. His breath was thick and stung my nose, as if I were smelling a glass of scotch directly.

I lunged, running farther down the alley, and skittered behind an electrical box about a quarter of the way down. I knelt, gasping for air, making myself as small as possible.

His voice echoed down the alley as they passed it, sending violent shivers throughout my body. "I'm gonna go find that bitch. I'm in the mood for some fun." His friends egged him on with jeers and laughs.

I snuck back to my spot where the alley met the sidewalk and waited to hear their voices fade and dissipate into the crowd. I visualized in my head how long it would take them to get into the house, and for the guy to make his way upstairs, careful not to wait too long. Then, as if in a trance, I tugged my hood as far in front of my face as I could, pulling the strings tight, and made a run for it.

The smell was what hit me first as I stepped into the house. The blend of sweat and beer heavy in my lungs. No one paid attention to me, and I bolted up the stairs, hoping to remember which door it was that I was looking for.

I opened the wrong door first, closing it quickly before the couple on Pete's parents' bed noticed me. The next one I tried was the correct one. I remembered the mosaic tiled floor of the bathroom too well.

He hadn't even bothered locking the door.

Before opening the door fully, I took a deep, shaking breath and yanked at one end of the string in my hood until it came all the way out. I knew what I had to do. In one swift motion, I swung the door open, stepped in, and closed it behind me.

Neither of them noticed me as I took in the scene before me; the sounds of the party were too loud. Graduation Me was bent over the counter with her head in the sink, blood spurting from a gash in her forehead from when he hit her head on the faucet. He had the whole weight of his body on her, his hand on the back of her head, pushing it down into the sink, elbow digging into her back.

My body. My head. My back.

She flailed and screamed, choking as he turned on the water to silence her even further.

"Hold fucking still." He strained as he struggled one-handed with the belt at his hips.

As if controlled by some invisible force, I took two big steps toward them. I wrapped the string from my hood around the guy's neck as tightly as I possibly could, winding it around my hands to get a better grip. I winced as it tore at the cut in my palm, but I kept going. The more it hurt me, the worse it hurt him.

"Run," I said to Graduation Me as the guy and I staggered backward, nearly falling into the bathtub.

Graduation Me stumbled away from the sink, wiping the water and blood out of her eyes. A wave of panic rushed over me as I realized my hood had fallen down. If she turned around, which I knew she was about to do, she would be able to see me.

I hadn't seen whose voice it had been that told me to run. It was one of the many questions that had burned in my mind the past year. Who had actually come to my rescue in this dilapidated bathroom at Pete's house?

If she saw me, it would change everything.

The terror running through my veins did its job. The prickling started at the base of my neck, and cut down my spine as I squeezed my eyes shut, willing the Jump to rush into every fiber of my being. I let go of the string and pushed the guy's heavy, limp body sideways into the tub, breaking contact with him just as the Jump consumed me.

As I scooped my hood back up over my head, I knew it wasn't just a Stop. A feeling similar to coming home after a long vacation filled my muscles as they released their tension. Except I knew I wasn't home. I was in the second-floor bathroom of Pete's house. The feeling still warmed me from my heart down through the soles of my feet, grounding me, the tug of being in the Past no longer hanging on my breath.

I checked my phone, and it said July 1, 2025. I had successfully Jumped back to my Present.

Just as I was stuffing my phone back in my pocket, the door to the bathroom swung open, revealing a girl around Maddie's age, her eyes wide in horror.

She let out an ear-piercing scream before shouting, "Mom! Dad! There's a burglar in the bathroom!"

I slammed the door in her face and locked it, pressing my back against it.

"Please let me Stop right now," I muttered, squeezing my eyes shut. Pete's little sister was still screaming outside the door.

A vision appeared before my eyes, replacing the darkness of my pinched eyelids. It was a beach, at sunset. I smelled wood burning on a breeze and felt sand between my toes.

My spine tingled once again, and my eardrums vibrated painfully as the Stop surged through and out of me. Everything fell silent.

As soon as I was able to open my eyes again, I pressed my ear against the door to make sure I couldn't hear anyone. I opened it ever so slowly and peered out. Pete's little sister was standing in the hall, looking toward the staircase but pointing in my direction, her mouth agape midscream. A grown man who I could only assume was Pete's dad was at the top of the stairs looking disgruntled.

I snuck past both of them and out the front door. I didn't Start again until I had reached my bedroom.

Surely it can't be this easy. I could get used to this.

CHAPTER TWELVE

I WAS STILL on a high from my successful Stop and Jump back to my present, and couldn't sleep. My mind was reeling from the realization I'd had in my Slip. It had been me all along. I was the one who saved myself from what could have been the worst thing to ever happen to me.

Yet I couldn't stop wondering if I had made a huge mistake. Because the fact that I got away from the nameless guy from Woodoaks High also meant that I had lost Tom.

When I closed my eyes, Woodoaks's hungry eyes flashed before me before switching to the redhead's face, sneering at me as she held the scalpel to my throat, not wavering as my blood pooled on her hand.

Around midnight, I was scrolling through social media profiles, digging way past six degrees of separation from myself, trying to find any clue as to who the redhead was. After what transpired on graduation night, I had often tried unsuccessfully to find Woodoaks on social media, but I didn't care about him anymore—he was no longer a threat to me. I felt empowered after saving myself from him, and it was time to tackle the person who still did pose a threat. The redhead.

I flipped over to my text messages and opened the thread between Adrian and me.

> Sloane: Hi Adrian, thanks so much for the lessons today. Could I possibly come back Thursday?

I didn't expect him to respond to me this late, but his reply came almost instantly.

> Adrian: Absolutely. Whatever you need, Sloane.

Another thing I hadn't expected was how excited the promise of more training made me. I felt an itch to use the powers, especially after what I had just accomplished. But they were still too unpredictable, and I was scared to deliberately use them, in case I screwed up and got myself stuck somewhere. But I wanted to train not only to reduce the likelihood of me making a mistake—I needed to be able to defend myself in case someone else caused me trouble.

☙❧☙❧☙❧

"So! You wanna try Stopping?" Maddie cut in like a ray of sunshine through fog. I was at Adrian's house that Thursday morning after having sent a vague email to my dad's secretary about not coming into the office that day. Not that she or anyone else cared, and I would probably not receive any acknowledgment of the email or my nonpresence.

"What, me? Like intentionally Stop? Now?" I said, panicking a little. As eager as I was to get better at it, using my powers, especially in front of Adrian and Maddie, still felt wrong somehow. Forbidden. Like it was this clandestine thing that I didn't share with anyone else.

"Yes, why not?" Adrian smiled. "No better time."

I narrowed my eyes at Adrian with a slight smile. "Was that a pun?"

"Pun, or simply a well-timed observation." Adrian laughed.

Adrian had started off by giving me the basics of Stopping. I had naively thought that time traveling and portaling through space came as a package deal. There was, in fact, no such thing as portaling through space. Wherever you were, you would stay in the same location, regardless of what moment in time you were aiming for when you Jumped or Stopped. Time Wardens had to physically travel wherever they needed to be to perform their duties.

I already knew that my powers were amplified by how strong my emotions were at any given moment, good or bad. The fact that they were connected to something so ambiguous and frankly, volatile, seemed to contrast just how many rules there in fact were around the whole business of manipulating time.

Another misconception of mine was that time travel had anything to do with dates or time in general. Adrian never spoke about days or weeks, months or years. Never minutes or seconds, just moments. While there were rules you had to follow, Adrian kept describing them as "best practices uncovered through eons of experience by Lunai before us." It always had more to do with feeling, rather than established time-telling conventions. The first rule, "Everything starts with a Stop," was the focus of today's training. I thought of the Stop I had executed inside my Slip in Pete's bathroom, but I had chalked it up to beginner's luck. I was too embarrassed to ask because that meant revealing I had Slipped again.

Damn emotions.

"So that's that? That's all I need to know, now I can just time travel?"

"Hah, no. Not even close. Like I said, I will teach you everything in steps. Trust the process, Sloane. There's the theory and the practical, which need to be understood concurrently. This is no crash course." Adrian always seemed to have an air about him as if he were a college professor, yet also your friend. He continued, "What you need to focus on first is learning the basic framework. Controlling your powers, getting to know them, recognizing them, so that you know how to steer them in the right direction if you Slip. Your biggest power is your Stop. You can always use it to get out of any situation. If you feel a Slip coming on or you actually find yourself in a Slip, you can Stop until you've calmed down enough to get back to the Present."

Maddie had not mentioned Sensing my Slips to graduation night, and I was not going to offer up that information.

"But, like, I don't know what to do—" I said, feeling stupid.

"You'll feel it!" Maddie said.

My phone buzzed in my pocket. I didn't want to be rude and make them feel like I didn't appreciate their time, so I just snuck a peek at the screen before silencing the call with the side button. It was Rebecca, for the fourth time that day. She would have to wait.

I looked between the two of them, not sure that I was ready. "But what if I get stuck? What if I can't, like, Start time again?"

"You'll take me with you. I'll show you," Maddie said.

"Take you with me?"

"Like I've done with you! You just need to hold my hand." She grinned.

"Skin-to-skin contact is the key here. Metal also works fairly well, but we'll get to that later," Adrian said.

"So you can Start again if I can't?"

"Yup!" Maddie was beaming. She was obviously very excited about the whole thing. I wanted to say that I'd rather have Adrian with me in the Stop, but that would've been rude. Besides, up until then, I had never actually consciously witnessed Adrian using his powers, but I had seen Maddie do a hell of a good job at using hers.

Maddie reached across the table and took my hand. "Ready?"

"What, right here?" I asked, indicating my sitting position at the table.

"Yes, it doesn't matter where you are!" she answered.

"But I don't know what to do!"

"You'll feel it," Adrian said, repeating what Maddie had said.

"But—"

"You'll feel it," he repeated, giving me a reassuring look.

I looked at Maddie for some kind of support, but she just nodded slightly, gave me the same look as Adrian, and tightened her grip on my hand.

It felt silly, but I closed my eyes.

Okay, Sloane. Feel. I guess.

For a while, I just sat there, not sure what I was feeling around for. I tried focusing, I tried spacing out, and I didn't know how long I'd sat there when I felt like I had stumbled upon a memory. No, not exactly a memory, more like an atmosphere. The image of a sunset at a beach popped up again, just like it had when I had to call on a Stop in Pete's bathroom. Everything was bathed in a red glow, hazy. There were embers floating everywhere from a bonfire I couldn't see. They came dangerously close to my eyes, but I wasn't afraid of them. The feeling of experiencing incomprehensible vastness filled my chest. Like I could see, and feel, to the ends of the world as I took in the ocean before me. As though my soul were trying to spread itself like a heavy, clingy blanket out over the expanse, to the outer corners of the world, and back again to my core. As if there were no other place in the world than exactly where I stood.

Sunset at the beach.

Embers from a bonfire floating in the air.

The feeling of having been out in the sun all day, your skin staying warm even as the sun's rays fizzle out.

A little voice that whispered, "This must be the place."

Just as I started visualizing this, a slow, almost painful shiver crawled down my spine, making the muscles in my back inadvertently clench trying to counteract it. My eardrums felt like they were going to burst, but then—

"Yay! You did it!" Maddie squealed.

I opened my eyes. Maddie sat there, smiling, bouncing up and down ever so slightly in her seat as a result of swinging her legs gleefully. Adrian was frozen, a patient expectant expression on his face. He seemed smaller somehow, being this unanimated. His shoulders seemed slumped when there was no life in him to hold them up. His eyes seemed wistful, where they hadn't given any such indication outside of the Stop.

"Whoa," was all I could say.

"Wasn't it easy?" she asked.

"I guess . . ." I said, after a small pause. "Now at least I know what I'm looking for."

"Exactly! You just gotta feel it! Everyone's transitional state is different. Yours is still a little shaky, it doesn't have to rip at you so hard—" She said the words like she was playing a snobby food critic on reality TV. "But we'll work on that."

"Transitional state?" I asked, poking Adrian's hand gently to see if I had actually done it.

"That place your mind just went. That sends you into your Stop," Maddie explained.

I stood up and went to the window, scouring for more signs of time being Stopped.

As if to give me a sign, I spotted a cat that had been skipping through the yard just as I Stopped. It was now frozen midair, all four legs off the ground.

"I did it," I said, semitriumphantly, as I sat back down at the table.

"*So* proud of you right now, Sloane," Maddie said with a sassy twang.

"So it's not always so . . . uncomfortable? When you do it yourself?"

"Oh no, don't worry," Maddie said, sure of herself, "it gets better with time. But everyone's Stop feels different. You'll see! Now, try going back; it's the exact same thing!" She grabbed my hand again.

I closed my eyes, and this time it was like the feeling rushed toward me. Like envisioning home, or some other place too close to your heart to forget.

Adrian's voice was the next thing I heard. "Has it happened yet?"

My eyelids lost their downward pressure, and I opened my eyes to Maddie smiling, Adrian oblivious.

"Just did," I said, smiling.

"Congratulations. Now go again."

※※※

We trained until late in the afternoon, and I was exhausted as I bid Adrian and Maddie farewell. As I walked to my car and plucked my phone out of my pocket, I saw that Rebecca had tried calling six more times and left a bunch of texts.

> Rebecca: Earth to Sloane! Am I just a lowly commoner to you now?
> Rebecca: Miss Big Shot Lawyer too good for her blue-collar gym coach friend?
> Rebecca: If you're seeing Dylan again, just know I may need to retain your dad because I will literally murder you!

Guilt sucker punched me in the stomach. I felt like the worst friend ever, but how could I possibly explain this to her?

As I drove, I started working up a lie in my head to tell Rebecca. I needed to come up with one fast and call her back. I felt sick to my stomach, but not in the same way the manifestation symptoms had made me feel. This was a feeling of being utterly sick with myself, all the lying I was having to keep track of. All the loved ones I was having to deceive.

The triumph and welcome exhaustion I had felt as a result of the successful training session I had just had was quickly replaced with plain old exhaustion. What was I thinking, running around with a bunch of nut jobs playing time traveler? Was this really worth losing out on the very few people I had left in my life who were always there for me?

The irony of the situation struck me as I realized that with these powers came literally endless amounts of time. I could have all the perceived time in the world in a Stop. But only by myself or with other Lunai.

Even though my best friend was desperately trying to reach out to me, I had never felt as alone as I did on the drive home that afternoon.

However, as soon as I arrived home, I found myself missing that feeling of loneliness. I was craving solitude, but when the front door of my house flung open before I could even reach it, I knew that wasn't going to be an option.

"Surprise!" Rebecca yelled, holding her hands out wide to greet me.

"Rebecca, what are you doing here?" I said, trying hard to match her enthusiasm as I embraced her.

"I got a long weekend for the Fourth, so I came home, duh!" Rebecca beamed, holding me by the shoulders and examining me. "Sheesh, Sloane. You really have been stuck in an office for the past month, haven't you?"

I assumed she meant my lack of summer glow. While it was true that I hadn't exactly been spending a lot of time in the sun, I knew my pallor was likely due to other reasons.

"I know you have *things* at the office keeping you *very* busy," she sassed. "But if you had answered my calls, you would have known I was coming."

"I missed you too, Becks." I rolled my eyes and laughed at her as I stepped past her and into the house.

Rebecca trailed me through the dining room and into the kitchen. Justin sat at the kitchen table and my mom stood by the island.

"So, what are we doing for the Fourth?" Rebecca asked excitedly and planted herself at the kitchen table across from Justin.

My heart sank. I had already promised my dad that I would go to the firm's Fourth of July party. He had invited me every year for years now, and I had always come up with an excuse not to go. Now that I worked for the firm, I didn't have it in me to bail.

"Uhm . . ." I glanced nervously between the three of them, all waiting for my response. "I'm so sorry, but I have a work party that I promised to attend."

Rebecca's shoulders slumped. "Ugh! Are you kidding me, Sloane? What am I supposed to do then?"

"I'm sorry," I wailed.

Amanda came skipping into the kitchen from the family room. "Mom, I need a sheet. A big one, like for the bed."

"There's my baby," Mom said cheerily. "What do you need a sheet for?"

"Mom," Amanda whined, drawing out the word, "I'm not a baby. I need a sheet because I'm going camping. Would a baby camp? I don't think so." Amanda's frustration made her last sentence come out in a staccato.

"Yeah, Lauren, babies don't camp," Justin teased my mom.

"You watch it," my mom clapped back jokingly. "You're still a baby yourself."

It warmed my heart to see the two of them interacting like this. It had taken a long time before Justin warmed up to my mom. He still called her Lauren, just like I called Neil, Neil. But she was his mom for all intents and purposes. The boy she never had, my makeshift Irish twin.

Justin laughed at my mom, but it was Rebecca who spoke first, in a mock-baby voice, "Aww, baby Justin." Justin mocked her back, and for a split second I felt like the rest of us were intruding on a private exchange. I glanced between the two of them as their eyes met for a fraction of a moment, so brief that I doubt anyone but me would have noticed. I tried to shoot Rebecca a confused look, but she didn't see it.

Then Justin met my eyes for a second, apprehensive almost, as he spoke. "Well, I'm going to a party at Nick's." He shrugged. "You could join. I don't know, but if that's not your scene, that's cool too, y'know."

I peered at my stepbrother. He was trying to play it cool, now avoiding my gaze as well as Rebecca's, but he was rambling. I had never seen him like this.

"That's so nice of you, Justin," my mother crooned, totally oblivious to what was going on in front of her.

"Sure, I'd love that," Rebecca replied to Justin, a small, mischievous grin plastered on her face. I could've sworn Justin blushed as his face lit up.

What exactly did I miss here?

"We can hang out on Saturday, maybe?" I interjected hastily.

Rebecca dragged her eyes away from Justin as she looked at me and responded, "I'm all yours."

Doesn't feel like it.

I stuffed my petulant thoughts away and beamed at her. "Can't wait."

CHAPTER THIRTEEN

THE FIREWORKS OVERHEAD lit up the underside of the low-hanging clouds, their blanket becoming an enormous ambient lampshade for the city. Wherever I looked, the impossibly tall sides of the skyscrapers surrounding the one I stood atop flickered under the violence of the explosions overhead.

The show had just started, but thunder threatened in the background, almost as loud as the man-made blasts. The warm, humid wind that was very uncharacteristic for Southern California picked up speed as lightning bolts started crawling on the bottoms of the clouds, easily competing with the multicolored panoply of the rockets.

The firm's annual Fourth of July party, held on the rooftop of the skyscraper in which the firm occupied a floor, was in full swing behind me. Bar-height cocktail tables were scattered around the rooftop patio, dressed in long white tablecloths held around the table legs with red, white, and blue bows. A hundred or so of my colleagues milled about, mingling and chatting, drinks in hand, their business suits swapped for something more fancy. Servers strolled around with tiny appetizers on trays. Live-flame torches were distributed evenly along the rooftop's edge, and I stood in between two of them, at a safe distance.

I kept glancing back to see if I could spot Eric. I may have secretly wanted Eric to see me dressed up, especially after the multiple highly humiliating situations he had witnessed me in over the past few weeks. I hadn't seen him much that week—he had been traveling, and without him the week had passed at a painfully slow pace. Thankfully, my symptoms seemed to be easing up.

The voices of the crowd went from murmurs of mindless amusement to a concerned, annoyed cacophony as raindrops started splattering the roof we stood on, reflecting the light show further in scattered fragments like a shattered mirror. Some people started retreating inside, but most retreated under canopies around the bar area. I looked around to see if I could spot my father, but the crowd was still dense around me.

The storm moved unbelievably fast, reaching the edge of downtown within minutes from when it first hinted at its proximity. I wondered if the fireworks show had been set on autopilot or whether they would eventually stop setting them off if the storm got in the way.

The droplets that were warm as they first made contact with my skin were now picking up with the consistent gust of wind rushing past me, sending shivers surging throughout my body. I welcomed the shivers, as they weren't from a panic attack or a stranger touching me.

"There you are," Eric said as he planted himself to my left. Lightning dipped out of the clouds to the west, taunting the fireworks directly below. My body tensed as he inched closer to me, leaning forward on the roof's ledge to match me. "The party is being moved to the lobby."

When I didn't say anything, he added, "I didn't take you for a thrill seeker."

I shot him a perplexed look, just then noticing how close he was. "What do you mean?"

"Sure, the tower's spire would in theory catch any lightning headed this way, but you're still very exposed out here."

"It's just so beautiful up here," I said, reluctantly dragging my eyes away from his face and to our surroundings. The mixture of different light sources from the various colorful firework displays, warm glows glinting in adjacent tower windows, and the sharp, cold flares of lightning crawling on the bottoms of the newly arrived clouds felt like a kaleidoscope curated just for me, and I wanted to hold on to the moment for as long as I could.

My thoughts went to Adrian and Maddie, and these powers I supposedly possessed.

Maybe I can?

Maybe, instead of being afraid of these powers, I can use them to hold on to moments like this?

"I know why I'm not worried about being out here. But I wonder if it's because of something we have in common." His voice held a hint of amusement as he brought me back to reality.

He raised an eyebrow as our eyes met, smiling as his hand found the back of his neck, giving away his slight nervousness.

"And what is that reason?" I turned to face him.

"Venture a guess?" he teased, sweeping his hand around in the rain.

I studied him, and for a moment I experienced an intense sensation of déjà vu—his smiling face obscured by the storm sending my hair flying into my face, the shivers so warm and welcome.

He took a step toward me, leaning casually with his elbow on the roof ledge. "I have reason to believe you want to tell me something." He was still smiling.

The wind gained further traction, and what was left of the heat outside was obliterated by the sheer force of the gusts. Thunder boomed overhead, drowning out the sounds of the fireworks. A blinding flash shot across the sky, casting sinister shadows across Eric's face.

Is he going to try to kiss me?

I looked around and saw the rooftop mostly empty. Maybe he was using the opportunity, now that we wouldn't be spotted by our coworkers.

Do I want to kiss him?

I shifted to match him, leaning on the ledge about a foot away from him, so that we were facing each other. I bit my lower lip as I tilted my head back to meet his eyes. He wasn't that much taller than me, but in that moment I realized how much I loved this view, his eyes fixated on mine from above, like he could envelop me and shield me from whatever might be thrown our way.

Yes, I definitely want to kiss him.

He moved a few inches closer as he continued, "I need you to say it."

My stomach did a twirl. We were soaking wet at this point, and I held my hand flat perpendicular to my forehead to minimize the droplets furiously bouncing against my face.

When I didn't say anything, he continued, "I think you and I have something in common. Something that you really want to talk to me about. I think I just have to make you believe it."

"Eric." I shook my head, half-smiling at his silliness. My heart skipped a beat, or two, as the weight of knowing my naive and potentially ill-fated crush being requited settled in my veins. My spine tingled violently, the hairs on the back of my neck rose, and it wasn't due to the weather. I wondered if I could maybe Stop for a moment, calm my thoughts. Still, I didn't give in, wanting him to be the one to take the leap. "I'm pretty sure you and I have nothing in common except where we work."

He just kept smiling. "You always make me work for it. And I never back down."

I furrowed my brow; he wasn't making any sense. I began, "What in the world are you talking—"

Lightning struck dangerously close to the tower, cutting me off. We were the only people left on the roof. He raised his voice to mitigate the earsplitting crash and grabbed both of my hands in his. "Fine, I'll show you!"

I had no time to react. The last thing I saw before my eyes closed was his beaming smile.

That smile that would have stopped me in my tracks even if he were on a rooftop a block away.

Recognition striking me as the nonweather-related shivers started crawling and gnawing at my hands from where he held them, continuing up my arms.

Quivering eardrums as the sounds of the storm and the show went mute.

Shivers flicking, gently, through the whole of my body in a single swoop.

Expecting the equivalent of a lightning strike but feeling butterflies instead.

Heavy, captivating butterflies.

My jaw dropped; I couldn't believe what was happening. My eyes opened, and it was like I had kept them closed my whole life.

Eric had just Stopped time.

The charge in the air was palpable, raising the hairs along my arms. A lightning bolt that had flashed just as my eyes closed lay half-dwindled, strewn across the sky. Frozen in its fury, it illuminated the surroundings softly with an ice-cold glow. A single burst firework loomed over the sky to my right, stopped midair like a claw hanging onto an invisible orb. The raindrops that had been swirling erratically lay perfectly still in formations around us, illustrating the breeze's shape upon which they had been riding just a half moment ago. They glistened under the lightning's sheen, as if a web of string lights were about to fall on top of us where we stood, catching us in its grasp.

Now I know what that feeling was the first time I saw him.

"What? Oh my god." I couldn't find a single word to describe my bewildered daze, so I just laughed and repeated, "Oh my god."

I know *him.*

Eric's smile, if possible, became even bigger as he bit his lower lip, "I know. It's wild! I've been waiting so long to tell you, but you had to figure it out for yourself. You had to talk to Adrian first. It's protocol. I've been watching your powers manifest over the past month, biting my tongue. Then when Adrian finally told me he had been in touch with you—I just—gah, finally!"

A million thoughts bombarded my headspace, and I couldn't finish one train of thought without three others invading.

I'm not going crazy after all. These powers are real.

"You know Adrian?" I said, breathless.

"Of course I do. He's the one who trained me. He's been my mentor ever since."

Taking in this new reality, a mixture of relief and terror washed over me. Relief, that I wasn't completely losing my mind. Terror, that now I knew without a shadow of a doubt that I was, in fact, capable of time travel. And so was Eric.

And the world as I knew it officially shifted.

The realization took over me, and I crumbled. I doubled over as a whimper escaped me, touching my forehead to our still clasped hands. "I thought I was losing my mind at first. This doesn't feel real."

"What?" Eric laughed sympathetically. "Oh no, Sloane. You have to give your brilliant little brain a little more credit than that."

He wrapped his arms around me.

And I let him.

I forced composure, hastily wiping away the two tears that had barged their way down my cheek to mix with the raindrops, my breaths shaky and sharp.

"What does this mean?"

I looked up at him, searching his face. He had the same unwavering calm about him as always, as if we weren't standing on a rooftop, frozen in time, in the middle of a thunderstorm.

He reached his right hand out and swiped at the raindrops hovering in the void. A gash formed in the static mesh of droplets, sending the ones he came in contact with flying in all directions. They collided with other drops and cascaded downward, showering the rooftop floor.

"It means"—he paused, and brought his palm up to rest ever so slightly on my chest, just below my collarbone, before continuing—"that violence in your heart? It's there for a reason, and it's nothing to be afraid of."

Our eyes met as if we were looking at each other for the first time. I wanted to memorize everything about him in this moment outside moments. He held my gaze, his expression serious but longing.

A thought came to me, and I burst out in laughter.

"What? What is it?" He looked panicked.

"Oh my gosh," I said breathily, still laughing, "At the all-hands meeting. The curtain. Was that you?"

His shoulders untensed with relief as he joined me in laughing. "Yes, yes it was," he answered between laughs, the joy in his eyes making them shine irresistibly. "I almost didn't pull it off. I was in that Stop for so long. I had to look forever in order to find a ladder!"

Our laughs dwindled and faded into nervous, excited smiles. I don't know who caved first. Maybe we both did at the exact same moment.

The way he kissed felt like the way he Stopped. Gentle but magnetic.

His breath on my lips was mesmerizing, as his hands made their way down my back, coming to rest on my hips. He lifted me off my feet for a brief second as our kiss deepened. Every touch felt electric, drawing its energy from the silent, static storm around us. I willed myself not to tremble from the newness of it all, but at the same time, it felt familiar. Like this was what I had been missing all along, this was the reason I had not been interested in anyone for so long—and I thanked the stars for the turn of events that led me to give in to what was there.

He pulled away abruptly, stepping back from me and letting go. The blood rushed in my veins from the contrast of being that close to him, drowning in him one moment, and the next feeling incredibly alone.

"Shit. I'm sorry. I shouldn't have done that—"

"No, no need to say sorry." I stepped closer to him.

"No—I really shouldn't spring something like this on you and then kiss you." He turned away, rubbing his temple with his left hand.

"Hey," I said, pulling gently at his arm to get him to turn back to me. "I wanted you to."

This time, I was the one who kissed him. I wrapped my fingers in his hair as I willed him to see how much I wanted this. I wanted to kiss him like the rain around us wanted to give in to gravity. Endlessly, helplessly, recklessly.

He let himself sink into the kiss for a while, but as he found his hands wandering, he stopped himself. He leaned his forehead to mine; his eyes were closed as he whispered, almost more to himself than to me, "You have no idea how much I missed this."

It was my turn to pull away.

"What do you mean 'missed this'?" I willed my voice not to break as my heart threatened to bruise my ribs with its pounding.

His expression changed from painful longing to terror. "Forget I said that. *Please* forget I said that."

My thoughts raced as I tried to make sense of what he was saying. As untrustworthy as my brain had been the past year or so, it would not betray me on something like this. I would remember if this had happened before.

"You've kissed me before, haven't you?" I said, my voice low as I took another step back.

Eric lifted his defeated gaze to meet mine. His face gave him away, and he nodded. His expression turned grave as he anticipated my inevitable inquisitions.

"Have you been to the Future?" I asked, my voice small, unable to conceal my annoyance at the situation.

He swallowed hard, and I wondered if he was hiding something else from me. He opened his mouth as if to say something, but then he seemed to glitch before my eyes, his figure flickering like a low-resolution video.

"Shit. Let's get off this roof before I lose the Stop and we get hit by lightning," he said.

He brought time back to us in one fell swoop. It was so effortless, nothing like the intense pain I had been in when it happened to me by accident.

The rain, the thunder, the lightning, and the fireworks attacked my senses as every movement around us started back up again, and we ran toward the penthouse.

"Eric, answer me," I said as the door slammed behind us and we gathered ourselves, shaking off droplets of rain onto the stairwell landing.

Eric tensed. "I have been to the Future, yes, but—"

"But Adrian said—"

"But you're the one who has been Jumping to the Past to see me. In my Present. The last few years."

Eric knows *me.*

Numbness gnawed at me, the weight of this confession threatening to send me into a Slip. Eric seemed to realize, and just then, a couple of waiters who were working the party came rushing up the stairs, chatting and laughing. They squeezed past us on the landing, giving us knowing looks. I hadn't noticed that Eric had grabbed my shoulders.

When the waiters disappeared outside into the storm, I spoke. "You need to explain. You need to tell me everything. Everything. Right now."

"I have already said way too much. I'm breaking approximately thirteen Warden Laws right now. I am not supposed to tell you about your Future," he ranted.

I wrinkled my brows and pinched the bridge of my nose. I tried to construct the situation in my mind. So Eric knew me before I knew him, except it was a Future Me.

He brought one palm to my cheek. "I could get in major trouble for telling you this, okay? I know this is a lot. Just try to not think about it too much. I'll be with you every step of the way."

He leaned in and kissed me again, letting the kiss linger and lengthen. As I pulled him in closer, adrenaline rushing through my veins, I forgot everything. I forgot that he was my coworker, I forgot that this was the last thing I needed—another secret relationship. I forgot that I apparently had a lot of time traveling coming up and that Eric had seen a part of my life that I had yet to live through.

I forgot that he was a widower, I forgot that I wasn't losing my mind and I could now do whatever it was that he just did to make time halt.

Instead, I allowed myself to sink into the kiss, into him, letting his arms envelop me in a sense of safety I couldn't ever recall feeling prior to that moment.

CHAPTER FOURTEEN

"So you've just been living your fairy tale over here while I've been stuck in the hellhole that is my job. I love that for you, queen," Rebecca crooned over video call after I told her about Eric and me at the Fourth of July party the night before. Leaving out the Lunai stuff, of course.

"Fairy tale is a little extra," I teased her. I had called her as soon as I woke up to make plans for hanging out that day.

"I *told* you he had a crush on you!" Rebecca laughed, bringing her phone back and forth a few times so her face got smaller and bigger as she glared and leered, one eyebrow arched.

"*Fine*, whatever." I laughed, rolling my eyes. "I'm sorry again for not being able to hang out."

"I guess I'll forgive you." She sighed. "But only because you got some action."

"Jeez—" I started, just about to broach the subject of whether Rebecca might be crushing on someone at the moment. But I completely lost my train of thought when a notification appeared at the top of my screen. I sat up in my bed and tapped it faster than my thoughts were moving as my heart leaped.

It was from Eric. My heart pummeled my ribs, and I had clicked on the notification before I had even finished reading the preview.

Eric: Hey there. Thanks for last night.
Eric: I just received word that there's gonna be an emergency Council meeting tomorrow.
Eric: At noon.
Eric: Wasn't sure if you heard about it.

Just then, another notification popped up, this time from Adrian.

Adrian: Your attendance is requested at a mandatory Council meeting tomorrow at noon.

Was Eric coming up with an excuse to text me?
Rebecca could tell I was reading something on my screen and not looking at her.
"Is that a booty call?" she sassed.
"You wish," I snarked, still reading Eric's messages.
"Totally a booty call!" Rebecca cheered.
"Stop it," I whined. "I'll pick you up in an hour or so?"
"Take your time," she leered, wiggling her eyebrows into the camera.
"You're incorrigible," I said as I hung up. Knowing fully well that my questions could be answered by Adrian, I reciprocated the excuse and texted Eric back.

Sloan: The what now?
Eric: Can I call you?
Sloan: Sure.

"Hey." His voice sent my stomach into a somersault.

"Hey," I said, and it came out with more breath than I intended. I thanked the stars he hadn't done a video call since I could feel a blush beginning to simmer in my cheeks.

"So. Council meeting," Eric stated.

Adrian's text had confirmed this was indeed Lunai-related, but just in case it was all a figment of my imagination, I feigned ignorance. "We're talking about... Lunai... stuff, right?" I stumbled over the words, wishing he would have been first to say it.

"Yeah." He laughed. "There's no Council at work."

I forced a laugh along with his even though I felt stupid. "Yeah, no, I figured. Do I need to be worried?"

"No! Please don't, not at all. We have regular meetings every three to four phases. It's mainly housekeeping. I'm not sure why they're calling an emergency meeting right now, but I'm guessing it has to do with the storms."

My brain was stuck trying to puzzle together his words as well as the fact that he now spoke so freely about the matter. I wanted so badly to shake the feeling that I was being pranked and that he was in on it.

"Phases?" I asked.

"Lunar phases. Sorry, I forget you don't know all the terminology yet." He chuckled nervously.

I was reminded of the fact that Eric knew me, but a different me.

"Sloane, you there?" he asked.

I had been silent for too long. "Yeah, yes. I'm here."

"You okay?"

How am I supposed to answer that question?

"Yeah, this is just... weird. Sorry." I added the last word out of habit.

"I know." Eric's voice was small.

"Can you tell me—are you allowed—to tell me anything? About me? Why I have been, you know, Jumping back?"

I heard him take a heavy breath, letting it out slowly. "Technically not. Since it happens in your Future."

It was the response I was expecting.

"No worries. I just thought I'd ask."

Awkward silence.

"So will I see you at the meeting tomorrow? It's at Adrian's," he said.

"Yep—yes. I'll see you there," I replied.

"Great," he said, adding, "all right then," indicating he was about to hang up.

"All right," I piped. "Goodbye, Eric."

"Hey, Sloane?" His voice stopped me from lowering the phone from my ear.

"Yeah?"

"Every time you Jumped to see me, it was for good reasons only."

༄༄༄

I spent the rest of Saturday physically with Rebecca, though my mind was entirely elsewhere. I wanted to fast forward to Sunday, when I could see Eric again. Too bad my powers didn't work that way.

Right before noon that Sunday, I sat at Adrian's dining room table in my usual spot, enjoying a much-needed cup of coffee as well as Maddie's company. I had been the first person to show up, but I also had a feeling I was the only Lunai who actually drove to Adrian's house. I nearly fell out of my seat when the second Lunai arrived.

Or rather, he appeared.

A middle-aged man wearing business casual clothes materialized in the house's foyer. He was plump and not very tall, his button-down shirt tucked into his khaki pants with way too much tension over his stomach. His clean-cut blond hair was in sharp contrast to his very tanned skin, and his thick clear-frame glasses made his eyes look abnormally large.

"Hey, Finneas," Maddie said in a bored voice. "Dad's downstairs."

"Thanks," the man, Finneas, said as he gave me a nervous glance. Maddie did not bother introducing me.

"We don't normally want the Temps to see a bunch of people showing up here at the same time, so we ask people to Stop somewhere down the street and just let themselves in, and Start again when they're inside. Parking can also be such a hassle here," Maddie explained after Finneas disappeared down the hallway toward the hidden elevator. "You should try it next time."

The closer to noon it got, the more people showed up in the entryway. It struck me how normal they all looked. Most were older than me, but one boy looked to be around three years old, accompanied by a woman whom I could only assume was his mother. He wore round, thick spectacles that looped around the backs of his ears. They looked entirely too big for his small stature, yet they did not conceal the contradictory mixture of boredom and curiosity that shone from his eyes. The woman was tall, strikingly beautiful with dark skin, her hair a short pixie cut, freshly dyed blond. I was curious to know which one of them was Lunai, or if they both were. I made a mental note to ask Maddie later.

"Hey, Maddie. You okay?" the woman asked her warmly.

Maddie nodded and forced a smile.

I thought I saw the woman's eyes linger on me a bit longer than the others' had. All of them had given me looks; a new Lunai was apparently not a common occurrence. But this woman looked like she had something she wanted to say to me. She stayed silent and ushered the little boy with her toward the elevator. As the Lunai kept pouring in, I kept a lookout for a redhead. No one even close to matching her description showed up. I didn't want to ask Maddie if she knew of someone who looked like her. Not yet at least. Not until I confirmed that my suspicions were correct.

Right at noon as Maddie and I stood up from the dining table and made our way to the elevator, a young woman, probably no more than two or three years older than I, appeared at the front door.

"Sorry! Sorry! I know, I know. Irony on two legs here, the always-late-Lunai." The woman looked flustered, but it didn't seem to affect her confidence. She oozed it. She had short light-brown hair and hazel eyes that had an inner glow about them, accentuated by sharp black eyeliner. Her face was round and friendly, with high cheekbones and a wide-set smile.

"But not the last Lunai," a voice from behind the woman chimed.

The woman swirled around and squealed, "Nico!"

The man who had just appeared and the short-haired woman embraced and swayed from side to side. They looked like old friends, albeit, not a likely friendship pairing. The man was in his late thirties to early forties, had pitch-black hair, a scruffy black beard, deep brown eyes, and what little of his rough face you could see was sunburned. He wore a motorcycle jacket and black skinny jeans.

"Jules, baby, you look ravishing," Nico said.

"And you look like you just came from Burning Man. Which one? Ninety-three?"

"Oh-six, sugar. Best one yet!"

"So contemporary," Jules sassed.

"I heard you went to Woodstock! That one was epic. Thinking of trying it again if I can figure out a way to remember where the heck I was the whole time. Then again, if I saw myself, I'd probably just think it was the drugs!" Nico roared with laughter, Jules joining him. She went on to gush about how yes, Woodstock had been epic.

The elevator bell dinged to announce the cab's arrival, and Maddie cleared her throat.

"Coming, coming!" Jules skipped the distance between us in a few steps.

"Wait a minute. Fresh meat? Adrian's text didn't say anything about fresh meat!" Nico boomed as he spotted me.

"Hi, I'm Jules," the woman said to me as she held out her hand. Her eyes shone even in the dimly lit hallway. Her wide-sleeved shirt slipped back to reveal a labyrinth of delicate tattoos along her forearm.

I shook her outstretched hand. "Hi, I'm Sloane."

Nico came up beside Jules and scooped my hand out of hers before she and I had a chance to let go, bowed theatrically, and kissed the back of my hand. "Welcome, darling Sloane. To what do I owe this immense pleasure? Who died?"

"We don't know yet," Maddie said smugly.

Jules and Nico collectively gasped as their eyes widened, looking me up and down.

"A mystery heir! Ooh, we haven't had one of those in a while. How exciting!" Jules clapped her hands as we gathered in the elevator.

Nico was staring at me with a smirk. "Nah, I think this one knows. She probably just hasn't put two and two together. Or—even better—she doesn't want *us* to know." He winked at me.

Maddie looked at me, a slight apprehensive glint in her eyes, as the elevator lurched into downward motion.

"I honestly don't know anyone who has died," I said in a shaky voice.

"Well, we'll see who's missing when we take attendance," Nico said. Jules laughed.

It surprised me how comfortable they were with the fact that one of their own might have died.

The lower level of the Sanctuary was packed with people. It felt like more people than just those I had seen appear in the foyer. I tried to be inconspicuous as I surveyed the room, yet again failing to spot any long wavy red hair.

Adrian was at the dais shuffling through the Horolog, not paying any mind to the people around him. Jules and Nico spotted someone they knew and joined them at the front of the hall. Without drawing too much attention to myself, I glanced around to see if I could spot Eric. He was nowhere to be seen. Maddie and I retreated to the TV alcove, which surprisingly was empty except for the young boy I had spotted arriving earlier. He was immersed in the cartoon playing on the TV and didn't notice us when we sat down on the couch across from him.

"These meetings are normally such a bore, but Dad's been weird lately. I think something's up." Maddie looked restless. She hadn't been acting like her usual exuberant, bubbly self.

"Welcome, friends." Adrian's voice and accompanying smile were warm like an embrace on a sunny day. His words rang across the hall clear like a chirp but smooth like honey, silencing all chatter instantly.

"Whoa, Dumbledore qualities much?" I whispered to Maddie, nudging her shoulder.

"What?" she whispered back, annoyed.

Embarrassed that she hadn't gotten my joke, I replied, "Temp humor. Never mind." I turned my head to face Adrian and the crowd once again, and something caught my eye at the entrance of the Sanctuary.

Eric was tiptoeing in and trying to close the heavy door behind him as gently as possible. He kept his eyes upfront and on Adrian as he meandered toward the crowd, stopping by one of the gray stone pillars and leaning against it, despite there being a ton of empty chairs.

His eyes glanced in my direction and my organs reshuffled with a jolt—and then he smiled. First a mischievous, sideways smile, which then transformed into that breathtaker of a beam, and I was done for. My cheeks burned and I wanted to sink into the ground, but in the best way.

I cannot believe that smile is meant for me.

I smiled back, biting my lower lip as I giggled under my breath.

He's not even my type!

Eric composed himself, needing to pay attention to the meeting. I tried and failed miserably to follow his lead. He wasn't doing a great job at it either, as we both kept glancing over at each other. Our eyes met for what seemed like the hundredth stolen glance, and I stifled a giggle, my insides somersaulting as my mind spun and my cheeks flushed.

To my surprise, I found myself bracing for an oncoming Slip—the threat of pins and needles starting at my spine as my breath caught. I took a deep breath, remembering where I was. I couldn't Slip here, not in the Sanctuary.

Still, the fact that I could still feel pins and needles bothered me. I willed myself to focus on what Adrian was saying. I had been completely distracted by Eric.

"... it is most likely that they are, indeed, related to some fluctuations in the Pattern."

The crowd gasped.

"There haven't been weather changes due to Pattern disruptions for decades!" A man sitting close to where Eric was standing sounded not only angry, but like he was in disbelief.

"He means the Pattern of Time," Maddie whispered in my ear.

"What? Sorry."

"Just—listen," Maddie snapped.

I was a little taken aback by her foul mood, but chalked it up to tween behavior.

A woman sitting close to where I was stood up. I recognized her as the little boy's mom. "I've been Sensing it, Charlie. So has Maddie." The woman gestured toward Maddie and me and all eyes in the room were suddenly on us. The boy peeled his eyes away from the TV to listen to his mom.

Maddie was still sitting with her arms crossed tightly over her torso, one leg bouncing up and down. She acknowledged the woman's claim with a wide-eyed nod, clearly as eager as I was to get the attention away.

"We all know your Sensing can be off, Malina. Are you sure there are discontinuations that would cause such wild weather anomalies? Isn't this just global warming?" A man stood up close to where Charlie was standing and spoke with a bratty dismissiveness.

Before Malina could defend herself, Maddie shot to her feet. "Victor, if two Sensors tell you they're Sensing the same thing, it's not *off*. I know what I felt."

She sat back down, cowering behind me a bit, looking like she regretted her mini-outburst. I for one was glad to see that she was still the same Maddie. She must have been acting off due to whatever she was Sensing—I just hadn't realized.

"Well what do other Sensors say? Have we contacted them?" Charlie asked, still frustrated.

"The Conservatory is currently working on confirming multiple reports of Pattern disturbances coming from Sensors around the globe," Adrian said, turning to Malina, "but it's not discontinuation, right Malina?"

Malina looked around at her fellow Lunai with fear in her eyes and shook her head ever so slightly. "It's something new. I've never felt it before."

"What are discontinuations? What's the Conservatory?" I whispered hurriedly to Maddie.

"When someone changes something in the past, it discontinues that string of moments. The Conservatory is where the big bosses are. It's in London. Now shush!" She nicked her chin to the front of the room, telling me to listen.

"Thank you, Malina and Madeline, for sharing your experiences." Adrian gestured for Malina to sit down, and Charlie and Victor followed suit, both in a huff. Adrian's eyes swept the hall with a worried look that I had never seen in them before. "This brings me to why I called this meeting, I'm afraid. I want to thank you all for making yourselves available on such short notice. The Conservatory reached out to me late yesterday evening with some very sad news. They cannot confirm whether this is related to the storms or the Pattern disturbances, but I am truly sorry to announce that three of our brethren have been murdered."

A wave of panic swept the group. Whispers and mutters were passed about, and the shock was palpable. I felt anxiety's icy claws clasp around my heart, a lump in my throat, but this time, knowing that I couldn't Slip didn't help keep it at bay.

"Who? Where? When? By whom? Did they have a transition agreement? Come on ol' bud, don't leave us hanging!" It was Nico, sitting front and center.

Adrian walked around the dais and placed his hand on the Horolog, facing us.

So that's what he had been doing. Inscribing the deaths of the murdered Lunai in the Horolog.

"Forrest Phillips of El Paso," Adrian began. Someone from across the room whom I couldn't see let out a wail and started sobbing.

Adrian continued, a pained expression on his face, "Makenzie Edwards of Little Rock, and Isaac Brewer of Santa Monica."

This time, the crowd's reaction contained more anger. People stood up to look around in search of their missing group member, coming up empty. Isaac Brewer of Santa Monica would have attended this meeting, had he been alive.

I spotted Nico staring at me again, smirking through the crowd. When our eyes met, he winked knowingly, pointing his index finger in my direction. I mustered my most angry, incredulous look and shook my head at him.

He was really starting to piss me off. Was he insinuating that this Isaac guy was someone I knew, who was now dead?

I thought about asking my mom whether some distant relative may have passed away recently. I still wasn't fully convinced that what they said was true, that someone had to die in order for another human to manifest powers. There was no one in my life even remotely close to me who had died recently. Let alone someone who would be thinking about me in their final moments.

My eyes wandered toward the pillar where Eric had stood, but I couldn't see him anywhere. People had dispersed from their seats and were huddled in groups. Varying emotions could be felt around the hall, none of them positive.

Adrian cleared his throat. "To answer your question, Nico, we do not know who the killer is. We can discern no rhyme or reason to who was killed, the time, the locations, other than them being Lunai, and all were killed in a similar manner. The police have not connected the murders, at least not that we know of. But the Conservatory believes there has been a leak, and this may be the work of Temps."

THE AFTER HOURS

"A leak as in, someone revealed us to the Temps," Maddie whispered.

"I got it," I semisnapped. I hadn't meant to, but her foul mood was rubbing off on me. That, coupled with this Nico guy, made my tone feel justified.

"The Conservatory has launched an investigation with the help of our friend Evan here"—Adrian gestured to a guy sitting in the front row on the opposite side from Nico and Jules—"who is scouring the dark web to see if there is any sort of organized planning going on, whether there is an identifiable group responsible, or if we may just be dealing with a single individual. Either way, these deaths are a horrendous injustice and loss to our community. May their powers find a peaceful transition, and may the Pattern keep."

"May the Pattern keep," the crowd repeated as one after Adrian before murmurs sprang forward again.

"Who was the last person to speak to Isaac Brewer?" Charlie was standing again as he addressed the hall. Nico looked over to me. I didn't give him the satisfaction of meeting his eyes.

"Probably me." A tiny, frail older woman with silver hair whom I had not spotted before stood up.

"What can you tell us?" Charlie asked, although it sounded more like a demand.

"So sorry, Babs," a voice from somewhere in the crowd said.

Babs took a deep breath. "Well, he would always check up on me on Saturdays. My house is on the way to Zuma Beach, where he liked to go surfing." Her voice broke, and she took a moment to recompose herself. "He would help me if I needed anything done around the house or if I needed an errand run." She sniffled, accepting a tissue from a woman in the row behind her. "He didn't stop by this weekend. I was sure he was just busy with his new girlfriend. I never asked him to come and never held him to it. He was just such a nice young man; he would even Stop for the labor-intensive tasks and get them done for me."

"So the last time you saw him was over a week ago?" Adrian asked.

"Yes." Babs cleared her throat. "Nothing seemed out of the ordinary. Except he mentioned his new girlfriend."

"Where was he found?" Charlie asked, directing the question to Adrian. Babs sobbed even louder and sat back down.

"A hotel room, downtown." Adrian knew better than to divulge any gruesome details if he knew them.

"Did he say who this new girlfriend is? Is she a Temp?" Victor chimed in, directing his question to Babs.

"I think that's enough speculation for now." Adrian held up a hand. "Let's let the Conservatory conduct their business. We will, of course, all be ready to help if our assistance is requested."

Charlie sat down again, a grumpy look on his face.

"Are we in any danger? Did the Conservatory say something?" Jules posed the question rather nonchalantly in contrast to the context. It made my stomach churn, and I wondered if I was in danger. Apart from the redhead.

"They did not. But I would like to remind all of you that you are, as always, welcome to stay here at the Sanctuary as long as you want and need," Adrian answered.

I looked up to the balconies above, all the doors leading to rooms that hadn't been occupied in years. Would I feel safer staying in the Sanctuary? No one could get in here by Stopping, Maddie had explained. If you tried to ride the elevator down it would break any Stop or Jump you were in. It would also send the elevator on a fritz, and Adrian did not like having to pay the extra amount it took to get a discreet elevator repair man to come fix it. One who wouldn't ask questions about the basement it led to.

It was tempting to get a break from the constant vigilance and looking over my shoulder. But how would I explain that to my mother? There was no way I could just take off for an undetermined amount of time and not go home in between.

The crowd dispersed and people huddled together talking in various pockets of the hall. I felt bad for being thankful that my status as "fresh meat" was overshadowed by the main item on the agenda. Maddie left me to go talk to Malina, the other Sensor.

I felt extremely out of place. I noticed that Eric had made his way to the front of the room and stood talking to Adrian. I stared at them, cursing the fact that I couldn't read lips, willing either of them to make eye contact with me. When that didn't happen after a good three minutes of staring, I felt too awkward to try and butt in to a conversation with these people I didn't know very well.

Everyone else knew each other, and I couldn't just organically slide into one of the discussions. I felt the intense need to make myself scarce before someone noticed how out of place I felt. A touch of indignation tugged at me at the fact that neither Adrian nor Eric had thought to engage with me. As I had expected, I went completely unnoticed as I left the grand hall, further cementing my rootlessness in this community I was supposedly now a part of.

What I had not expected was how much I ached to be a part of it. Just as I reached the elevator, a voice echoed from down the hall, calling my name.

"Sloane, wait up!" It was Maddie. She ran to catch up with me, panting in a slightly exaggerated manner as she came to a halt in front of the elevator doors.

"So," she said breathlessly, "we need to talk."

"Oh?" I said in an amused tone.

"I know your secret," Maddie teased in a singsong voice as the elevator chimed and the doors slid open.

My chest tightened at her words, but Maddie's demeanor was too jolly for me to be overly worried.

"Eric revealed himself to you, didn't he?" Maddie squealed.

It felt like my nerves were overtensed guitar strings that someone strummed on with violent force. It didn't help that with every inch the elevator moved upward, my powers flooded my being once again, threatening to send me Slipping.

"Wait, how long have you known?" I asked, still a bit taken aback. Eric had mentioned knowing Adrian, but I had assumed it was only a formality.

"Gosh, I don't know. Only, like, forever," Maddie answered, flippant.

Annoyance pricked at me. I felt like I was the last to know about something very obvious. I was also starting to question whether I had trusted these people too easily, which made me even more annoyed—at myself.

"So—you guys know him well?" I stuttered.

"Oh yeah, he's the last person we trained!" Maddie beamed at first, not reading the room at all. Then it was as if she realized that my energy wasn't matching hers, and she followed up with, "You like him, right?"

If you only knew.

"Yeah, no—yes," I muttered awkwardly. I couldn't tell an eleven-year-old how much I actually liked him. Or in what way I liked him.

Maddie cocked her head, eyes narrowed, lingering behind me for a few seconds after the elevator doors opened and I stepped out into the hallway.

"Is something wrong, Sloane?" she then asked, stepping out of the elevator.

I gulped tiny sips of air through my nose as I lied through my teeth, "No—no. Just a fun coincidence."

Why wouldn't they mention another Lunai they knew was in my life?

I quickly changed the subject. "Can I ask you something?"

"Always!" Maddie beamed, following me through the front door and out onto the porch.

"How come only you and that woman downstairs—Malina—have these Sensing powers?"

Maddie's smile disappeared, and I immediately regretted asking her.

"It's okay if you don't want to tell me," I added.

"Oh no, it's fine," Maddie said with a forced laugh and a dismissive wave of her hand. "So it's a girl power thing. Assigned-females-at-birth only. If you're a girl born to a girl Lunai, and then she transfers her powers to you when she dies, you develop the Sense."

I regretted asking her even more.

"I'm so sorry, Maddie."

She waved dismissively again, unconvincingly. "I told you, it's fine. My mom died giving birth to me. Not like I have a mom to miss or anything."

My heart broke at her words, and I reminded myself to give my mom a long hug when I got home.

"I'm still sorry. That's awful."

"Well if that hadn't happened, I wouldn't have been adopted by Adrian and gotten to live at a Sanctuary!" Her voice was back up to its regular octave. She smiled a smug smile before adding, "At first I was put here because I was too young to have powers, but then Adrian decided to keep me."

"Oh, so did you not manifest until later, or . . . ?"

Maddie laughed hysterically. "Heck no! I manifested before I was a year old. That's why I was kept in the Sanctuary. Can you imagine controlling a toddler with Lunai powers?"

Maddie kept on laughing, and so did I as I imagined my sister Amanda with time-traveling powers. One tantrum and she could change something that would later wipe out humanity.

Yet the sadness I had in my heart for Maddie just grew. Her life couldn't have been easy, growing up without a mom, having powers she wasn't allowed to use but also another set of powers that she couldn't control or help, all confined to what was essentially an underground bunker.

I hugged her tightly before saying goodbye, and she acted bothered, but I could tell she needed it.

As she let go and stepped back, she quickly hardened her demeanor. "If you tell anyone I let you hug me, I'll have you Stripped. Can't have people think I'm going soft." She laughed.

I gave her a mock salute to acknowledge her request before asking, "Adrian mentioned something about that but didn't explain. What's Stripping?"

She chuckled, walking back toward the front door. "Oh—Strip you of your Lunai powers. But don't worry, I was just kidding. I like you too much."

CHAPTER FIFTEEN

ADRIAN HAD PROMISED me more robust homework, but when I opened the email from him, it wasn't what I had hoped. Nothing about Lunai history, just elementary articles on lunar phases. I wanted to reach out and ask for something more challenging—I felt frustratingly far behind, especially compared to Eric—but I was afraid I would start sounding like a broken record.

I sat in my window seat that Sunday evening, where I could just glimpse the (waxing gibbous) moon through the old oak tree in our front yard. The articles Adrian sent were nothing you couldn't find on amateur astrologer profiles on social media or learn in basic astronomy classes in high school, with a handful of Lunai-related commentary.

New Moon
Waxing Crescent
First Quarter

Waxing Gibbous
Full Moon
Waning Gibbous
Third Quarter
Waning Crescent

I was thoroughly bored. As I knew, Lunai powers were magnified during full moons and dampened at new moons, growing and decreasing correspondingly and proportionately between the two. It went on to explain:

For the most accurate Jump, aiming for lunation identical of the Present you Jump from has proven most successful. Obviously, the closer both Present and Destination are to Full Moon, the more precise you will find your Jump.

I wanted to be making more progress. I knew I should trust the process, and lunar phases were a foundation, but something gnawed at me. It felt like I wasn't being told the whole truth.

Regardless of my lack of enthusiasm for the material, I decided to commit them to memory by copying the list from the article. My mother had always told me that writing things out by hand helped you retain better, so I never took notes on my laptop.

I searched my room for my lavender journal. The longer I searched, the more I started to worry whether someone had gotten their hands on it. I hadn't taken it with me to college, so there was nothing recent in there. The latest entries, apart from the formulas I had been practicing the other day, were a string of horrendously bad poetry inspired by my breakup with Dylan. It had not been the catharsis I had been looking for; instead it had just made me feel bad about my poetry writing skills. I would be mortified if it fell into the wrong hands.

I was about to lift the mattress off my bed when I spotted the journal on the floor under my nightstand.

It lay open to a spread far back from where I had left off. The pages should have been empty, but they weren't.

598 s spring st apt 1849
3/2/23

It was my handwriting. I rushed back over to the window where my laptop sat, quickly typing up the address in a map search, while simultaneously opening another tab, searching for "lunar cycles."

The address was to an apartment building downtown. Not too far from my office. I found a site where you could look up lunar phases based on the date. Today's date, July 6, showed waxing gibbous, and illumination at 80.79%. Distance, 251,261 miles from Earth. The moon would be full in four days, the Buck Moon.

I hastily looked up March 2, 2023.

Waxing gibbous, illumination 81.49%. Distance, 251,506 miles. Five days before a full moon.

Doesn't really get much closer than that. If I was ever going to aim for a Jump to March 2, 2023, now was the time. I knew I was supposed to be careful, but a little practice couldn't hurt? After all, it was me who wrote that, and I wouldn't tell myself to perform a Jump if it was unsafe. My Present and the date in my journal lined up too perfectly. The lunation was too similar, and the full moon would bolster me. I had no doubts in my mind I had left that note for myself for a reason. It was no coincidence that I had stumbled upon it just as I was tackling this lunar phase homework.

I had to trust the process, after all.

༄༅༄༅༄༅

I stood in front of 598 South Spring Street and looked up at the tall building. Up there on the eighteenth floor, something was waiting for me. In the corner of my eye, the moon taunted me, competing with the streetlights.

THE AFTER HOURS

The lobby of the building was bigger than I had anticipated, with old green marble columns, new Scandinavian-looking furniture, three elevators on the left-hand wall, and a concierge desk on the right. To the back of the room, doors labeled Trash Room and Maintenance flanked a wall of brass-colored mailboxes.

The doorman didn't pay any attention to me as I strolled in. He was playing a game on his phone, feet up on the desk and chair leaning dangerously far back.

I walked confidently toward the mailboxes, sneaking a peek at the elevators as I passed them. I let out a frustrated sigh when I saw that there were no elevator call buttons, just pads where residents could swipe their keycards. To further my disappointment, the mailboxes were only marked with apartment numbers, not the occupant names. I looked back at the doorman, then glanced up at the ceiling to see if there were cameras.

I'm an idiot. Why should I bother looking for cameras?

I turned toward the mailboxes and closed my eyes.

"Please let this work," I whispered under my breath.

Beach.
Eardrums stretching.
Sunset.
Crackling Spine.
Fire.
Pins and needles.
Embers adrift.
Eyes burning.
This must be the place.

The sounds of the lobby were put on mute, a mellow pop song playing on the tiny battery-operated radio I had noticed on the doorman's desk, cut off awkwardly. I opened my eyes and looked out the glass doors at the front of the building. The bustling street was frozen.

I memorized the way my feet aligned with the travertine tiles below them, to make sure I could Start again in the exact same spot.

Taking care to not knock the doorman over, which wouldn't have been hard with his precarious positioning, I carefully removed his keychain from the loop on his belt. But before I would let myself up the elevator, I needed to make sure whatever was waiting for me in apartment 1849 was what I thought it was and not, perhaps, the redhead. I brought the large silver keyring with me back to the far wall and started testing brass keys matching the face of the mailboxes in the keyhole marked Master.

The third key I tried worked, and I thanked the stars the building was still using analog mailboxes. The massive brass door swung open in two parts, its opening in the middle. The mailbox for apartment 1849 was in the second to the top row, seven boxes down from the left.

My heart jumped when I saw the name, partially out of satisfaction because I had been right, and partially out of excitement. It was handwritten on a white sticker, taped over a pile of other older stickers, burying the face of the tiny placard that hung down from the roof of the mailbox.

E.C. Baxter

I hurriedly closed the mailbox wall, removed the keycard off the doorman's keychain, and returned it to his belt. I walked back and placed my feet between travertine squiggly number one and squiggly number two, staring directly at the number 1849, and closed my eyes.

Beach, sunset, fire.

The pop song and traffic noise reverberated around the lobby once again as I strode to the elevators, careful not to make eye contact. I called one of the elevators by swiping the card against a black plastic casing on the wall in between them. A small light in its corner turned green for a split second and the contraption chimed.

I watched the doorman as the elevator doors closed behind me. He didn't look up.

Once alone in the elevator, I glanced quickly around to see if I spotted any cameras. There were no obvious ones, but I could never know what the ornate decorative ceiling and multiple control panel covers held. I didn't care too much though; I was too giddy. I let out a small squeal, pulled my shoulders up to my ears, and allowed myself to smile from ear to ear.

I fucking did it. I am fucking doing it!

A little over a week earlier, I had struggled with whether I actually believed these powers existed.

But in that elevator ride, I felt invincible.

Once on the eighteenth floor, a sign clearly articulated which apartment ranges were in which direction, and Eric's was to the left. It was almost to the very end of the narrow, carpeted hallway. Glancing both ways down the empty hallway and up into the ceiling to check for cameras, I took a deep breath to ground myself.

"This is my Present, I won't forget, and I will be back."

I didn't know where the mantra came from. I just wanted to have something to remind myself that even though I was technically sneaking around, I was okay, and I wasn't using my powers to hurt anyone. Why that was even a concern of mine was another question.

"You can do this," I whispered, reminding myself that today and the date I was aiming for were lined up perfectly, and I was ready.

Beach. Sunset. Fire. Spine. Fire. Sunset. Beach.

I let out a frustrated sound and opened my eyes quickly to make sure no one had appeared in the hall before clamping them tightly again.

Beach. Sunset. Fire. Burning spine. Embers. Painful spine. Extremely painful spine.

The pain caused me to start hyperventilating. I wanted to back out of the Jump, but it was too late. My eyes wouldn't open, but the Jump wouldn't come to me.

I cursed under my breath and tried to remember something to anchor me to the moment I was aiming for. In March 2023, I was a junior in high school. It was a particularly rough patch in my friendship with Rebecca, as she chose to spend most of her time with other cheerleaders. My relationship with my mom hadn't been great either. I had spent more time at Tom's house than my own—

I willed the atmosphere of that era of my life to wash over me, and the Jump ripped through me with scathing force, and for a second I thought I had actually come in contact with a flame as I yanked my hands to my chest, fingertips burning.

I opened my eyes, gasping for air as I reached for my phone.

8:28 p.m.
March 2, 2023

The feeling of triumph was indescribable, but it was starkly overshadowed by the crippling anxiety I had over whether Eric would recognize me or not.

I didn't have to wait long because he opened the door before I had a chance to knock.

"Hey babe," he said with an ease, as if it was something he did every day. "Happy belated Valentine's."

He was so young. Just twenty. His skin didn't hold the glow of summer, but it did have a glow of happiness. His green eyes glistened, the subtle crow's feet I was used to seeing barely visible. His hair was shorter than what I was used to, but it suited him extremely well, sharp against his forehead. He was clean shaven, accentuating his jawline. He wore a tight-fitting black V-neck shirt above loose gray sweatpants, the shirt revealing every curve of the muscles underneath. Despite this, it was his smile that struck me. The same smile I caught him giving me at work. The same smile he had on the rooftop when I first kissed him. It lit an entirely different fire within me. I flung my arms around him, half-startling him, kissing him as we stumbled into the apartment.

༄༅༄༅༄༅

I lay on my stomach in Eric's bed, propped up on my elbows, tangled in his sheets. I knew I had never been here before, but everything about his apartment felt familiar. From the texture of the walls to the smell of his sheets. While it didn't feel like home, it still felt like it was mine, somehow.

"Wait okay, so if this isn't the first time I've Jumped to you, when was that exactly?" I was extremely confused about the logistics of the whole ordeal.

"You know I can't tell you since it hasn't happened for you!" he said.

"Ugh, I'm sick of not being in the know here—you have to give me something! Otherwise it may not happen! And that will throw the Pattern completely off and fire and brimstone and all that," I said, bending my knees and swinging my legs back and forth. I made an exaggerated sad face, blinking my eyes rapidly.

Eric smiled, sighing. He shifted closer to me in the bed. "Fair point." He kissed me softly, quickly, as if he were utterly used to kissing me. It not only left me wanting more, but also torn as to how I felt about the imbalance.

Do I like that he's already so comfortable with me?

Or am I setting myself up for heartbreak?

Eric continued, "It was in October of last year. You scared the shit out of me, then Malina told me you were legit, and I ran with it. No regrets." He intertwined his fingers in mine, every touch still charged with tension. At least from my end.

While I was relieved that he didn't regret taking a leap of faith when he had first met me, I couldn't help but feel annoyed that he had needed convincing. And that the person who had convinced him was someone I didn't know at all. I thought back to the Council meeting and what Maddie had said about Malina. My frustration compounded at the thought of how out of place I had felt toward the end of the meeting, and if Eric in 2022 knew and trusted Malina, 2025 Eric could have maybe introduced me to her, or something. But I couldn't dwell on it. I needed to gather more information so that I would know when to execute a Jump to Eric that would be his first time meeting me.

October 2022. I will at some point need to Jump back to October 2022.

It was insane to even think about the fact that when I was just starting my junior year of high school, Eric already knew me. Not Junior Me, of course. But a Future version of me that I didn't even know yet.

I had found a new and improved use for my journal, as I had to keep track of these Jumps somehow.

"Did I look different? Was I, like, thirty or something? Come on, give me some hints." I bit my lip as I lifted my leg over his.

"More like forties. Total mess, boils everywhere, so much plastic surgery—"

I hit him in the head with his pillow as he laughed at his own joke.

"Okay, okay! No, you weren't much different at all. Your hair was shorter though." He let his fingers find a lock of my hair that lay down over my chest, grazing the mattress in front of me. He twisted the strand loosely around his finger with a wistful look in his eyes before letting it go. I couldn't imagine cutting my hair anytime soon, so that was weird, but I didn't press him for more information.

"Do you even know how old I am?"

His turn to bite his lip, wincing. "Why?"

"Just wondering if you know what my Present is, is all." I said, teasingly. I had no idea how many of these visits I had yet to make, but I knew this was the youngest I'd ever be.

Panic flashed in Eric's eyes. "Oh god, please tell me you're over eighteen."

I fell back to my side of the bed laughing.

"Not funny! I'm not about to pull some *Time Traveler's Wife* thing here!" he exclaimed, but he was still smiling. He leaned in over me to meet my eyes and smiled as he asked, "So, babe, how old are you?"

I calmed down from my fit, taking in his face, wanting to remember every part of this moment, before saying, "I'm nineteen."

"Goodness." He paused, surveying me as if he were seeing me for the first time before leaning in to kiss me. But he pulled back abruptly after a while. "Wait. So you're from 2025?"

"Mhm."

"Did I pass the bar yet? Wait—no—I'm way off, that won't be until 2027. Also, don't tell me that. There might be a tsunami over LA when you get back to your Present."

Little did he know about the strange happenings that were already occurring in my Present.

We were still inches apart. He kept staring at me, inspecting me, and while this would normally have freaked me out, I was surprised to find that I didn't mind. I wanted to remember him this way forever, too. His thumb stroked my jawline and tucked a strand of my hair behind my ear. He might have been comfortable touching me, but his touches still resembled those of someone handling an extremely valuable item—reverent, savoring the seconds before eventually having to hand it back.

I opened my mouth to say something, but he placed a finger on my lips and beat me to it. "Shush, you." Then he kissed me again.

I hated not being able to just tell him everything. These rules sucked.

I knew I should have felt more connected to this Eric, him being so much closer to me in age. But he was still light-years ahead of me it seemed—he was already a widower. He already knew so much more than me about being Lunai. He had already had experiences with me that I had yet to have with him.

Eric stepped out to grab us some food from the bar on the first floor, and I was left to study his apartment. It was an open loft, everything in one space except the bathroom. The ceilings were at least twelve feet high, and the one window in the apartment looked original to the building, spanning the entire exterior wall, single pane, with a large operable partition in the middle. It was tilted open just a tad, letting in cool air and the noises of the street below.

He didn't have a lot of furniture; I knew he hadn't been living there very long. But he had books. Shelves lined the entire wall next to where he had a living room set up, reaching all the way up to the ceiling, brimming with books. I had barely read a fraction of them.

The shelves were almost completely stuffed with books, but some pockets held knickknacks of varying beauty, or law books stacked horizontally, ready to be referenced at a moment's notice. One of the stacked horizontal books caught my eye, bound in gold-colored leather, almost certainly the oldest book in the collection.

It was a copy of the Horolog. It wasn't as large as the one Adrian had, and certainly not as thick. But it was definitely the Horolog. I recognized the sigil on the spine, the same one marked at the top of every page of Adrian's Horolog, except this one was vertical, running parallel to the book's spine. I flipped through the pages quickly—they weren't as old as the ones in the Sanctuary Horolog. There were no empty pages toward the end, just chapters on Lunai history, Laws, codes, ethics, instructions, diagrams, explanations, theory. The inside of the front cover was inscribed:

August 2022
My warmest welcome to you, Eric.
May this help you get started on
your journey, and when you're well
on your way, may this remind
you that help can always be found
at the Sanctuary.

Adrian

Why did Eric have this? Or a better question, why did I not have my own copy? I closed the book and stared at Eric's front door. He would be back soon, so I really didn't have time to make up my mind. I dashed to where my handbag was sitting on one of the barstools up against the kitchen island and stuffed the book inside, feeling utterly vindicated in purse size choice, something Tom had often mocked me for. At the thought of Tom, a searing shock went tearing through my body, and my hands, busy closing up my handbag, vanished right before my eyes, for the tiniest fraction of a moment. My eyesight then went black for a similar amount of time, coming back slowly, film burn spots swimming in front of my eyes. My feet felt as if they needed to reland on the floor beneath me.

Eric entered the apartment, large paper bag in hand, a huge smile on his face. It quickly disappeared when he looked at me.

"Hey, everything all right?" he asked, placing the bag on the counter and hurrying over to where I stood.

"Yeah, yeah I think so—" I looked down at my feet, willing my eyes to focus, the spots slowly diminishing.

"You're shaking. Did you Flicker?" he asked.

"Do you lose your eyesight when you Flicker? If so, yeah probably."

"Yeah, did your body seem to disappear for a second?" He stroked my back, heat radiating out from wherever his hand made contact.

"Yup," I replied.

"Ugh, I'm so sorry. Flickering is awful. I know you've been here a while already." He said this as he pulled me into a hug.

"What does that have to do with it?" I looked up at him without leaving the embrace. "Sorry, Adrian really has taught me very little."

"That's weird. I would have thought he would teach you Flickering on day one," Eric said, looking confused. He tightened his grip on me and buried his face in my hair as he let out a contemplative, "Hmm."

Add that to my list of things I felt Adrian was dropping the ball on.

"Well, Flickering is totally normal. It happens when your powers get fatigued, if you have too many After Hours at one time, if you're feeling under the weather, attempt a Jump that's too much for your powers to hold up, or you get overwhelmed with emotion. That sort of stuff," Eric said reassuringly, still not letting go of me.

"Okay, that makes sense."

"You've already been here for hours. It happens to the best of us. I'm surprised you didn't Flicker before . . . you know." He nicked his head in the direction of the bed.

He smirked and heat flooded my cheeks. My heart fluttered as he surveyed me, arms still wrapped around my waist. But just as my pulse accelerated, pain tore at me once more and I knew it was time to say goodbye.

"I don't want to leave," I said, burying my face in his chest.

"I don't want you to leave either," he said, and kissed the top of my head. I could feel him inhaling my smell as he squeezed me tighter. "But this is how it works." His voice was small and somber as he looked down at me. Our eyes met and I pushed myself up on my toes to kiss him.

I wished more than anything I could curl back up in his bed and spend the night sleeping with my head on his chest. It was so unfair to have to ruin this moment because of the restrictions of our powers.

As we came out of the kiss, I pressed my left cheek against his chest and my eyes roamed over to my purse on the barstool. At least I had reading material now.

"At least you are going back to a Present where you know me. I'm going to have to wait for your next visit," he said. I could tell he was trying to lighten the mood and make me feel better, but it only made me feel worse.

Worse because he truly had it so much worse. I could call Eric up as soon as I got back to my Present if I wanted to. This Eric could not under any circumstance contact me in his Present.

My heart broke for him.

But what made me feel even more horrible was that the thing I most looked forward to doing when I got back to my Present wasn't calling him.

I just wanted to read the book that I was stealing from him.

CHAPTER SIXTEEN

T HE NEXT DAY, I was still riding the high from my successful Jump to 2023. I scoured my journal for any other notes indicating a time I should aim to Jump to but came up empty. I was dying to try another Jump, hungry for the rush of it, but I was scared to try to Jump somewhere if I didn't know it was safe.

I sat on the window seat in my room poring over the stolen Horolog. I tried to memorize the formulas, doing my best to commit the rules to memory. I wanted to figure out if my escapades during graduation night could have possibly done some damage that I wasn't aware of yet.

The first thing I learned was the meaning of the sigil that ran along the book's spine and sat at the top of every page. Each corner of the diamond symbolized where Lunai moments could take place: the two corners inside the infinity symbol loops represented Past and Future Jumps. The ones sitting above and below the center of the infinity symbol, where the lines crossed, represented Present and Stopped time, respectively.

I stared at the formula for Past Jumps and transcribed it into my lavender journal, replacing the words with an estimate of how long I had spent in the Past in my Slips to graduation night and my visit to Eric the night before.

PAST JUMP:
($6 \text{ HOURS}^2 + 6 \text{ HOURS}$) + 19 YEARS, 26 DAYS = 19 YEARS, 27 DAYS, 18 HOURS
LIFESPAN = NEW LIFESPAN (NO CHANGE)

I was probably overthinking it. It didn't seem too bad once you did the math. So I was almost two days older than I should be right now. And some change, if I counted my other Slips. It didn't seem like a big deal.

The only thing that still worried me was the fact that both of my Jump-Slips had been to the same place in time, graduation night. There were already three of me overlapping at some point that evening. I pulled out Adrian's drawing that he had given to me the first time he took me to the Sanctuary. I studied the diagram of the pocket one creates when creating After Hours in the Past. I replicated the diagram in my journal, except I made two overlapping pockets over relatively the same spot on the straight line that represented the Past.

I knew I had to be really careful moving forward.

But I'm hungry for that rush.

My own thoughts took me by surprise. Adrian had warned me about this part of it. The powers, as uncomfortable as they were when manifesting could, in some instances, become somewhat of an addiction for people. It was rare, but when it happened, it was stronger than most substance addictions. Lunai had stopped living in their Present, even lost it altogether, not knowing where their Present was anymore. Just trucking along in Stops and Jumps until they had no idea where they had begun.

A little practice wouldn't hurt though. He did say I needed to master my Stop. To protect myself. You couldn't overpractice self-defense, could you?

Staring out into the street, I cursed the sleepiness of my neighborhood. Nothing ever happened here.

Headlights appeared at the corner at the far end of my street. "Perfect," I said into the void. I waited to make sure the car would gain momentum toward me, and then closed my eyes.

I was back at my beach. It was sunset, and the whole world seemed to be at my feet. The image swept me away and engulfed me as soon as everything went dark, the sun dipping past the horizon, setting the ocean ablaze. Conjuring the scene took no effort. The vibration in my eardrums even sounded like the visual's theme song. I took a deep breath and let it linger in my lungs before releasing, and the sensation of the Stop exited my body through the tips of my fingers and toes.

"This must be the place," the little voice in my head whispered, excited. I opened my eyes and smiled. The car was stalled.

A quick few breaths with my eyes closed again, and I had Started. The car continued to mosey down the street and past my house.

The rush wasn't just exhilarating, it was empowering. Still high from it, I chucked my journal toward my bed and squeezed my eyes shut.

Sure enough, when I opened them, my journal was frozen midair, its previously flailing pages stuck in immobile curls.

I chuckled to myself and closed my eyes again.

The golden-red sunset burned against the back of my eyelids. But the little eardrum theme wouldn't come. I cocked my head, eyes still closed, wondering what was happening. The sky blazed and started to quiver, the orange rays of the setting sun rippling and twisting until they changed and took on a texture, contrasting their normally smooth, hazy quality.

Red hair.

The Start shook through me, sending me tumbling off the window seat onto the floor. I wasn't sure which one was more painful, the blow to my shoulder as it hit the floor, or the rattling, piercing shock of the Start.

My eyes flew open as I cradled my shoulder, my breath coming in ragged, shallow gulps.

What the fuck was that?

I hobbled over to my bed, sweeping the journal to the floor before getting under the covers. It landed face-up, open on a blank spread, against the wall in the corner of my room.

That's enough practicing for now.

⸘⸘⸘

I fell asleep fairly quickly; it was the first time in over a week that I had been able to fall asleep effortlessly. But it didn't last. I hadn't been asleep long when I woke up on top of the covers, drenched in cold sweat.

The dream I had just been having was twisted in my mind, slipping away from me fast. But it had something to do with the redhead, of that I was sure. Her evil sneer was the only thing that remained branded on my brain.

I looked at the clock on my bedside table, utterly confused. I was certain I had fallen asleep after midnight, yet my clock said 10:45. It was still dark out; I had definitely not slept through till morning.

I ran my hands along my sheets around where I sat and under my pillow, frantically searching for my phone.

June 7, 2024.

"Fuck! Not this again," I exclaimed, falling back and letting my head hit the pillow, covering my face with my hands.

"Okay, I can do this. I did this in my Slip. And I'm really good at Stopping now. I can do this." I gave myself a pep talk, my hands still over my face.

I closed my eyes, and nothing happened.

I willed my beach back to me, but my mind kept losing the image.

I let out a frustrated growl and stood up. I had to use the restroom, might as well get that over with. I was in my own room. Just not my own time. The glass I had dropped on my toe the prior week in my Present was still on the floor.

It must have landed on my toe just as I Slipped, and gone with me into it. It was the same one I always kept in my bathroom and should probably have been brought downstairs to the dishwasher more often than I did. I placed the one from the floor next to its twin—clone—on the counter.

As I sat on the toilet, I stared at the two identical glasses and realized we didn't own two of them. I would remember if there had suddenly been two on my counter after I got back from being out on graduation night. I needed to bring the glass back with me, to my Present.

Maybe that's why I Slipped here yet again. I needed to fix this.

As I turned the sink off, my ears picked up on muffled voices from downstairs. I recognized them as Justin's and my mother's. I ran to my bedroom door and pressed my ear against it.

"Did you have fun?" my mother asked.

"Yeah, it was all right." Justin was not good at conveying fake enthusiasm. "I'm gonna change and go meet up with the guys though."

"It's almost eleven o'clock." This was Neil.

"Yeah, and I'll be back before midnight, just like always," Justin snapped as I heard him bolt up the stairs. Midnight was our curfew senior year, and Neil made no exceptions even for graduation.

I realized there might be another reason for why I had Slipped back to this night yet again.

After the party, I hadn't come home until the early hours of the morning, yet neither my mother or Neil had said anything about it, and there were never any repercussions. It might have bothered me more at the time if I hadn't had so many other things on my mind. Like hiding the gash on my forehead and dealing with the aftermath of what happened with Tom.

I lifted my ear from the door, gently, and hurried over to my armoire. I changed clothes quickly, pulling on black yoga pants and my trusted old black hoodie, string intact.

"Return these clothes. Take the glass back. Return these clothes, take the glass back," I muttered to myself as I finished getting dressed.

I leaned back against the door, just in time to hear Neil say, "See you in sixty-three minutes or less!"

Justin didn't reply, but I heard the front door close rather harshly.

I didn't hear anyone come up the stairs, and I knew both my mother and Neil were still on the lower level of the house. I snuck out into the hall, tiptoeing down toward the primary bedroom, passing Justin's and Amanda's rooms.

Finally, I could use the spiral staircase how it was meant to be used. Too bad I couldn't brag to Justin about it.

The old, rickety metal staircase creaked and bowed under my weight. It was one of the few things Neil hadn't bothered remodeling when they bought the house when Justin and I were in middle school, claiming it would never be used anyway, before shooting Justin and me a stern look.

Finally safe on the ground below, I skittered across the grass along the east side of the house to the side gate. I glanced at my phone; it was eleven o'clock sharp. Perfect timing.

I walked as inconspicuously as I could up to the front door and swung it open.

"I'm home!" I called into the house, heart racing.

"Hi, baby." My mother appeared in the family room, walking in my direction. "Did you have fun?"

"Yup. Just hung out with Tom," I said. The words felt wrong on my tongue.

"I'm glad you had fun, whatever you were doing." She smiled a smile that didn't make it to her eyes.

"I'm exhausted, going to bed. Love you." I hugged her tightly, remembering Maddie's story. I made another mental note to also hug my mother in my Present.

"Love you, sweetie. Sleep tight."

I ran upstairs and repeated the act. Changing out of the black outfit, back into what I had been wearing in the Present. I nearly forgot the glass in the bathroom, stuffing it in my pocket before heading back down the upstairs hall and out to the balcony. I took a deep breath and half-ran, half-skidded down the stairs as fast as I could. I wanted to kiss the ground once I reached it.

There was no going back now. No way to stop what was about to happen to Graduation Me since she had free rein to stay out all night. But I could try.

CHAPTER SEVENTEEN

After the guy had cornered me in the bathroom at Pete's house, I had run directly out into the street, soaking anyone I encountered with the mixture of water and blood that dripped from my face and hair. Just as my feet hit the sidewalk, Justin and his friends had pulled up to the house. I had never seen Justin move so quickly, not even as a running back. He jumped out of the car before it came to a proper halt. A squabble ensued.

Justin asking me what had happened.
Me pleading with him and his friends to not go after the guy.
Justin insisting on taking me to the hospital.
Me rationalizing that I was okay, it wasn't as bad as it looked.
Justin insisting again.
Me telling him he needed to be home in less than an hour and I was not about to get our parents involved. I would be fine.

Tom showing up, equally frazzled by my appearance.

Justin and Tom bickering about who would take me home when they realized I would not agree to the hospital. The most words they had ever exchanged.

Tom winning the fight by hitting Justin where it hurt, telling him to stop trying to be my brother.

Me pushing them apart before someone else ended up injured.

Pete, apologetic, bringing us some towels and a six pack of beer.

Tom having had too much to drink to be able to drive.

Me cleaning up in the visor mirror of Justin's friend's car.

It honestly wasn't as bad as it looked.

Me making Justin pinky promise he wouldn't go after the guy, telling him to just go find Rebecca and tell her what had happened and that I was okay.

Tom and I walking the long way back.

I had run the scenario over in my head enough times to know that was what was in fact going on at Pete's house that very moment I was making my escape down the spiral staircase for the second time.

I took off sprinting down the street, neighborhood watchdogs be damned. I knew it was no use returning to Pete's house—I had already done everything I could there.

I stopped to catch my breath about three blocks down from my house.

Bad things have happened when people lose their Present.

"I'm nineteen, I Jumped, uhm, Slipped—from July 7, 2025. I'm not in high school anymore. I don't belong here," I whispered, trying to move my lips as little as possible so I didn't look like I was talking to myself.

Okay, I cared about the neighborhood watchdogs just a little bit. My mother was friends with all of them.

I knew what I was doing was reckless. Stupid. The more time I spent here, the likelier I was to screw something up. But there must have been a reason for why I kept Slipping back to this night, and this night only. I didn't intend to interfere with anything like last time. I had gotten lucky, because my actions when I came to my eighteen-year-old self's rescue had happened all along, I hadn't changed anything. But my intuition was telling me I had unfinished business here.

Closure.

I found myself at the end of the street, at the entrance to the hiking trail. To the left, Pete's house. To the right, Tom's house.

Also to the right, our bench, that we would be sitting on in not too many moments.

I walked in a trance toward it, drawn to the atmosphere, the nostalgia. I hadn't been there since that night, the one I kept finding myself in.

It was one of the last conversations Tom and I had as friends.

The last conversation where everything was normal.

Before everything changed.

I reached the bench, and our initials were still there. No heart. Just "T & S." I started tracing their worn, smooth outlines with my finger, until a noise down the path startled me.

I flung myself into the bushes that separated the trail from the greenbelt and houses beyond, praying there wasn't a snake or scorpion in there.

I watched from my hiding spot as Graduation Tom and Graduation Me made their way to the bench. Graduation Me didn't look as bad as the last time I'd seen her, when I'd tightened my hood string around Woodoaks's neck.

Graduation Me should have just gone home to bed. She had been stubborn, and in denial, not wanting the night to end because of some nameless douchebag. Not wanting that to be the way the night ended. The way high school ended. Rationalizing that if she just put some time between what had happened and when she went to bed, it might not leave as much of a mark on the night.

She had been right. Because she had left the night open for way worse things to happen. My brain scrambled, trying to make sense of the fact that what I had done to the guy—and him to me—had just taken place, maybe half an hour earlier. But that was now a Past Me. Anxiety pricked at my pulse as I realized I now had four versions of myself running around at various points in time during this evening.

They sat down on the bench. I remember feeling like we were still twelve, despite working on the six pack that sat between us.

Apart from the incessant chirps of crickets and the occasional faraway coyote howl, there was a comfortable silence around them. Like it always had been between Tom and me. Now being a spectator, it filled me with both ease and sorrow. I hastily wiped a tear that escaped down my cheek.

I wished I could just tell her to go home. And hug her. I really wanted to hug her.

Tom was the one to break the silence. From my hiding spot, I could hear him loud and clear, even with the crickets.

"I'm so sorry things got so bad for you Sloane. I wish I had known," he said, talking about the rumors and slut-shaming I had been on the receiving end of since the school year had started.

"It's okay. Not like I wanted to talk about it." She smiled and gave his hand a quick squeeze.

"When did life get so complicated?" he said into the void, taking a swig of his beer. "Since when are there things that you and I can't talk about?"

"Life just got messy, I guess." She shrugged and followed suit, taking a couple big sips.

"I hate that," he said, shaking a finger at her. He always got a little animated when he had been drinking. "I hate that there's shit that you and I can't talk about. And why? Just because you're a girl and I'm a guy? Seriously."

She smiled an apologetic smile. Truth be told, I hated it too. I didn't know when it had become that way because I used to tell Tom everything. Then around the fourteen-year mark, that had changed. Around the same time people started teasing us about whether we were a couple. It was like those words from other people, external to our friendship, had built a wall between us, brick by brick, that only grew with age. It made me sad and made me question the resilience of our friendship to begin with.

"I'll try and be more open, in the future. If that's what you want? I didn't think you'd want to hear, you know—" she began.

"About your sexual conquests? Not really." They both burst into laughter. He recovered first, and continued, "But no, for real. I don't want you to keep stuff from me, especially stuff that you're going through."

"If it makes you feel any better, I didn't even tell Rebecca about Dylan until way late," she said, matter-of-factly.

"Really? I thought girls called each other within five minutes of it happening. That's what guys do. Or you know, send a level up message or something."

They laughed some more, the sound of their combined laughs almost too bittersweet for me to handle. I missed it so much.

"No, that's really not how it went down. I kept it to myself for a while. Rebecca was mad about it though."

The silence was still comfortable.

"If we're going to be more open"—he paused, taking a few more gulps of beer—"then I should probably confess something." He made a mock-wincing face.

She raised an eyebrow. "Oh?"

He held up a fist and then snapped his index finger out of the fist and up into the air, saying, "Level up." Still grimacing, embarrassed.

"No way!" she shouted, her jaw dropping. "Who? Where? When?"

"A girl whose name I won't try to pronounce out of respect for her. When my parents dragged me to Italy last spring."

She made an exaggerated, drawn-out gasp. "Last spring? Dude, you beat me to it!" she exclaimed as she fist-bumped his shoulder lightly. "And with a foreigner!"

"Ehemm." He cleared his throat as if he were offended. "Excuse me, why is that so hard to believe? Have you seen me?" He gestured with a flat hand, and made a circle around his face, looking smug.

They laughed so loudly that they probably woke someone up in one of the neighboring houses.

It wound down, and the silence was still comfortable. And stayed that way for a good while.

"I always thought it would be us, though." His voice broke the silence with a bang despite its soft resonance.

My heart skipped a beat as I heard his words. I had forgotten about this part of the conversation. Or maybe I had never remembered it in the first place. By the looks of it, Graduation Me was taken aback too.

"Uhm, what?" she said, followed by an unnecessarily loud nervous laugh.

He sighed heavily. "When we were younger, and I hadn't started thinking about girls *for real*, I always thought you'd be my first." He turned his head and their eyes met. I could tell he was freaking out a little, wondering what her reaction would be.

I remembered now. I remembered hoping it was just the beer talking.

When she didn't respond, he turned away from her and spoke again. "Relax, Slo." He chuckled, staring straight forward. "I'm not confessing some decade-long crush." He finished his beer in one drag, and immediately got busy opening another.

"Thank goodness," she replied, and they burst into laughter again.

Crickets again. And I could have sworn the silence was starting to get contaminated with tension.

She lifted her right leg onto the bench and folded it under the other, turning her whole body to face him. "But why us then?"

He shifted so that he was facing her too, laying his left hand along the back of the bench, his hand inches above where I knew our weathered initials were posted. He had a cool, calm manner about him I hadn't remembered. He was looking down at the beer bottle that rested on his knee, picking at the label with his right thumb.

Without looking up he said, "I don't know, honestly. It was a really long time ago and, like I said, I didn't even really know anything about it. I guess I just thought that it should be with someone I trusted. And you were the only girl I ever imagined trusting."

I couldn't see her face anymore after she turned to face him. I couldn't remember my reaction.

Then he grinned before adding, "You have to admit, the rest of your kind are dragons, Sloane. Even you breathe fire and become a little terrifying sometimes."

She threw her head back, laughing. Leave it to Tom to always find comic relief.

"Shit, Sloane, you're bleeding," he said as she faced him again. He leaned in and examined her forehead, tucking her hair behind her ear.

She flinched as his finger hit a sore spot. He pulled back and her hand replaced his.

"That's nothing," she said, pulling her hand down to assess the amount of blood transferred to her fingers.

"Are you sure you don't want to go and get checked out?"

"Yes. I'm fine, honestly."

"You could have a concussion."

"I'm *fine*."

"Someone needs to cut that guy's balls off," Tom said angrily.

"You know what?" She started laughing, composing herself slightly before finally getting the words out. "That makes *so, much, sense!*" she exclaimed, straightening her back, hitting the back of the bench with a flat palm to the beat of the last three words.

He mustered a, "Huh?" from behind the bottle, not stopping his sip. He swallowed and said, "It makes sense to cut his balls off?"

"No!" She exclaimed, waving a hand, "Well yes, but I'm saying, you know, at this point, I would've probably wanted to lose it with you, too." Her voice was matter-of-fact, and I could glimpse a silly smile on her face.

He brought his bottle down after another gulp as he cough-laughed a couple of times. "What?"

"Oh, relax Tom," she teased. "I'm not confessing some decade old crush. I'm just saying, it would have made sense to have some sort of . . .

arrangement. Like if it hadn't happened before we went off to college, we'd get it over with."

It was his turn to have a fit of laughter. "An arrangement?" he asked between laughs.

"Well what would you have called it?" She sounded a bit uneasy.

"No, no. You're right! It makes sense!"

"*So* much sense."

"Just get it over with." He made a theatrical swoop with his hand, and she found her laugh again.

"Yup!"

"Take the stress out of the equation." Another exaggerated swipe.

"Ugh, the stress!"

"Right?"

The laughter continued comfortably for a while before it smoothed into silence. The silence still held a speck of strain, something brand new poking at its edges. A muffled, far away voice saying, "Everything just changed."

I had only retained this part of the conversation in bits and pieces, probably due to the alcohol. But the memory gaps were filling in fast as I watched it unfold. I knew what she was thinking, and it made me sick to my stomach. I couldn't watch anymore.

I made my way out of the bush away from the trail, and dashed silently down the manicured greenbelt grass, meticulously maintained by the neighborhood's homeowner's association. Their voices faded and I was about to reach a bend in the trail where it would curve out of view from the bench, where I could sneak back through the bushes. But a rustle behind me made me turn around.

Her red hair stood out against the dimly lit, dark green surroundings like flames against the sea.

CHAPTER EIGHTEEN

A HARSH WIND slapped me in the face with the scent of vinegar and roses. I bolted through the bushes, branches and nettles catching on my clothes and scraping against my face. I could hear her gaining on me when my forehead came into contact with something hard. I stumbled back, falling hard against the rocky trailside. Static blurred my eyesight, as I found myself wishing, yearning, *willing* a Slip to wash over me to take me out of there. Not even back to the Present, just anywhere. But it didn't come.

"Where do you think you're going?"

It was her.

I staggered to my feet, wobbling, squinting my eyes to focus. She was somehow in front of me, and she was holding a baseball bat.

Of course, she Stopped and went around me. How stupid was I to try to outrun her?

"Who are you? What do you want from me?" I screamed.

"The fact that you don't know makes it even more important for me to kill you and take back what's mine. You've had it long enough."

"I don't even know who you are. How could I have something that's yours?" I yelled, taking slow steps backward.

"And *I* don't know who the fuck you think *you* are. You're on a need-to-know basis, bitch." Her figure flickered before my eyes. In an instant, she had closed the gap between us with a Stop, and I found myself face-to-face with her, about three feet between us, her bat held high above our heads.

I braced myself for the inevitable pain as a sensation started at my core, tearing through me and out to the edges of my being in a fraction of a second. I fell backward into the tall grass with a painful thud, dirt and pebbles digging into my palms.

I need to Stop.

She charged at me, lunging down to where I lay. I let go of the ground beneath me and placed both hands, instinctively, on her face, digging my nails in. There was no way I could focus enough to be able to execute a Stop. I had to let my body shift from flight to fight mode if I was going to survive this.

She threw the bat to her side and placed her hands around my neck, squeezing. She was too strong despite her haggard appearance. My lungs screamed from lack of oxygen and my muscles burned from exertion as I tried desperately to push her away so that her grip would loosen. But she had the literal upper hand, gravity working in her favor. I was considering giving in, letting myself pass out when something—someone—tackled her from her left.

She grunted as she landed on her right side, a male figure pinning her down by her wrists.

"Oh, hey babe. I'm not in a mood for rough right now; maybe later tonight?" She giggled. She sounded completely unhinged.

"That is *enough*, Alicia," the man growled.

"Eric, honey, it's you who can't get enough of me. Why else would you be hunting me?" Her last word bled into maniacal laughter.

Eric?

I scrambled to my feet and away from them, but as I stood up someone grabbed my elbows from behind and restrained me, tearing at the fabric of my sleeves.

Eric looked in my direction, a pained expression on his face from holding the redhead down, his eyes not showing any signs of recognition as they passed over me.

"Malina, get her out of here!" he screamed.

"What? No!" I shouted.

I noticed that the redhead—Alicia—looked even sicklier than when I had last seen her. She was wearing faded black leggings and a light gray, hooded sweatshirt that looked like it hadn't been washed for a very long time. Despite this, she seemed to have plenty of strength to go around. She writhed and contorted her body until she was able to get one leg free from Eric's weight, lifting it up and jamming her knee into his torso with a nauseating thud. Eric let go of one of her wrists, clutching his lower ribs. Alicia got ahold of the bat again and swung it, hitting him in the shoulder. He fell to the ground, and as soon as he lost contact with her, Alicia was gone.

The person holding me let go, and I slithered to the ground. I looked up and it was indeed Malina, the other Sensor I had seen at the Council meeting. Except her hair was long and pitch-black. She was thinner, younger.

Eric limped over to where we stood. "I told you to get her out of here."

"I wanted to make sure you were okay first," Malina said, her voice cold.

Eric winced and turned to me, his eyes still empty, and frighteningly so. "Forget everything you saw. No one will believe you anyway."

"Uhh—what?" I stuttered.

Malina cut in, "Eric, you should go have that checked out. Jump back and let Julianne take a look at you. I'll meet you there."

Eric narrowed his eyes at her. "Why can't you just—"

"Go. Now." Malina's voice was even icier, if that was possible.

"Close your eyes," he said to me. His nostrils flared and he looked livid. I had never seen him like this before.

"What?" I spat, thoroughly annoyed.

"Are you deaf or something? I said, *close your eyes!*" he snarled, taking a threatening step toward me. As he did, he stepped into the beam of light from the nearest lamppost lining the hiking trail. It flashed across his face to reveal an Eric that I did not know. This Eric had smoother skin, his stubble sparser. He looked even younger than in my visit to him the night before. He seemed scrawnier all around, like he was missing muscle.

"Eric. Chill, man. Don't take it out on the Temp," Malina implored.

Temp? This Eric doesn't know me, either.

Malina placed her hands on my shoulders, gripping tightly at the fabric of my shirt. This seemed to satisfy Eric as he nodded. Malina spun me around, and I knew that was his cue to Jump.

My eyes met Malina's. They were full of concern, contradicting her stern demeanor.

"Girl, what have you gotten yourself into?" she asked.

I didn't know what to say, how much to divulge. I myself wasn't even sure what I had gotten myself into.

"Are you okay? Did she get you?" Malina pressed, surveying me.

"No, I'm fine."

"Okay, well." Malina took a deep breath that she blew into her cheeks before letting it squeeze out through pursed lips. "Eric thinks you're a Temp, but I can Sense you. When are you from? Is this your Present?"

"No, I'm from 2025." My voice was small.

"Yikes, I shouldn't even be talking to you. I'm from 2022."

"I figured."

I was about to ask her how Eric knew this Alicia person, when Malina's face tensed. She swallowed hard. "I'm so sorry," she said, holding up a finger before placing her hand over her mouth. "Excuse me."

She lunged to the side of the trail and threw up in the bushes.

"I'm so sorry," she said again after the last heave.

"Don't worry about it. Are you okay? Your powers new?" I asked innocently.

Malina chuckled, "I wish. Manifestation nausea beats morning sickness any day."

"Oh! Congratulations!" I blurted. I did the math; if she was from the year 2022, it made sense if she was pregnant with the boy I saw with her at Adrian's house.

"Listen, I'll keep your secret. I don't know what Alicia wants with you, and I don't want to know. Whatever mess you've gotten yourself in, you best get yourself out. And don't breathe a word about her to anyone."

Her commands did not leave space for questioning. I swallowed hard. "Okay."

"Can you find your way back from here?" she asked.

"Uhm—" I didn't want to admit that I was actually in a Slip. It would reveal how weak and untamed my powers still were.

I didn't need to; she saw right through me.

"I got you. What's your Present, what's the phase?"

"Uhm—I Jumped from July seventh. I'm not sure of the phase—"

"July 7, 2025? Right before the Buck Moon, all right. No wonder you came all this way. All righty, should be no problem. What time?"

"Right around one a.m., I guess."

Malina grabbed my hand; hers was cold to the touch, and I could feel her bones where they pressed into the webbing between my thumb and index finger. But she let go almost immediately, jerking her hand back, a terrified look on her face.

"What?" I asked in a panicked voice.

"Sorry." She grabbed my hand again, less eagerly this time. "Again, none of my business. I don't want to know."

"Is there something wrong—"

I couldn't finish my question before my eyes shut on me. Her Jump was like a pleasant breeze, like lying in bed while someone lifts and lowers a sheet above you.

THE AFTER HOURS

She let go of my hand as if it were on fire. "All right, my job here is done," she said as soon as the heaviness in my eyelids subsided. "Now listen to me closely. Whatever you do, do not tell anyone you saw me, you hear? Not a single soul. I keep your secret as long as you keep mine."

I had a million questions for her. "But, wait—"

"Stay out of trouble, kid."

She was gone.

༺༻༺༻༺༻

Alicia.

Her name is Alicia. That was something to go off of, at least.

But Eric knows her. Eric in 2022, knew her.

I was already searching my wits away on all my social media platforms on my phone, for any sign of an Alicia, but my battery was dying, and staring at your phone while trying to walk fast was not conducive. I was utterly exhausted, my eyes dry in the nighttime heat. About two blocks away from my house, my phone shut down just as I was opening another app.

She had called him "babe."

Once safely up in my room and after making sure that there wasn't another version of me asleep in my bed—about to Slip—I plugged my phone in, threw my clothes off, and yanked my laptop from my desk before collapsing into bed.

Instead of social media, I typed "Eric Baxter Alicia" into the search bar in my browser. It returned roughly nine million results, but the top one was all I needed.

Alicia Jayne Baxter (née Stoddard) Obituary
January 14, 2003–February 10, 2022.

Alicia was born on January 14, 2003 in Minsk, Belarus. She was adopted by Timothy and Beth Stoddard at the age of two, and spent the rest of her life living in sunny California. An only child and apple of her parents' eyes, Alicia excelled in school and extracurriculars. She started playing piano in kindergarten, was on the varsity gymnastics team, participated in color guard, and was an avid theater fan.

Alicia was adored by friends and family, and found love at a very young age in her high school sweetheart, Eric Carson Baxter. They wed in a private ceremony last fall.

Alicia's memorial service will be held at the Woodoaks Church and Cemetery at 11 a.m. on Friday, March 18. In lieu of flowers, please consider donating in Alicia's name to Children's Hospital Los Angeles or the UCLA Comprehensive Cancer Research Center.

"Holy fucking shit."

CHAPTER NINETEEN

I HAD DEVOURED every detail about Alicia Baxter that was easily discoverable on the internet. There wasn't much. More memorial pages with the same stories. The same three photos of her used over and over. One from a yearbook, one of Alicia in a color guard uniform, and one of her and Eric on their wedding day.

He could have at least told me that his ex-wife was also Lunai.

Then, I proceeded to tear through Eric's copy of the Horolog for hours into the night, despite my exhaustion. I contemplated Stopping first to keep reading, in order to have hours left in the night to sleep. But I decided against it, as I knew there were more important things to age myself for by completing them in a Stop. Like college coursework, come fall.

I pushed the thought of the rapidly approaching school year off to the side, guilt scraping at my insides.

The Horolog held so much information that I was hungry for—I felt like I couldn't devour it fast enough. I focused on the parts that felt most important to know right away, so I didn't read in order or take notes. I knew I probably wouldn't retain a lot of it.

I figured I could Stop to sleep, but I soon reconsidered that idea when I read one of the first technical Lunai rules.

Frustration pulled at me as this rule was yet another thing I felt like Adrian should have conveyed already, and that was to never, ever, fall asleep in a Stop.

You were almost guaranteed to Slip once you hit REM sleep, and it often had disastrous consequences, sending Lunai as far back as the Jurassic era. Or forward into the Future, but the book didn't go into any detail on those incidents.

One section in particular that piqued my interest:.

To Strip a Lunai of their Power of Manipulation

In extreme cases, a discontinuation is needed in a heritage line without ending the life of a Lunai and transferring those powers onward. Temporal electroshock therapy, aimed at the dorsolateral prefrontal cortex, has been proven successful for the purpose of this. The Stripping Ritual can be performed at any lunation, but must happen outdoors, preferably at a New Moon for maximum results. Multiple sessions may be needed.

It seemed almost too simple. There had to be a catch.

I had no idea how long I stayed up reading. I didn't even remember falling asleep, and I was borderline enraged as my groggy voice answered the phone around seven the next morning after I had silenced it three times already and whoever was calling wouldn't let up.

"Hello?"

"Hey, you."

His voice made me perk up. I knew this Eric was my Present Eric. Not one of the other two versions of him whom I had last interacted with. But what happened two nights ago was now a shared memory of ours, one I hadn't known about. I was finally catching up. I blushed thinking about all the memories he may have that were like that night I Jumped to, while I had been oblivious, thinking he was just my coworker.

"Everything okay?" I asked, reflexively. I kicked myself, remembering I was supposed to be mad at this Eric.

"Finally you pick up. Council meeting at noon. I thought maybe you'd like to grab brunch with me before we go? I'll come up with an excuse for us at work." I could hear his anticipatory smile through the phone.

I cleared my throat, getting rid of some of the raspiness.

"Oh, sorry, did I wake you?" he added quickly.

I steeled myself, willing my voice to come out as stiff and authoritative as possible. "No, no absolutely not. I was—I didn't have my phone with me."

"I know your sleepy voice," he said, his own voice buttery.

I didn't want him to feel comfortable speaking to me that way. Yet, I loved that he knew.

"That's unfair," I protested.

"Sorry." He paused, "It's not been easy for me either, acting like I don't know you."

"Mhm."

"But that's the life of a Lunai, I guess . . ." he said, the spark gone from his voice. "Hey, is everything okay? You sound . . . off."

"Yeah I don't think brunch would be a good idea right now. I'll see you at Adrian's." I managed to get the words out without my voice breaking, but as soon as I hung up, a guttural sob escaped me. I pulled my comforter over my head and buried my face in my pillow, clutching my ribs as if someone had kicked me repeatedly.

I had told him what the person who attacked me at the coffee shop looked like. I had every reason to believe he knew it was her. His ex-wife.

His dead ex-wife.

How could have I let myself fall for this guy?

৩৩৩৩৩৩

I was beyond exhausted as I parked my car around the corner from Adrian's house right before noon. I struggled with the Stop. My beach just didn't want to come to me. The day was gloomy and muggy, just about the opposite of my transitional state. I finally mustered up the brain bandwidth needed to conjure it, but the Stop was extremely painful. Wincing as my eyes fluttered open, I then walked to the house in Stopped time and entered.

The atmosphere was heavy, even in Stopped time. A handful of Lunai stood waiting for the elevator, one of them Jules. Standing awkwardly in the house's foyer, I called time back, the Start zooming through me with insolent force.

This must be the place.

The voice suddenly crept into my head without me even trying, and the Start washed over me, smoother than it ever had before.

"New girl!" she exclaimed as I appeared. Her enthusiasm pierced the heaviness that draped over the hallway, and one of the middle-aged women in the group rolled her eyes.

"Hi, Jules," I said, walking the few steps from where I had Started, joining them.

Jules was laughing to herself. "Man did you pick a time to join us. Bizarre stuff going on."

"Do we even know what this is about?" another woman asked as we filed into the elevator.

"You didn't hear?" Jules toned it down a bit. "Charlie's dead."

The group gasped in collective shock.

"*No—*" a guy at the back of the elevator said. He looked to be in his midthirties. But then again, he was Lunai. He might have been twenty-five with a lot of After Hours.

"So sad," Jules said, although her voice didn't really convey the content of her words. It was more like a matter-of-fact observation.

Once down in the Sanctuary, Jules insisted I come sit with her in the front row.

"So, have you figured out who died yet? Who you got your powers from, I mean," she leaned in and whispered in my right ear once we were settled.

I cleared my throat and shifted in my seat. "Uhm, no."

I have way more important shit to deal with.

"Damn this is juicy. We've never had anyone with unknown lineage before. I'll give it a couple more weeks. Lunai deaths never go unnoticed. Maybe Malina can help you; she's good at lineage stuff."

She was starting to really get on my nerves. I regretted agreeing to sit with her. I myself was perplexed enough as to who could've left me their powers without her constant badgering.

"Hey, did I miss anything?" Eric's voice sounded from my left. He sat in the empty seat next to me. I didn't acknowledge him.

"Eric!" Jules exclaimed, dragging out the word, "What is *up* dude? When are we going to catch up?" She was leaning over me to get Eric's attention, almost as if I wasn't there.

"Hi, Jules. Nice to see you," he said dryly.

Maybe I wasn't the only one she irritated.

Once convinced he managed to dismiss Jules, Eric leaned in and whispered to me, "Hey, can we talk? After?"

I didn't give him the satisfaction of looking at him, making sure he wasn't even in my peripheral vision. "I need to get to the office; I didn't go in this morning," I said without looking at him. This was partially true. I hadn't been to the office that morning, but I didn't exactly need to go in. I wasn't sure whether Eric knew the lax attendance requirements that were part of the deal with my father. But I wasn't about to tell him.

"Oh, all right. I'll catch up with you later then," he said, hurt and confusion dripping from his words. It took everything in me to keep from glancing at him.

He left his seat without another word.

A few horrendous minutes of biting back tears later, the hall was nearly full, filled with ambient sounds from varyingly distressed conversations happening throughout it.

Jules leaned in after a moment and whispered in my ear, "What is up with that Eric guy? Jeez."

I shot her a wide-eyed glance.

She kept rambling. "I've tried so hard with that guy. Like, *threw* myself at him once. He wouldn't budge. It's always the hot ones." She leaned in even closer before adding, "But then again, I hear he likes them older." She nodded in Malina's direction, catching her eye and sending her a big smile and wave, both of which Malina returned.

My blood boiled. I managed a chuckle and sent Jules a polite smile, just as Adrian emerged from one of the rooms off the side of the hall. He looked like he hadn't slept much either.

"Fellow Wardens," he said, clapping his hands together once. Everyone settled within seconds, but not everyone sat down. Some stood toward the back of the crowd, most with arms crossed, attention on Adrian as if they knew to brace for bad news.

"Thank you for assembling on such short notice, again. I regret to have to bring you some more dreadful news," he began. The crowd tensed. "Five more members of our wonderful community have been found murdered. Our brother in the FBI, Theo Adair, has started a task force for the case preemptively, before Temps in the police start piecing things together, in order to steer the investigation. He has promised to keep us updated, and is fairly certain he has a lead to the group responsible for the killings. The Conservatory's suspicions seem to have been correct; it is highly likely there has been a leak, and that multiple Temps are now aware of our existence. Theo has been able to pinpoint one group of Temps with a questionable past; most of them have been branded as conspiracy theorists by Temps, but we will still be digging into them further."

"Who died? Anyone from here?" a woman on the opposite side of the hall from where I was sitting asked as she looked at those around her.

THE AFTER HOURS

Adrian took a deep breath, his knuckles white where he clasped the dais.

"Charlie Stanford."

The crowd burst into outrage, some yelling, some crying. All looked terrified.

"We have to do something!" a female voice yelled from the back of the room.

"D—Do we know who caused the leak?" a man in the row behind me stuttered nervously.

"Why hasn't the Consul said anything?" another voice growled angrily.

Adrian clapped his hands again, just once. The wrath emanating from the Lunai dissipated into disapproving murmurs, letting Adrian have the floor.

"Annika Hail, San Diego. Yara Caldwell, San Diego. Adelle Shepherd, Encinitas. Jordana Britton, Temecula." Adrian read up the names and locations of the murdered with a pain-stricken face before adding, "May their powers find a peaceful transition, and may the Pattern keep."

"May the Pattern keep." The collective grumble rang throughout the Sanctuary.

"Wait. It's getting really localized. All here in SoCal. And didn't Charlie live in Orange County?" Jules asked, and for the first time since I met her, I could hear a hint of apprehension in her voice.

"San Juan Capistrano," the man with the ambiguous age from the elevator responded.

"That's super close to San Diego. Do we think the killers are targeting someone specific? They must still be in the area." Eric, now sitting next to Malina, spoke with a calm, clinical rhythm.

An infuriating wave of guilt and shame surged through me at the sound of his voice.

"We don't know anything yet. But you are correct; it does look like the killer, or killers, have concentrated their efforts here." The tension flitting through the crowd was palpable as Adrian spoke.

"Did Charlie have a transition agreement?" the man from the elevator spoke again.

"His son. We are working hard to track him down. We are unsure whether Charlie's wife knew about us; she's a Temp."

"She should know. I can try and get a hold of them, if you want." The man's voice was drenched with grief. "I'm friends with the family and live pretty close."

"Thank you so much, Pablo." Adrian's voice was soothing. "We must prepare for an influx of new Wardens. I've requested support from a couple Sensors from the Bay Area Council. They should be here in the next few days. In any case, and just as a precaution, I am invoking a mandatory Sanctuary stay for the Los Angeles Council through the weekend. You will find your room and task assignments on the flyer Madeline is handing out. Please come see me if you have any questions about the assignments. You can go home and get what you need, but the Consul has set a curfew of six o'clock. And thank you, Eric and Malina, for helping us organize so quickly and moving furniture around. Sanctuary business takes more time than most because you can't Stop."

Adrian stepped down from the dais, concluding his speaking, and the crowd dispersed into smaller clusters, conversing in hushed, concerned tones. I promptly stood up and made my way over to Maddie, whom I spotted toward the back of the room, handing out light blue papers to everyone in attendance.

"Hi Sloane!" Maddie chimed when she saw me.

"Hey. I gotta go. Can I grab one of those?" I pointed to the stack in her hands.

"Of course," she said, handing me one.

I scanned to find my name, my heart lurching uncomfortably as I spotted it, along with the name below it.

Sloane Becker Room 413 Task: Dishes
Eric Baxter Room 414 Task: Dishes

The rest of the list had tasks such as dinner preparation, trash collection, floor sweeping, hall cleanup, lookout duty.

"Can I switch?" I asked, following Maddie around as she continued her disbursement.

"Room or task?" she replied.

"Uhm... both? Preferably."

Maddie glanced at the paper. "Why? We put you with Eric—"

I surprised myself how fast I was able to come up with a lie. "I just hate doing dishes." I gave her an impatient look. "So can I switch or not?"

"I'll talk to Dad." She turned away to begin handouts in the next huddle of people, but quickly turned back and grabbed my arm, fear shining in her big blue eyes as she added, "And Sloane? Hurry back, please."

༄༅༄༅༄༅

"Sloane, wait up!" A voice from behind me echoed down the hall after me, where I was briskly power walking to the elevator.

I didn't stop.

"Sloane!" I heard his footsteps turn into a jog.

I pressed the button to summon the elevator just as he reached me and placed a hand on my shoulder. I spun to face him, and swung my arm at his, sending it flying off me.

"Don't touch me," I snapped.

"Slo— What the heck?"

I stayed silent as I boarded the cab, Eric following my every move. I acted as if he wasn't there the whole way up, staring directly at the door.

"Please talk to me," he pleaded.

I exited the elevator, turned to the right, and just as I was about to reach the front door of the house, I came to a halt. I turned my head to see behind me, shooting Eric a glare before closing my eyes deliberately, making sure he could see what I was doing. He tried to grab my hand again, but I was too quick.

Beach-sunset-fire-ember-numbness-thunder.
This must be the place.

I took in the sight of him frozen, reaching to me, his hand inches away from mine, and proceeded out the door.

CHAPTER TWENTY

Sloan: Rebecca, can i ask you a favor?
Rebecca: Well well well. The prodigal daughter returns.
Sloan: Can I tell my mom I'm staying at your place tonight?
Rebecca: ???
Rebecca: I'm not in town?
Sloan: She doesn't know that
Rebecca: She will if she talks to my mom
Sloan: That's a risk I'll have to take.
Sloan: I just need an excuse.
Sloan: Please?
Rebecca: Then why do you even need to ask me?
Sloan: . . .
Sloan: Guess I don't
Rebecca: Please don't tell me you're seeing Dylan.
Sloan: Promise

Rebecca: Okay . . .
Rebecca: Where are you going?
Sloan: Gonna stay with some friends
Rebecca: What friends?
Rebecca: Why do I not know these people?
Rebecca: Is this why you've been ghosting me?
Rebecca: Hello?
Sloan: Friends from work
Rebecca: OMG. Eric???

Despite the gnawing guilt in my stomach over using Rebecca as my alibi, I let the conversation drop there.

When I arrived back at the Sanctuary, deliberately not until right before six o'clock, the main hall was fuller than I had left it, many people having brought along their kids or pets, and a ton of luggage. The space was bustling: groups of Lunai were rearranging tables, laying out stacks of plates and beverage bottles. A large white projection screen had been set up on the front platform behind the dais, and two men were busy getting the projector set up.

I spotted Maddie quickly among the group of kids who had gathered in the TV area off to the side, her white-blond hair sticking out against a sea of more pigmented shades.

"Reporting for duty," I said as I reached the group, still carrying my heavy duffel bag, weighed down by my lavender journal, my laptop, and Eric's Horolog.

"Oh hey, Slo," Maddie said in a cool voice. "Everyone, this is Sloane, our newest Warden. I rescued her from her first Slip." She was playing it cool in front of the other kids, but I could tell she was bursting with pride at the fact.

The kids stared at me as if I were an alien; only a few piped their hellos. I wondered which ones actually had powers and which ones were Temps accompanying their Lunai parents.

"Were you able to switch me?" I asked, taking my eyes off the kids.

"Oh!" She jumped to her feet. "Yes. Yeah. Not the room though. But I put you on lookout."

"Lookout? Are you sure I'm the best fit for that?"

She waved her hand dismissively. "Psh, it's no biggie. Not like anyone is gonna come here."

"Does that mean I have to stay up all night? I had a late-night last night and I'm really tired."

"No, you take turns, two at a time. Don't worry so much, Sloane!" Maddie turned back to the congregation by the TV, continuing whatever story she had been telling the wide-eyed kids.

I made my way up the tight spiral staircase to the fourth, and highest, level of balconies that flanked the grand hall, trying not to think about how high up I was. I made my way as fast as I could down the hall, pressing as much as I could up against the wall and away from the railing, which felt way too short to be safe. Just thinking about the distance down to the main level made me dizzy. Rooms 413 and 414 were next to each other.

Room 413 had white walls, a light-colored wood floor, and white baseboards. A fluffy rug began under the bed and filled up most of the middle of the room. The bed was pushed to the left side, with a desk and chair along the right wall. Frames with what looked like stock photos of moonlit night skies hung above the bed. A small nightstand stood next to the head of the bed, a small lamp flanking an outdated digital alarm clock, black with big, square, shining red letters stating 06:03.

I closed the door behind me, grimacing at the fact that it didn't have a lock, and proceeded to dump my duffel bag on the bedspread and lie down, catching my breath from hauling it up the stairs. I must have been even more exhausted than I realized. Or maybe it was the stillness of being in the Sanctuary, but I passed out within minutes.

When I woke up to a knock at my door and glanced at the clock which read 09:58, realizing I had missed dinner, I was glad. One less opportunity to run into Eric.

"Becker? Your turn for lookout. Two minutes." The face of a man I had never seen before appeared in the doorway, along with the back of a clipboard. He was small and mousy-looking, the clipboard almost too big for him.

"Coming. Coming," I replied, embarrassed that he had caught me sleeping.

"Cool. I'm Greg by the way."

"Hi Greg. Sloane."

"I know. Your lookout partner is already upstairs." He turned to leave.

"Hey, Greg! Who—?" I called after him, wanting to ask who I was paired with, but he was already gone.

※※※※※

The nap had proved surprisingly restorative, but the weight of my powers settling back into my veins was heavier than ever as I made my ascent up to the house above. But something else was bothering me, and I didn't know what it was until I turned the corner into the living room, where Eric sat on the couch with Malina and Victor. They were having a heated yet quiet discussion. I cleared my throat to announce my presence. Malina was first to notice me, glancing over as she stood up, followed by Victor.

"We'll see if we can get an exception from curfew to go get Charlie's son right away. It shouldn't take long if he is where his mom said he'd be and where Malina is Sensing him," Victor said, taking slow steps toward where I stood, gearing up to leave.

"Sounds good," Eric said, placing both hands on his knees before standing up.

"I just have to go check if someone can keep an eye on Darius. I'll be right back." Malina directed her words to Victor.

"I'll go chat with Adrian," Victor responded, and left.

"Hi, I don't believe we've met. I'm Malina," she said as she turned her back to Eric to face me, and stuck her hand out.

I hesitantly reached for it, remembering what had happened when she first touched me in my Slip.

"Sloane. Pleasure," I said stiffly as I shook her hand.

She didn't flinch at the contact, but she did squeeze my hand so tightly I thought she was trying to break it. Her eyes bored into mine as she remarked, "Very nice to meet you, Sloane."

She let go and disappeared down the hall. It took everything in me to hide from Eric how much my hand hurt.

"Howdy, partner."

I cringed at his words.

"I think there's been a mistake. I asked to switch—"

"And I switched right along with you. Didn't want to do dishes anyway." He shot me a small smile, testing the waters.

I let out an audible sigh and rolled my eyes at him. "Learn to take a hint."

"What is going on with you?" he asked frantically, his voice breaking in the middle of the sentence. His expression dripped with hurt, and I found myself wishing he were angry instead.

Still, I shot him an incredulous scowl before walking away, heading to the kitchen. It didn't do much since he followed me like a puppy.

Adrian and Victor were finishing up a conversation when I arrived.

"The Consul says it's fine. Getting him here is more important, especially since he may have been exposed." Adrian was reading from his phone. He added, "It can't be easy losing your father in such a brutal manner and then starting to manifest right away."

"Great. Thanks, Adrian." Victor gave me a nod before heading back to the front hall.

"Is there coffee?" I asked Adrian, ignoring Eric.

"Of course. Always," he chuckled. He reached into the cupboard for a mug. "Cream?"

"I'd also like to request another switch please," I said, deadpan.

Adrian looked back and forth between Eric and me.

"Sorry, Sloane, I'm not sure I know what you're talking about," Adrian said.

"Maddie said she asked you. To switch my task. I don't want this one, I'd like to go back to dishwashing."

Eric groaned, reaching for the fridge to grab the cream. He was more at home here than I knew.

"I suspect this has less to do with the task at hand than it does the two of you. Trouble in paradise?" His voice was appropriately concerned, but I thought I caught a glimpse of amusement in his eyes.

I looked at Eric, horrified.

"He knows, Sloane. Of course he knows," Eric explained in response, shrugging.

"About—?"

"About us."

"I've known for a while, actually." Adrian wasn't hiding his amusement anymore.

I closed my eyes and pinched the bridge of my nose as I barked, "I am so sick of this. Could the two of you please tell me when I will go back to being the person who knows the most about myself? Because right now it seems like I know the least. Hmm?"

Adrian's eyes went wide, avoiding my gaze and clamping his lips as he handed me my mug. He left the room silently as he mouthed something to Eric, thinking I wouldn't notice. Which made me even more furious.

Once we were alone again, Eric handed me the creamer. I begrudgingly snatched it from his hands.

"So... wanna talk about it?" He reached into the same cupboard Adrian had and pulled out another mug.

"Nope." I poured way too much creamer into my coffee.

"Wanna talk about anything else?"

"Like what? Why do you want to talk so bad? So you can spew more lies?"

He looked genuinely confused. Pain shone from his eyes as he ran both hands halfway through his hair, stopping at the nape of his neck. He glanced around, as if looking for an answer. He exhaled loudly and let his hands drop to his sides.

Before Eric could formulate a response, Greg, who I learned was the stay's self-proclaimed task coordinator, poked his head into the kitchen and asked if someone had shown us the armory. I tensed at the thought of needing weapons—I had taken Maddie's word at face value for the lookout being "no biggie"—but the armory turned out not to be as formal as it sounded. The house's coat closet, located under the stairs that led to the second floor, had a wall of fairly nonthreatening-looking gadgets hidden behind a row of coats. From rope, baseball bats, pepper spray, and a couple innocent-enough-looking knives to a single crossbow that looked as if it had never been used, none of the contents surprised or worried me. Except the far end of the closet, where the floor to ceiling height reached its highest point. The whole wall was covered in tasers.

The tasers tugged at something in my mind. I felt like I was experiencing a glitch in the matrix, the Baader-Meinhof phenomenon. Like I had seen a taser somewhere recently and now I was seeing them everywhere. I racked my brain. I knew I hadn't been watching any TV where I could possibly have seen one lately. Neil kept one in his bug-out bag and had taught Justin and me how to work it in case of a home invasion, but that was years ago, and I knew better than to dig around in his stockpile.

When I remembered what I was connecting it to, it wasn't so much a lightbulb as a lightning bolt that hit my brain.

Temporal electroshock therapy, aimed at the dorsolateral prefrontal cortex, has been proven successful for the purpose of this.

The Stripping Ritual. It didn't mention tasers, but it spoke of electroshock therapy used by Temps. The tasers in the closet must've been for that.

"Good to know. Thanks so much, Greg," Eric told him as he finished his very short tour. His voice sounded like the one he used at work. Greg shuffled into the elevator cab, not looking up from his clipboard.

I stalked into the living room and sat down with my coffee in a green velvet armchair situated by a paned bay window. I kept my eyes firmly on the front yard, blinking away tears and grinding my teeth against the overwhelm threatening to consume me. I could see Eric's reflection in the panes as he inched his way into the room.

"Sloane?" My name didn't sound that good in anyone else's voice.

I clamped my lips shut, my gaze locked on the glass.

"*Sloane*," he begged.

I was too angry, too tired, and too impatient to keep my wall up. I needed answers. I snapped my head in his direction, letting him see me. All of me. Then, I stiffened my features, careful to keep the most neutral expression I could. Then I said the last word he wanted to hear out of my mouth. I took care to pronounce it sharply, deliberately, my emphasis nearly adding a syllable to it.

"Alicia."

And I saw him. I saw him break. His jaw went slack, then he took a breath and squeezed his eyes shut for just a second. When he released the breath and opened his eyes, his shoulders slumped and he made his way over to my chair, bending down in front of me. I could tell he wanted to reach out and touch me, but he didn't dare. Instead, he dug his fingers into the fabric of the armchair.

I peered down my nose at him, letting my disgust poison my words. "You told me you were a widower. You didn't tell me about *her*. How long have you known that it was her that day at the coffee shop?"

Eric's tanned skin went pale. I knew he knew.

"Sloane, I had to protect you—"

"Protect me how?" I boomed. "She nearly *killed* me Eric! On multiple occasions! In what world is it okay to not tell someone you're involved with that your crazy *dead* ex-wife is running around in the Present making Jumps from over three years ago? Huh? You could've at least told me she was Lunai once I knew about everything."

"She's— You saw her again?" Eric stuttered.

"I didn't just see her. She nearly bludgeoned me to death with a baseball bat last night."

Eric had kept his eyes down while I went off on him, but something piqued his interest. "Baseball bat?" he asked, his eyes lifting to meet mine.

"Yeah?" I snarled.

He stood up hastily, pacing. "On a hiking trail up by where you live?" He placed his clasped palms on top of his head, licking his lips nervously.

"Yes?" I crossed my arms, not bothering to conceal my impatience. He obviously knew which moment I was talking about. I knew he hadn't recognized me then, but I wasn't going to help him figure it out.

"Oh my god, that *was* you." Eric stood up and started pacing back and forth across the room, avoiding eye contact.

"Yeah. That was me," I snapped.

"Sloane, listen." His hands found his temples, illustrating his helplessness. "You cannot tell Adrian what you saw. He doesn't know about my past and I need to keep it that way. Okay?"

"What is with all this secrecy? Aren't we supposed to trust Adrian with all Lunai matters?"

"Yes, but babe—" he pleaded, coming back to a kneeling position in front of me.

I shot up, stepping right past him and putting space between us. "Don't fucking 'babe' me. Who do you think you are?"

Eric let out a groan and covered his eyes as he stood up to face me. "Sorry. I'm so sorry. That was douchey. I'm sorry. I'm just so used to calling you that."

"I don't care. You don't get to lie to me about something this monumental and then speak to me like that." I didn't know where the confidence was coming from. It was probably something I had wished I had been able to say to Dylan, now finally being directed somewhere.

"Sloane, please—"

"How could you not tell me about her? What else have you been keeping from me?"

Eric collapsed onto the couch, scrubbing his face with a frustrated moan.

"So Adrian doesn't know?" I asked, my tone harsh. But not harsh enough.

"No, and it needs to stay that way."

"Why?"

"I can't tell you, Sloane. I'm sorry."

I stormed out into the entryway. Eric came right after me as he realized I was leaving. I slammed the front door behind me, but he caught it. It had started raining, but I didn't care. I charged into the downpour.

Eric caught my hand halfway down the path. "Sloane, please. Okay, I'll tell you everything. I promise."

I spun to look at him, droplets furiously showering my face, but didn't say anything. Just glared.

Eric let out a heavy breath, letting go of my hand and averting his gaze before he began in a shaky voice, "We were together in high school, and then she became really sick. Like immensely sick. She was diagnosed with multiple types of cancer, autoimmune disorders, neurological issues, degenerative diseases, you name it. We were still in high school. Her dying wish was to get married. So I married her." Eric's brow furrowed as he closed his eyes. He scrubbed his face with one hand and let his cheeks puff out as he exhaled, and I couldn't tell if the retelling pained him or angered him.

"I was nineteen, she was eighteen. She was never actually my *wife*. She never even left the hospital after our wedding, and she died three months later."

While his story tugged at my heart strings, I was determined to keep a straight face. When I didn't respond, he continued.

"She had lost her mind toward the end. I couldn't even stand to be in a room with her. She would zone out, and come to with all these stories that made absolutely no sense. She was convinced she would live forever. She told me we would be together forever, and she would never let me go. Little did I know, she meant what she was saying."

"So, are you?" I chided.

"Am I what?"

The wind picked up and despite the muggy, thick air, the rain made me shiver.

"Not you. You and Alicia. Are you still together?" I realized I was being irrational. But nothing would have surprised me at this point.

"No!" Eric exclaimed angrily, his nostrils flaring. "Of course not. Fuck!"

"So what does this have to do with me? Why am I being dragged into this mess?" My voice sounded more pleading than I had intended.

Eric gave the house behind him a furtive glance before lowering his voice. "She was the one I inherited my powers from. After she died, I thought maybe what had made her sick had been contagious after all, and I had caught it from her. But they were just my manifestation symptoms. Then she visited me, from the Past, and told me all about it and how she had already set our whole life up, and we'd be together forever. She had all these plans for how I was supposed to Jump back to see her, and she would Jump forward to be with me."

My heart raced, making my skin sizzle under the pelting raindrops. None of this could be true.

"But— You can't do that. Jumping into the Future like that—"

"I know." I had never seen Eric look as defeated as he did right then. Not even in my Slip the night before, when he was in a Future Jump, fighting Alicia.

"Can we sit down? Please?" He beckoned to the porch. My clothes were nearly soaked through at this point, so I reluctantly followed him to sit on the steps, shielded from the rain.

Eric glanced at the house again, double checking the door and the windows before speaking. He ran his hands through his wet hair nervously. I mentally scolded myself for noticing how handsome it looked, sopping wet and swept to the side.

Eric continued in a whisper barely audible over the gaining momentum of the storm around us. "Alicia was never trained. She didn't know about the Warden Laws. She's not in any Horolog."

My eyes went wide.

"Adrian doesn't know the truth about whom I inherited my powers from. And it needs to stay that way. I did a lot of messed up things before I met Adrian and was recorded in the Horolog and learned the Laws."

"What kind of messed up things?" I asked, my voice barely a squeak. I found myself wishing his indiscretion wasn't something I couldn't live with. I wanted so badly to trust him.

"Everything I did, I did to stop Alicia. She was messing up my life. She honestly thought that even though she was dead in my Present that she could just show up and live her life with me. When I wasn't showing up for the Jumps she had planned out for me—she became unhinged. But I had no idea how to stop her, since she did all of this before she died.

"So I did anything I could. Each time she came to see me became more and more dangerous. I never knew which version of her I would get. The healthy one from when we first got together, or the deranged sick one who was incoherent and unpredictable and had completely lost a grip on her own chronology. I'd come out of class, and she'd follow me around campus like nothing ever happened—like her death hadn't happened. One time she even showed up barefoot in a hospital gown, IV punctures bleeding and electrode wires dangling. She couldn't understand why I wouldn't have lunch with her. She became more and more obsessive, the more I refused to act as if this was normal.

"It started out as small-time sabotage, using her powers to screw up my life. Stealing papers I had already turned in, causing me to fail classes. She just wanted my attention. One time, I came home to an empty apartment. She said that if I didn't want to let her live with me then I didn't deserve to live anywhere. It escalated from there to the point where she was convinced that I was no longer worthy of her powers, and needed to give them back to her. So that she could live forever."

I gasped and inadvertently placed my hand on Eric's arm. I thought about pulling back, but I didn't want to. As mad as I was, my heart was still breaking for him. "She was trying to kill you?"

THE AFTER HOURS

Eric shot me a sideways glance, pain tangible in his features. He stared back out through the rain and into the street before continuing, "It turned into a hunt, and I'm not sure which one of us was hunting who. It's not like I could kill her. She was already dead."

He crossed his arms and looked away from me for a moment, regaining his composure before continuing, "When I finally met Adrian, I learned about the effects all of that Jumping has on you, and I put two and two together. I knew she had done this to herself. By constantly Jumping into the Future to be with me, she had made herself sick. She killed herself trying to control her life."

The sky shook with thunder. I pondered if maybe he was the person I needed to stay away from in order to get my life back on track. We seemed forever destined to conjure storms.

"Please come inside, Sloane. It's dangerous out here. And not just because of the storm." He stood up and held a hand out to me. I looked up at him out of the corner of my eye.

His normally bright green eyes were a dark shade of sage, with circles forming underneath them that I had never noticed before. I wanted so badly to trust him. Despite having thawed considerably, I still wasn't convinced I could.

Too bad my body was betraying my conviction in every way possible. I wanted nothing more than to fall into his arms and apologize for making him relive his trauma.

But the problem was, it was becoming my trauma, too. I let him help me up, but quickly let go of his hand and led the way back inside.

Eric shivered as he sat down on the couch in the living room. He grabbed his coffee cup and warmed his fingers on it. I settled back into the armchair, deliberately keeping some distance between us.

"You have to believe me Sloane. I haven't seen her in my Present in years. I thought she was done. The last few times I saw her she had grown so frail, I knew she was close to death in her Present. She had completely lost her Present by the way. Doubling up on After Hours to the point where she didn't even detect time passing anymore. It was horrendous. Eventually, she stopped showing up. I figured she had literally, and physically, run out of time, and that all of her Jumps were finally over. Until you told me what happened in the coffee shop that day." He shot me a pained, apologetic glance.

"But I refused to believe it was her. She was too weak toward the end. She couldn't put anyone into a chokehold like you described even if she mustered all her strength. I don't know what Present this version of her is from. But I am so, so sorry that she found out who you are. She always threatened to do this, but like I said, I thought she had run out of time."

"Threatened to do what?" I asked with a puzzled look.

"Well, her main reason for continuing to Jump and see me after she was dead in my Present, was because she didn't want me to move on. She said she would kill any girl who tried to come between us. She just truly believed in her heart that if she continued to Jump into the Future past her death, we would stay married as if nothing happened."

"And did she? Kill someone?" I avoided his gaze. I didn't really want to know the answer.

"She always talked a big talk. But I don't know if she would be capable of actually killing someone." Eric's eyes met mine for a split second before he turned his gaze back out the window and into the street, through the torrent and the thrashing tree branches. "But— I hadn't dated anyone since her, for fear that she might do this. But when I met you, I thought you would be safe, because you were coming from the Future."

The realization that someone could kill me during Stopped time and I couldn't do anything to prevent it—I wouldn't even know it was happening—terrified me.

"This may be a stupid question..." I paused, feeling just that, ignorant. "But why doesn't she just Stop and kill whoever she wants to kill? It seems too easy."

Eric shrugged. "In theory, she could. But I guess she just has so many After Hours stacked that she maybe can't handle Stopping within a Jump? I don't know."

"Eric, we have to tell Adrian. He can help us. We can bring her to the Sanctuary to disarm her—"

"No." He grabbed my hands in his and turned to face me, his expression a mix of ferocity and panic. "Sloane. You cannot under any circumstance tell anyone about her. She is—was—whatever—unregistered. Rogue. Has Adrian not told you?"

I shook my head, apprehension clouding my thoughts.

"That's . . ." Eric trailed off, letting go of my hands as he glanced in the direction of the dining room. I wondered if that's where he, too, had received most of his training, like I had up until then. He looked pensive and slightly bewildered, as if he were trying to recall something. A few times, he opened his mouth as if to say something, but each time it was like he talked himself out of it.

When he finally spoke, his demeanor shifted as he stated, matter-of-factly, "They were called the Tellurian, at least by the original Lunai Councils. Tellurian, because they denounced the need to connect to the moon. They considered themselves firmly belonging to the Earth because they did not need to rely on moon phases to amplify their powers. They also did not want to adhere to the Lunai Laws. They used to wreak havoc with their powers—causing wars, genocides, natural disasters, torturing Temps. They used their powers for financial gain, relentlessly Jumping to the Future, manipulating stocks, getting winning lottery numbers, even influencing some election outcomes by simply manipulating ballots in Stops." He caught his breath, his recount of the story seeming to have swept him away. He recomposed himself, shifting to a grave tone. "They were a different breed of Lunai. Something about how their powers were passed along early on. The more powerful they got, the more power hungry they were. They had no regard for human life, and believed that Lunai powers should only be given to those deserving of them. In order to eventually reveal their existence—and become a superior human breed."

I took in what Eric was saying, annoyed that Adrian hadn't bothered sharing this with me. This seemed like Lunai History 101.

Maybe I was just not there yet. I had let it get to my head, thinking I was invincible already with the little information I had. When, in fact, I knew nothing. I was still just a weak newbie.

When I didn't react, frankly, because I was having a hard time processing all of this, Eric continued, "They were wiped out around the middle of last century, or at least that's what the Conservatory says. The Conservatory was established to regain control over the Lunai population after the Tellurian were defeated. Register, train, regulate. I have no idea who Alicia got her powers from, but they were *strong*. She's strong. She was adopted from an Eastern European country when she was a baby, with no records of who her birth parents were. She told me she had had her powers as long as she could remember."

He paused, his eyes boring into mine, begging me for some sort of reaction. When I didn't give in, he pressed, "You have to let me handle this, Sloane. I will handle it. I won't let anything happen to you."

It took everything in me to not cave in at his words. Instead, I pivoted. "Belarus."

Eric narrowed his eyes. "Yeah. Belarus. How—?"

"I found her obituary, Eric Carson Baxter."

Eric let out a small mirthless laugh. "Guess I haven't told this version of you what the C stands for."

"But I don't understand. If having these rogue powers is forbidden, why wouldn't that help us plead our case to Adrian?"

"Because, Sloane." He let out a long breath as if bracing himself. When he continued, his voice was shaky. "I've got her powers. They would kill me."

CHAPTER TWENTY-ONE

I WILLED MY voice to come out strong but failed miserably, sounding more like a child than my normal self. "Eric, I'm worried. I'm scared. I don't know how you've done it for all these years, but I sure as hell can't live like this."

"I told you, there's nothing we can do, Sloane. I wasted months of my actual life and countless, endless After Hours trying to stop her, to no avail. I have to accept that her lifespan ended, so her Jumps will too. Eventually." His despondent demeanor matched mine, but he spoke with much more reassurance.

I took in the sight of him in the silence that followed. The shape of his body, still so foreign, yet still so *mine*.

"I'm sorry," I murmured. "I'm still mad at you. But I'm also sorry."

"I'm sorry too. I thought I was doing the right thing." He looked at me with his tired eyes, his jaw cocked to one side, before resting his chin on his fist, elbow propped on his knee, staring straight ahead.

The rain slowed outside the window, the thrum of it decreasing as if it were controlled by a volume dial, until we were left with the sounds of straggler splats dripping off the roof's parapet.

A terrifying thought popped into my head, leaving me no grace period before it made its way out. "But wait. Forget about Alicia for a second. What if they find out about you?"

Eric straightened his back. "That won't happen," he said sharply.

"How can you be so sure?" I objected.

"Are you going to tell them?" he snapped, slightly startling me. "Didn't think so. The secret is safe."

Taken aback by his sudden sharpness, I stared into my lap as I muttered, "I sure hope so." After a moment, I slowly raised my gaze to meet his, my brows furrowing. "But how do you know you've tried everything if you haven't even brought it up to Adrian? He might have all sorts of tricks up his sleeve that you don't know about. Did you even try the Stripping Ritual?"

"The what now?"

"The Stripping Ritual. In the Horolog. You know, to remove a Lunai's powers," I said, his expression telling me clear as day that he had no idea what I was talking about.

He hadn't even studied the book that I was so jealous of him for having.

He seemed to recollect. "Oh yeah. That. I've never heard of that being used, honestly. I don't even know if it works. My Horolog went missing years ago, and I didn't have the heart to tell Adrian. But I'm glad to hear you're reading yours."

I gulped down against the tightening in my chest, knowing I was the reason his Horolog went missing.

We sat in an uncomfortable silence for quite a while, until the remnants of rain outside were louder than the hum of traffic down the block.

My voice was raspy when I spoke. "Do you know who gave me my powers?"

Eric had been staring straight out into the street, but his face shot in my direction at my words. "You don't know?"

My face became a mixture of anger and confusion. "No! Not a clue. Don't you think I would have mentioned it? If I knew, I could get Jules to stop bugging me about it."

He studied me with a concerned expression for a good long while, before averting his eyes back to the street and then answering, "No, I have no idea. I'm sorry. Maybe Malina can help you figure it out. She specializes in Sensing lineage. She's great; I've been meaning to introduce you to her."

About time you thought of that.

I wanted so badly to tell him about meeting Malina in my Slip. But the way she had crushed my hand in hers earlier, her stare saying more than a million words, was enough to deter me. I couldn't tell him I knew she helped him hunt Alicia years ago. And she had saved me from my Slip, in exchange for my silence.

"Can I ask—is there—or was there—something between you and Malina?" I asked, my voice small.

Eric looked genuinely perplexed. "Malina? No, never. She and I are *just* friends. Always have been. Malina was the one who Sensed me and brought me to see Adrian for the first time. She was the first Lunai I met after I manifested. She's the only other person who knows where my powers came from." His eyes still gleamed with genuine incomprehension. "I told you—I haven't been with anyone. There hasn't been anyone but you, Sloane."

I averted my gaze. His pull on me was too strong.

"How am I supposed to believe that?" I grumbled. I had so many questions, and they just kept spilling out of me. "You literally just waited for me to make Jumps? What did you do in between? Were single but secretly committed to a Future version of a girl who was in high school at the time?"

Eric let out the smallest laugh and shot me an apologetic smile. "I mean, yeah. I guess. When you put it like that . . ." He narrowed his eyes at me again before lowering his voice, his smile growing ever so slightly. "Wait a minute. *You Jumped!*"

I opened my mouth to protest—but nothing came out except a long, defeated sigh.

"Come on! You did, didn't you?" he pressed, leaning forward with his elbows on his knees.

I raised my eyes to look at him as I sipped on my cold coffee. I knew keeping silent wasn't enough—he saw right through me.

"Yes!" he exclaimed, letting himself fall back into the couch, grinning from ear to ear. "When? You have to tell me when."

"Isn't that forbidden?" I asked.

"No, that's the genius part! I've been waiting for this forever. It's in both of our Pasts now. We can talk freely! We finally have a past together!"

"That's so fucking unfair!" I whined. "I want you to tell me about the stuff I don't know *now*—and I had the hardest time keeping my mouth shut with you back then!"

Eric burst into laughter, and soon I was laughing with him. I could not for the life of me stay mad at him.

And it terrified me.

"So?" he asked in a singsong voice.

"What?"

"Which time was it?" He was growing impatient.

"Do you keep a log of my visits to you? Because if so, that would be helpful," I quipped.

He groaned. "No, and even if I did, you know I wouldn't be able to share it with you."

I let out a *hmph* and crossed my arms. When I still didn't respond to his question, he made a mock-begging face.

I caved, laughing softly, my inner turmoil over the conversation still not fully releasing me. "Ugh! Fine. March 2, 2023."

Eric bit his lip as he smiled. Our eyes met, and I could tell the same memory was playing behind all four of them.

"*What?*" I wailed.

His smile turned crooked, making it even more irresistible.

He nodded his chin to the side and looked down as if reveling in it, before shooting me a knowing glance and saying, "I can't believe *that* was the first time."

⋇⋇⋇

At midnight, Greg and another man I remembered seeing at the first Council meeting I attended, Finneas, came to relieve Eric and me from our shift. I noticed how much they looked alike, and small talk confirmed they were brothers. I figured they were likely one of the cases where a Lunai had been able to transfer their powers to two people at once.

I let Eric hug me before we stepped foot into the main hall.

I bade him good night, and he went to join a group of people who were sitting up. I could feel his eyes linger on me as I made my way up the spiral staircase. Once in my room, I reread the passage about the Stripping Ritual in my secret copy of the Horolog, not gleaning any more than what I already knew. I looked up the dorsolateral prefrontal cortex on my phone, to see if I could connect it to something. One article did state that it was the part of the brain that had the most to do with how humans perceive time. It was located at the front of the brain, on either side, between the middle of the forehead and the temples.

I remembered feeling like it was too simple to work. Maybe Eric was right—maybe the description wasn't accurate. Maybe there wasn't a way to Strip someone. Plus, Adrian kept reminding me that the Lunai Laws were nothing more than a best guesstimate. Maybe the Horolog was all out of date and they had stopped giving copies out to new Wardens? But then Eric wouldn't have assumed that I had received one. Maybe the tasers didn't have anything to do with Stripping and were just a weapon of choice to subdue people when needed? My brain hurt, and I knew there was no use lingering on the topic. I could tell my brain was trying to come up with any excuse on Adrian's behalf for seemingly withholding information from me. I wanted so much to trust him. I needed someone to trust.

I scanned through the table of contents, deciding which reading material I wanted to fall asleep over.

The second page of the table of contents held the word *Tellurian* a few lines down, indicating it was almost at the end of the book. My interest piqued, I turned to the given page number.

But it didn't exist. In fact, the pages that were supposed to hold the Tellurian chapter had all been ripped out. The tail end of it was still there, before the next chapter began.

One of the ways the Tellurian used to manipulate their power transfers was by killing their own or captured Lunai in the Past, thus transferring powers to individuals whose Present they had Jumped to. They would also frequently travel back to Strip or kill their enemies in the Past, causing massive Pattern shifts and essentially rendering their victims powerless without them knowing.

Their go-to for Temporal manipulation was transporting them while Stopped, Starting again with the Temporal placed in some sort of peril.

In worst-case scenarios, the Tellurian practiced trapping Temporals in Stops, never to be redeemed. This practice was considered particularly gruesome and could be identified by the following sequence of events:

The Tellurian would perform a Stop while maintaining physical contact with a Temporal, hence Stopping time for them. The Tellurian would then Start time without making physical contact with the Temporal. This led to the Temporal being stuck in Stopped time.

The corpse of the Temporal would then appear, returned to their Present upon their death, often much older than they had been going into the Stop, having lived out the rest of their lives in Stopped time. The Temporal's death would consequently be ruled as being from natural causes, unless they did not have the means to feed themselves in the Stop, in which case they would pass from starvation. Some committed suicide, and I wasn't surprised. The time I had been stuck in a Stop without knowing what was going on was the most terrifying thing I'd experienced, despite the perils unstopped time held for me.

THE AFTER HOURS

The Tellurian were also known for their ability to create Pattern Gaps, where things, or even individuals, could be banished, never to be recovered, their existence ceasing in every moment in the Past, Present, or Future. It was still unknown how a Pattern Gap was created, but its identifying marker was an implosion of energy, often causing immense heat and even flames, scorching anything in direct contact. The object or person would then slowly fade from existence over a string of moments, enough moments to be observable by the naked eye, unlike Stops and Jumps. Hence an observable gap.

As I finished reading the passage about Pattern Gaps, my transitional state hijacked my mind for a few moments. The embers on the beach attacking me. I felt a hollowness, similar to a Flicker, and gasped to catch my breath as the wind got knocked out of me by some invisible force.

"What the heck," I muttered. I was in the Sanctuary; you couldn't Flicker down there. Besides, I wasn't even in a Stop or trying to use my powers.

"I'm probably just tired," I said to myself, shaking out my shoulders.

I turned the page and cursed. The chapter had ended. I started flipping the adjacent pages back and forth, hoping the missing pages about the Tellurian had been placed somewhere out of order. I held the book by its cover and shook it, hoping loose pages would fall out, but none did. I wanted so badly to see what they said. Even more so because they had been removed.

I contemplated sneaking downstairs to borrow the big Horolog from Adrian's dais, but I was fairly certain the hall wasn't going to be empty anytime soon. Conversations still drifted up from the group gathered there, sliding underneath my door. I fell back onto the pillows, letting the cacophony whisk me off toward slumberland, finding comfort in being surrounded by all these people who were the same as me and focusing on the silence in my body from the Sanctuary's dampening effects. Just as I started to drift off to sleep, the sounds of a separate conversation started interrupting the comfy rumble from downstairs. And this one wasn't coming from under my door. It was coming through the wall opposite my bed.

Eric's room.

I hurled myself off the bed, flattening myself against the wall to press my ear up against it. I heard a deep voice—Eric—and another, lighter, more feminine but still powerful. They were so muffled that I couldn't tell what the words were.

If I was lucky, my room wasn't the only one in the Sanctuary without a lock.

I didn't even stop to think about what I was doing before I bolted out of my room. I felt stupid; this wasn't how I wanted to portray myself. Yet I couldn't stop. I didn't know if it was because Eric had already broken my trust once, the indiscretion still being too fresh, or if I was perhaps letting past issues steer me.

Before I could even cringe at my own behavior, I found myself standing in front of the door to room 414. The brass doorknob was loose in its placement and gave way easily, the door swinging fully open at the touch of my fingers.

Inside, Eric's room was identical to mine, apart from his personal belongings and the extra guest.

Malina and Eric sat on his bed, embracing, neither of them noticing me for a full ten seconds.

"Sloane!" Eric exclaimed, throwing himself away from Malina.

Malina looked at me with a mixture of pity and dismay.

I had never run so fast down a spiral staircase, slipping and sliding on the asymmetrical, too shallow treads. Once on the lowest level, Eric caught up to me. We were in plain view of the group sitting at one of the hall tables. It had grown considerably smaller, but their eyes stung me regardless, their chatter coming to a complete halt.

"Sloane, please—" He grabbed my hand, and in turn, I grabbed his forearm and squeezed, letting my nails dig in.

"Don't. Cause. A. Scene," I said between gritted teeth.

Eric lowered his voice to a whisper. "Please, *please* don't do this."

I let go of him, yanking extra hard to get out of his grasp as well.

"Do what, exactly?" I whispered furiously, "I will not be played like this. Running to her as soon as you had me fooled. As soon as you secured a visit from me in the Past. Enjoy the memory, asshole. There won't be another one."

He didn't follow me out of the hall.

༺༻༺༻༺༻

Once back above ground, I wanted to collapse. I wanted to shrink into a cocoon of self-pity and cry until my body shriveled up. But I couldn't, not here. I had already caused quite the impression with the display Eric and I had put on in the Sanctuary hall.

But I was not about to let my life be controlled by a crazy, jealous ex of a guy who obviously couldn't care less about me. A crazy, jealous, *deceased* ex. If he wasn't going to take action, I would. With the help of the Horolog, which I was feeling less and less bad about stealing, I knew what I needed to do. Or try to do, at least.

Greg's and Finneas's voices drifted out from the kitchen. I peered around the dining room doorway to see them sitting at the small kitchen table that sat under a window facing the backyard.

They didn't notice me coming up. Perfect.

I dashed across the hall and into the coat closet, diving through the coats. I grabbed a taser from the back wall, made sure it had charge just like Neil had shown me, and stuffed it in my pocket.

Here goes nothing.

If I could Strip Alicia, I could not only prevent her from ever attacking me again, but she would stop coming after Eric. He would emerge from the Sanctuary tomorrow without his powers, because she wouldn't have any powers to transfer to him when she died.

Beach, sunset, fire, embers, haze—

This must be the place.

The Stop came more naturally than it ever had before. My emotions probably had something to do with it, and the proximity to a full moon, but I didn't care. I felt empowered. I felt determined.

I felt unstoppable.

❦❦❦

I parked my car across the street from the coffee shop Eric had taken me to. Where I had first seen Alicia. It felt like a lifetime ago, but it had only been a few weeks.

Unable to rely on lunar phases, the destination I was aiming for being too close for that, I willed myself to fill my being up with the sensations and energy I had felt that day.

Confusion. Excitement. Awkwardness. Rage at Alicia. Warmth and safety at Eric's reaction. The thrill of newness and nervousness at his touch.

At the same time I let these feelings devour me, I vowed to never let myself feel that way for him again.

I stepped out of the car to make sure I didn't bring it with me into the Jump. From what I had read in the Horolog, I learned that machines worked in Stops and Jumps as long as you remained in contact with intent. I realized it was how my car had still worked the day of the hurricane. But I couldn't risk taking it with me into the Jump this time, since another car could potentially be parked in this spot in the moment I was aiming for.

Crossing the street, I planted myself in an alley two doors down from the coffee shop before calling on it.

Beach-sunset-fire-ember.

Vast, exquisite nothingness.

I opened my eyes. It was daytime. Checking my phone, I let out a tiny yelp of triumph when I saw it state:

3:35 p.m., Friday, June 27, 2025

I had Jumped successfully, and not a moment too late. As I got my bearings, reeling from the intensity and swiftness of the Jump, I heard a sound that I regretted knowing all too well.

Alicia's laughter.

I poked my head out of the alley, looking toward the coffee shop, but she wasn't there.

Her evil howl echoed again, this time coming from the alley behind me. I spun around—

"Hi, *Sloane*." She said my name with a whiny, nasally sound, as if to convey that just the word was somehow annoying. "I wasn't planning on sticking around, but then I heard you were here to see me." A sinister giggle escaped her where she stood about halfway down the alley, the sneer on her face just the same as I remembered.

She wore the same clothes as the day I had first seen her in the coffee shop. White tank top, black jacket, light wash jeans. The white of her tank was dotted with blood. There were streaks of blood on her thighs. I got a better look at her now than I had that day, and I couldn't help but pity her, knowing now why she was here.

Why she was doing this to herself. Her face was weathered, probably beautiful at some point, but now just vile.

She coughed into her sleeve and spit a ball of red slime on the ground next to her. I tried to take advantage of this, storming in her direction, but she was still too quick. She was behind me before I had even closed half of the distance between us, laughing hysterically.

I knew I couldn't outpower her; I had no idea if I was even strong enough to perform a Stop within a Jump. So I would have to outsmart her.

I ran again, this time away from her, toward the opposite end of the alley. She showed up as expected, right in front of me in a split second, except her body was a bit to my right, and she held her hand straight out in my path, getting ready to send me hurling backward once I would crash into it.

I lunged, wrenching the taser out of my pocket, and aimed for her forehead. Between the middle and the temple.

"You fucking bitch!" she managed to yell before crumpling to the ground beneath me, convulsing and writhing as I dug the prongs into her dry skin, straddling her torso.

She started coughing with the convulsions, blood sputtering from her mouth. For a second I worried I was doing this to her, the shock of the violence before me created by my own hands breaking something in me. But I knew it was the sickness she brought on herself with all of her After Hours.

The shaking in her body subsided, and she managed to wriggle and grab my arm, sliding her bony fingers under my shirt sleeve to get a good grip with skin-to-skin contact. She let out a frustrated growl when she realized whatever she was trying to do wasn't working. The rush of victory swept through my body momentarily, until the taser stopped clicking.

I jumped to my feet and bolted as fast as I could out into the street. I glanced back down the alley for a split second, the figure of her heap exactly where I left her. I sprinted to where my car was parked in the Present, and called it back to me with ease, aided by the adrenaline thrashing in my veins.

CHAPTER TWENTY-TWO

"Got it out of your system now?"

Adrian's voice had never been as devoid of warmth as when it rang across the craftsman's foyer after I Started from the Stop I used to sneak back into the house. It sent a palpable chill through my body. He sat on the couch in the unlit living room, his figure illuminated just barely by the moonlight coming in through the old windows.

"Hi, Adrian. Sorry, I was just—"

"Save it. I know what you were doing." His words pierced through my chest; I couldn't fill my lungs.

A figure emerged out of the even-darker back den. It was Maddie. Her eyes were red and swollen, her normally glowing skin splotchy and dull.

"I'm sorry, Sloane. I had to tell him the truth," she sobbed.

"Maddie, honey, please go to bed. I'll be right down." Adrian's voice held affection for his daughter, but his eyes stayed on me with an unwavering fury.

Maddie avoided my gaze, sniffling as she shuffled past me to the elevator.

"Sit down, Sloane."

He directed me to the armchair where I had been sitting earlier that evening. I made my way over there, my chest tightening with every step. I was certain I was going to pass out from lack of oxygen.

"I have never, in my entire career and time as a Lunai, witnessed such utter stupidity from a new Warden as I did this evening from you, Sloane."

I chewed the inside of my cheeks, breathing desperately through my nose, bracing for what was going to come next.

"I heard commotion in the hall, and went out to see what it was. When our fellows told me it had been you and Eric, I was hoping they were mistaken. Until Madeline woke up screaming and shaking from the force of whatever she had been Sensing. You do realize that Sensing is not a comfortable act and is often completely out of the Sensor's control? Their readings come and go as they please, and can either be relatively unnoticeable or an immensely difficult experience?"

Part of me wanted to retort, come to my defense. Tell him that of course I hadn't known that, he had kept me in the dark about it, as with so many other things. But I was too scared to utter a sound.

"When I didn't find you in your room or anywhere else in the Sanctuary, and Eric told me you had stormed off, I knew that whatever Madeline was Sensing must have been at your hands, and I started mentally preparing myself for the worst. A leak, a death, a cataclysmic Pattern shift—heck, I even prepared myself for the possibility that I'd be alive one moment and not the next. You do realize that's what could've happened, right Sloane? You do realize you could have changed things so catastrophically and irrevocably that we would never be able to come back from it?"

I had begun to shake forcefully under the weight of his words, shattering piece by fragmented piece as his tone got louder and louder.

When I didn't answer, he roared, "Do you, Sloane?"

"Y—yes. I'm sorry. I—I realize that. I—I'm so so sorry."

He started pacing as he continued to rant as if there hadn't been a break. "Especially when you could have run into yourself. That's part of what Maddie Senses. Do you know what running into yourself outside the Present can do to you? Huh? You can lose your mind. You can forget which one of you is your Present You. You'll feel so drawn to and protective of your other versions that you can end up hurting them or yourself or both because you just feel this immense need to be one with them. Your soul longs to be in one place."

I remembered the gnawing ache in my chest whenever I had watched my Past self go about her life, as if I missed her. As if I missed the essence of myself.

"While I do not want to know where you were or what you were doing, I know that Madeline sensed a disruption in the Pattern. You changed something. I want you to understand that if whatever the ramifications are come to light—which they almost always do when you change something in the Past—you leave me no choice but to Strip you."

I'd had enough. I needed to point out his hypocrisy. "You haven't even told me what Stripping is, and now you're using it against me. Don't you think you should have told me more of these things already? I need to train, not sit around and chat. What if I decided to take a nap in a Stop—it's very likely I would get that idea—but it's actually something that's really dangerous! And you told me nothing, not even something as basic as that. You didn't even tell me about Flickering. You were even gatekeeping the Horolog from me, despite me constantly asking you for homework or reading material!" I stopped myself before I wouldn't be able to.

Adrian turned to face me in the moonlight, the dark circles under his eyes a deeper shade than I had ever seen them. I could tell he was hurt, and it broke my heart. He had never been anything but kind to me, despite his shortcomings in training. I just knew he was capable of more than what he was giving me.

We stared at each other for several long moments. I thought about mentioning that I have apparently yet to use my powers multiple times to visit Eric, seemingly with no consequence, and I wondered if he knew that. But I didn't know if he was allowed to know that. Because of Eric, I had no idea which versions of the truth were floating around, and I despised it.

When he still didn't speak, I couldn't stop myself from continuing. "I know the other Lunai get to use their powers for their own entertainment. That Nico guy used his to go to a festival—"

Adrian cut me off, his voice thundering over me. "Nico is a senior member of our Council. He has privileges that you do not. And he knows not to risk running into a Past version of himself."

His words stung. I had rarely felt so small.

Adrian looked utterly defeated. His chest lifted as he took a long, steadying breath before speaking. "I'm afraid I'm going to have to place you on probation, Sloane. Effective immediately, until further notice."

"Probation? What does that even mean?" I spat.

"It means there will be no further training for the time being. You are banned from all Council activity as well as the Sanctuary itself. If you use your powers, it will be grounds for an immediate Stripping." He was somber, but dead serious.

"Adrian, you can't be serious. There's a murderer out there targeting us. Where am I going to stay if not downstairs?" My voice started to shake at the realization of how vulnerable I would be.

"Go home. Go out of state. Go to Saturn. I don't care—it's no longer my problem. But you can't stay here. You do not have the privilege of Sanctuary when you are on probation for breaking Lunai Law."

He walked over to the den where Maddie had appeared, and reached for something on the floor. My duffel bag.

He carried it over to where I stood, his features sunken, hands shaking. "I gathered your items. Everything that belongs to you is in there."

I took the bag from him. It felt lighter than when I had lugged it with me to the house. I shot him a perplexed look and zipped it open, digging my hand in.

The Horolog wasn't there.

I looked up at him, my confusion turning to anger, about to demand he return it to me, but he beat me to it.

"Like I said: everything that belongs to you is in there."

CHAPTER TWENTY-THREE

I CRIED THE whole way home from Highland Park. First out of frustration. Then out of sadness, and last, fear.

Fear that a killer was out there targeting Lunai, and I was the only sitting duck left in the Los Angeles area to be targeted.

Fear that if Alicia showed up, I'd risk losing my powers if I used them to defend myself.

But I had Stripped her powers. I must have. She had tried to use her powers and failed. Which meant every time I saw her after that was from before whichever Present she was Jumping from during the coffee shop incident.

I knew that ideally she would have needed to lose her powers much earlier in life in order to prevent the brunt of the Jumping she had done in her lifetime. But Eric said that she kept getting sicker and sicker until she stopped showing up, so hopefully this prevented at least some of the damage she had done. But more importantly, any further damage to me. I knew what I had done was wrong according to the Warden Laws, but frankly, I didn't see a point in these powers if we weren't allowed to use them for good. To protect ourselves along with the Pattern.

I groaned with frustration at Adrian. I had so many questions, and I now knew for a fact that he was keeping things from me. I desperately wanted to know if my actions in the alley had worked, but the Horolog didn't say anything about how to check if Stripping was successful. At least not in the section I had read. But now I didn't have a Horolog to check if it may have been mentioned somewhere else.

The only way I would know for sure if the Ritual worked was if Eric didn't have his powers anymore, either.

ᘓᕒᘓᕒᘓᕒ

"Wake up, Slo."

"Sloane. Wake *up*."

It took me a while to figure out that I was in my own bed. I felt like I hadn't slept at all, or for days for that matter.

"Go away," I murmured into my pillow.

"Not a chance. We need to talk."

At this second voice, I sat up with a jolt, my vision taking longer than my body to reorient itself, the outlines of two people sitting at the foot of my bed, hazy.

"What the fuck?" I asked, rubbing my eyes.

"It's noon already. And we need to talk." Justin's face came into focus. His brows were furrowed, a slight scowl on his lips.

"What are you doing here? Why aren't you in Vegas?" I turned to Rebecca and my heartbeat picked up, dread clasping at my lungs. She looked exhausted, her hair in a messy bun on the top of her head, no makeup on. Rebecca never left the house without makeup.

"What happened?" I said breathlessly, bracing myself for the worst.

"We were hoping you would tell us," Rebecca said quietly.

Confusion rattled around my mind like a pinball, furiously zapping back and forth, not allowing me to string my thoughts together into anything cohesive. The exhaustion I felt probably had something to say there as well, but what did she mean? Had I done something in my sleep?

Oh god, did I reveal my powers somehow?

Justin cleared his throat and shifted nervously, sitting up better where he was perched to my left. "We know something's going on with you, and we're worried. So we wanted to check in." I could tell he was pitching his voice softer than he would have liked.

"What in the wo—" I began.

"Sloane, please don't insult us by trying to play dumb. I could tell something was going on with you all the way from Vegas. I've seen you through some dark shit, but this is another level." Rebecca's voice was sharp, the tone she reserved for defending herself or her inner circle from those who were outside it.

"You've been acting weird ever since you came back from campus. I don't know if it's your job, your dad, or something else. But we know we're the ones who are going to have to pick up the pieces when you eventually get in over your head and—I just don't want to see it come to that," Justin said, his features grim, yet concerned.

"Wow. So you guys have been plotting behind my back? For what reason exactly?" I said, indignation swelling in my chest.

"We're not plotting against you, idiot! We care about you," Rebecca snapped.

"Since when do you guys even talk?" I retorted.

"That's none of your—" Rebecca started to complain, but Justin cut her off.

"Since we needed to. Because of you! Okay?"

I looked between them, bringing my knees and covers up to my chest, frustrated tears stinging uncomfortably in my eyes. As if I didn't have enough going on, now my best friend and my brother were ganging up on me.

"Please just talk to us. You know there's nothing you can't tell us," Rebecca pleaded.

Yes, there was. There was a whole world I couldn't tell them about.

"I don't know what you guys want to hear me say!" I yelled. "I'm *fine*! I've just been busy with work and—"

"Where were you last night? You said you needed to lie about staying at my house," Rebecca said, pain lacing her words and concern darkening her eyes.

Justin had been looking at Rebecca as she spoke but turned his gaze back to me when she finished. His eyes seemed less angry now; I could tell he was worried.

"I told you: I was staying with some work friends. But I wasn't feeling it, and I came home early." The lie burned on my lips.

Rebecca sighed, and she and Justin exchanged a look across my bed. For some reason it infuriated me seeing them communicate like that. It compounded my bitterness at the current situation.

"Justin told me Tom showed up at your birthday. Why didn't you tell me?"

The sudden pivot in subject surprised me. "Because it didn't matter? I kicked him out as soon as he got here."

"What did he want?" she asked.

I groaned, "Not this again. You"—I motioned to Justin—"already asked me and my answer stands. I don't know."

"Slo." Rebecca placed her hand on my knee, over the covers, and gave it a little squeeze. She almost never called me that. "Justin told me."

"Yeah, then why are you asking?" I barked.

"No, Slo, I told her what happened between you guys."

The lie. The lie about why Tom and I stopped being friends. The one I had so masterfully kept away from Rebecca. She and Justin weren't meant to talk to each other.

It had been the safety net I had counted on in order to contain the truth, and my lie.

Rebecca, looking devastated, continued her plea, "Why didn't you tell me? I know I didn't exactly notice—or care—and I'm sorry for that. I just figured you guys grew apart."

That showed just how little Rebecca knew about my friendship with Tom. It wasn't the kind you grew out of.

My phone buzzed, and I glanced automatically, any reprieve from the ongoing conversation, welcome.

> Eric: Please give me a chance to explain.
> Eric: Please let me know you're okay.

It wasn't a welcome reprieve. Eric had been sending apologetic texts at regular intervals ever since I stormed out of Adrian's house, even in the middle of the night. I hadn't answered any of them.

And I had no intent to answer Rebecca either. Instead, I channeled all my anger in Justin's direction. "I told you to keep that to yourself. That was not your secret to tell." Panic stung at my chest as I contemplated how in the world I was going to perpetuate, and contain, the lie. Now that Rebecca knew, my safety net was gone.

"I know that. But you have not been acting normal since he showed up on our doorstep, and I am fucking worried about you, okay? I had to tell her my reasons."

"And what are your reasons, exactly?" I spat, narrowing my eyes at him.

"I don't know, Sloane! I think him showing up made you remember what happened—between you guys—I'm worried it's making you do some stuff you'll regret. Or could hurt you." Justin cleared his throat aggressively this time, clearly uncomfortable.

"What sort of lame-ass conclusion has your mind been jumping to? I haven't been doing anything I'll regret. I've been working and I've been making new friends—"

"There's more," Justin said, his expression pained. He turned to Rebecca and nicked his head in my direction while telling her, "Show her."

Rebecca's jaw clenched and she let a long breath out through her nose, keeping eye contact with Justin before turning to me. "Sloane. Babe. I'm only going to ask you once and I want you to be totally honest, okay?"

I glared at her.

"Are you in some kind of financial trouble or something? Or, like, doing shit for other people on the internet or something?" She held her phone, unlocked, tightly in one hand while holding the palm of her other hand over the screen, blocking my view.

"No!" I roared. "I don't know what the fuck you're talking about. What were you going to show me?" I gestured at the phone in her hand.

Justin looked away from us both, staring at the door. She passed me the phone and her hands went straight to her face, covering her mouth and nose, as if she had handed me an explosive.

And it kind of was.

The site she had pulled up was rudimentary, an old-school style chat board with simple fonts and archaic emojis. The top post in the thread was an embedded video. I recognized it instantly as the same video that had been playing on my computer my first day at the internship. I had almost forgotten about it in light of everything else that was going on. Self-hatred seethed in my veins over the fact that I hadn't done something more about it.

Because my suspicions about what it was had been correct.

But even just thinking about it had sent me Slipping last time. I couldn't have that happen again; I already had way too many After Hours piled up on graduation night.

Because that's when this video was from. Tom's bedroom, where I had stayed on graduation night.

CHAPTER TWENTY-FOUR

I SAW RED.

I had never been so enraged in my life. I didn't just see red, I saw flames. My whole body was flames. Flames of shame, humiliation, pain, and a thirst for vengeance that I was sure nothing in this world could quench. I had deleted that video from the camera I had discovered hidden on Tom's bookshelf. I had even made sure that there was no memory card in there to back up the internal memory of the camera. There was no doubt in my mind, and the memory of it was clear as day.

Groggy eyes.
The initial collision of disbelief.
Hands shaking furiously.
The feeling of breaking apart from the core.
The lash of reality as I knew it, leaving me in the wake of its destruction.

Panic to get it done before he came back.

And then the screams.

There had been six different videos, each reaching the maximum duration the camera was capable of recording at a time. Six separate stabs to my heart as I clicked on each to erase. The tap of a finger felt so inadequate for such a paramount task. The weight of the videos needed to be vanquished with the fury of a thousand volcanoes—violently, with reckless abandon. Instead, it had come down to taps in trembling hands.

✧✧✧

The scene of the crime hadn't changed at all since that night. The bushes lining the path up to the house were probably trimmed to the same quarter-inch increment as they had always been for all the years I had joyfully skipped past them. I hadn't needed to knock on this door since early elementary school years, and nothing in me felt the need to start. I knew he was home alone, as so many times before, based on the plastic-wrapped newspapers littering the front porch. He would always wait till the day his parents were scheduled to arrive home to pick them up.

I charged through the front door, not bothering to knock. The two-story foyer looked smaller than I remembered as I yelled up into the heights of it with all the air I could muster out of my lungs, "Salinger!"

Thundering footsteps sounded from the second-floor slab, but Tom stopped dead in his tracks when he saw me.

I stomped up the stairs, not waiting for him to acknowledge me.

"So you had an automatic backup, huh? A cloud folder? A separate memory card?"

"Sloane—what are you—" He stood frozen in place, eyes like saucers, terrified.

"Shut up. Do not open your mouth unless it's to tell me what you did with them." I had reached him by this point, where he stood on the walkway between the two upstairs wings. I walked straight up to him, shoving him backward with both hands. "Where did you post them? Do you have any idea how many places they could be in by now?"

I kept shoving. He kept letting me, a pain-stricken look on his face.

"Do you have any idea how much you ruined my life?" I sobbed. I couldn't control it anymore. The shoves turned more into punches on his chest with the sides of my fists, and all I could do was hope that I wouldn't Slip.

He grabbed my upper arms, holding me at arm's length, stronger than I remembered him being. I wriggled and thrashed, but the initial rush of adrenaline was plummeting, and I was no match for him.

"Sloane, please calm down. Please calm—What are you going on about?" His eyes searched my face, full of fear and concern and *Tomness*.

"Let me go! Don't touch me!" I swung my shoulders from side to side and he let go.

I stormed past him to his room. I knew he wouldn't admit it. I knew I'd have to pry it out of him. His room looked the same. Everything was as if no time had passed. The spell of being back in his room was stronger than I had experienced in all my trips back in time. I felt more like a time traveler now than I had in any of them. I beelined to his desk and didn't bother sitting down. I stood at the table as I grabbed his mouse, clicking through folders furiously, local and cloud alike.

"What are you doing? Stop!" he begged, but I didn't care.

I switched to his browser and scrolled through his browsing history. I was so delirious, I wasn't retaining anything. Still, I kept going.

"What are you trying to find?" his small voice said from behind me.

I swallowed hard as the tears continued to stream down my cheeks, silently. They piled up on my lower lash line and blurred my vision to the point where I didn't really see what I was doing on the screen.

"S—please talk to me."

I whirled around to face him, my lips pressed together against the cry wanting to escape.

"What did you do with them? How many sites have them?" I said through gritted teeth. I knew it was no use; it wasn't like he could know. Once something was in one place on the internet, you had to assume it was everywhere.

"I really, really, have absolutely no clue what you're talking about," he said, earnestly, all my old signals firing, indicating he was telling the truth.

"The videos. Of us." A sob escaped me—I had never said it out loud. I couldn't elaborate, all I could muster was a whimper, "*Why?*"

Tom stood in silence, giving me a similar look to those that Justin and Rebecca had given me. Pity, worry, apprehension.

"Why?" I yelled, barreling into him again, shoving him with each word. "Why, why, why, why?"

I snapped out of my fit when I heard the lock on his bathroom door click behind me. He had stood entirely still under my strikes, but he stepped to the side and straightened up as he watched the person emerge from the bathroom. I spun to face the door too and instinctively let him shield me.

"What's that ruckus, babe?"

I had heard that "babe" before. The sound of the word was like being hit by a truck. It sent my head spinning, nausea rising in my chest.

Tiptoeing out of Tom's bathroom, drying her wet hair with a towel and wearing only a bra and underwear, was Alicia.

She noticed me and smiled. Not the sneer that was normally her weapon of choice against me, but an innocent, friendly smile, as if she were a normal person.

She looked more normal. Not as weak. Not as sick. It was terrifying.

"Hi, I'm Alicia," she said, taking a few steps toward us. "Babe, why don't you introduce us?" She held out one hand as if she wanted to shake mine, still squeezing her hair with the towel in the other. My eye was drawn to something above her thin, blond brow. Faded taser marks.

I staggered backward, tripping over the corner of Tom's bed. I yelped as I fell on the floor, crawling backward toward the bedroom door, mumbling incoherently as I tried to regain my footing.

"No—no, no, no," I mumbled, eyes darting and finger pointing back and forth between the two of them.

"Hey, Slo—come ba—What is going on with you?" Tom said, more annoyed than concerned this time.

I managed to get my feet under me again and ran out of the room, Tom on my heels.

I flew down the stairs, two steps at a time, and didn't bother closing the front door behind me as I charged out. I ran so fast I had no control over my legs as they gained more and more momentum against the asphalt of Tom's street, but he still caught up with me.

He grabbed my arm at the elbow and yanked, his fingers slipping down as I pulled against him, until he caught me at the wrist. He dug his heels into the ground against my running, managing to stop me. I fought, but his grip was locked.

"How could you? Do you have any idea—" I screamed, but the force I put into the words took away from my torque against him.

He tore at me with a jolt, grabbing my other shoulder and pulling me into him. Once he had me close, he wrapped one arm around my shoulders and the other under my arm and around my upper back, holding tightly. I collapsed up against him, fully bawling.

"Hey, hey. It's okay. It's okay. You're okay." He placed his hand on the back of my head and his head on my shoulder, and for a split second his cheek stroked against mine.

A split second of skin-to-skin was all that was needed, and the Slip washed over us.

The pins and needles rushing back and forth between our bodies felt like a million tiny razor nicks. I felt his knees buckle. The pressure on my eardrums pierced through my skull, and my brain was on fire. Everything was fire, and then my eyes shot open.

The hot breeze that had been lapping the valley we called home was immobile around us, suffocating. The palm branches and brush stalks lining the front yards around us, static, midway. Sprinklers on the lawn next to us were silenced, their latest sputter of water stuck in a rigid arc, waiting to be let down to fulfill its purpose.

My breath came in heavy gasps, my chest pushing against Tom's, but it wasn't just me. He still had not let go of me, his inhales and exhales matching mine.

I stepped back and out of his grasp, horrified as our eyes met. His shoulders undulating from the force of his breaths, he looked just as scared as I was.

I saw him glance around, noticing the stalled still-life around us, his eyes growing wider, his breathing getting even more aggressive.

"I don't—" he started.

"Shush!" I said as forcefully as I could. I grabbed his right hand and squeezed it between both of mine, thrusting my eyes shut, squeezing until it hurt.

Sun, fire, embers, embers getting closer.
Darkness.
Darkness?

The Start threatened to give me whiplash, but it was deliberate, and not as painful as the Slip had been. I took a rattling breath as our eyes opened to meet once more, and threw his hand away from mine. Tom's gaze was disoriented as the sounds of the environment spilled over us.

"Don't utter a word to anyone. If you want to stay alive, you keep your mouth *shut*." I willed my voice to be as menacing as possible. "And don't *ever* speak to me again."

CHAPTER TWENTY-FIVE

"**P**ICK UP PICK up pick up," I muttered under my breath as I half jogged back to my house, holding my phone to my ear. How could I have been so stupid as to think that I could just perform a Stripping Ritual by myself with no experience whatsoever?

You have reached Adrian Lex Curatorial Services. Please leave a message with your name and callback number, and the best moment to reach you. I will return your call just as soon as time allows.

I roared when I reached his voicemail for the fifth time and hung up. I had to tell him that I Slipped, before he thought I had been using my powers on purpose.

Even if it meant having to tell him why.

Sloan: Adrian please call me back ASAP I really need to talk to you.

I also needed to tell him that I had inadvertently revealed myself to Tom. I had no idea what the protocol was in these situations. I was most definitely going to be Stripped. But maybe if I got ahead of it, I could prevent that from happening.

Sloan: Please.
Sloan: I know you don't want to help me.
Sloan: But I'm really scared that I fucked up.

Coming to a halt just before I reached the line of sight from my house, I tried to call him one more time, hoping he'd take pity on me after seeing the texts. Voicemail again.

A text came in and I yelped in anticipation, but my hopes were crushed as fast as they came on; it was just Eric again.

Eric: I can't stand this. Please answer me.

I switched my phone's front camera on, checking the damage to see if anyone could tell I had been crying. The signs were there, but not as noticeable as I would have thought. I took a few deep breaths before I rounded the corner and strolled up to my house.

My mom was in the kitchen when I arrived. I could've sworn she had some sort of sixth sense about someone going in and out of the house, because even though she couldn't see the entryway from where she was, she called out.

"Hello?" Her voice pulled at my heart, all obliviousness and love. I wanted so badly to run to her and crumble in her arms, have her fix all my problems with forehead kisses and Band Aids and hot chocolate.

She appeared in the dining room when I didn't respond. "Hey honey, where'd you go? Rebecca was here looking for you."

"Oh just—for a walk."

"Are you staying over at her house again tonight?"

Despite her front door sixth sense, she still hadn't noticed that I had actually slept in my own bed and how out of character it was for me to just go for a walk with no reason. Thankfully.

"No, she needs to go back today actually. Did she leave?" I asked, genuinely curious.

"Yeah, she and Justin went to the diner, I think," she replied, all smiles.

"Gotcha. Cool." The fact that Justin and Rebecca were hanging out without me was far from cool but also far from being my biggest problem no matter how much it irritated me.

"Is everything okay sweetie? You look a little tired," my mom cooed.

"Yeah, just... tired. Rebecca and I were up late watching movies."

"Okay, sweetheart. Well don't turn your clock around; you've got work tomorrow."

As if I was going to work tomorrow. As if I was going to subject myself to being around Eric. I knew I needed to just tell my father that I quit.

"Yup. No worries," I muttered, and shot her the most convincing smile I could muster before heading upstairs.

༺༻༺༻༺༻

The steaming hot shower was no match to the disgust I felt in my body. I wanted to keep crying. I had fully planned on crying more once I was alone again, but the stream of emotions ravaging my body left me with numbness.

She had called him *babe*.

I tried Adrian's number again as I stepped out of the shower. It went to voicemail before I had even finished drying off. I cinched the towel around me and wrapped another into a turban on my head. Crawling under the covers, I knew I wouldn't be able to sleep, but I just needed to disappear. I needed to match the vast emptiness that threatened to become a black hole and swallow me if I were to even begin processing what had just happened.

What I hated the most was that there were countless alarm bells going off in my mind telling me that Tom was telling the truth. That he truly hadn't known what I was talking about when I mentioned the videos. My rational brain wanted to punch the emotional one. I needed to believe it was wishful thinking. I wanted so badly for none of this to have happened, that my intuition was misfiring—trying to justify any possible scenario where he would not be culpable. It had to be wishful thinking.

Because Alicia was there.

Alicia, the redhead.

Eric's Alicia. The Alicia who apparently was from a long line of Lunai that were so noxious, they had to be eradicated.

Dead Alicia.

Dead Alicia taking a shower in Tom's bathroom.

Dead Alicia wearing only underwear in Tom's room.

How had this happened?

Despite the desolate haze fogging my mind, a flash of clarity hit me as I had my first sensible thought since being jerked awake by Rebecca and Justin's intervention.

Alicia must have infiltrated Tom's life to get access to me. To get back at me, for Eric. Or simply get closer to me, so she could kill me. It was the only reason that made sense.

I tried Adrian's number one more time, unsuccessfully, before rushing to get dressed.

I was certain I was going to be Stripped anyway, and I had to use my powers wisely while I still had them. I had to stop her. Tom may have betrayed me, but he did not deserve what inevitable horror would ensue if she was in his life.

CHAPTER TWENTY-SIX

Beach. Sunset. Fire.

It wasn't working. I wondered if the Stripping Ritual was maybe something they could do to me in Stopped time and my powers had been taken away without my knowledge.

The thought of being powerless and unable to defend myself rattled me to the core.

Cold beads of sweat pricked every inch of my skin.

Beach. Sunset. Fire. Dwindling flames.

I let out a frustrated sigh and slumped down lower on the bench. I had waited until it was dark outside to leave the house, but the stifling air around me still made everything sticky, and my bare thighs caught painfully on the rough wood.

Beach.
Sunset.

Maybe I was trying too hard to get to a moon phase that had no correspondence to the current moon phase. I racked my brain, trying to remember what I had read in Adrian's measly reading material as well as what I had gleaned from the Horolog. Maybe I wasn't able to get the feeling right. I was sitting in pitch darkness with no lights to aid me in conjuring up the image of a sunset. The only illumination came from the dim lights along the hiking path and the tiny specks of quivering lights in the windows of the neighborhood's houses.

I had avoided this place in the Present for so long, afraid of the pain it would cause. But sitting there in that moment, all I felt was frustration. Frustration over time wasted. Frustration that such a mundane location could hold such power over me. The nostalgic surge of reactivity that the environment caused in my brain felt surprisingly unwelcome. I did not want to drown in it; it was drowning me.

I crossed my arms over my chest with a huff and squeezed my eyes shut as tight as I could, so much so that the pressure on my eyeballs hurt. I had to be here before Graduation Me and Tom showed up. I had to be here before Alicia was here so I could take her by surprise and prevent her from getting to Me from two days ago who had Slipped here. What I would do after I ambushed her, I had no idea. If I had to wrestle her baseball bat from her and use it, I would. Anything to stop her from ever knowing Tom.

But it would be infinitely harder without any control over my powers.

This is all my fault. I led her straight to Tom, exposing him with all my Slips back to graduation night.

Beachsunsetfireembers—
Inferno.
This must be the place.
This is *the place.*

The Jump tore through me and knocked me off the bench. I fell to my knees, panting, and barely managed to blindly place my hands on the ground in front of me so that I wouldn't fall flat on my face. My eyes still wouldn't open, and I gritted my teeth as my body spasmed against the pain. The moment was so hard to grasp onto, and I knew it was because I had already visited it way too many times as my essence became thinner, weaker, completely ungrounded.

And then it was over.

I caught my breath, adjusting to the feeling of not being fully there. There were fewer crickets now, and the air was slightly cooler and easier to breathe, but the darkness was the same. Everything else was the same. The bench, the brush, the bleak glow from yellow lamppost bulbs.

I stood and gingerly dusted away the sand and pebbles embedded in my palms before reaching for my phone.

11:27 p.m., June 7, 2024.

I had made it.

I knew it was only a matter of time before Me from two days ago would wander down the path from my left, followed shortly thereafter by Graduation Me and Tom. I also knew that Alicia was lurking somewhere to my right. I had to find a good hiding spot where I could see her approach, or appear out of nowhere. No one was standing between this Alicia and Me from two days ago. She was going to chase me down and eventually get tackled by Eric. But if I got to her first, she would never see me coming.

It had to be now.

About twenty yards down the trail to the right, the greenbelt that separated the hillside trail and the neighboring residential streets was cut off abruptly by a cliff that reached up higher than the rest of the landscape. The trail wound around it and out of sight from the houses and the bench, slicing into the hillside between the cliff and the rest of the hill. A few yards closer to the bench, a couple of large boulders sat on the side of the trail close to where the hillside had been sculpted to accommodate the flat surface needed. They were probably remnants of the excavation, and were the perfect hiding spot for me to have enough oversight to catch Alicia before she could reach either version of me. Or notice Tom. I settled behind one of the boulders; it was more than large enough to cover me. I grasped the porous surface as I lowered myself to a seat on the edge of the trail, but my hand seemed to lose its grip for a split second and I stumbled. My hand seemed to quiver on sight, but I was holding it perfectly still. A hollowness spread through my body, whipping in on itself and culminating all my awareness into my spine, which tensed and crackled in a sickening burst. My sight went black for just a moment, returning slowly, reluctantly. I realized I must have just had a pretty violent Flicker.

As I regained the feeling in my body, my stomach churned as the gravity of the situation dawned on me. There were now four versions of me existing in this moment, and earlier this evening held yet another.

"My Present is July 9, 2025. I won't forget and I will be back," I whispered, closing my eyes for as long as it took me to say the words.

A hand clamped over my mouth. My whispers became a scream into someone's palm as an arm wrapped around my torso and I was dragged farther behind the boulder.

I kept screaming, hoping to get someone's attention. But I knew it was no use; I didn't remember hearing a scream as either version of myself that night. But maybe I could change that. Changing the Past, with all its consequences, sounded much better than dying right there. I started flailing around, fueled by the anger at myself for letting her ambush me again at the same time as I willed myself to try to Stop, Jump, Slip—anything. That was when the last voice I ever expected to hear in that moment whispered into my ear.

"S, relax, it's me."

Tom's voice sent a bigger shock through my body than when the hand had been placed over my mouth. He slowly eased this grasp on me, and I flung myself away from him and spun around.

"H—how? What the—" I started, and hurriedly peeked around the boulder down the trail to see Graduation Me and Graduation Tom getting settled on the bench.

There are two Toms.

Tom held a finger up to his lips and proceeded in a low voice, "I'm like you. I don't know how—and I know you don't want to talk to me, but please hear me out, okay?"

I stood in silence facing him, looking him over. I knew he was from the same Present as I. He wasn't wearing his glasses, his hair was styled differently, he filled out his shirt more than the version of him down the path. The panicked look in his eyes looked foreign without his glasses framing it, but I still knew it all too well. Like looking at a painting that had hung in your house your entire life. Something so ingrained in you that you never thought twice about it until someone moved it to a different wall. You know the painting, but the context throws you off. Still, I knew he was telling the truth.

"Who transferred to you?" I asked. It was the most practical, nonemotional question I had.

"Transferred to me?"

I knew it couldn't have been Alicia. She transferred her powers to Eric when she died. But could she have been thinking about Tom as well? I didn't have time to unpack that. Tom was obviously not part of the Los Angeles Lunai Council, which put him at risk for being determined to be rogue, a Tellurian, like Alicia.

"Yes, transferred their powers to you. Gave you your powers. Who died?" I asked, impatiently.

"See, that's the thing, I don't know, Slo. I don't know what I've gotten myself into. I'm fucking freaking out." Tom fidgeted and grabbed his upper left arm with his right hand, sliding his fingers underneath his sleeve. Some things about him had stayed the same. "But after you came over to my house and I accidentally Stopped in the street and then you got us out of it—"

"Wait, that was *your* Slip?" I interrupted.

"Slip? Is that was you call it?"

"Yeah, that's what happens when you use your powers involuntarily," I answered him, eager to hear more of his story.

"Yeah, so, I Slipped and you fixed it and that's how I knew," he said in a shaky voice. I knew he wasn't saying everything he wanted, or needed, to say.

"How did you know I was going to be here?" I asked, fighting the temptation to blurt out everything I wanted to tell him. I had to figure out how much he knew before I could judge if he was to be trusted or not.

"I didn't. I came with Alicia. You know—the girl who was—"

"Yeah yeah yeah, I know," I interrupted.

"We were walking down the last cul-de-sac before the trail, and she started saying she needed to go. She was acting all manic, and I caught her hand just as she Jumped. She hurried off, Stopping and Starting to get away from me, and I lost track of her." Tom took a long, shuddering breath before continuing. "Then I saw you. On the bench. But I knew it wasn't you from high school. I remember what you were wearing on graduation night. So I came after you."

A discomfort pricked at my edges at the hidden meaning of his words.

"So where does she think you are?" I asked, hoping the nervousness in my voice wouldn't reveal how absolutely terrified I was that Tom may have led her straight to me.

Tom shifted his weight from one foot to the other where he stood, arms crossed, peering around the boulder down toward the bench, seemingly just as nervous as I was.

"That's what's freaking me out. I don't know what's going on with her. It's like she's an entirely different person every day. One day she'll act all normal and she looks all pretty and put together, and the next—it's like she's been using drugs for, like, a decade. She's all deranged and out of touch with reality and—When you came to my house earlier, after you got me out of that ... *Slip*, I went back to my house and she had completely morphed into some other version of herself." He pinched the bridge of his nose and heaved a deep sigh. "Do you and her know each other?"

"Not exactly," I answered.

Tom didn't look convinced, but his desperation overpowered his need for explanation. "You have to help me, Sloane. You're the only person I can trust with this."

Part of me wanted to snap at him. Ask him why the hell I should help him.

But I couldn't do that to him. I knew the reason Alicia was the way she was, but he obviously had no idea. He had no idea of the danger he was in.

"No secrets then," I declared. Our eyes met, and I held the gaze longer than I would have considered safe with him. But his held just as tightly.

"No secrets."

I took a deep breath that shook me more than I intended it to, before speaking. "So. You have no idea that she's actually dead, do you?"

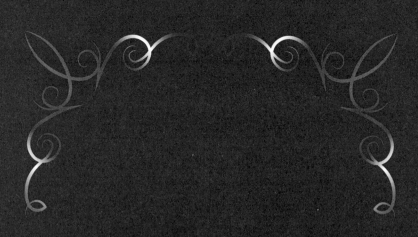

PART THREE

"We have learned that trauma is not just an event
that took place sometime in the past;
it is also the imprint left by that experience on mind, brain, and body.

This imprint has ongoing consequences for how
the human organism manages to survive in the present."

—Bessel van der Kolk

CHAPTER TWENTY-SEVEN

"I WANT TO believe you Sloane, I really do. I mean we're time travelers for f—"

"Wardens. Time Wardens," I corrected him.

"Yeah, whatever. I mean this whole situation is wild and all, but she can't be . . . *dead*." He whispered the last word as if it would offend someone.

"She's of course alive when you see her, but she died in 2022. I'm telling you," I started as I hastily typed into my phone, before holding it up to show him. "This is her obituary, Tom."

The cold glare of the screen illuminated Tom's face at a peculiar angle as he studied it, distorting his features. He scrolled back and forth a couple of times with his index finger as I held the phone. I could see his jaw muscles tighten as he became convinced.

"Well okay. So she's dead. But why is she bothering with all the recruits then?"

I narrowed my eyes at him. "What do you mean, recruits?"

"You know, like me and you. Recruiting new people to have powers."

"Uhm, no, Tom. There's no such thing as recruiting new people. You inherit these powers. When someone dies."

Tom's eyes went wide. I had already explained to him that I was being trained, there was a formal structure to the Lunai, a Sanctuary, rules to follow. I explained that she was rogue, something called Tellurian, without going into too many of the nasty details.

It hadn't surprised him, since Alicia always talked about "the others" and how she didn't want to "be a part of their cult." But it was harder to convince him the more I got into specifics.

"So a person somewhere in the world dies, and new powers get made, right?" he asked, weak hope trickling through with his words.

"No, Tom. A Lunai dies and their powers get transferred to the person they choose as their successor. I don't know where she is getting the powers for these recruits, but the powers aren't meant to multiply. Very rarely does one Lunai transfer to multiple people." If the situation had been different and not as grim, I would have been pretty proud of myself for how well I had managed to memorize from my readings of the Horolog.

Tom pinched the bridge of his nose, again, and looked down at our feet, before whispering angrily, "Fuck!"

"I'm sorry." My voice was small as I waited for him to look back up.

"No. I'm sorry. I'm sorry for letting her brainwash me—I should've listened to my gut when I felt something was wrong. It all makes so much sense now." Tom had never had a hard time admitting he was wrong. Even when we were young kids. It was one of his best traits.

"What is she doing, Tom?" I asked, not bothering to hide the fear in my voice.

A roar of laughter coming from the bench interrupted us. I heard my own voice exclaim, "No way! Who? Where? When?"

Tom and I peeked around the boulder, watching ourselves from a year ago. She fist-bumped his shoulder, he gestured at himself, their collective

THE AFTER HOURS

laughter echoing off the nearby hillside. Then a crisp silence reset the air, allowing his next words to chime clearly down the path to where we were hiding.

"I always thought it would be us, though." Graduation Tom's voice danced along the night breeze, distant but clear, hitting us both with an uncomfortable jolt. I hurriedly tucked myself back behind the boulder, not wanting to hear more of the conversation.

Tom backtracked into the brush to where he had been standing, fidgeting and avoiding eye contact with me.

"What is Alicia doing, Tom?" I pressed him for an answer.

"I should have realized sooner." He was still avoiding my eyes. "She keeps introducing me to people, calling them recruits, as if they're going to be part of some sort of group she is putting together. But then some of them, I never see again. And she always has a story of where they went, or she manages to dodge my questions. But that usually coincides with some recruits getting their powers." He let out a long breath before he spoke again. "Slo, I think she's killing them."

"It wouldn't surprise me," I said, looking at him deadpan as our eyes found each other again.

Tom's face held a world of pain at that remark, and I felt so bad for him. I could tell he, at some point, must have cared for her.

"Yeah. I'm starting to agree with you," he admitted.

"Have you met any other Lunai that are not one of her recruits?" I asked to make sure, even though I knew Alicia was most likely working alone. But if there were more Tellurian Lunai out there, that made the situation even scarier.

"No. Just a bunch of recruits. She said I was one of her first."

"How did she turn you, Tom?"

Tom looked surprised at the question. "Uhm, I don't know. I woke up and she told me it was done. Then I started having all these symptoms—nosebleeds, nausea—"

"I'm familiar." I scowled.

Tom opened his mouth as if to say something and wrinkled his brows.

"What?" I asked.

"I think I actually did meet someone who wasn't a recruit, now that I think about it," Tom said, still obviously contemplating.

"Who? Were they also trying to find new recruits?"

"No—" Tom began, still lost in thought. "She said it was a friend of hers, and that he was like us. I remember being kind of pissed off at her because they seemed to be way more than friends."

"What?" I exclaimed, narrowing my eyes. A twinge of panic pricked at my heart as my mind went straight to Eric.

"Yeah . . . we met up with him downtown and she was flirting up a storm, right in front of me." Tom swallowed hard, biting back bitterness before he continued. "Then I stormed off, and she apparently spent the night in his hotel room. But she swore nothing happened between them." He let out a heavy sigh. "I decided to believe her."

As if I couldn't be more disgusted by this person. But my brain was too busy putting two and two together to focus on her promiscuity. Something else about Tom's story was tugging at my mind.

"Tom, what was the guy's name? Do you remember?"

Please don't let it be Eric.

"How could I forget? We had a big fight about him. His name is Isaac Brewer."

The words sent a visceral shockwave through me.

"Tom. Isaac Brewer was found dead a few days ago. He was murdered in a hotel room downtown."

Tom sank down to the ground, taking a seat with his legs bent up in front of him. His shock was palpable.

"You okay?" I asked in a small voice.

"When?"

"When what?"

"When was he found dead?" Tom asked, without looking up at me, one hand over his mouth and nose.

I racked my brain for when my first Council meeting had been. "I think it was last weekend. Sometime over the Fourth of July weekend."

"Fuck." Tom buried his face in his hands. "That's when she was with him."

"Did Alicia say why she came here, to this moment?" I asked carefully. I didn't want to be inconsiderate of what he must have been dealing with in that moment, but I needed more information out of him before I became Alicia's next victim.

He lifted his gaze, letting his palm and fingertips drag, scrubbing his face. "No, she just said she had some business to take care of."

"Do you know where she went?" I tried to hide the panic in my voice.

"No. Like I said, I lost track of her. Then I saw you and decided to follow you instead."

"Okay, we may need to get out of here. What was she wearing when you followed her?" I asked frantically, wondering whether there was more than one version of her here. If Tom had followed the same version that attacked me the last time I Slipped here, the Me who was currently hiding in the bushes closer to the bench, then there was hopefully only one Alicia. But if he had followed a different Alicia, I was both in trouble, but also had a better chance at catching her off guard.

Tom looked confused by the question; I doubted he even paid attention to what she had been wearing. "Uhm . . . she was just wearing normal clothes, I guess. A hoodie? But like I said, she looked really off after she came back today. Like she was sick or something."

"A gray hoodie?" I asked as the memory of her and Eric struggling on the ground flashed before my eyes. I was certain she had been wearing a gray hoodie.

"Yeah. Yes, like sweatpants gray."

"Well, she's going to be here any second then. She's here for me."

"What? What do you mean? You said you guys didn't know each other—"

"Well she still wants to kill me. Long story."

Tom peered around the corner again to look at Graduation Us before speaking. "But, you're fine. You came home with me and—"

"It's not that Me she's trying to kill," I interrupted. "I came here the other night. One of Me is over there hiding behind the bushes."

Tom's eyes went wide. "How many of you are there?"

"In this moment?" I said, scanning the other edge of the greenbelt where Alicia had emerged from in my Slip. No sign of her. "Just three. Total this evening? Five."

"Jesus Christ . . ." Tom whispered under his breath. "That's gotta be dangerous though."

"Yup," I replied, not looking at him. "We really need to get a move on. They—we—are going to start walking in this direction at any moment"—I gestured toward the bench—"and I want to catch Alicia before she catches up to Me."

"Wait, what? You're not making any sense—"

Graduation Tom's laughter made its way down the trail along with the words, "An arrangement?" He kept laughing.

Our eyes met for a moment where we stood behind the monolith. Graduation Tom's words hung in the air, and all the other unsaid words teetered in between.

"You shouldn't have said that," I blurted, without thinking.

"I know," he responded, surprising me.

"We have to go now."

Tom protested, but I had already bolted out from behind the boulder, across the greenbelt to the edge of the nearest backyard. "Sloane!" I heard Tom call from behind me as I took long, quick strides over the grass, bending low and beckoning for him to follow me. He complied, begrudgingly, and followed me through an unintentional gap in the fencing surrounding the neighborhood and into the nearest cul-de-sac.

We came to a halt behind an RV that sat in the driveway of the house closest to the greenbelt. From there, we could see down the trail, the bench, and approximately the location where Alicia had ambushed me in my Slip.

"What are we doing?" Tom asked, frustrated.

"Alicia is going to be here any moment. I told you, she showed up when I was here the other day."

"Well, the Alicia I followed is probably far away from here at this point. She went in the other direction," Tom mumbled. I didn't have time to argue with him.

"Look, smartass," I snarked, pointing toward the trail.

You could just barely make out the outline of a Past Me trying to slip away through the brush. Graduation Me and Tom were getting up to leave, their figures tiny compared to the vantage point we had previously had. But one figure that had appeared seemingly out of nowhere was unmistakable even from afar. Alicia's red hair gave her away instantly as she made her way toward Past Me.

"What the—" Tom began.

My heart ached. I wanted so badly to come to my own rescue.

. . . you can end up hurting them or yourself or both, because you just feel this immense need to be one with them. Your soul longs to be in one place.

Adrian's words and the angry memory of him stung just as hard as the ache in my heart.

Tom and I watched Graduation Us make our way up the trail and disappear behind the boulder and the subsequent hillside. Soon, Alicia and Past Me would disappear around the other bend in the trail, in the opposite direction.

"Come on, we have to follow them," I whispered, stepping into the street.

"Why on earth would you do that? Didn't you just say she came here to try to kill you?" Tom was having the hardest time keeping his voice low.

I raised my eyebrows at him in disbelief. "Uhm, yeah? That's why I'm here. To get her before she gets me. Or before she manages to escape, at least."

"You don't seem sure what you're doing. Is that what actually happened? Did you see yourself?"

The tug to run down the trail was almost unbearable. I wanted to scream at Tom where he stood, still behind the RV, feet firmly immobile.

"No, dude. I'm trying to change things here. It's for everyone's good," I snapped.

"Sloane. Listen to yourself. Are you saying you're going to change the Past? And do what, actually *kill* her?" he said with a look of disbelief.

His mocking infuriated me. "No! Okay, maybe I don't know exactly what I'm going to do, but I know I can't do *nothing* anymore! She has to be stopped!" My voice was fully out of whisper at this point. "And since when are you the Lunai rule keeper? You just learned the correct name not even half an hour ago!" I added. It was unnecessary, but I was annoyed with him.

"Okay." Tom threw his hands up in defeat. "I get it. You want to do something. I want to as well—that's why I came to you. But Slo, you're only going to cause more damage by trying to interfere where you know you'll be changing the Past." He took a few steps down the driveway and into the street. "And you're not violent." He chuckled. "You're not a killer. But it's highly likely that she is."

The tug to Past Me lessened. The tug to Tom, who had always managed to talk me out of any craziness, increased. My instincts had been right. They must have been, since Tom suspected it too.

Alicia was a murderer, and I couldn't sink to her level in order to stop her. Like Eric said, she died in 2022. Until that became her Present, she was essentially untouchable. Unless I changed the course of absolutely everything.

"You need to think about this, Slo. And if what you're saying is true, we really should get out of here before she comes back," Tom continued when I didn't say anything.

"Well, let's just get back to the Present then," I conceded, reaching out a hand to him. It felt strange to speak freely about Jumping around him. My brain hadn't fully wrapped itself around the fact that he was like me. The thought excited me at the same time that it sent a wave of panic through me.

"Actually . . ." Tom began. He fidgeted nervously, rolling his shoulders and glancing away from me as if he didn't know how to say what he needed to say. I wanted to shake him and tell him to spit it out. But I made do with raising my eyebrows and shooting him an impatient look, that did the trick and got him talking.

"I was actually hoping to show you something that's happening now, tonight. We have to stay here a bit longer." His voice quivered ever so slightly.

"Where?" I asked, my voice small again.

"My house."

I narrowed my eyes at him and instinctually took half a step backward. "You want to show me something that happened *tonight*, graduation night, at *your* house? Where you and I *just* headed?" I cocked my thumb toward where Graduation Tom and I had disappeared behind the hillside.

"Trust me," he pleaded.

My eyes met his and held the stare for a long moment, staying silent. When I didn't say anything, he spoke again.

"No more secrets, Slo."

I made him wait longer than I should have before responding, sighing defeatedly, "No more secrets."

CHAPTER TWENTY-EIGHT

Tom's house was among the largest in the neighborhood and resembled an old southern estate with its wraparound porch, navy blue shutters, and white wood siding. It stuck out like a sore thumb in the sea of beige and brown stone-clad McMansions that lined the subdivision streets.

Tom stopped a couple of houses down from his home and sat down on a transformer box on the edge of the sidewalk. The streetlight above went out as soon as we came too close, covering us in darkness.

"So what are we waiting for?" I asked impatiently, standing next to the transformer with my hands on my hips, the lack of forward momentum making me restless.

"You'll see; just keep watching the house." Tom's gaze didn't waver from the house.

I glanced at my phone; it was almost two o'clock in the morning. Nausea pricked at my chest as I thought of the irony of having to relive these very moments. I knew exactly what was going on inside that house, but I wished I didn't.

Me being stupid, wanting to erase everything that happened at the party earlier that evening.
Replace it with something better. Rewrite the story. Regain control.
Tom being the responsible one.
His hands on my bare skin.
Him asking me a million times if I was okay.
"Are we screwing things up?"
How surprisingly soft his lips were.
"This isn't an arrangement."
The subtle smell of his cologne, like a warm breeze after traversing through a forest.
Promises made to not let anything change between us.
His arms around me as if there was nowhere else I should ever have been.
My favorite memory, that I'd tried so hard to forget.

He wasn't wearing that cologne now, and I wondered if he changed his smell for Alicia. Nausea doubled up on me at the thought of them. She was so different from me. Tall and thin, angled features, fiercely and frightfully confident.

How could he be attracted to such polar opposites?

Maybe he was never attracted to me.

My mind wandered to Eric. He had also fallen for the two of us, so maybe it wasn't so far-fetched. The incestuousness of it all made me shudder. I looked at Tom, still not used to seeing him without his glasses. It felt as though he couldn't have been further away from the person he was a year ago. Whom Graduation Me was sharing a bed with at that very moment. Then again, I hadn't been my true self that night either. I had felt upset and unloved, so I looked to the only person I knew loved me unconditionally: Tom. But a drunken quasi mistake wasn't what ended our friendship.

Justin had been correct to be skeptical of my lie. Our friendship was so much stronger than that. What had been its downfall was what came next.

"What's the point of all this? I don't want to see myself—" I began.

Tom held a finger to his lips and gestured for me to look.

Someone had opened the front door of the house, taking one step onto the front porch and glancing up and down the street. The person knelt down and rummaged around in the pile of newspapers on the porch, checking each and every one of them.

"Is that—?" I squinted to try to see better.

"Me. Yup," Tom replied.

"What the—"

"My second to last secret is that there are actually three versions of me here. I uhh—Slipped again—earlier today. After you left. I'm checking the dates on the newspapers to get an idea of where I am."

The fact that he Slipped to this moment meant he'd been thinking back to this night after I told him to never speak to me again and then left him in the street—and in a way that stirred his emotions enough to cause a Slip. I couldn't help but feel a bit of satisfaction at the fact, given that I had already Slipped back to this night three times already.

I peered again and saw that this Tom didn't have glasses. He was telling the truth. Graduation Tom needed his glasses to find his own nose. He could never make it down the stairs and out the door without them. Plus, he was wearing the same clothes I had left him in.

"You can check your phone, you know. They update for some reason," I said, my voice monotone.

He pulled his phone out to test my theory. "Yeah, well, I didn't know that," he huffed.

"Okay, so you Slipped here. And what?"

"Just wait."

Tom from the Past returned inside the house and closed the door behind him. A few moments passed and I was starting to get pissed off. The silence around us was harsh and buzzing.

But then, a figure appeared on the front porch where Tom from the Past had just been. A figure with long, wavy, red hair. It was not the same Alicia we had seen by the trail. This one was wearing a pale-yellow dress underneath a denim jacket. I took two rushed steps in the direction of the house, but Tom caught me and yanked me back behind the transformer box and farther into the yard we were trespassing on, hiding us from Alicia's view behind a row of immaculately trimmed hedges.

"Let me go!" I whispered sharply.

"Absolutely not."

I struggled against his grip, but my attempts quickly became half-hearted.

"I think there's a reason I Slipped to this moment," he began as his hold loosened.

I yanked my arm free with a final tug, but didn't go anywhere, indicating I was willing to hear him out.

"I had no idea what you were talking about when you came over earlier. Honest. I thought you were mad at me because"—he stole a glance toward the house—"because of what happened between us."

I felt my jaw clench involuntarily. I wanted so badly to believe him.

"And then you started talking about some videos, and I just had to get to the bottom of it. And I figured it must have happened this night, because we were fine up until then."

I could still see his house through the hedge we hid behind, and I caught a glimpse of Alicia letting herself into the house.

"So," Tom continued after a deep breath, "right now, Past Me is in there, freaking out because I barely managed to hide before Alicia saw me. I'm currently hiding in the coat closet off the downstairs hall."

"What's your point here, Tom?" I kept my voice deliberately soft.

"I followed her upstairs. And I think we should too. Right now. Are you able to Stop?"

I weighed the option for a moment. It felt strange to be the stronger one in a pair after all the time spent with Eric, Adrian, and Maddie. I wasn't sure I could Stop in a Jump. Still, I hadn't Flickered since earlier behind the boulder by the trail. In fact, I'd barely felt a tingle. Like I was becoming more and more grounded in this moment.

Which was probably not a good thing.

"I think so," I said, nodding.

He reached his hand out to mine. Sparks radiated out from where our fingers grazed each other, but instead of fizzling out, they turned into a wave of smooth, static energy that swept through us like a warm embrace. Our eyes fluttered shut, and for a moment I felt weightless, as if I was being swept along by a lazy current.

This must be the place.

As our eyes opened, they immediately made contact. I let my gaze linger a little longer than normal, reveling in the comfort of being able to look into his familiar face before I let go and started looking around for evidence of my Stop being successful. There wasn't much to go by; the night had been so silent already. But the dry desert breeze that never seemed to cease in the valley where we lived no longer swept along the sides of my temples, making my flyaways twitch annoyingly. There was a still, eerie, uncomfortable silence now.

I realized we were still holding hands just as Tom let go. He nicked his head in the direction of the house, telling me to follow him.

We entered the Salinger house like so many times before. But this was the first time I had been scared to walk into his house. The last time I had exited the house I had also been scared. For the same reasons.

"Oh jeez, this is so fucked up," Tom exclaimed as soon as he closed the door behind him. I looked at him to see what he was talking about, and he pointed down the hall. Sure enough, just like he had said, Past Tom from earlier in the day I had Jumped from was peeking his head out of the coat closet, his gaze directed to the second floor above.

I laughed. For the first time in what seemed like a lifetime, I let myself laugh. My voice rang and echoed throughout the vast, two-story entryway, bouncing off the paneled walls and barrel vault ceiling. It was unsettling to know that the amount of sound I was making, the sheer energy I was letting into it, would never exist again. This Stop could never be visited again; it existed outside of time. It was almost as if elements that required time to exist, like sound, never existed to begin with, except for the person in the Stop. It could just as well have been in my head. But that also meant that it was kind of like Tom and I were sharing thoughts, something we weren't that unfamiliar with.

Tom laughed with me before saying, "I will never get used to this. Seriously. Seeing yourself is just too whack."

"I know."

Tom's face changed suddenly as he stepped closer to the coat closet version of him, becoming more and more concerned.

"What is it?" I asked.

Tom came to a halt right next to the coat closet door, so close he could touch his other version. "I don't know. It's weird. I just had this bad feeling." He turned to look at me. "Is it weird that I want to hug him—erm, me?"

I smiled, happy to be able to put Tom's mind at ease. "No, that's not weird at all. It happens when you see yourself. Especially if you have multiple After Hours stacked like you do right now."

"After Hours?" Tom asked, looking more concerned.

I shook my head. "Forget that. Sorry. I'm info dumping. All you need to know is, it's normal. It's your soul wanting to be in one place."

Tom's eyes widened. "Okay yeah, enough info for now." He chuckled nervously before pointing up the staircase. "Shall we?"

My stomach lurched. I didn't want to see what was happening upstairs. But I had to trust Tom that it was important.

"Sure."

As we scaled the stairs, my heart beat steadily faster with each step, and I started to worry whether I'd be able to sustain the Stop. It was tugging at me a little bit, making me dizzy. Holding a Stop inside a Jump was tremendously taxing.

"Okay, so," Tom said breathlessly as he stopped at the top of the stairs to turn around and face me. "Me from downstairs is about to come up here and see what we're about to see, except not in a Stop. She didn't notice me, but I did bolt back down the stairs rather ungracefully, so she's probably gonna know something's up in just a little bit. It's your call if you want to Start again and see her in action, or if you want to stay, you know, Stopped."

It still felt so weird to be having Lunai conversations with Tom. He seemed, despite his self-proclaimed lack of ability and improper usage of some of the terminology, to have caught on pretty fast. Maybe Alicia was teaching him well. The thought annoyed me. But Tom probably had an easier time filling in the gaps than I did, having watched way more sci-fi movies than I would in an entire lifetime.

Suddenly, nausea hit me like a brick wall, and I Flickered.

"Slo, you okay?" Tom placed his hand on my shoulder, and I instinctively pulled away even though I immediately regretted it.

"Yeah, I uhm—so you're telling me that it was her all this time? She was *here* on *graduation night*?"

Tom nodded ever so slightly and gestured for me to follow him down the hall. As I looked in front of us, I saw where Alicia stood with her ear on Tom's bedroom door. In her hand was a DSLR camera.

"She's not even in a Stop! It's like she's not even trying to be careful," I growled.

"She's about to Stop before she goes inside. She comes back out without the camera. If we were to Start time, in a few moments you'd see Other Me watch her from the top of the stairs," Tom explained, pointing to the top of the staircase. "But yeah, she's basically nuts. Probably craves the thrill of the possibility of being caught." Tom shot me a pleading look. I knew I had to help him.

I didn't take you for a thrill seeker.

Eric's statement poked at me, and anger blossomed in my chest. I didn't want to be anything like her.

"I'm sorry I thought it was you." My eyes filled with tears almost instantly, surprising me. "I'm so, so, sorry."

"I know. It's okay. I forgive you." Tom's voice was the softest it had been since the night we were currently visitors in. And I realized just how much I had needed to tell him that I was sorry. I wondered if I had known deep down all this time that Tom would never do something like that.

Suddenly, I Flickered again, catching myself completely off guard. It ripped at me with a searing pain.

"I can't stay here. I can't be this close to her. I'm going to lose the Stop and expose us."

Tom closed the distance between us with one step and placed an arm around me, the other reaching for my hand down by our sides, making sure to hold it skin-to-skin, readying himself to take us back to the Present.

And for the first time in almost a year, I finally felt home again.

CHAPTER TWENTY-NINE

"Y<small>OU UNDERSTAND THAT</small> in order for me to help you, I have to get Adrian—the Curator—involved." Tom and I sat in his car. Tom had managed to Jump us both back from the Stop we were in on graduation night. I had wanted to walk home from Tom's, but I was exhausted from holding both the Stop and the Jump for so long.

"You trust him?" Tom asked.

"Of course!" I exclaimed, offended at his suspicion, but also, not entirely sure.

"Sorry. I just really don't know who to trust here. Alicia has made *them* sound like criminals."

I felt for him. Being unsure myself of whether I could trust Adrian—or Eric—I knew the turmoil he must have been going through. But I hoped he trusted me enough to follow my lead.

"Just trust your gut. You know what she's capable of. You came to me because it didn't feel right. And your instinct was correct."

THE AFTER HOURS

Tom nodded, but I could see his knuckles turn white where he gripped the steering wheel.

As much as I wanted to get the confrontation over with, going to the Sanctuary would have to wait. It was well past midnight, and if I was going to show up there while on probation, I wasn't going to do so in the middle of the night. I almost laughed at the irony of the situation: someone with my powers having to deal with such temporal time restrictions.

But alas, I was also exhausted; the Jump, Stop, and Flickers had taken a toll.

"Let's get some sleep and then we'll head over to the Sanctuary. Sound good?" I tried to sound as reassuring as possible, even though I was scared as hell what they would do to Tom when they found out about him.

He was unregistered; he might have Tellurian powers for all I knew. I just had to trust that they wouldn't punish him for what Alicia was responsible for. Especially if he cooperated and gave the Council valuable information.

"Sounds good." Tom smiled at me, his eyes tired.

I turned to get out of the car but stopped to look back at him with my hand on the door lever. "Hey. I really am sorry I didn't believe you."

"I wouldn't have believed me," he said, his smile growing.

I smiled back and bade him good night before climbing out and softly closing the door behind me. I stood in place on the sidewalk, watching his car mosey down to the end of my street before turning left at the stop sign. I chuckled to myself at the thought that there were millions of stop signs around the world with a hidden meaning known only to a few. If only the Temps knew.

෬෨෬෨෬෨

Sloan: Trying one more time . . .
Sloan: Okay. I get it. But I can't keep your secret. I'm sorry.
Sloan: I have to tell the council.

Tom hadn't picked up his phone or responded to my texts all morning. At first I thought he was probably still sleeping. But by one in the afternoon, I realized that maybe he'd had a change of heart. Either about seeking help from the Council—or simply about me. I refused to take it personally. I had spent a year without him, and I would not miss him this time around. I refused to.

At least, that's what I told myself, in a desperate attempt to shield my heart. Was I hurt that I had gotten my hopes up after the night before, that our friendship might actually have had a chance of returning to what it once was? Of course I was. But I was also just annoyed with myself for setting myself up for disappointment.

The important thing was to bring the information I learned from him to Adrian as soon as possible. Not only would it help the Council, but maybe, just maybe—it would get me back in their good graces after my screw-up.

I parked my car by a grocery store a few blocks away from Adrian's house. I knew I was supposed to Stop and let myself in so that the neighbors wouldn't see me, but that also meant using my powers. If Maddie hadn't already Sensed my Jump from the previous night, she would for sure Sense me Stopping and Starting now.

Would it be worse to have them know I was still using my powers? Or would they be angrier if a neighbor spotted me?

"Fuck it," I muttered, and drove the car out of the lot and around the corner, finding the parking spot closest to the house. Once parked, I strolled up to the porch, but before I could even knock or open the door, it flew open.

"You really shouldn't be here." Maddie's face was the most concerned I'd ever seen her. She looked incredibly tired. It was hard seeing such a young face look so exhausted.

I threw my hands up and pitched my voice low. "I know, I know. I'm sorry. But I have to see your dad. And the others. I have some really important news."

Maddie's expression turned from concerned to pained, but she stayed silent.

"Please, Maddie. I swear, I have information on the murders."

I could tell her interest was piqued, but she still didn't say anything.

"I know who has been hunting and killing Lunai. Possibly even been creating new ones. Unregistered."

Now Maddie's eyes went extra wide. "New Lunai? Here in LA?"

"Yeah," I answered, breathless. I had been holding my breath without realizing. "Is that what you've been Sensing?" I was probing, but my instinct turned out to be correct.

"It's only been keeping me awake for, like, ever," Maddie huffed. "I can't figure it out though, so I haven't told Dad. It's almost the same as with you—I didn't Sense anyone dying and transferring their powers to you. You were just there one day, poof! New powers. Malina doesn't seem to be noticing it either, and I was starting to think there was something wrong with my power." Maddie's voice broke at the final words, which got her to stop rambling.

"Hey, it's okay—" I hesitantly put my arms out, hoping she would let me hug her.

She fell into my arms and squeezed tight. "I will kill you if you tell anyone I let you hug me."

I thought about making a teasing remark, that it was more her that was hugging me, but I let it be and instead tightened my arms around her. I could tell she needed it.

When we stepped into the Sanctuary, Adrian's eyes found me immediately from where he stood at the dais, handling the Horolog. The hall was half full, the tables and chairs still in a dining hall formation, except instead of food and coffee cups, the tables were littered with thick books, notebooks, maps, papers, pens, and laptops. It looked like they were preparing for war.

Various Lunai were gathered around the different tables, busy with whatever work they were doing, but as Adrian continued to silently look at me, his recognition seemed to spread out and infect those around him, until all eyes in the hall were on me and Maddie.

I spotted Eric sitting at a table close to the entrance of the hall, poring over a large map with a group of other Lunai. Our eye locked, his holding a look of disbelief, like he was trying to find the right words to say.

I forced myself to tear my gaze away from him, redirecting it toward the front of the hall and Adrian. I couldn't take the accusing stares and ruinous silence, and before I even had time to think the decision over, I started to speak.

"I know I'm not supposed to be here," I said, marveling at how my voice sounded as it reverberated off the stone walls of the hall. It was like the hall was built to magnify the voice of a single speaker.

No one said a word. Or blinked, for that matter.

"I know I broke the Laws, and for that I'm sorry. But I have information about the murders. Information that could help us stop the killer. That killer is the reason I broke the Laws to begin with."

My eyes met Adrian's once again. His expression had not wavered since he first spotted me, but he had stepped down from the platform and was now situated by one of the front tables. I glanced at the Horolog; it was the first time I had seen it unguarded by Adrian. My skin prickled as I wished I could just do a tiny little Stop and go read the pages that had been missing from Eric's copy.

But I found myself compelled to continue speaking. Until someone stopped me, I would tell my side of the story. "I'm not saying that as an excuse. And I will accept whatever punishment the Council deems fit for my mistake. But the fact of the matter is, I know who the murderer is, and it is the same person who has been stalking me for weeks."

A murmur rang through the crowd.

Maddie tugged at my sleeve before asking, "What are you talking about? Why didn't you say anything?"

My eyes went back to Eric, and his expression changed instantly. "I was told that the situation was being taken care of. But I guess not."

"Well who is it then?" it was Victor, the ever-vocal Council member. He was sitting at Adrian's table.

My eyes were still on Eric. He glared at me, shaking his head back and forth ever so slowly, his movements so minuscule I doubt anyone in the hall but myself noticed.

"The killer's name is Alicia Stubbert. Also known as Alicia Baxter."

Furtive glances piled in Eric's direction. His eyes locked on me, livid. He stood up in one movement, sending his chair flying off behind him, not bothering to push it back under the table. All eyes stayed on him as he stormed past me and out of the hall, nostrils flaring and jaw clenched, avoiding my eyes when he got closer. I had the hardest time keeping my guise determined. I needed to tell him that I had no choice but to speak up, but that would have to wait.

The hall erupted into chatter. My fellow Lunai had expressions that ranged from confusion to frustration, from disbelief to terror. I heard a few people ask their neighbors who I was, where I had come from. I couldn't blame them; it's not like I had made an effort to introduce myself to people during the little time I had spent at the Sanctuary.

"And how do *you* know this?" Victor's voice boomed over the rest of the crowd. He stood now, hands on his hips, an annoyed look on his face.

"Yeah, who are you even?" A young black-haired woman next to Victor stood to match him, her voice patronizing.

"Can everyone be quiet please?" Adrian delivered the polite request at a surprisingly high decibel, and the crowd became silent almost instantly. His eyes were cold as they locked onto me. He continued, "Everyone, this is Sloane Becker. The newest member of the LA Council. She is on probation for Pattern interference and is not supposed to set foot in the Sanctuary."

"I say we hear her out."

The voice came from the right wing of the compound, from the second story balcony. Eyes all across the hall drifted upward to find its owner.

Malina made her way toward the spiral staircase and took her time with each stair, her thick-heeled boots thudding loudly on the thin metal treads. She came to a halt next to me, and I noticed then that Maddie had made herself scarce.

The little traitor. I thought I wasn't standing alone.

"I say, we hear what she has to say. See if her sources are credible. We don't have much else to go by anyway." Malina spoke with the ease of someone with authority.

"Thank you," I said quietly, begrudgingly.

Malina's head spun in my direction. She was much taller than me, but she was mere inches away. Her eyes were furious as she whispered so no one else could hear, "Don't."

I narrowed my eyes at her. I could tell she wanted me to be scared of her. But I had come to expect this demeanor. I was ready to retort, despite it being out of character.

"I know exactly what I just did. Eric will have to deal." I pitched my voice to match hers, all low tones and sharpness.

Malina let out a low, unamused chuckle and shook her head before turning back to the crowd.

"All in favor of hearing what Sloane has to say?" Adrian posed.

Malina's hand shot up. An obvious majority of hands followed, albeit some more reluctantly than others.

"Sloane, you have an audience," Adrian declared and sat down.

Malina went to join Adrian, and I was suddenly very aware that every person in the enormous hall was waiting on what I was going to say next. The initial rush of adrenaline of being there, seeing Eric, saying Alicia's name out loud, was wearing off quickly, and with it came a wave of withdrawal causing my very bones to shake.

"So—" I began, hating myself suddenly. "My best friend, Tom Salinger, was supposed to be here with me to tell you in his own words. But he couldn't be here—"

Victor let out an angry scoff of disbelief so loud it echoed across the hall as he rolled his eyes.

I willed my voice to steady before I continued.

"He has Lunai powers. Yet he doesn't know who they came from. But he's been—he was introduced to Alicia a while ago. She is the one who allegedly got him his powers. But it's not only him. She's been actively recruiting."

Faces across the hall softened into curiosity; even Malina seemed to perk up and take notice.

"Recruiting?" Adrian asked.

The fact that Adrian interacted with me willingly made my heart flutter hopefully. "Yes. Tom told me that she keeps introducing him to new people, some of whom disappear shortly thereafter. This coincides with a handful of other new people gaining power."

Displeased tones skittered across the hall.

"So where is this friend of yours?" I glanced to my left and spotted Nico at one of the tables, his rough voice unmistakable with its signature hint of mocking no matter what the words were.

"Like I said, he couldn't be here right now. But he fully intends on cooperating and telling us everything he knows." I could feel tiny pearls of sweat form at my hairline.

"I call BS," Victor boomed before returning to the laptop he was working on.

"Do you have any tangible proof to show us to support your case, Sloane?" Adrian asked dryly.

My eyes scanned the crowd as my heart threatened to break my ribs. Expectant glances started fading to disappointed, judging stares the longer I stayed silent.

"Well, no. Not on me at the moment. But my friend—" I couldn't control the shaking in my voice.

"I've been Sensing it," Maddie said, standing up from where she had blended into the crowd at one of the tables.

"Madeline?" Adrian looked at his daughter with intense concern.

I hadn't wanted Maddie to have to come to my rescue, but relief washed over me all the same.

Maddie let out a long, dramatic sigh. She didn't mind the spotlight. "I haven't been able to figure it out exactly, so I was going to keep it to myself until I knew what I was Sensing. But what Sloane said makes sense. I've been Sensing lots of new power but also lots of power disappearing."

"Any discontinuations?" a woman at Maddie's table asked.

"No, that's the weird part. There's usually at least a shift when power gets transferred. But the lineage is muddled. Like, I don't know. Like I said, I'm not sure what it is but it makes me want to believe Sloane." Maddie plopped herself down again, clearly stating that she was not welcoming more questions.

"Malina? Your Sense is keen to lineage. Can you tell us if you have been picking up on anything strange recently?" Adrian turned to face Malina as he asked.

Malina's eyes met mine for a fraction of a second, but it was enough to get her message across to me. I was not to say another word.

"I have reason to believe that what Sloane is saying is true. I can confirm that Tom Salinger has indeed manifested powers. As far as I know, he is neither registered with the LA Council nor any other Council. Neither is this . . . Alice?" Malina directed her question at me; I could tell she was throwing the others off. Playing dumb. She knew what Alicia's name was.

"Alicia," I corrected.

"So . . . she's rogue?" Victor inquired.

"Well then, what are we waiting for? We gotta bring her here! Stop her from using her powers—" the black-haired woman spoke, her voice shaky, but Adrian cut her off.

"No. We won't take any drastic actions. It might be dangerous. She might be Tellurian." Adrian stood up and made his way to the Horolog on the dais.

A wave of discomfort engulfed the people in the hall.

"Tellurian? But how could that be? They haven't existed in decades—" a blonde woman sitting at a table to my left said, panic lacing her words, but Adrian ignored her.

"Tellurian protocol is to involve the Consul and the Conservatory immediately. Besides, if, and only if, we are truly dealing with a Tellurian, the last thing you want to do is to bring them to a Sanctuary." Adrian's voice was grave as he continued to flip through the ancient pages in front of him.

"What? Why?" Victor asked, not bothering to conceal his annoyance.

"Because the Sanctuary's effects may not be enough to subdue their powers. We'd essentially be rendering ourselves powerless, but not them." Adrian paused his perusing of the Horolog to look up at Victor.

A couple people gasped and muttered under their breaths. But no one was more surprised than I was, and I had the hardest time keeping my chin off the floor.

"You heard her, fellow Wardens. Alicia Baxter. Let's see where the lead takes us," Adrian ordered as he stepped down. He headed to the kitchen off the side of the hall, closing the door behind him without another word. I couldn't help feeling hurt that he didn't come over to speak with me one-on-one.

The crowd sprang into action and got back to their planning, but not without shooting glances in my direction. Out of the corner of my eye, I saw Victor charge toward Malina and me.

"Adrian and Malina may want to believe you, but you're still on probation. Come on." Victor gestured for me to follow him toward the Sanctuary exit.

"I'll escort her," Malina's voice came from behind me just as I turned to follow Victor.

"Thanks, Mal. Get back quick; we need you," he huffed.

Malina didn't say a word to me, just kept walking past me and out into the hallway that led to the elevator.

I wondered if the elevator was cursed. Or maybe I was. Each time I had used it, there had been some sort of tension in the air. But this ride took the cake. Malina's iciness was like a straitjacket. I rushed outside, stepping out onto the front porch of the craftsman, but once again the door didn't close behind me as I had expected.

Much to my surprise, Malina was now following me.

"Keep walking," she said through clenched teeth.

My heart pounded as I made my way out to the sidewalk, and I contemplated whether I should lead her somewhere other than my car. I yearned to use my powers in that very moment, anything to get me out of whatever confrontation Malina was planning.

We were just about to my car, and I was panicking over whether I should stop and get in or keep walking, when Malina spoke again.

"Sloane. I think we're far enough."

I spun around to face her, taking small sips of air through my nose.

"Whatever you have to say, let Eric say it for himself. Don't be that girl who does her boyfriend's dirty work." I was trying so hard to keep my voice steady that it almost sounded robotic.

Malina's face morphed into complete bewilderment. I shot her my best "what are you going to do about it" look, willing my face to stay stiff.

Then she burst into laughter. Wholehearted, shoulders shaking, belly-clutching laughter. I'd never seen her smile that way, her pearly white teeth a sharp contrast against her dark complexion. She really was very pretty.

"Oh, Sloane. You are misunderstanding the situation on *so* many levels."

CHAPTER THIRTY

"Didn't I tell you to stay out of trouble? It can't have been too long for you—you still look just like I remembered you," Malina said, once she came out of her laughing fit.

"It was, like, three days ago." My voice came out grumpy, but I didn't care. "Good times. Sorry I puked in front of you."

I acknowledged her apology with a grunt and crossed my arms over my chest as I leaned back on my car, the soles of my shoes balancing on the edge of the curb.

"Listen to me. Don't worry about Eric. There's never been anything between us and never will be. He's literally smitten with you, Sloane. And you're breaking his heart right now."

"Fine." I sighed. "Let's say I believe you. Then what was that I walked in on in his room?"

"Well, Eric was telling me that Alicia was back. And I told him I was sorry and hugged him. As a friend would do."

She was matter-of-fact but wasn't doing a good job at hiding her amusement.

"So you know the whole story about Alicia?" I guessed. I knew Malina had been helping Eric in 2022, but I didn't know how much he had filled her in on Alicia's motivations.

Malina took a deep breath and joined me in leaning on the car. "Okay, story time," she began, and I shifted nervously; she had positioned herself a little too closely for me to comfortably look her in the eye while she was talking, setting me on edge. Instead, I stared straight ahead at one of Adrian's neighbor's fences.

"So you know how I'm a Sensor, right? Well, back before Maddie started practicing using her Sense, I was the only Sensor in the LA area. For a few weeks, I kept picking up on some super weird activity that was increasingly sporadic, and I could never pinpoint it. It wasn't like normal manifestation symptoms or anything where the person keeps Slipping. It was more like these explosions of power that then fizzled into nothing. Then one day, I managed to track it well enough that it led me to Eric. When I got to him, I understood why it had been throwing me off. I'm not like Maddie—that girl tracks like a bloodhound—my specialty is lineage.

"But that day, I found both Eric and Alicia, Eric having some of the gnarliest manifestation symptoms I've ever seen and Alicia, of course, Jumping from the Past from before she died. Eric being her powers' heir, they were both expelling the same power signature, so of course it came off weird for me."

I glanced sideways at Malina, who was also looking straight ahead as if she were reading off the chain link fence and the overgrown bush beyond it. What she was saying made sense, but I still had so many questions.

"We worked so hard to try to stop her. Get her to stop stalking Eric, stop acting as if she could just live in the Future, accruing so many After Hours. She refused to believe that she was killing herself. That her actions were why she died so young.

"Eventually, her visits became fewer and farther between, and then they stopped altogether. We figured she had run out of time, that she hadn't managed to squeeze in any more Jumps before she died. But since she's back now, she probably just started focusing on Jumping to another time. Which would be now. Our Present."

"Wait, why didn't you guys get Adrian and the Council involved back then?"

Malina glanced at me with a stern look. "Because that would have been a surefire way to have Eric Stripped, or worse. Tellurian lineage is strong, and the Stripping ritual doesn't always work on them. There's a reason the Tellurian were eradicated, not just Stripped."

She was skirting around the words, but I knew she meant that the only way to stop a Tellurian would be to kill them. It dawned on me that my feeble attempt to Strip Alicia had never stood a chance to begin with.

"So when I introduced Eric to Adrian and the rest of the Council, we made up a story about how Eric had inherited his powers from an older lady visiting from another country, someone whose name we wouldn't know. We told Adrian there had been a car accident and Eric was the first to discover it, had stopped to check on the victims and call 911. The lady had died while Eric was trying to comfort her and, as it turned out, she was Lunai."

"And Adrian believed this?" I asked incredulously.

"Well, it's my job as the LA Council Sensor to tell the truth. So yeah, he believes it."

"Why are you keeping his secret? Why risk your own neck and your position with the Council?" I asked, suspicion still gnawing at the back of my mind. It sure sounded like they were more than friends for Malina to put herself in that position.

Malina's eyes met mine, and I could tell she was contemplating whether to be truthful or not. "Let's just say I have some secrets too. And the only other person who will ever know them is Eric, so don't bother asking."

I decided to take what she said at face value. I wasn't entitled to her secrets. Even if I felt like I was.

"Okay. So I get why you were . . . upset, that I revealed Alicia to the Council. I didn't mean to get you in trouble—"

"Oh, I'm not angry at you, that was an act. It's not me you have to worry about."

"Well Eric—"

"Not just Eric." Malina pressed herself off the car and came to face me on the sidewalk.

"What?" I asked angrily.

Malina stayed silent but didn't break eye contact with me. Her eyes told me that whatever she meant, I had to figure it out myself. It made me even more annoyed.

"What? Tell me!" I exclaimed after a while, "I'm not here to play games—"

"You really don't know how to keep yourself out of trouble," Malina said cryptically, in stark contrast to the truth dump she had just provided. I wanted to storm off.

"You can't just tell me all these things but not tell me the whole truth," I snarled. "If there are consequences I need to know about—"

"I'm sorry, Sloane. It's your Future, and I can't tell you. All I can say is that you need to trust me."

I growled in frustration, "I fucking hate when people say that. I'm sick of it. And it's not working anyway! Look where it got me!"

Malina chuckled. "Don't worry. Eric and I hadn't planned on this, but I think we can still make this work in our favor. We just have to be smart about it. Keep up the act, okay? Let me take the lead, and we'll all be fine."

"How?" I looked at her suspiciously. "They're going to figure out that you and Eric were lying because of what I said. How are you not mad?"

Malina was smiling a small smile. "Look. Yes, you may not have done it in the best way, but it was bound to happen. Especially if your suspicions about her breeding new Lunai is correct. The Council should know what she is up to, otherwise she's just going to continue to kill, right?"

"I guess?"

"So there are two outcomes here: either we get the Council's help to stop her once and for all, and then we plead our case and take our chances afterward. Or, we let her continue to kill and wreak havoc in our lives, and the secret might still get out. I know which option I would choose."

"If you are so certain of this, did you know it was her all along?"

"I knew Alicia was capable of some outrageous stuff, but I never fathomed she'd become a murderer. But when you said her name, I knew that the time I met you years ago wasn't the only time you'd had to deal with her."

Still feeling suspicious and indignant, I was at a loss for words. I hadn't noticed that I had my arms crossed tightly, as if I were cold, which was far from being the case in the afternoon mugginess that enveloped us.

Malina gently touched my upper arm in a reassuring way, smiling. "Don't worry Sloane. I got you. Any friend of Eric's is a friend of mine. Especially someone he holds in as high regard as you. Besides—and I really shouldn't be telling you this—but I've known you since early on in your Jumps back to see him. You and I are actually pretty good friends." She laughed, obviously relieved to be able to share this tidbit.

I knew she could still be lying, but I really had no other choice than to believe her. She was right: either the Council helped us and Eric's lineage would most likely be revealed, or we let Alicia continue killing and creating new unregistered Lunai.

I hated that something in me wanted to give keeping Eric's secret priority over stopping the murders.

CHAPTER THIRTY-ONE

Sloan: It's done. the council would like to meet you.

Sloan: I'm going back there later to help with a gameplan. They are already requesting that Lunai from other states come to help, which is really huge!

Sloan: You can come with me later.

Sloan: They can also help you.

Sloan: These are not the people you need to be afraid of.

Sloan: Okay well, I guess you're getting second thoughts on this whole thing.

Sloan: But Alicia is dangerous.

Sloan: And I'm not just saying that.

Sloan: I'm like genuinely worried about her hurting you.

Sloan: Okay, attempt number 78436 . . . now I'm just worried about you in general.

Sloan: I'm kinda freaking out so . . . gimme a call.

Sloan: Just please lmk what you wanna do. I won't be mad if you back out.

By the time I got back home that evening, Tom still hadn't answered any of my calls or texts. I wanted to be mad at him for bailing on our plan, but I wasn't. I was just worried. It wasn't like him to not respond for a whole day. He had seemed too genuine in his plea for help the night before.

My heart was heavy as I sat at the dinner table with my family. It was probably the last time I was going to do so for a long time.

Malina had gone and spoken with the Council. I knew from experience she could be very persuasive. She also was trusted by everyone in the chapter, and her pep talk seemed to have done the trick. Adrian had allowed me back into the Sanctuary; he had even asked my opinion on formulating a plan.

"Go home and come up with a story to tell your family for why you will be gone for some time," he had said.

Each word lashed at me as I had lied to my mother, Neil, Justin, and Amanda that I was going to go with Rebecca back to Las Vegas for a few days. Justin's eyes had narrowed suspiciously. I still wondered just how much he and Rebecca were talking these days.

Part of the uneasiness I was feeling also had to do with the fact that Eric still hadn't returned to the Sanctuary, and no one knew where he had stormed off to according to a text from Malina.

The Sanctuary dwellers had been speaking about him in varyingly pleased tones after the revelation that Alicia and he shared a last name. They had probably done some internet searching just like I had and put two and two together.

I got my phone out of my pocket and sneakily typed out a text to Eric under the table, even though my mother had a strict no-phone rule at the dinner table.

Sloan: Let's talk.

The phone buzzed almost immediately after I sent it, but my mother caught me.

"Phones away, please."

Her wholesome little rule felt so banal in the grand scheme of things.

As we were finishing up and starting to gather the dishes, the doorbell rang. Neil answered it. I glanced out into the foyer from the kitchen and was startled to see two sheriff's deputies on the porch. Neil nodded as he said something I couldn't hear, and then gestured for the cops to enter.

"Mom," I whispered, "it's the cops."

My mother gasped and hurriedly sat down the stack of dishes she was holding before heading toward the foyer. My curiosity was almost going to kill me, but nothing could have prepared me for what came next.

Neil appeared in the kitchen doorway, looking pale. "Sloane, these officers are here to see you."

The police officers appeared behind Neil, looking out of place and too large in their uniforms for their current domestic setting.

One of them spoke. "Are you Sloane Becker?"

I felt my mother move behind me and grab my shoulders. I swallowed hard and answered, "That's me."

"The detectives at the station would like to speak to you regarding a matter they are investigating," the deputy droned as if he were bored.

"What is this about?" my mother asked sternly, her grasp on my shoulders becoming tighter.

This time, the other deputy spoke. "The detectives will explain everything at the station. We need you to come with us please, Ms. Becker."

"Excuse me, you cannot expect her to come with you to the station without telling her what this is about," Neil argued.

I wiggled my way out of my mother's grasp and came around the island I was standing by, still facing the deputies. Neil was right, I had no obligation to come with them. "Am I under arrest?" I surprised myself how cold and steady the question came out. I had nothing to hide. Well, except my power to manipulate time.

"No, you are not, but—"

"Then I don't see the need to bring me to the station. The detectives can speak with me here," I interrupted, unsure of where my confidence was coming from. But I knew my rights.

The deputy who had had been first to speak was holding a tablet; he started scrolling and typing something into it. The second deputy stepped back into the foyer and out onto the front porch, but I could hear him page someone on his radio. Their silence was infuriating, but I also had the right to remain silent. When the second deputy came back, he made a noise to his partner indicating for him to proceed.

The first cop read off the tablet, "What is your relationship with Mr. Thomas Salinger?"

My heart stopped, lungs incapable of drawing in any air. I barely managed to stutter, "He—we're friends. Best friends." I didn't know why I added that. "Why? What happened?"

The officers glanced at each other before the second one proceeded, "Well, I'm very sorry to inform you, Miss Becker, that Mr. Salinger was found dead in his home earlier today."

My mother caught me on the way down. I gasped for air, demanding my body obey me and not send me into a Slip with my mother clinging to me. The rest was a blur. I remembered bits and pieces in between the static feedback that threatened to short-circuit my mind.

"It did look like a suicide."

Neil asking why they would need me for questioning.

My mother yelling at the officers that they could have at least told us to sit down.

"However, we have reason to believe that the circumstances around his death are more complicated than that."

"Can't you see she is completely distraught? She just lost her best friend!"

"Ma'am, your daughter is a person of interest, and if she resists cooperation she can easily be escalated to suspect."

Justin and Amanda joining us in the kitchen, both of them looking equally perplexed.

Noticing my tears only when they hit the tile floor below me.

"Sir, your daughter will still need to come in for questioning. It's protocol."

My mother, yelling that their protocol was inhumane.

Justin shouting obscenities when my mother filled him in, and her proceeding to scold him for his language in front of Amanda.

"Your daughter is of age, so we really have no obligation to involve you. If you and your wife continue to impede our investigation, we will be forced to arrest you both for obstruction."

My mother looked at Neil as she threw her hands up, pain in her expression.

"Ms. Becker, please come with us," deputy number two said.

I didn't move. I couldn't move. I couldn't speak.

Tom is gone.
Suicide?
Tom is gone.
Circumstances are more complicated?
Tom is gone.
Person of interest?
Tom is gone.

The deputies were done playing around. They grabbed each of my arms and lifted me to my feet, which barely supported me.

More yelling came from my mother and Neil. Amanda was screaming. Justin kept cursing.

A searing gust of hot wind hit my face as the officers dragged me out the front door. The sun shone sharply in my eyes as its last rays clung onto the horizon for dear life. This, coupled with the sight of the police car and the neighborhood watchdogs reporting for duty on the sidewalk, pulled me out of my stupor.

"Mom! Call Dad!" I yelled, struggling to look behind me to find my mother's eyes as the deputies pulled me with increasing force toward the squad car. "Call Dad and tell him to bring Eric! Eric Baxter!"

CHAPTER THIRTY-TWO

THE SEATS IN the back of the police car were made of hard plastic. Behind each front seat, the plastic was molded into what could only be described as butt prints, with a small section sticking up in the middle to go between your legs. The middle and the edges toward the doors were higher than the base of the seat, and every turn the officer made sent the sides of my thighs squishing painfully up against the rigid material.

As we drove, my mind raced a million circles around what the officers had said. Something wasn't right. How could it be a suicide, yet more complicated? There must have been a mistake. Tom would never do this. Not to his parents.

Not to his friends.

Not to me.

I could feel it in my heart that he wasn't actually gone, and I knew what had to be done.

THE AFTER HOURS

൭൬൭൬൭൬

The room at the police station that the officers escorted me to was very different from what I had imagined an interview room to look like. I had expected a cold, gray room with a large one-way mirror-window into an adjacent room, a metal table bolted into the floor with uncomfortable chairs flanking it.

Instead, I found myself in a room with three white plaster walls and one red brick wall. I had been let in through a yellowing wooden door, but there was no one-way mirror-window. The room was furnished with wide-set wood chairs, their seats covered with rough material that nearly matched the blue carpet flooring. A table stood in the middle of the room, but it was neither metal nor bolted down. It was the same yellowing wood that the door was made of. Two fluorescent light fixtures hung below stained ceiling tiles, making everything in the room look even yellower. On the walls, cheesy inspirational posters in cheap plastic frames hung beneath a thick layer of dust that had collected on the top edges. It smelled like someone had forgotten sweaty socks in there for weeks. To my surprise, there were no obvious cameras in there, so either there weren't any, or they had some very incongruously high-tech gadgets at work.

The officers had taken my cell phone away from me in the car. I had no idea if my mother had called my father or not. Whether anyone was on their way. I had no idea how long I was going to have to wait for someone to come talk to me, let alone let me go home. A clock on the wall behind me was well past eight o'clock when the door was flung open, letting in a brighter, colder light from the hallway beyond.

"What the fuck have you gotten yourself into?" Eric said as he hurried in and closed the door behind him.

I couldn't utter a word. It was both so good and so painful to see him. I wanted to just crumble into his arms and cry for weeks. Months. Years.

"It's Tom—" I started.

"I gathered," Eric interrupted as he took a seat next to me.

"He—" I choked on the words. "Alicia got to him. They were—involved."

Eric shushed me sternly, but then his face softened as he whispered, "You told the Council that he had gotten to know her and she had facilitated him getting his powers. You didn't say they had dated."

I wanted to tell him that I hadn't wanted to speak the words out loud. But I decided to circumvent revealing just how much it weighed on me. "I didn't think the nature of their relationship mattered."

"Bullshit, Sloane—" Eric started, but was interrupted by the door opening again.

"Give me a few minutes with my client first, please." My father directed his command to someone in the hall whom I couldn't see.

His expression as he came in and closed the door behind him was a mixture of annoyance and something else. Something I had never seen on his face before.

Disappointment.

I had made it nineteen years without disappointing my father. Mainly because he was never around *to* disappoint. But it still hurt that there had to be a first.

"Hi, sweetheart." His voice was dry, tired. He looked tired.

He dragged an extra chair from the corner of the room and had a seat at the head of the table.

"I'm so sorry, Dad. I don't know what's going on."

"Well, the detectives didn't want to tell us much either. But, this guy—Thomas Salinger—isn't that your best friend Tom?"

My eyes burned and my lower lip trembled. I clenched my teeth together before nodding.

"I'm so sorry, honey. I know how close you were," my father said, his voice surprisingly warm now. Eric, on the other hand, seemed confused at his remark. As if he hadn't realized Tom and I were close enough that even my father knew him. I didn't bother correcting him that it had been over a year since we had been close. It didn't matter now. All that mattered was fixing this.

"Listen, we're just going to sit here and hear what they have to say," my father continued, "and then we'll get you right back home, okay?"

"It's extremely important that you don't say anything, Sloane," Eric interjected.

"That's right. We're here to listen, not to talk. They will phrase things in a way that will make you want to answer. But you are not here to do that, all right?" My father pulled his briefcase from the floor and placed it on the table, flipping open the clasps.

"You guys are acting as if I have something to hide," I said, glancing at Eric. I couldn't read his eyes, but I knew what he was thinking. I definitely had something to hide, and so did he.

"No, sweetie. Not at all. This is just strategy. The detectives won't think you're guilty of something because you don't speak."

I wanted to believe my father so badly, but I couldn't shake the feeling that I'd be better off with some other lawyer.

Someone more experienced with these situations. Not just scandals and money feuds.

"You're not under arrest, so they aren't going to read you your Miranda rights. But they can still use anything you say against you." Eric looked as if he had more to say but was interrupted by the door to the room opening.

A woman with short brown hair poked her head in and asked impatiently, "Are we ready?"

"Yes," my father answered.

The woman, who looked to be in her forties, was followed into the room by a much older man; in fact, he looked so old I wondered why he wasn't retired already.

"I'm Detective Jill Cassidy, this is my partner, Detective Roger Berns," the woman said as she and the man sat down in the chairs opposite Eric and me.

"What is the purpose of this interview, detectives?" Eric began.

"We would like to ask Ms. Becker some questions. If we have time we can see if we can answer some of yours." Detective Cassidy kept her voice calm, but the message was clear: Eric was not going to be able to lead this conversation.

"Some questions about what?" Eric asked, unfazed by the detective's demeanor.

She shuffled some papers in front of her on the table and shot Eric a warning look, also glancing over at my father, who was, strangely, quiet.

"Ms. Becker, when was the last time you spoke to Thomas Salinger?"

I looked back and forth between my father and Eric, trying not to come off as panicked. My father asked, "Is my client currently a suspect?"

The old man, Detective Berns, was sipping a gas station soda from a comically large cup and hadn't said a word. He peered over the top edges of his glasses and observed us.

Detective Cassidy was obviously annoyed with both Eric and my father. Had she hoped to be able to interrogate me without any lawyers present? She snapped at my father without looking at him; her eyes were fixated on the papers below her.

"At the moment, your daughter is only a person of interest. That can change any minute, just so you know."

"My client." My father's voice now matched the hostility in the detective's voice. "And I am well aware of the police whims that affect the statuses of individuals during investigations."

This was not going well. My father's pride was making me look bad, and I wasn't getting anywhere closer to what had happened to Tom. Or rather, *when* it had happened.

"Let's try this again," Detective Cassidy began. "Ms. Becker. When did you last speak with Thomas Salinger?"

"Last night," I answered. I felt Eric's and my father's eyes on me.

"My client will actually not be answering any—"

"And what is the nature of your relationship with Mr. Salinger?" Cassidy continued.

"We're best friends."

"Sloane." Eric hissed.

THE AFTER HOURS

"Since you were his best friend, are you aware of Mr. Salinger dealing with any mental health issues?" Cassidy was furiously scribbling something I couldn't read from my vantage point onto a yellow notepad. I hated how she spoke about him in past tense.

"Can we have another minute—" my father began before I cut him off with my own question.

"When did he die?" I asked. Cassidy's eyes looked up at me even though her head didn't follow.

"Like I said, we will be asking you some questions and then if we have time—" Cassidy said.

"You must have good reason to believe my client is a person of interest. Kindly share this with us." My father did not look at me; instead, he stared down Cassidy.

"Mr. Salinger was found with a gunshot wound to the head that we at first believed was self-inflicted." This time Berns finally chimed in. I did my best to not let the nausea his words caused take over me. "However, upon preliminary searches of his electronic devices and his room, we found some evidence that directly links Ms. Becker here to the situation." He reached for a piece of paper from Cassidy's stack and pushed it over to our edge of the table. Cassidy looked as if she was about to breathe fire.

The piece of paper Berns showed us was a printout of a black and white photograph. In it, a hand held a cell phone. The cell phone's screen was open on the notes app and read:

If something happens to me, it was Sloane Becker.

My stomach did a flip.

"The time stamp of the note says it was written early this morning. Which is why it is very important for us to know exactly when you last spoke with him," Cassidy said, almost through gritted teeth.

"When did he die?" I repeated my question. I had to know.

In my peripheral vision, I saw Eric's eyes boring into me.

He knew what I was doing.

"We don't know. The autopsy hasn't been performed—" Cassidy began, sighing.

"Well then, when was he discovered? You must have a timeframe. He was one hundred percent alive last night when I last saw him, so that should help you narrow it down." The feistiness came out of nowhere, and I spoke so fast I was afraid the words were almost incomprehensible. But I didn't have time to think about that because as soon as I had spoken, I felt my right arm yanked down below the table and Eric's hand clasped in mine. My eyes closed—

Summer breeze. Sun-singed skin. Star-filled skies.

"What the hell are you doing?" Eric growled as our eyes opened to meet each other.

"I need to know when he died so I can go back and stop it from happening. He was murdered, Eric. Tom would never commit suicide."

Eric sighed. "Sloane, you can't be serious. You know you can't do that."

"They're probably going to Strip me anyway! I might as well use my powers while I have them."

"Slo." Eric's voice was stern, but what he said next was not what I had expected. "Why would there be a note on his phone saying that?"

"Don't you think it's obvious?" I answered.

Before Eric could protest, I grabbed his hand and Started.

Is this the place?

"Asking questions like this won't make me believe that you don't actually know the answers yourself, you know," Cassidy snapped. Her hands were crossed in front of her on the table and she leaned her face in to come closer and closer to me as she spoke.

My father stood up, pushing his chair back harshly. "We're done here."

Eric shot me a concerned look, and I knew the time to act was soon going to pass.

I needed to get into a Stop by myself to be able to look at the papers Cassidy had.

Beach. Sunset. Embers. Blaze.
This can't be the place.

Eric was too fast; he managed to have the back of his hand touch mine right before the Stop washed over me.

"Eric, what the fuck!" I exclaimed as soon as I opened my eyes.

"Sheesh," he said, ignoring my complaint. He rolled his shoulders and shook out his hands, trying to get rid of the aftermath of my Stop.

"Well don't grab me when I'm Stopping then!" I yelled.

"I cannot let you do this," he warned.

I was already digging through the stack of papers that Cassidy had brought with her. My hands trembled uncontrollably. Most of the papers were forms, logging activity, logging evidence collection, logging personal details of Tom, his parents. There was even a sheet dedicated to me.

"Sloane," Eric pressed, trying to grab the papers from my hands.

I turned the next page to find a thicker, glossier type of paper beneath it. It was a photo of Tom's room. Of his bed. Blood-stained sheets below an inhuman form—

I let out a scream as I swept the papers to the ground before burying my face in my hands, still shaking. Eric tried to place an arm around my shoulders, but I swung at him to leave me alone. I got out of the chair and let myself fall to the floor on all fours. I opened my eyes to see the photo I had just looked at, right below me on the floor. I let out a frustrated growl and sloppily folded the photo and stuffed it in my pocket.

I proceeded to rummage through the papers, now flinging any photos away from me without looking at them. I had to find when he had been discovered, otherwise I couldn't pinpoint my Jump well enough. If I Jumped too late, I'd miss it. If I Jumped too early, I might not have the strength to stay there long enough. I couldn't risk having to Jump multiple times either, especially after having completed my longest Jump ever just the prior evening.

"Sloane."

"Shush!" I yelled.

I finally spotted a form I hadn't seen before. A coroner's field report form, scribbled in messy block letters.

> *Arrived at 11:43 a.m. to single family residence...*
> *Upstairs bedroom...*
> *Initial impression of external blood coagulation puts estimated TOD somewhere between 3 a.m. and 8 a.m....*

"Got it," I whispered, but in the silence of the Stop, Eric of course heard me.

"I'm not going to let you do this." Eric sounded tired.

"You can't stop me," I retorted.

"Yes, I can."

I glared at him. Every bone in my body buzzed with adrenaline. It helped the pain that otherwise threatened to engulf me.

"Sloane, *come on*. Do you not realize how crazy you sound? Do you realize the extent of damage you could do to the Present, even if it hasn't been twenty-four hours, by changing the trajectory of someone's *life*? I know this is hard for you babe, but these are the things that we have to accept. Everyone has to accept death, even us Lunai. Look at the bright side. Maybe he planned some Jumps to you."

Eric's voice had a hint of hurt between the exhaustion. I realized suddenly that back when he was married to Alicia, he had to go through the pain of losing her. It wasn't until after she died that she became a danger and he started wishing she would stay dead.

"I'm sorry Eric, but this is not the same as when Alicia died. She had gotten way too close to Tom already. He had no idea what she's actually capable of, but last night, he came to me asking for help. That's how I know what she's up to with recruiting people. This isn't just a death that we need to accept. She must have found out that he went behind her back and talked to me. She must have had something to do with this."

"Technically, Alicia's death wasn't something that needed to happen either," Eric said in a small voice. I'd never before sensed in him an inkling of compassion for her. It infuriated me.

"She did that to herself. Tom didn't do this."

"You don't know that."

"Neither do you."

Eric remained silent, his sleepy eyes unwavering, locked on mine. After a while, he said, "Well I won't stop you then, but I can't know what you're doing. I can't condone it or know what you're planning to do. I'm not letting you risk my status within the Council more than you already have."

His words stung, but I knew he was right, which was why I chose to ignore the hurtful part. "Don't worry, I won't tell you my plan because I don't have one."

"This is— I can't believe we're doing this." Eric was hastily picking up the papers I had strewn across the interview room floor.

"Why are you even bothering with that?" I asked.

"Do you want to have to come back here to do this? We can't just Jump and all of a sudden no longer be in the room and the papers are all over the place. Surefire way to reveal ourselves."

"Good point," I said. "It would be kinda cool though." I stifled a smile as Eric shot me a disgruntled look. I helped him pick up the rest and we carefully placed them back in front of Detective Cassidy.

"How were you sitting?" Eric asked as he sat back down in the chair next to my father who half-stood, frozen, glaring at the detectives.

"Uhm, I don't know... does it matter? I just sat in the chair."

"Yes it's important Sloane. Your dad and these cops are going to see it like a glitch in a movie. I think you had one elbow on the table and one hand hanging down." He gestured to show me what he meant.

"So? It'll be over in a second."

"For one person, that might be okay. For three persons collectively? Not so much. They'll get suspicious. And we don't know where they're hiding the cameras." He glanced nervously around the room, and it surprised me that he was so certain there were cameras since none were visible. "We cannot afford to take any chances, Sloane."

"Fine," I said, sitting back down in my chair and mimicking the posture he had prescribed.

Eric grabbed my hand that hung down by my side. "Ready?"

Harsh, hot summer wind. Sun-singed skin. Furious flurries of warm raindrops.

"We're not done with our questioning, Mr. Becker," Cassidy said the moment the sounds of the scene came rushing back to my eardrums.

"Yes, you are," my father said, pushing his chair back to the corner where he'd found it. "Sloane. Baxter. Let's go."

"Well, all right then. I will note that your daughter refused to cooperate." Cassidy sent my father a threatening look.

"You cannot punish my client for following her attorney's advice. I'll have you thrown off this case, Cassidy," my father said as he ushered Eric and me out.

"Not if I indict her first, Becker."

☙❧☙❧☙❧

The three of us stayed silent all the way out to the parking lot. I wanted to get going, still fueled by the crush of seeing those pictures of Tom. I needed to get back to the prior night.

But I had a million questions.

"Do you know that detective, Dad?" I asked.

My father let out a deep sigh. "Yes, unfortunately. She was a rookie detective back in the day when I represented Missy Spencer's family. She's as crooked as they get. I'm sorry about this mess, sweetie. I'll call my buddies and get this all settled."

"Sloane. Why would Tom have a note in his phone with that text?" Eric repeated his question from our conversation in the Stop. My father and I both stared at him in surprise.

I narrowed my eyes as if to tell Eric, "I already told you; it's pretty obvious" before I replied, "I don't know, Eric."

"Well, if we're going to be able to help you, we need to know your whole side of the story—"

"Thank you, Baxter. But there's no need to worry. I'll handle it from here." My father's voice was neither threatening nor patronizing, but I could tell Eric was embarrassed. "Let's get you home, sweetheart. Maybe stop somewhere for food? I'm so sorry for all of this. Losing your friend is hard enough."

My father embraced me from the side, the only way he knew how. He had his moments.

Eric, however, seemed to have completely forgotten that I had just lost my best friend. His expression held no sympathy. Maybe because I could still try and stop it.

I had to try and stop it.

"Thanks, Dad," I said, moving around to the passenger side of his car. As I passed Eric, he grabbed my hand.

Darkness. Star-filled skies. Snow flurries that stung at my spine.

"You're in a mood!" I barked at him as my eyes opened. His Stop was harsher than I'd ever felt it, and I knew it had to do with the emotions he was feeling at that very moment.

"I can't let you go with him. I can't let you Jump."

"I thought you didn't want to know what I was doing."

Eric let out a long breath and glanced off into the distance. "Well, I *do* know. So I can't let you do it by yourself."

My heart skipped a beat. Everything would be so much less frightening if I had Eric with me. "So you're saying—?"

"I'm coming with you."

CHAPTER THIRTY-THREE

IN ORDER TO keep my father from being suspicious, I told Eric to leave fifteen minutes after my father and me. That would give me enough time to placate my mother and convince her I just wanted to go to bed. At least let me slip upstairs for long enough to Stop and get out of the house.

My father was oddly quiet the whole ride home. Every time I thought about the crime scene pictures and the fact that in this timeline, Tom was dead, it felt like a punch in the gut. Like someone was squeezing every last bit of air out of my lungs. Like the wiring in my brain was giving off sparks, about to short-circuit.

But I couldn't cry. I was determined to go back and prevent this from happening. I knew in my soul that this was not how things were supposed to go. I knew this had something to do with Alicia.

It was too much of a coincidence—it happened just hours after Tom told me everything and agreed to go to the Council. Even if I ended up changing something with catastrophic consequences that would leave me Stripped of my powers and cast out from the Lunai, at least it would be worth it if Tom was alive.

I knew I was being selfish. But I couldn't help it. I had always wondered how the other Lunai resisted the urge to go back in time and change things they regretted. The only people I knew of who seemed to Jump for pleasure were the annoying two from the Council, Jules and Nico.

But me—ever since I started believing in these powers, I had dreamed of all the things I could go back and change. Heck, part of me was probably trying to, because I always kept finding myself Slipping or Jumping back to the same night: the night I graduated from high school. I had even accidentally given in to the urge to protect Past Me in the bathroom at Pete's house. Thankfully, that had been me all along.

But the only thing that was really stopping me from going back to all the times I wished I could've acted differently, couldn't find the right words to say on the spot, gotten a bad grade on a test, made a fool of myself, or dated the wrong guy—or even walking into a bank and swiping a few stacks of cash—was the fear of being Stripped and shunned by the Lunai. If that weren't a real threat, I would have probably broken the honor code a long time ago.

Then there was the fact that I had yet to Jump and visit Eric multiple times. As my father stopped his car by the curb in front of my house, a lightbulb with the strength of a lightning bolt went off in my head.

Eric said I had Jumped back to visit him multiple times before. I had only visited him once so far—which could mean that I wasn't going to be Stripped after all. It could also mean that whatever I was about to do could get me Stripped, causing a ripple effect back many years, eradicating all the times I had visited Eric. Possibly even making him forget me.

"Do you want me to come talk to Mom?" my father asked.

"No that's—" I began, but I realized this would be a perfect way for me to dodge my mother's smothering. "Yeah. Yeah that would be great. I'm really tired."

"Of course, sweetie." He shifted to park and killed the engine. "We'll get this sorted. Don't worry."

I managed a small smile in his direction before I stepped out of the car.

※※※

After the minimum amount of hugging I could get away with was over, I excused myself under the pretense of going to bed and did my best not to run up the stairs.

Eric: Here.

My phone buzzed in my pocket as I entered my room. I surveyed the street from my window and noticed a dark sedan parked about a half a block away, lights still on.

Beachsunsetembers.
This must be the place.
Blaze.

Even at my best, my Stops were still more painful than Eric's at his worst. But it got easier every time.

※※※

As we walked closer to Tom's house, my insides tightened. Yellow police tape surrounded the entire front yard. No lights were on in the house.

"This must be it?" Eric asked.

"Mhm."

"Have you thought of a plan?"

"Mm-mm."

Eric sighed.

The full moon cast an icy glow on the otherwise dark house, overpowering the warm rays of the streetlights. The mid-July air outside was muggy and hot as ever, despite the sun having been down for a few hours already. So when I started to shiver uncontrollably, I knew that, yet again, it wasn't from being cold. My eyes burned before everything went black. Not from my eyes closing, but my sight simply vanished. My bones sizzled, sending a painful wave out from my spine to my fingertips and back again.

My sight returned, bits and pieces, almost pixels at a time.

"Thought I'd lost you to a Slip for a second there," Eric said. "You okay?"

I swallowed as hard as I could, my mouth dry. My voice was still shaky as I replied, "Can you—you know? Can you do the Jump please?"

Eric studied my pleading expression, his own face grave. He let out a frustrated sigh and grabbed my hand. This time, instead of just making enough contact to include me in his Jump, he brought my palm in his, intertwining our fingers.

"The things I do for you, Sloane Becker."

Sun-singed skin.
Star-filled skies.
Fluttering leaves on a warm breeze.
Sprinkles of balmy raindrops.

I could have stayed in Eric's transitional state forever.

He grabbed his phone out of his pocket and showed me the date and time. Three in the morning, July 10, 2025. Barely twenty-four hours from our Present.

I nodded, acknowledging he'd hit the correct moment.

"You're lucky it's a full moon. Makes it much easier to navigate short distances because of the energy that's already here," Eric said.

Part of me was intrigued by this tidbit. I thirsted for more Lunai knowledge. But another part of me was immensely sad, knowing that what I needed to do next could very well cause me to never fully receive all the Lunai training I was meant to have. I'd miss out on all the times Eric could have taught me something like this.

"Thank you, Eric. I don't know what I'd do without you."

The yellow police tape had vanished from around the yard, and my heart ached knowing that if I failed to do what I came here to do, it would be back up again in a matter of hours.

Tom's house looked the same as it always had—pristine and quiet. As if no one lived there, but someone kept the lawn manicured.

"My Present is July 10, 2025. I won't forget and I will be back," I whispered to myself so Eric wouldn't hear.

"You still don't have a plan, do you?" Eric asked as we made our way up to the house.

"I'm going to prevent Tom's death."

To my surprise the door wasn't locked, so I let myself in like usual.

"Tom!" I shouted up into the foyer, my voice carrying throughout the house.

No answer.

I beckoned for Eric to follow me and tiptoed up the stairs. The door to Tom's room was slightly ajar, and I could hear snoring. A rush of relief washed over me. If he was snoring, he was alive.

I barged in and sat down next to him on his bed, grabbing his shoulder and shaking it. "Tom. Tom, wake up."

"Sloane!" Eric exclaimed from his perch by the door.

To my right I heard the unmistakable sound of a gun cocking.

My head shot to the right, but I already knew what I would see. The red glow of her hair had already infiltrated my peripheral vision. I staggered backward from the bed as she leaned into Tom, thrusting the barrel of the gun into his temple.

He stirred and rubbed his eyes, then sat up with a jolt when he realized he wasn't alone.

"Tom, don't move," I squeaked.

Alicia laughed. The forced intimidation in her laugh was gone though; this laugh seemed like it belonged in an asylum, its pitch and tempo all over the place. Tom tried to push himself backward away from her, but all of a sudden, within the same moment as he was scrambling under his sheets, his hands were out at his sides, each handcuffed to the headboard of his bed. Alicia had the gun back at his temple.

I scrambled backward off the bed and whimpered as I realized that if she pulled the trigger right then, what I'd be looking at was nearly the exact same scene as the one in the photos detective Cassidy had.

"What the fuck? Alicia, let me go!" Tom yelled.

I felt Eric's presence by my side. "Alicia, put the gun down. Tom's not your enemy."

She let out an unamused chuckle, disdain plastered on her face as her nostrils flared and she jeered, "Oh I know. But you guys are. And the fact that you're here means that you really don't want me to pull this trigger, doesn't it?" She smacked her lips sarcastically. "It would be a shame, wouldn't it? But tell me, Eric, how does it feel that your girlfriend cares more about another guy dying than she cares about you?"

"I do not—" I began, but Eric squeezed my shoulder, hard.

"Don't take the bait," he whispered, before resuming a normal volume and addressing Alicia. "Alicia, you got us where you wanted us. Now, what do you want?"

As Eric dropped the last word, I felt myself being flung forward, landing on Tom's bed again. I turned around to see Alicia now behind Eric, the gun mere inches from the left side of his head.

"What I want, is to play a little game. It's called *Watch Sloane React.*"

Before I could protest, an earsplitting bang rang through the room. Instinctively, my hands found my face and my lungs seemed to collapse in on themselves from the shock.

As my eyes regained focus, I saw Eric bent over with his palms over his ears, his features twisted in pain. Alicia resumed her laughing. I wasn't sure which sound was more disturbing: her laughter or the gunshot.

THE AFTER HOURS

"Eric!" I stumbled off the bed in order to catch him before he hit the floor. But he never did.

I looked up and saw Alicia now had both of her hands on the gun, still holding it in place midair where it had met Eric's temple, except one hand hovered toward the end of the barrel and two fingers grasped something.

Eric straightened up and turned to Alicia, one hand still over his left ear. "Fucking crazy bitch! Haven't you done enough already?"

I stood up next to him and peered at Alicia's hands. She laughed and took whatever she was grasping and threw it up in the air, catching it again in the palm of her hand. It was a bullet.

"That's no way to talk to your beloved wife, Eric." She giggled as she continued throwing and catching the bullet with one hand.

I had been an absolute fool to think I could ever take her on. She was way stronger than I could fathom. I didn't know if I'd ever have the strength and control needed to do what she had just pulled off. Pulling a trigger but Stopping and catching the bullet before it moved even a few inches.

Eric appeared behind Alicia, struggling to hold her hands behind her back, trying to knock the gun out of her grasp. They then proceeded to appear in different locations across Tom's room in various positions of struggle, each of them apparently taking turns Stopping and Starting. How long they stayed in each Stop was impossible to know, but Eric was already looking extremely fatigued.

I turned to Tom, my voice low as I asked frantically, "You don't happen to know where the keys to these are?" indicating the handcuffs.

He shook his head. "Probably close to the vest. Literally."

I glanced over at Eric and Alicia, who were like an old-time movie that was missing every other slide from the projector. One of Tom's bookcases was suddenly lying on its side, books splayed across the ground. It was uncomfortable to watch things happen outside of time, and I realized what Eric had meant earlier at the sheriff's station, how it would appear as a glitch.

I needed to rummage through Alicia's pockets. She had quite a few. She was donning her jean jacket over black jeans and a long, weathered

T-shirt that had probably been blue at some point. She seemed healthier than I had ever seen her. Her skin was glowing, her eyes weren't bloodshot. It looked like she had gained some weight, filling out her cheeks, making her look almost friendly.

I took a deep breath and set all my intentions toward taking myself out of this moment.

Beach.
Sunset.
Sunset.
Sunset.

My spine seemed to twist independently inside me, and all I could feel was pain. Not the normal uncomfortable tingling. Beads of sweat materialized on my forehead as my eyes flew back open and I gasped for air.

"Come here," Tom said quietly. "Let me."

I stood up and walked over to the head of the bed by the nightstand. The last time I had stood in that very spot was when I had discovered the camera on Tom's bookshelf. The moment that changed everything.

I grasped Tom's handcuffed hand with my own and let him lead, closing my eyes preemptively.

A meadow with tall grass.
A forest beyond.
Tall snow-capped mountains beyond that.
The breeze that smelled like him.
Sunshine piercing through cool air, warming but sending shivers all at the same time.

Our eyes were locked as we opened them in the Stop. But something was off. The air in the room had become static. We looked over at Eric and Alicia. Alicia was kneeling, the gun still in her hand, pointed to the ceiling.

THE AFTER HOURS

Eric was trying to restrain her, pushing on her back with one hand and reaching for the gun with the other. They were frozen, but they were still only halfway there.

"Shit." Tom muttered.

They weren't transparent, they weren't missing any part of their forms, they weren't Flickering. They were just not entirely in the moment Tom and I were in.

It was like my eyes couldn't focus on their shapes, but I also couldn't shake them. It wasn't a visual effect; it was more of a distortion in the way I was perceiving their presence in the moment.

"You must have hit the exact moment they were Starting or Stopping," I said.

"Yeah," he breathed.

"Do you think I can still check her pockets?"

"You can try."

I carefully made my way over to them. As I got closer, I noticed Eric now had a gash over his right eyebrow, and a nasty bruise was forming on Alicia's cheek. I reached out to grab at her jacket, lifting it away from her chest.

My sight went black. I could still feel the rough material under my fingertips. I yelled out for Tom, but no sound came out. A hum started in the back of my skull, increasing sharply like someone had turned the volume up all the way in a split second, until it took over my entire mind and I screamed soundlessly, breathlessly in pain.

Just find the keys. Use your hands and find the keys.

My fingers fumbled with the flap on the jacket's chest pocket, the cold metal button underneath it sending false triumph signals to my brain. Then, my fingers clasped around something small, cold, jagged, but I couldn't hear anything so I didn't know if it jingled like keys should.

As soon as I let go of the jacket, my eyes opened and I was propelled backward by an invisible force, landing hard on my back, my head colliding with the floor with a searing thud.

"Slo! Are you okay?" I had never been as happy to hear Tom's voice.

I rolled to the side, raising myself up to a sitting position, rubbing the back of my head with my left hand.

"Yeah. Yeah I'm okay."

My right palm, flat on the floor propping my upper body up, suddenly felt like it was being held up to a flame and I winced as I jerked it toward my body.

"Shit," I muttered, looking at the floor where my hand had been. A pair of small narrow keys on a thin keyring lay on the floorboard, glowing red hot as if they were being forged in flame.

I quickly yanked one of Tom's T-shirts off the bed's footboard and used it to pick up the keys. The heat emanating from them quickly seeped through the material, and I ran to unlock the handcuffs, not bothering to go from one side of the bed to the other, instead jumping feet first over Tom. Anything to release him from the location that had been captured on the photo in my pocket.

He hadn't been handcuffed in the photo, but this made it so that he was already in the spot he was going to die. I felt like I couldn't breathe until I got him free.

As soon as I unlocked the handcuffs, I threw the keys and the shirt on the ground, shaking out the hand that had been holding them. Part of the weight in my chest lifted as soon as I saw him move freely.

"What the hell?" Tom asked as he stood up.

The keys were now entirely melted, glowing an iridescent orange, the shirt catching on fire beneath them. Tom leaped to stomp on the shirt, but I yanked him back. Something in me told me he shouldn't be touching them.

A flame ignited, devouring the keys, fizzling out as fast as it had conjured. Tom's shirt was left on the floor, scorched and ashy.

"What. The. Hell," Tom repeated.

After a moment's silence when Tom looked at me in disbelief, I cleared my throat, not knowing where the words were coming from. "Pattern Gap."

"Again, what?"

My voice shook, because I knew in my bones what had just happened. "I think I just banished the keys from the Pattern. A Pattern Gap."

"Is that even possible?" Tom began.

"It is. It is if you're Tellurian."

CHAPTER THIRTY-FOUR

T OM FLICKERED, AND I grabbed his hand, encouraging him to start again. Thrashing started at the other end of the room once again, but suddenly Eric and Alicia disappeared altogether.

We heard commotion in the hallway and hurried out of the room.

Eric had Alicia bent backward over the railing that lined the second-floor landing. The gun was still in her hand, but Eric now had hold of both the gun and her hand.

"It's over, Alicia!" Eric boomed, his voice bouncing off the foyer walls. "This is not your time—you're dead! You have to accept that before you kill one more person!"

Alicia let out a giggle that did not suit the situation at all. "Babe. That's where you've got it wrong. Killing people is exactly how I stay alive."

Even in profile, I could see Eric's brow furrow. He looked in our direction for a split second, and Alicia seized the opportunity. She brought her feet up and kicked him in the gut with both feet, causing him to stumble backward. Alicia flew backward over the railing and down, plummeting toward the hard marble floor on the first level.

Tom and I ran to the railing, Eric, clutching his ribs, close behind us.

I looked down into the massive entry hall just in time to see Alicia disappear midair and reappear on the floor below. She half knelt, with one fist on the floor to steady herself, the other hand still clutching the gun. She raised her head slowly to look up at us, leering.

I had no idea how she had managed to brace her fall within the Stop, the possibilities were endless. A surge of jealous, angry curiosity tore through me, I wanted so badly to know how to replicate what she had just done. But I didn't have time to ruminate on it because someone materialized next to her. A young man about Eric's age whom I had never seen before. He stood with his feet in a wide stance, his arms tightly crossed over his chest, an empty expression in his eyes as he stared straight forward. As Alicia rose, another man, equally stiff and dull looking, appeared on the other side of her.

And then another. And another.

Soon Tom's entryway held probably twenty people, lined up next to and behind her.

She was breathing heavily and unsteady on her feet. She coughed, sputtering blood over the light-colored stone floor below her. Wiping her mouth with the back of her hand, she asked, "Who's next to ascend? Who wants to live forever with me?"

Eric and I exchanged terrified looks. A woman from the back row standing closest to the front door stepped forward.

"I'm ready."

Alicia smiled before turning around to see who had spoken. "Come here," she said as she held her hands out, her voice suddenly a sinister sweet tone.

The woman walked up to her and took her hands. Alicia stood still for a moment before she leaned in and kissed the woman. In the same moment, Alicia suddenly had her hand at the woman's back.

"Fucking shit," Eric growled and lunged down the stairs.

"Eric!" I yelled.

He turned around and held up one finger. "Do *not* follow me."

I saw now what Alicia was doing. A knife had materialized in her hand, the product of a Stop undoubtedly, and she had thrust it into the woman's back without breaking the kiss.

The others all turned to the staircase that Eric was bolting down, forming a human wall, blocking him.

Eric tried to Stop and leap over the handrail, but the others caught him. Three of them tackled him, Stopped, and hurtled him back up the staircase. What Tom and I saw was him appearing for a blip over the railing, and then crashing with a painful thud against the edges of the stair treads, his head hitting the adjacent wall. He skidded down a few steps before coming to a halt halfway down the staircase, his body limp.

Alicia let the woman sink to the ground, blood pooling out of her, her body stiff, eyes wide open, and mouth slightly ajar. Blood covered the lower half of her face, and I wasn't sure if it was hers or Alicia's.

The others didn't seem too bothered; only a few looked slightly unnerved at what they had just witnessed.

"For those of you who are new, welcome to your first ascension ceremony."

Alicia bent down and took the woman's hand. In an instant, the woman was gone, and Alicia reappeared: standing, sturdier, stable. She seemed rejuvenated after killing the woman.

"Marcie has been taken to her rightful place time! There, she will reawaken with her life renewed and never-ending!" Alicia addressed the crowd standing in front of her. The most determined-looking ones started clapping, quickly joined by the ones who had seemed unsure at first. They started gathering around Alicia, asking questions and wanting to hug her. She seemed to revel in the attention.

Ascension ceremony? Right place? Renewed life?

None of this ever came up in the Horolog.

I looked at Tom, who was staring with a horrified look at the scene below. I nudged him in the shoulder before saying, "Tom, is this what she's been doing? You know this is bullshit right? You know she just killed that woman."

Tom swallowed hard and turned to me, his eyes still about to pop out of his skull. "I knew she was doing something called ascensions and I was skeptical because I'd never see anyone who ascended ever again. But I didn't know"—he gestured to the foyer—"*this*."

I looked over to Eric. He was stirring, looking even more exhausted than before, and seemed on the verge of passing out at any moment. He was the one holding the Jump we were both in and he had used his powers extensively already on top of that, to try and subdue Alicia. I begged any higher power that would listen that he wouldn't lose consciousness and, consequently, the Jump.

I grabbed Tom's hand. "Tom, you have to Stop again. I need to keep my powers unused in case Eric loses the Jump we're in."

Tom stuttered, "I—I don't think I can."

I let out a frustrated sigh, squeezed his hand tighter, and closed my eyes.

Sunset.
Please let this work.
Sunset.
I've never needed this to work more than I need it right now.
Sunset.
Come on!
Blaze. Scorched ground. Horizons on fire.
This must be the place.

"Whoa. And *ow*," Tom gasped as we opened our eyes.

"Sorry." I rolled my shoulders back, shaking out my arms. "I need your help. I don't know how long I can hold the Stop." I glanced down at where

Alicia stood, thinking how easy it would be to just end her then and there. Not that I knew *how* exactly I would go about that. Tom was right: I wasn't a killer.

But I was also too terrified to go anywhere near her, in case I lost hold of my Stop, like that day when I had my first Slip at the office. I'd be handing myself to her on a silver platter.

We raced down the stairs to where Eric sat, each of us grabbing him by the upper arms. His stiff body was insanely heavy, and there was no way we were able to carry him gently. It was either drag him up the stairs or not at all.

"Ugh, this is going to be so painful for him when we Start again," I grunted as we pulled him onto the landing. A painful Flicker shot through me. Tom noticed and winced at the sight of me.

"Here," Tom said, holding his hand out to me once we reached the top of the stairs. "I can do it."

My face held a pained but grateful expression as I took his hand.

He brought time back with an effortless blink.

"Now, remember how I told you guys about the little bitch who tried to steal my husband?"

Alicia's voice rang through the hall and a groan came from the ground where Eric lay.

"Eric. This is all lies, right? There's no such thing as ascensions. She's just flat out lying to these people, right?" I bent down to his level and held his shoulders, resisting the urge to shake him. He was in so much pain I wasn't sure whether he heard me, but I needed an answer, and I was still not confident in the amount of knowledge I had self-assembled. He managed a silent nod.

"Well, she can keep him for all I care." The maniacal, hysterical laughter was back. "Not much left of him anyway, thanks to you guys!" She sounded like some sort of twisted motivational speaker.

The crowd cheered. My heart raced; I couldn't get enough air in my lungs.

If she didn't care about Eric, what did she want from me?

"However! This bitch thinks she can walk around using *my* powers—" Alicia's crowd let out a roar of disapproval, some of them shooting me murderous looks.

> The confirmation of my suspicions hit me like a brick wall.
> Making the keys go up in flames and disappear.
> The uncharacteristic recklessness.
> The selfishness I was so ashamed of.
> Malina's reaction to touching me.
> I had Alicia's powers. Tellurian powers.
> But how?

"Yup, you heard that right. This bitch stole my husband *and* my powers. Thankfully, I was saved by ascension! Coming back from the dead as you all have witnessed." The crowd chanted in excitement as Alicia kept spewing her lies.

"We have to get him out of here. *We* have to get out of here," I whispered to Tom, who grabbed Eric's other arm, and we began to drag him toward Tom's room, when I realized that was the last place I wanted Tom to be. The closer he was to his bed, the likelier it was that my plan to keep him alive wouldn't work. "Wait, Tom," I said quietly, my voice strained from dragging Eric's weight, "We can't go to your room."

"Why not?" he wheezed.

"Spare our traitor friend Tom though. I want him for myself," Alicia declared.

"Let's just try to Stop okay?" I had no idea if it would work. Tom had even less control over his powers than I did, but he wasn't in a Jump to begin with. My powers were not complying, and I was also not in my own Present. But it was our only way out. As long as Alicia and her minions didn't follow us to wherever we Started again. "If we can Stop and hold it long enough to get—"

Tom interrupted me. "Slo, look." I looked up to see him pointing downstairs.

"Now, get her for me so I can close the loop. Restore my powers to their rightful home: me." Alicia finished her rally and the others had started up the stairs, their eyes set on one thing: me. But then I noticed the front doors had been flung open, and through them poured another, larger, crowd of people. Terrified, I braced myself for the fury of an even larger crowd, but a white-blond head that drifted lower in the air than everyone else's caught my eye.

It was Maddie.

CHAPTER THIRTY-FIVE

AN ENORMOUS NUMBER of things happened in an instant. Maddie, Malina, and Jules appeared beside Tom, Eric, and me on the second-floor landing. Alicia screamed at the crowd below to come back down and help her. Alicia's minions and the Lunai Council members started trying to capture one another, their Stopping and Starting sending them scintillating across the space, appearing and disappearing in different spots within the same moment, some pouring out into the front yard, some reaching the top of the stairs where we were. Some of Alicia's crew obviously didn't have powers yet and wielded an array of weapons from baseball bats to knives to guns. Thankfully, the Lunai were dodging them masterfully.

"Sloane. Let's go!" Maddie exclaimed, but I was mesmerized. The powers emanating from the group set the space aglow with energy.

Alicia's group was no match for the Council, and before long, I started seeing a few of them subdued. The Council members had brought tasers, using them mercilessly on the rogues' temples to render them powerless. At least for the time being.

"The tasers only work for so long. We gotta get Eric out of here," Malina said, grasping my shoulder. I could see her visibly shiver as her finger accidentally came in contact with the skin on my neck. It all made sense now.

"My powers. The Tellurian you're Sensing. They're from Alicia," I whimpered hastily, and to my surprise, tears stung at my eyes for the first time since entering Tom's house.

What surprised me even more was Malina's reaction. She didn't blink. Instead, she hugged me tight. "I know, girl. I've always known." I stared at her in disbelief as she let me go, but she left no room for discussion. "We gotta go. *Now*."

I glanced down. Adrian and Alicia were now engaged in their own Start and Stop standoff. I realized that it was the first time I had ever seen Adrian use his powers, and it was striking. His movements and the way he weaved in and out of Stops were like a choreographed dance. There was subtlety and softness in the sheer power he exuded, and I could tell Alicia was getting tired. Meanwhile, Adrian looked completely relaxed, yet seething.

"Alicia, if you come with us now, I can help get all your friends up to speed. No one else needs to die. There won't be any consequences. But this has to end. Now," Adrian begged.

Alicia flashed behind him, but he was too quick: he was back to the other edge of the room. Alicia roared in frustration. "Come with you? And live like mole rats in a cellar, controlled by factitious limitations you impose on yourselves? Forget about it!"

Adrian swung to the side, appearing behind Alicia again, managing to grab her in a chokehold. "Offer still stands," he said, voice only lightly strained.

They flashed in and out of sight for a few moments, both managing to knock the other over but also stand up again. As their forms became whole again, they stood, mere feet apart, in the middle of the foyer.

"I have no interest in becoming subhuman and denying myself my right to live freely and fully with my powers. So thanks, but no thanks." Her voice was sarcastic and threatening, frightfully confident and calm.

"Well, you leave me no choice then," Adrian said.

Suddenly, I wasn't on the landing anymore. I was on the floor, lying down, somewhere completely different.

Tom's room.

Nauseous inertia hit me violently and mercilessly, but before I could do anything about it, Maddie was beside me on the floor, holding a trash can in front of me.

"Sorry. I know the inertia can be so bad. Malina made me move you. You weren't listening." Maddie's childlike voice felt so out of place in the midst of all this violence.

I succumbed to the nausea. I had absolutely no control over it. But as I lay hurling into the trash can, I noticed the sounds of someone else retching too.

I looked up and saw Tom lying on his bed, throwing up into a plastic bag Malina had brought him.

"Tom! Get off the bed!" I screamed, wiping my mouth with the back of my hand, stumbling to my feet.

Malina grabbed me before I reached him. She was too strong. Or I was simply too exhausted. "Sloane, let him be. The inertia has to get out of the system."

"No. No. He has to get off the bed. *Now.* You don't understand—"

At the opposite wall, under a window, was a couch. Eric's limp form lay splayed across it, and Jules sat on the edge next to him. I hadn't noticed them until she spoke. "Mal. He's not doing so good."

Malina let go of me and hurried to his side.

I dragged Tom to the ground. He was still hunched over, clutching the plastic bag.

"What the fuck, Slo," he said in between retches.

"Stay off the fucking bed!" I shouted, and stumbled over to the couch.

Eric was paler than I had ever seen him. I wondered how sun-kissed skin could just lose its color like that.

"What's wrong with him?" I demanded.

"We don't know. It could be internal injuries. It could be power fatigue," Jules answered. Her usually cheerful and carefree face held a pain I didn't think it was capable of. She glanced up at Malina with tears in her eyes. "Mal, I don't know what to do. I always know what to do. I've always been able to heal him."

Eric, you should go have that checked out. Jump back and let Julianne take a look at you.

"He's holding the Jump we're in. I can't believe he's managed to hold it this entire time," I muttered, more to myself than to the people around me. I knelt down next to Eric, placing one hand on his cheek, leaning in and kissing the other. "I'm so sorry I made you do this. Please get better. Please come back to me," I whispered into his ear, willing him to hear me. But he lay still, his breaths ragged and inconsistent.

A loud boom sounded from downstairs.

"Alicia has a gun," I said, looking between Malina and Jules. "She's not afraid to use it."

They exchanged panicked glances, but before they were able to react, Maddie was already out the door.

"Maddie!" Jules yelled, bolting after her, Malina on her heels.

"This is so fucked. What are the cops going to think? What are my parents going to think?" Tom was rambling. He sat down on the edge of his bed and buried his face in his hands.

"Tom!" I yelled. "I said stay off the fucking bed!"

"What is your deal?" he snapped.

Before I could answer, I was interrupted by a haggard-looking Adrian entering the room. Maddie clung to his arm, and he had what looked to be Alicia's gun in the other. Relief washed over me knowing he was safe.

"It's done." His eyes stayed on the floor in front of him, a look of deep shame etched on his face.

"What do you mean 'done'?" I asked hesitantly.

"She's gone," Jules said as she entered the room. Behind her, Malina joined us.

"Gone?" It was Tom's turn to question. As he turned to face the door, I used the opportunity to yank him off the bed again. He swore at me but kept waiting for an answer.

"I managed to get hold of her gun, and a bullet hit her square in the chest. She disappeared nearly instantly. That amount of pain sends you right back to your Present. Or at least, it should. If not the pain, then death." Adrian explained the ordeal he'd just witnessed calmly, as if he were presenting one of his lessons.

I heard shuffling behind me, and to my surprise, Eric spoke next.

"She didn't die of a gunshot wound."

Adrian looked at Eric, astonished. "Really?"

He seemed relieved.

"Nope. She died in her sleep. I was with her." Eric's voice was raspy. Jules was back at his side, clasping one of his wrists with her fingers and staring at her watch.

"And you're not experiencing any discontinuations?" Adrian asked.

"Not as of right now. She must've healed from it somehow," Eric said, trying to sit up.

"Thank goodness." Adrian let out a long breath.

I could tell his heart wouldn't have handled it if Alicia had ended up dying by his hands.

A disheveled Finneas poked his head into the room. "Uh—Adrian? They're waking up. They're Stopping or Jumping as soon as they regain consciousness. But not the Temps of course. Do you want us to stop them or . . .?" Finneas's voice was shaky as he asked how to handle the rest of Alicia's minions.

"Let them go," Adrian replied.

"Adrian. We can't. When will we ever have them rounded up like this?" Malina protested.

Adrian's voice was firm and devoid of any empathy as he responded, "And what do you suggest we do? Keep them subdued and imprison them at the Sanctuary?"

"For example!" Malina threw her arms up.

"No. We don't operate like that. We do not take people into custody. We have to take this to the Conservatory. We have to get assistance. This is more than some psychopath targeting individual Lunai..." Adrian trailed off.

"They would be safer at the Sanctuary though." Eric struggled to get the words out. "She's breeding them, Adrian."

Adrian shot Eric a confused look.

"She's breeding them in batches by killing one at a time. But then she uses them to transfer their powers back to herself."

My jaw dropped. What Eric was saying made so much sense, I was surprised I hadn't thought of it myself. Probably because it was also batshit crazy.

"Power compounding? But that's not possible," Malina interjected.

"More like power hoarding," Maddie muttered.

Eric shrugged. "I don't know. Maybe it is if you're Tellurian. We have no idea what she's capable of. Whether it was a placebo effect or not—she sure seemed refreshed after killing that poor woman."

My eyes met Eric's for a split second and a jolt went through my body.

"Is that whom the puddle of blood downstairs belongs to?" Jules piped.

"Yup," Eric professed. He looked so defeated, his complexion still devoid of color. All I wanted to do was to just hold him until he got better. And tell him I was sorry a million times over.

I looked hesitantly at Adrian, not knowing where we stood. What I had just done was way worse than what he put me on probation for.

He has to understand. Now that he's seen it for himself.

I cleared my throat, but my voice was still barely a squeak, "She—she said something about me. About closing the loop and taking her powers back from me."

Adrian's expression was stony as he shifted his gaze to meet Eric's eyes. "Eric, care to enlighten us, since it seems you and her are... acquainted?"

I helped Eric get to a seated position. He said, "I remember it now. From before she died. She told me she knew of a way to live forever. That if she managed to transfer her own powers back to her, she would become powerful enough to live forever. I, of course, took this as ramblings of a madwoman; I had no idea what she was talking about at the time. I'm sorry I kept this from you, Adrian."

I stared at him, slack-mouthed.

This is why she never just finished me off. She had to make sure I transferred the powers back to her.

The room had gone completely silent. Eric continued, his voice strained in between winces. "I think she had always planned to have me do it. That I was just a pitstop for her powers."

"But that means—" Maddie breathed, the horror in her words, devastating in her youthful cadence. I saw Jules's jaw drop in shock as she wordlessly came to the conclusion she was so desperately seeking, about the origin of my powers.

Adrian finished his daughter's sentence, his own fear palpable. "That means, that whenever Eric's existence ends, he will transfer his powers to a Sloane who already belongs to the Past."

CHAPTER THIRTY-SIX

"WE SHOULD ALL head back to the Sanctuary," Adrian said, turning to Tom and adding, "Thomas, you're welcome to join us."

"Yeah, thanks. I was going to come with Sloane—" Tom's voice quivered nervously.

"However," Adrian cut Tom off. "We have no idea what Present we are actually returning to, so I suggest we travel to my house before Jumping back."

"Wait, what?" Tom asked, utterly perplexed.

Everyone in the room fell silent, their eyes alternating between me and Adrian.

"Thomas, you are the only person here who is currently in their Present. The events that just transpired are guaranteed to have caused a disturbance in the Pattern. I suspect the consequences to our Present are grave, since you should not even be alive."

"Excuse me?" Tom asked, the color quickly draining from his face.

Adrian kept his eyes on me but stayed silent.

"Sloane, what is he talking about?" Tom demanded.

I swallowed hard, attempting unsuccessfully to keep myself from crying as I spoke. "That's why Eric and I are in a Jump. I came here because—you died."

Malina shifted nervously. "And we came here when I Sensed the discontinuations Sloane was making by coming back here."

"What—what do you mean I died? How?" Tom pleaded, terror visibly rattling him.

"I don't know!" I yelled, my voice breaking. I shoved my hand into my pocket and pulled out the crumpled photo to show him. "All I know is it was made to look like you'd done it yourself, but some note on your phone made the cops think I did it. Look!" I pushed the photo into his hands.

Tom stared at the photo, and then at me, his face blank. "What am I supposed to be looking at?"

I ripped the photo back from him and looked at it. It was not the same photo I had seen at the sheriff's station. It was of Tom's bed, but there was no Tom, no blood, no gun.

"I—I don't understand—" I stuttered.

I stared at the photo again. Right before my eyes, two pairs of handcuffs appeared hanging from the bed's headboard in the photo, just as they were in reality in front of me. I had safely saved Tom.

"If that's a photo you brought with you from the Present and it doesn't look the same, it's because our actions have already begun to have consequences."

Adrian's voice was livid, and I could feel the anger seeping off him as his eyes locked on me.

"Adrian, come on. We saved a life," I begged.

"Sure, one life. But who knows how many countless other lives will be or have been lost in the Present? We don't even know what the Present that we have to return to now looks like."

"It was me."

Everyone's gazes shot to the back of the room to Eric where he sat on the couch, still clutching his ribcage but regaining some of the color in his pained face.

"What was that, Eric?" Adrian asked, stepping closer to him.

Eric shot me a look and I shook my head vigorously, mouthing the word "no."

"I decided we would save Tom. I couldn't stand to see Sloane accused of murdering her best friend—something she absolutely didn't do—so I authorized the Jump. In fact, I executed the Jump."

Adrian gave Maddie a look and nicked his head in Eric's direction, giving her silent instructions. She shuffled over to Eric and placed her hand on the nape of his neck, closing her eyes briefly.

When she opened them again, all she said was, "He's telling the truth. He's holding the Jump."

I, of course, had already told them this, but I didn't think Eric was going to use it to take the blame for me.

Adrian sighed a long, exhausted sigh as he held Eric's gaze. "We'll deal with this later. I need the Conservatory's input on all of this. Come on everyone, let's get back. Travel in groups within Stops, for safety." Adrian's authoritarian tone was irrefutable. "Thomas, since you are the only one here in your Present, you will have to let the moments pass. Meet us at this address at ten o'clock, tomorrow evening. We should all be back by then." Adrian handed Tom his business card, then proceeded to exit Tom's room and call for the other Lunai to return to the Present.

Malina, Jules, and Maddie shot me sympathetic glances before disappearing into a Stop together, their presence extinguishing just a half heartbeat before their forms did, replaced by the golden-red beams of the sunrise leaking in through the curtains.

I made my way to Eric's side.

"Why did you do that?" I said in a small voice, sliding my hand into his and interlocking our fingers.

"Because I love you."

The look in Eric's eyes left no room for doubt: he meant what he said. I sat there, frozen, head spinning, and realized I needed to reply. Before I could, Tom spoke.

"I'll uhh—leave you guys to it." He hurried out of the room, his room, closing the door behind him.

Eric beat me to it. "You don't have to say anything. I've known you a lot longer than you've known me. But I wanted to say it and I don't believe in holding these things back."

My inhale shook me and tumbled out of me as I breathed the words, "I love you, too." The words felt both familiar and foreign on my lips, just like Eric always had. Keeping me craving him like my life depended on it. "But we need to talk about the other thing you're going to do."

Eric smiled and stroked my wrist with his thumb, inspecting our intertwined hands. "For all we know, one-hundred-year-old me Jumps back and transfers his powers to nineteen-year-old you. Please don't worry about that now."

I opened my mouth to argue, but before I had a chance to rebuke, Eric squeezed my hand and I felt my eyes close. Then, he whisked me off into his transitional state.

Summer skin.
Warm rain.
A million stars falling from the sky like a net cast to capture me.

"Whoa!" I heard Tom's voice and a ruckus of something falling before I even opened my eyes.

It was dark outside again. Tom was on the floor next to his desk, stumbling to get to his feet. Eric seemed relieved, color returning to his face as his Present crept back into him.

"Sorry, bro," Eric said, "didn't mean to scare you."

Tom laughed. "I *literally* fell out of my chair. I don't know if I'll ever get used to this."

I checked the time on the large clock on the wall; it was around nine in the evening, the same time it had been when Eric and I showed up on the front lawn of Tom's house before executing the Jump.

"Tom!" a voice sounded from outside the room. I recognized it instantly as Tom's mother's voice. A sting shot through my heart, realizing that Tom's parents must have come home from their trip today and had found their son dead.

But I had fixed that. Tom was here, and he was alive.

"Shit. I'll go talk to her; you guys stay here." Tom hurried out and closed the door behind him, leaving Eric and me alone.

"We should Stop before we leave the house since we're not alone," Eric stated.

"Yep." I didn't want to come off short, but the turmoil in my body wouldn't let me put more energy into my answer. I couldn't understand how I was supposed to just ignore the fact that whenever he died, he would be thinking of me—and all the weight that this fact bore.

I heard murmurs of Tom's conversation with his mother from beyond the door, but that wasn't what held my attention. What did was perhaps the only thing that could take my thoughts off Future Eric's intentions.

Something familiar had caught my eye on Tom's computer screen. I walked over, leaving Eric on the couch. My heart pounded as I saw what he had open, as it was the website that Rebecca and Justin had showed me. But there was no video.

Tom returned. "What's this?" I said, holding my breath. His response could either send my world crumbling yet again, or finish constructing the rickety fortress of hope I had so hastily allowed back up when Tom sought me out and explained to me that it had been Alicia all along.

"Oh! Good news. I got it taken down." Tom smiled.

I stood up from his chair and flung my arms around his neck, causing him to stumble, but as he regained his balance, he embraced me back.

"Thank you," I whispered into his shoulder, trying to steady my breath and not cry. I had done enough crying.

THE AFTER HOURS

"What are we talking about?" Eric asked, prompting me to let go of Tom.

"Nothing. I'll explain later," I said, wiping a stray tear that had escaped my lashes.

"Should we get going to this—Sanctuary place?" Tom asked, uncertain, pulling the business card out of his pocket.

"Yeah, yes, let's get going. I'm gonna use the restroom first." I stopped by Eric on the way to the bathroom door. He was standing now, albeit shakily. "You okay?"

"Yeah, I'm good." He smiled warmly. "See you soon."

CHAPTER THIRTY-SEVEN

I LOCKED THE bathroom door behind me and turned the water on, resisting the urge to sink to the ground and collapse in a heap of exhaustion and overwhelming emotions. I lifted my gaze to meet my own eyes, and I nearly didn't recognize myself. The circles under my eyes were the darkest they'd ever been, my hair resembled a tumbleweed more than it did a head of hair, and it felt like it had been days since I put it into its current ponytail. I was pale—way paler than I had ever been in July, and my cheeks seemed to have lost some of their volume. As I started thinking about it, I realized a lot of my clothes were actually feeling pretty loose these days. For the first time in what seemed like forever, I was able to look at myself in a bathroom mirror without feeling like someone was going to come up behind me.

I splashed the ice-cold water on my face, welcoming the chill it sent down my spine. Despite the situational trigger having been removed, my mind couldn't veer from the direction this action sent it spinning down,

THE AFTER HOURS

and the memory engulfed me before I could even take a breath. This action was nearly identical to what I had done the last time I was in Tom's bathroom, on graduation night.

"Ugh, not this again," I groaned.

The shudder in my spine from the water quickly turned into an unwelcome sting, and I clutched the countertop, wincing and cursing as the Slip spilled over me, ravaging and ruthless, splitting me in half. I didn't even reach my transitional state, my brain just burned with a pain so crushing that all I could do was curse under my breath and will my lungs to do their job. When my eyes opened, the bathroom was completely dark, the only glint of light coming from Tom's bedroom through the now slightly ajar door.

I grabbed my phone out of my pocket, but it was dead. I had no idea where I had Slipped to. But I had a strong suspicion.

"Great."

I took a deep breath, centering myself. I needed to focus. Whatever moment I had landed in, I was probably not supposed to be in Tom's bathroom, and if it was the middle of the night, which it looked like, I couldn't risk waking him up. I needed to find out what moment I was in, and I needed space to try to execute a Jump back. But in order to do that, I first needed to Stop to get out of there.

Sunset.

"Come on," I said under my breath through tightly clenched teeth. Not a hint of a Stop was present anywhere in my body.

Sunset.
Beach.

I let out the quietest sigh I could muster, puffing my cheeks out as the air escaped soundlessly through my lips

"Fuck this."

I tiptoed toward the door and opened it wide enough for me to fit through. Thankfully it didn't creak. I snaked around the corner and into the room, staying as close to the wall as possible, as if that would somehow help. I was still in plain sight from the bed, where Tom most likely lay asleep.

Except he wasn't alone in his bed.

I froze, holding my breath. The two beings were fast asleep, deep breathing and light snores alternating from under the covers. I willed my eyes to focus through the dim light, to see if I could spot who was in his bed with him. If it was Alicia, I knew I'd spot her hair from a mile away in any lighting.

I took a step closer to the bed, stretching as far as I dared toward the bed. The figure that lay closest to me shifted suddenly, making my heart stop. The person turned over to their left side, so I was able to see their face.

My face.

I pressed my fingertips hard into my eyeballs, until all I could see was a checkered pattern on the inside of my eyelids.

Why, why always *this night?*

As I opened my eyes again, I surveyed the room, knowing what I'd find. My clothes from that evening strewn on the floor, my shoes—and on the bookshelf on the adjacent wall, a tiny, blinking red light shining from between a book and a wooden box.

Once again, I found myself being tempted by the all too easy solution in front of me. One that would eradicate so many of the problems I knew the girl asleep in the bed next to me would have to endure over the coming months. I could just steal the camera then and there, and the Me in the bed would never know. Tom and I would remain friends. And we wouldn't be in this mess.

But that was my Tellurian-tainted blood talking.

I stared at the little blinking light that the girl in the bed was about to discover when she woke up. That little blinking light was going to send her world crumbling. I remembered handling the camera like it had happened yesterday. My gestures exaggerated and harsher than needed, my breath not reaching the bottom of my lungs. Double and triple checking everything was deleted. Checking the memory card slot—

And then it dawned on me.

I tiptoed up to the bookshelf and picked the camera up carefully, turning it over to flip open the memory card slot. Sure enough, there was a bright yellow card in its designated place. A bright yellow card visible even in the half-darkness of Tom's room. A bright yellow card that would be removed sometime in the next few hours before the girl in the bed would ever notice the camera.

Alicia had wanted me to find the camera the next morning. All she had to do to cover her tracks was Stop before the girl on the bed woke up and grab the camera. But instead, she only took the card. It was outrageously obvious, really.

About as obvious as it would be for me to just steal the camera, card and all, in that very moment.

I know, girl. I've always known.

Malina had known this whole time that I had Tellurian powers, but still she treated me with kindness and empathy, even when I was putting her at risk. I harshly wiped a tear from the corner of my eye after replacing the camera in its hiding spot. I swore to myself that I would never give in to the worst part of my powers, the reckless selfishness, ever again.

I hurried to the door, silently, casting one glance back into the room before exiting. I still had an hour or so to go before two extra versions of Tom would come snooping around, one of them accompanied by an extra version of me. I could easily make my escape out through the front door, and onward to my house to attempt to Jump back to my Present there. I couldn't manage it here, not in this environment, not in these moments. I'd call Eric and Tom and explain.

The heavy night air caressed every bare inch of skin as I stepped out onto the porch. The wind was moistureless and harsh in its beeline, but I gulped it nonetheless. The ornate streetlamps cast hazy shadows across the perfectly manicured lawns and smooth sidewalks, rendering everything in a little bit lower definition than it really was.

As I made my way down the hydrangea-lined path, I jumped as I heard a loud engine roar. Two beams of light rounded the far corner, and a car came hurtling down the street toward me. My heartbeat surged even higher as recognition struck me. I knew that car all too well. It screeched to a halt in front of where I stood on the sidewalk.

"Sloane! Thank god!"

Dylan Archer, looking more flustered than I had ever seen him, called to me from his car.

He didn't even bother closing the door behind him as he bolted from the driver's seat and up to the sidewalk where I stood frozen. He hugged me tight, and I was so flabbergasted I didn't even register to reciprocate.

"What happened to you?" he asked as he pulled away, placing one hand on my left cheek and stroking it with his thumb. He examined my face as one would examine something fragile after dropping it on the floor. I knew I looked worse for wear, but I also realized that this Dylan was expecting a Me from 2024.

I focused on the air flowing through my nostrils in little sips, willing my face to not look like I had seen a ghost. For the tiniest instant, I had forgotten what moment I was in. I had forgotten that this was not my Present. I hadn't understood why Dylan was here and what he was saying.

But now I realized: he had come here on graduation night, and instead of finding me, he found another me.

The me I was now.

But I was still confused. He was supposed to be in New York.

"What are you doing here?" I asked.

"I got back in town today and I swung by this party to meet up with the guys. I heard you had been there and something messed up happened, so I came to find you—" he rambled.

I held up a hand to silence him. "*Why* are you here, Dylan?"

Disappointment flashed across Dylan's face before he replied, "To see you. I was hoping we could talk?"

I sighed, knowing what I had to do. The Sloane who was asleep in the house behind me had no idea Dylan had come after her. All she knew was he went to New York and never looked back. Not a phone call, not a single message. Just party pictures and shenanigans with pretty girls with private social media profiles.

Something gnawed at me though. The compulsion to get a do-over pulled at my being. I could play along, say all the words he wanted to hear. Let things run their course and give Past Me what she so desperately wanted: to be with Dylan again. The shameless selfishness of giving in to my own whims and wishes at the cost of literally everyone else in the world. It would be so easy.

When I didn't say anything, Dylan spoke again. "I figured, you're eighteen, so—" He trailed off, reminding me that this Dylan was under the impression he was speaking with last year's me. His voice was barely a whisper as he added with a shrug, "Happy belated birthday."

I know you said I'd learn to love it, but New York's not for me.

I knew now why I had Slipped to this night again. I hadn't taken care of everything yet. This was the last challenge, and possibly the hardest.

"Dylan, you have to go back. We're done."

Pain and confusion struck Dylan's features with a fierce intensity as he took a step back from me.

"Wait—what?"

"Go back to New York. You'll learn to love it—"

"I've been there for an entire school year, and I hate it," he protested.

"Give it a chance, trust me."

He narrowed his eyes at me. "You've never even been to New York. What is this really about? Why—"

"We're over, Dylan. I'm so sorry." I did my best to be warm, to be fair to him. I knew the turmoil his heart was in, and it was the most painful thing.

"I knew it. That's why you're here, isn't it? I *knew* there was something more between you and Salinger!" he yelled.

But what startled me in that moment didn't come from Dylan.

"Mhm! Yummy! Where do you find these guys, Sloane? I mean, I'd understand if you were super pretty or something, but not with that face."

The voice was tattered, almost robotic, intermittently cutting off as if on a call with bad reception. Ice crawled through my veins as I watched Dylan's expression change from frustration to horror.

I spun around, Alicia was mere feet away from me, barefoot, wearing a dirty hospital gown, looking closer to death than I had ever seen her. Her eyes were so sunken, you could almost see the outline of her skull at her brow, her lips were chapped and flaking, her skin flushed in patches and gray in others. She doubled over in a fit of coughs, blood spattering the sidewalk and the front of her gown, adding to its collection of stains. The sight of her seemed to drift in and out, unable to come into focus as she Flickered frantically. She held what looked like a scalpel, dull and dirty, barely catching the beams of the streetlamp above her. I knew that this was yet another version of her existing in that night that I hadn't been aware of until now.

"Well now, I'm not exactly thrilled to see you either, but you can at least say hi before I kill you."

I felt Dylan step up next to me, his elbow brushing my upper arm. I held my hand in front of him to stop him.

"You can kill me, but I will *never* transfer my powers back to you," I kept my voice monotone, bone-dry like the wind.

Dylan stifled a panicked sound of incomprehension. I didn't pay attention to him.

Alicia laughed her signature, psychopathic laugh for a split second before it quickly turned into a cough.

"Alicia, you cannot compel me to relinquish my powers to you. You'd know that if you had ever reported to the Council and actually learned—"

She just kept laughing, coughing in between, her Flickers getting more and more prominent. "Ahh, you stupid little bitch. You think you have all the answers, don't you? With your fancy *laws* and damn *books*," she snarled. "I have perfected my method to be able to absorb the power of anyone whose life I personally end." Her coughing calmed down and she started pacing, leisurely almost, a look of unhinged glee plastered on her face. "Now, I'll be the first to admit that I'm not perfect. In the beginning, eye contact did the trick. Make sure the person has their eyes locked on their successor. It could get tricky, especially if people realized what was about to happen. But as you know, Sloane, I had a workaround for that. Being the nonkilling version in the moment is also super fun." I shivered as I remembered being in my car, restrained by one Alicia, while staring at another Alicia standing outside my car.

She hacked and spit blood onto the pathway that led to Tom's house. "But then I figured out that my power sources actually needed a bit more . . . *persuasion*. Since then, it's really been quite simple to have any power I want."

I wouldn't let her have the satisfaction. I didn't know if what she was saying held any truth to it, but I kept a straight face.

"You're lying."

Alicia's Flickering seemed to have calmed back down and she started tiptoeing in circles on the sidewalk, squishing the droplets of blood into partial footprints. She smiled again and tapped her temple. "How do you know I haven't been to the Future to confirm that my plan works?" She stuck her tongue out as her sinister smile reached its peak before keeling over with laughter.

Any chance of me keeping a straight face was extinguished in less than a heartbeat. I couldn't know. I couldn't compete with someone who didn't fear Jumping to the Future.

Dylan started yelling before I had a chance to rebuke, "What the actual fuck is going on, Sloane? How do you know this lunatic? What is this talk about powers? We need to call the cops!"

"Dylan, please." I pressed my elbow into his ribs, still holding my hand in front of him.

"You need to leave, now. I'm calling the cops," Dylan threatened Alicia. She laughed. "Well at least wait until the cops have a reason to come."

Alicia charged. She was still Flickering, and I knew she wasn't strong enough to try to outpower me, because instead of her usual move to Stop and appear behind me, she came barreling straight toward me. I ducked, sending her flying into the fence that lined the sidewalk.

"Get in the car!" I screamed at Dylan, and he scrambled, half running, half crawling, to the other side of the car.

Alicia roared and lifted herself off the ground. Her nostrils flared as her upper lip curled with disdain, her eyes lighting on fire. I braced myself, pressing my back against the car door, ready to kick her away as soon as she got close enough.

But just as she got up, a shape came flying into my line of sight and tackled her, both of them landing harshly on the Salingers' front pathway. As I realized what was happening, a sickening sensation of déjà vu ravaged me.

Eric growled as he pinned her down, holding both hands. However, Alicia's Flickering was back to projector-esque levels, and she was now disappearing for a full second or two at a time. Eric found himself grasping at nothing but the pavement beneath him as Alicia used her Flickers to wiggle away.

"Eric!" I screamed.

"Get *out of here!*" he shouted in my direction, not meeting my eyes but tilting his head toward me enough so I could catch a glimpse of him. This Eric was not the Eric who had just told me he loved me. This Eric was disheveled, with a full beard, lines in his skin I wanted to get more familiar with, shoulders broader than any earlier version of him.

It was in that split second that he turned my way that Alicia lunged out from under him. The next thing I knew, she sat, straddling him with her legs pinning his arms to his sides where he lay on his stomach. She thrust his head down, but he managed to turn it to the side, facing me.

Everything seemed to slow down.

She held the scalpel tightly in her right hand and swung it down in a sweeping motion across Eric's body. I couldn't move fast enough, I couldn't get my body to comply.

I needed to Stop, sprint, scream—something.

But she was too fast. Too resolute.

The scalpel tore at Eric's neck, the ripping sound unlike anything I had ever heard, slicing deep into him with a squelch.

"No!" I screamed, flinging myself forward, but Dylan appeared behind me, his hands gripping me painfully, keeping me in place.

I kicked and screamed, mainly directing it at Alicia. Eric's body lay motionless, eyes wide open, blood pooling below his mouth.

There is no way he can survive this.

"Oops," Alicia said in a blood-curdling, childlike voice, before turning to me and shrugging. "Oh well, I had to get rid of him eventually. He was seriously getting in my way." She giggled, sending shockwaves of rage through me. She jabbed the scalpel once more into the side of Eric's neck, right into the carotid artery, causing the blood torrent to triple in size. "For good measure," she sneered.

She yanked the knife out of Eric's neck with a nauseating slosh, and let it drop onto the sidewalk. Blood sprayed my shoes as the knife tumbled in my direction.

What struck me more than the blood, the lifeless pallor of Eric's unfamiliar, yet *so* familiar face, was the acute extinguishing of his presence. As the weight of reality settled in on me—*Eric is dead*—I collapsed forward, Dylan struggling to keep me upright.

Dylan's grip on me relaxed and I sank to my knees, sobs with no breath behind them shaking my body. Sirens sounded in the distance.

"Sloane, we have to go. *Now.*" He placed a hand on my shoulder.

I swung him away and yelled, gasping for air, "No. No. I have to fix this. This is all my fault—"

"Sloane. Get in the fucking car right now. The cops will be here any moment and we are pretty much in possession of a murder weapon right now." And before I could catch my breath, Alicia's eyes widened as she tore her gaze away from me. She and Eric disappeared, leaving only blood, and a knife.

As I scrambled to my feet, I looked up to where Alicia had been, and my eyes came to a stop on Tom's front porch, where two figures wrapped in blankets, stood staring at us.

Graduation Me and Graduation Tom.

I instinctively covered my head with my arms and threw myself into the passenger seat of Dylan's car. My head was about to burst as Dylan floored it and his car lurched into motion, tires squealing so loudly that if there had been any neighbors left asleep, they weren't anymore. The memory of waking up to screams, coming downstairs, seeing myself on the sidewalk by a pool of blood, seeing Dylan—memories I had never had before—etched themselves into my mind. My breath came in rapid bursts as Dylan was the first to speak.

"What the *hell* was that?"

"I—I can't," I stuttered, clutching my head in my hands.

"How the fuck did those people just disappear like that?" Dylan sounded terrified. He made the turn out onto the parkway, tires screeching, zooming in the opposite direction of at least five police cars that were headed into the neighborhood.

"Dylan," I said, interrupted by a dry heave, the pain in my head too intense. Not bothering with hiding the semantics, I begged him, "Dylan you have to stop the car. I need to get out of this Slip. I'm not supposed to be here."

"There is no way in hell I am going back to New York now." He drove even faster as my mind continued to stitch together new memories.

Polluting old ones.

Changing details.

Blurring the order.

Scrambling my truth.

"My—My Present—" I wailed, face buried in my palms.

I couldn't remember. I wasn't even sure there was a Present to go back to. As the pain in my head reached a new height, I let everything go black. My eyes fell closed, not to Slip, but to settle into the Presentless purgatory I had created for myself, and probably the rest of the world.

EPILOGUE

THOMAS SALINGER LOST a lot more than just his best friend the night Sloane Becker disappeared.

After countless attempts and many months of trying to convince his parents, Sloane's parents, the police, his teachers, his friends, enemies, and even strangers on the internet, that the footage on the mysterious camera he found in his room was genuine, all he had gained was a few stints in the psychiatric ward, and a handful of labels that would last him for life.

"Weirdo."
"That dude who lost his mind."
"Liar."

There had been two Sloanes in the footage. One sleeping over at his house—the real Sloane—and one intruder Sloane wandering aimlessly around his room, picking up the camera and doing something to it before returning it to the shelf and exiting the room. The footage had looked like that straight out of the camera.

It didn't matter how many experts he hired to validate the footage, no one believed him. They all said it was either two actresses who looked the same, or that the video had been edited.

He had watched the last ten or so minutes of it so many times, he could recite it by heart.

Intruder Sloane messing around with, and then eventually putting away, the camera on the shelf, after having surveyed the room.

Real Sloane waking up in pain.

"Tom, it feels like my head is going to explode."

"I knew I should have taken you to the hospital."

Indistinct screams from outside the house.

"What was that?"

"I'll go check it out."

"I'm not letting you go alone."

Tom bursting back into the room, alone, lunging for his phone on the nightstand.

"Nine-one-one what's your emergency?"

"My friend—she's gone. She disappeared. We were standing on the porch and she fucking just disappeared and there's blood everywhere outside and I have no idea what happened—please help me."

What was even stranger was the book he found on his nightstand. The book must have been some weird type of fantasy novel—it spoke about humans with the power to manipulate time, humans who killed people and tortured. Caused pandemics and burned down cities. Bred underlings with ferocious aggression and weaponized their own children. It mentioned Stopping and Jumping with capitalization, and that bad things could happen if people who shared the same power signature existed in the same moment in time.

Tom had read his share of fantasy, and he did not recognize this from any fictional world he knew of. His first year of college, he spent more time searching for clues on the internet and in library books than he did doing schoolwork, causing his grades to tank. But he didn't find any matches or references to the book's content, anywhere, fiction or not.

But what was perhaps the strangest, was the handwritten note on the book's first page that read:

Dearest Sloane,

I apologize for gatekeeping this from you. I couldn't risk you figuring out where your powers came from before you were supposed to. This copy has all the pages—including the ones I removed from Eric's copy. Please know everything I've done is to protect you. You deserve to read this now that you know what you are. You don't need to be afraid, I'm here to help you.

Just remember to not lose your Present.

Best,
Adrian

ACKNOWLEDGMENTS

If you are reading this, that hopefully means you read this book, so my gratitude goes first and foremost to you.

For decades I've wondered who you might possibly be, and now that you're here, I couldn't be more grateful and honored. I hope you'll stick around!

To my husband, who has put up with the Lunai and my late-night writing sessions since long before we were married. As cliché as it is, you always believed in this story even when I didn't believe in it myself. When I told you I was getting published, the first words out of your mouth were "I knew it!" Thank you for being my biggest fan, the best dad, and the best life partner a person could ask for.

To my kids, human and canine alike, I'm somehow capable of stringing together hundreds of thousands of words, but I'll never be able to find enough words to describe how much I love you. I'm so proud and lucky to be your mom.

To my dad, thank you for showing me what it truly means to be creative and leading by example. For making Sloane's absent father a really hard character to write since you are the exact opposite.

To Taylor Munsell, the best critique partner a writer could ask for. This story would still be a collection of incohesive Scrivener scenes if it weren't for you. You literally helped me birth Sloane—without you, her name would still be *you-know-what*. I've never known a friendship like ours, where I can share every part of myself and all you do is fangirl. Thank you for always rooting for me, harassing me to write, and being an endless source of inspiration. I wouldn't want to be on this journey with anyone else. You are the CP Veronica Roth told me to find.

Speaking of—Veronica Roth, you don't know me, but you signed my copy of your book once at YallWest. While you were doing so, I asked you what your one piece of advice was for an aspiring author. You said to "pick a critique partner who roots for you, not someone who is harsh." This seems intuitive, but for someone who had only ever had the wrong CPs, this advice gave me the confidence to seek out those who rooted for me. This book wouldn't exist in its current form if it weren't for that seemingly simple recommendation from you, so thank you.

To Jason Khoury, thank you for being one of the first people to read this story, for nerding out over it, and for sharing your dog with me.

To my editor, Elana Gibson. Thank you for making this entire process one of the best experiences of my life. Your brilliant editorial vision, kind words, and all-around excitement for my story made working on revisions all the more fulfilling. Thank you to the entire CamCat team for being so wonderful to work with, for seeing the magic in my story and not being afraid of a little time travel—I know it's a beast. Special thanks to Maryann Appel, for capturing my exact vision for the cover, and my copyeditor Penni Askew, for your incredible and invaluable attention to detail.

To Sue Arroyo, thank you for making my publishing dreams come true. I feel honored that your voice was the one who gave me that coveted "yes." Thank you for the incredible community you built.

ABOUT THE AUTHOR

Raised in the Pacific Northwest, Aspen Andersen now calls the hills of sunny Southern California home. She will, however, always miss the rain and trees of the PNW. She shares her life with her high school sweetheart and three kids, two human and one canine. There's also a cat there, but she doesn't really know why.

During business hours, Aspen is a project manager at an engineering consulting firm. She holds a bachelor's degree in Creative Writing and a Master of Architecture. She is obsessed with finding ways of challenging human nature with fantastical powers. When not preoccupied with this, she spends her moments exploring the Southern California hillsides with her family, doing yoga, and reading. Her ultimate goal in life is to write books while living on a ranch converted into a nursing home for elderly dogs to live out their golden years.

If you liked
Aspen Andersen's *The After Hours*,
consider leaving a review
to help our authors.

And check out:
Meredith R. Lyons's *A Dagger of Lightning*.

CHAPTER ONE

If you don't know where you're going, fine, just make sure you know what you're looking for. —Solange Delaney

"Im. Imogen! You're okay. You're all right, you're okay."

I awoke gasping, my ears throbbing as if my heart had established satellite locations. My eyes immediately locked onto a familiar shape, the feather swaying back and forth, dangling from the chain on our ceiling fan. *I'm safe. I'm in bed. With Keane. I'm okay.*

The orange glow of a streetlamp filtered in through the open curtains. I reached up and lightly clasped Keane's forearm, his warm palm still gripping my shoulder, although he had stopped shaking me. I turned my head toward him, trying to take slower breaths. He'd angled himself just far enough away so that I wouldn't accidentally strike him. I must have been flailing.

"I'm awake. Sorry. Was I loud?" I never remembered these dreams when I woke. Only a sensation of falling and some vague knowledge that my grandfather had been there, either falling with me, or trying to keep me from falling, or . . . something . . .

"You didn't shout or anything this time, just thrashed around." Keane flopped back onto the pillows, sliding an arm beneath me and hauling me to his side. I let him, even though I was very warm and wanted air. The sheets beneath me were damp with sweat. I shoved the comforter down to my waist.

"Sorry I woke you. I've been trying to rest my ankle and didn't run yesterday." I always slept better if I was exhausted. I didn't process emotions the way most people did, and if I was unable to channel them physically, they liked to ambush me when I was unconscious.

"That's all right." Keane sighed, trailing his fingertips up and down my arm. Keane had been a good friend since college. Neither of us had ever married, in spite of cycling through many long-term relationships. At some point, after spending a mutual friend's wedding together as bridesmaid and groomsman for the umpteenth time, Keane had suggested that if we hadn't found anyone by forty, we should just wed each other. I'd drunkenly agreed. Now I was forty-five, Keane was nearly fifty, and six months ago he'd finally gotten my yes.

I accepted a ring after insisting upon dating first, living together first, then living together for at least a year . . . until I'd run out of excuses. There were none. Keane was great. We got along great. Sex wasn't bad. Cohabitating was cheaper and made maintaining a home easier. And it was nice being on his insurance plan.

Settling, Imogen. You're settling is what you're doing. She'd been gone sixteen years and I could still *hear* my grandmother's exhale, could practically see her tossing a gauzy scarf over a small-boned shoulder as she gave me a *look* from beneath her lashes.

But what was wrong with that at my age? I'd come to the conclusion that *true love* was a fantasy—although my grandparents had sure seemed to have it. Perhaps it wasn't in the cards for everyone. I'd looked around long enough. Fortunately, I'd never wanted kids, so I'd never felt that pressure.

"So, what are your plans for today?" Keane yawned, still lightly stroking my arm.

My stomach tightened. He had some kind of agenda. "Some more job applications, maybe—"

"You know, you don't have to get a job right away—"

"I *want* a job. I need to contribute—"

"I know, Im, and you will, but you don't need one in the next twenty-four hours. Your dad's coming in next week, and"—he rolled toward me, pulling me even closer—"the guest room is still a mess."

My eyes dropped away from his. I turned my face skyward again and focused on the feather. "I know." The guest room would have been nice if it weren't for the large pile of cardboard boxes. All mine.

I *had* tried to whittle them down. But I didn't know what I'd need. I didn't know where I'd fit in this new place. Keane had received a dream job offer in New Orleans. He'd convinced me that this would be a great life for both of us. Wasn't I tired of the cold in Chicago? Wasn't I able to find friends wherever I went? Weren't we going to get married now? I had no good arguments, so I went with him. It made sense. We were engaged. Why not? I rolled my shoulders against the tightness threatening, trying to make a little more space between us. I didn't want to go through the boxes downstairs. Going through them meant getting rid of them, and I hated to let go of those little parts of myself.

I'd never found my calling. I liked to hop around. I was good at a lot of things, never great at any one thing. I never had a "crowd," but I was good at getting along. I'd find a job here too. Find things to like about it. I was good at adapting. I could wedge myself in.

Grandma would have told me to keep searching. *You're different, Imogen, and that's okay. But you have a place. We all do. You'll know it when you find it. Just keep looking.* Well, she wasn't here. Besides, maybe this would be it.

"Okay," I said, taking a deep breath. "I'll go through the boxes today. Try to put some away."

"You could make a donation pile too," Keane said, pulling the covers back up around us. "What about all that martial arts stuff? You haven't fought in over a decade."

Something twisted at my center. "I liked fighting though," I said, quietly. I had loved sparring. It was another effective outlet for emotions packed down too tightly. And I'd been good at it. Although I was technically too old to fight competitively anymore, I could still train. "Maybe we could find a place here, we could do it together—"

Keane chuckled. "I'm still sore from soccer two days ago." He yawned again and pulled me even closer, eliminating any space I'd created by wrapping his arms around me. He pressed a kiss to my forehead, one hand rubbing my back. "You know, I was thinking when your dad's here next week, we could set a date for the wedding. Like, an actual date. Maybe something in the fall."

I felt myself go rigid in his arms. "Not the fall," I said. Keane's hand stilled on my back, but he didn't let me go. This was the only thing I had ever pushed back on consistently.

"Imogen—"

"My grandma disappeared in the fall. I don't like the fall."

"Imogen." Impatience simmered under his voice. "Everyone on Earth has lost a grandparent—"

"Lost, yes, had one disappear, no."

His chest inflated against my arms where I was still smashed against him. He exhaled slowly. "She was one hundred and two, Im. You know she died. She probably left because your grandpa had just passed on and—"

"Her car was still there. All her stuff was still there. And she left me that message." The muscles between my shoulder blades tightened painfully.

Keane sighed. "She was quoting Stephen King—"

I knew exactly where this conversation was going and how I would feel afterward, but I couldn't help it, I took the bait. "No, she said, 'There might be other worlds to see,' not 'There are other worlds than these,' there's a diff—"

"So she misquoted—" Keane cut himself off when I started pushing out of his embrace. "Okay, baby." His voice lifted on the second word like he was asking a question. He held me slightly away, pushed my short hair back from my face, then tilted my chin up so I was forced to look at him. "I know you don't like to talk about this, so I'm not going to push it but... it's always something. First, you wanted to wait until I was sure about the job, then you wanted to wait until after the move, and now I just feel like you're making excuses."

"Just not the fall," I said. "Any other season—"

"How about this summer then?"

It was already June. Summer was technically days away.

"You want to get married in summer in New Orleans?" Honestly, this far south it felt like summer had been sitting on us for months already.

He didn't answer, just stared into my eyes, his fingers still at my chin, his arm at my waist, still holding me to him. Keane knew how to wear me down. If it was this important to him... what difference did it really make when it happened?

"Fine. Summer," I said, although a surge of distress simmered beneath my skin. "We can talk about it when Dad's here."

"Really?" Keane grinned, the corners of his eyes crinkling. My heart softened. He really was a handsome guy. And he was good to me.

"Really," I said, smiling back.

He kissed me softly. "I love you, Imogen."

"I love you, too." The words came easy. We'd been saying them to each other as friends for decades. I forced another smile, the distress coalescing into eels tossing against my stomach. "I'm gonna head out for my run. The sun's gonna come up soon."

"Okay." He gave me a squeeze and released me. Keane knew what I was doing. And he was letting me. "Text me when you're close, and I'll go out and get coffee for us." He snuggled back into the downy comforter.

"'Kay." I rolled out of bed and padded to the dresser in the soft brown light of near dawn. I snatched up some running shorts, a sports bra, and socks and slipped into the bathroom to get dressed. My sore Achilles still ached in spite of my rest day, but I ignored it. I couldn't get out of the house fast enough.

I stopped long enough to do a few heel drops on the front step to warm up my ankle before setting out, but that was it. The sky had lightened to pink by the time I hit the pavement. I loved the warm June mornings. Although I was leery of hurricane season, I couldn't complain about being warm all the time. No more treadmill-exclusive winters. I took off toward the levee. Running along the top at dawn was my new favorite way to greet the day.

I tried to shake off the tension from this morning's conversation as I ran. No one understood how hard I had taken my grandma's disappearance. We'd had a different bond. Even my father had said that he felt like an interloper sometimes when it was just the three of us together. I had a nagging feeling that Keane had used that attachment when he suggested the fall to push me into a summer wedding. I shoved that thought away. If he had, it was done now.

My mother had died when I was eight, which was about when I'd stopped emoting in the "normal way." I had to let it out physically. Running, fighting, acting. I wasn't a crier and I wasn't a talker. I think it was one of the things Keane liked about me. If something upset me, I waited until I felt safe to let it out, or I channeled it through my body.

Not for the first time, I wished my grandma was around so I could run this wedding thing by her. Ask her why I had these conflicting feelings about what was so obviously the right decision. I mean, I'd already followed the guy across the country.

Keep looking, Imogen, she would level her green eyes at me. *Keep exploring. No need to pin yourself down to this one. You've got time. I don't care what anyone says.*

Never mind that she'd met my grandfather at eighteen and married him shortly after. Well, look where all that exploring had landed me. I had the most eclectic résumé on the planet and was now a forty-five-year-old fiancée.

"Get outta my head, Grandma. Keane's great and I'm doing this." I turned up my music, ignored my aching ankle, and picked up the pace.

Running was one thing I'd always done, always loved, and always been good at. And Keane was obviously the right choice. Wasn't he?

I'd only logged about three miles when I had to stop to stretch my protesting Achilles and glanced up at the rising sun. Good clouds today. I pulled my phone out of its pouch to take a picture and noticed a text message. Odd for this early. Maybe Keane needed something. I clicked on the app and my heart lifted a bit when I saw it was Al from our soccer team.

I liked Al, although I was surprised to receive a text from him at dawn. Keane and I had joined a rec league this spring to meet people, and Al was another charming newcomer. We'd gotten close with the team, and I'd enjoyed harmlessly flirting with Al, even though I was probably technically old enough to be his mother.

He gave back as good as he got, which was fun for me, and he and Keane got along like a house on fire. Didn't hurt that he was easy on the eyes and fun to talk to. The first time the three of us had hung out alone, we'd stayed up until midnight. My five a.m. run the next morning had been rough, but I hadn't regretted it.

Al: Hey! I know it's early, but since you're an early bird, I took a chance you might be up. You feel like meeting for some coffee? My treat.

My finger hovered over the screen, and I started walking toward the next trailhead, almost absently. Keane was supposed to get coffee for us later. But Al had never asked me to coffee before. Maybe he needed to talk. And if I were being honest with myself, I wanted someone to talk to who wasn't Keane. Seeing Al was always fun. It would give my morning a lift. And I was feeling a little reckless.

Me: I am up! On a levee run actually. Which coffee shop are you going to? I'm less than a mile from the next trailhead and I could run there.

Al: What trailhead are you near? I'll come meet you. We can go together!

Directions given, I tucked my phone away and continued my run, my pace a bit faster—in spite of my Achilles—in anticipation of seeing my friend. *Calm down,* I told the tendon. *We'll have a shorter run than planned and a nice rest at coffee.*

When I approached the trailhead, Al was already waiting. He waved. I waved back, slowing to a walk as I reached him. Strolling toward me. Wearing... a tunic and pants? Odd. His long blond hair was pulled neatly back, and he was sporting the laid-back grin of a confident twenty-something without a care in the world.

It was impossible not to smile back.

I pulled my earbuds out and tucked them into the pouch with my phone, shutting off the music. "Hey! Fancy meeting you here. Do you live or... work around here?" I gestured to his attire. Come to think of it, Al had never mentioned where he worked or what he even did.

"Not exactly." He smiled and reached for my left hand as if to shake, which I automatically extended. He cupped it in both of his.

I laughed. "Sorry if my hand is sweaty."

"It's not." His amber eyes glittered. The wind blew his earthy, sandalwood scent in my direction. I was positive that I smelled of nothing but sweat, but if he noticed, he didn't seem to mind. "I'm glad you were out. Thanks for meeting up."

"Sure. How can I help?" I pushed sweaty strands of my choppy, chin-length hair out of my face with my free hand and planted my foot on a rock, taking advantage of the pause to stretch again. He clocked the movement.

"Ankle?"

"Always." I smiled, pulling slightly on my hand. He gave it a squeeze and let go. His eyes dropped to my engagement ring as his fingers brushed over it. "Ankle, shoulder, uterus... getting old is no fun."

He moved closer. "Maybe I can help with that."

"With . . . my ankle?" I stepped away from the rock, fiddling with the zipper on my pouch, a warning bell pinging. Was this weird? It felt weird. I glanced around for Al's car and realized there wasn't one. Had he walked here?

"Among other things." His gaze flicked to my fidgeting hands then bounced up to my face. Something flashed behind his eyes. "How'd you like to know more about your grandmother?"

I froze. My stomach turned in on itself. "What are you talking about?" I tried to remember if I'd ever talked to Al about her, riffled through my memories of postgame bar visits.

Al cleared his throat, eyes on my nervous fingers, speaking quickly as if he could sense that I was ready to bolt. "I knew her. And I know you want to know where she went and where she came from. I can tell you everything about her."

I stilled, my heart hammering. How was it possible that Keane and I had just been talking about her and Al would show up minutes later claiming to know what happened to her?

Grandma would have called it a sign.

"I can tell you about where that part of your family originated and what they were like," Al spoke again when I remained silent. "And you'll get to learn everything you want about Solange."

He knows her name.

He glanced up at the sky then back at me. He tilted his head. The corners of his mouth turned up. "All you have to do is come with me."

"Come with you where?" Electricity bounced through my chest. *How could he know my grandma?* "Al, this is—"

His eyes flicked toward the sky again, brow furrowing. I followed his gaze. *Is it supposed to storm or something?* I saw nothing.

I shifted my weight from foot to foot. My heart desperately wanted answers. My atrophied practical side scratched at my subconscious, telling me something was off, urging me to ask more questions. "Can we go tomorrow? How far is it?"

"I have to go now, Im. I promise you'll learn all about Solange, but it has to be your choice to come. If you really want to know." He swallowed again, his jaw bunching with tension. "Some of it is probably going to be hard to hear. Up to you." He held out his hand to me. An invitation.

I hesitated. These were questions I had asked myself for so long. And was it possible . . . could she still be alive somewhere? *There might be other worlds to see . . .* No. That was ridiculous. But . . . if I could get closure . . .

"I do want to know." Why was I even trying to pretend? "Okay, I'll go," I said. I could text Keane on the way. I reached for Al's hand. My fingers closed around his. "How far—"

He yanked me forward, pulling me hard against him. The earth fell away. The levee disappeared. We were plunged into blackness so thick it was almost tangible. I sucked in a sharp, panicked breath, my stomach lurching. There was no ground, no horizon, no sun, nothing but tumultuous current. Adrenaline punched through my veins as I instinctively scrabbled to cling to Al, the only solid, visible thing around me as we shot through a void of black wind. He hugged me tightly, chuckling. "You're okay, Im. I gotcha." I could do nothing but hang on as the entire world vanished.

MORE HEART-POUNDING READS FROM CAMCAT BOOKS

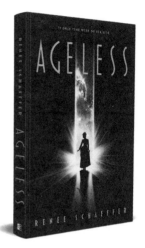

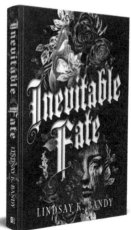

Available now, wherever books are sold.

VISIT US ONLINE FOR MORE BOOKS TO LIVE IN:
CAMCATBOOKS.COM

SIGN UP FOR CAMCAT'S FICTION NEWSLETTER FOR
COVER REVEALS, EBOOK DEALS, AND MORE EXCLUSIVE CONTENT.

CamCatBooks   @CamCatBooks   @CamCat_Books   @CamCatBooks